The Lizard's Smile

The Lizard's Smile

João Ubaldo Ribeiro

translated from the Portuguese by
Clifford E. Landers

Atheneum
New York 1994

Maxwell Macmillan Canada
Toronto

Maxwell Macmillan International
New York Oxford Singapore Sydney

This a work of fiction. Names, characters, places, and incidents either are the product of the author's imagination or are used fictitiously. Any resemblance to actual events or persons, living or dead, is entirely coincidental.

First published in 1989 in Brazil as *O Sorriso do Lagarto*

Atheneum
Macmillan Publishing Company
866 Third Avenue
New York, NY 10022

Maxwell Macmillan Canada, Inc.
1200 Eglinton Avenue East
Suite 200
Don Mills, Ontario M3C 3N1

Macmillan Publishing Company is part of the Maxwell Communication Group of Companies.

Library of Congress Cataloging-in-Publication Data
Ribeiro, João Ubaldo, date.
[Sorriso do lagarto. English]
The Lizard's smile/by João Ubaldo Ribeiro; translated from the Portuguese by Clifford Landers.
p. cm.
ISBN 0-689-12125-3
I. Title.
PQ9698.28.I165S613 1994 93-38774 CIP
869.3—dc20

Design by Laura Hammond Hough

Macmillan books are available at special discounts for bulk purchases for sales promotions, premiums, fund-raising, or educational use. For details, contact:

Special Sales Director
Macmillan Publishing Company
866 Third Avenue
New York, NY 10022

10 9 8 7 6 5 4 3 2 1

Printed in the United States of America

The Lizard's Smile

1

This may not be clear for some time, but a conscientious examination of the facts that led to the major events of this account demonstrates that its opening scene unfolded on a date now somewhat distant, with no one at the time knowing what it augured. It took place on a warm and motionless morning that began with the crowns of the trees stone-still, a day of a heat front. A "heat front" manifests itself after a confluence of natural events that only the wisdom of a handful of older folk knows in its entirety. Suddenly, in the midst of a conversation about nothing in particular, one of them squints as if in an effort to make out something in the distance, rubs the skin on his arms and face, sniffs the wind, and comments that, judging by the moon, the air, the tide, the texture of his skin, and a multitude of other signs, tomorrow will be a scorcher. And in reality the next day dawns covered in a dull metallic luster that turns the sea at the opposite side of the island into stagnant quicksilver, veiling the ledges of the facing land in translucent mist. Very early, the sun spreads itself over the mirror of the water, imparting an unnatural sheen to faces, causing the boatmen to disappear from time to time behind the flashes of light from the silvery wake they open in the sea as they slowly navigate away from shore. On land everything is sluggish also, and it seems like a miracle when four swallows manage to cleave swiftly through the diaphanous swelter smothering the world to evaporate in the haze, as synchronized as an aerial squadron.

In the midst of that great heat front a man in brown denim pants, a white dress shirt, and a brimless straw hat veered his motorboat and decided to make one last run in both directions along the north shore of the mangrove swamps that he soon planned to circle. Surely it was because of that oppressive day, without a doubt it was, that he began to experience an inexplicable sadness and dejection and no longer felt like collecting specimens as he had earlier planned. He geared down the motor and approached the shoals around the swamps. At that time of day, when the crabs come out to warm themselves and all the creatures of the muddy bottom are left exposed by low tide, there should have been many birds hunting insects, but he saw only a group of bemtevis, perched in the branches of a dead *gaiteira* tree, take raucous fright at the boat's passing and disappear behind the densest fronds. With the motor off, he let the boat glide over the dark water until it stopped and became as motionless as its surroundings. He reached for the stone anchor, then changed his mind, for it wasn't needed. He slid to the other side of the bench in the stern without getting up and listened for a time to the water lapping against the hull, more muffled and briefer each time, but even so reverberating like a thunderclap amid all that silence. Wasn't there anyone fishing, anyone looking for crabs or hunting for mussels, some fisherman following the mullet run at the mouth of the river? He looked about him; no living thing showed itself, not even the silhouette of a canoe in the distance. His eyes fixed on the unyielding vastness of the mangrove swamps. Fear? The desire to flee, to take shelter, to be nowhere at all? What is this uneasiness that makes him so anxious, almost to the point of palpitations? Now that he looked closely at the swamps, which stretched before him like an aggregation of dark caverns bristling with thorns, reminiscent of carnivorous mouths, he couldn't say it was actually fear that he felt, but he did feel something similar, a heavy foreboding, a sinister imminence, the impression that a relentless siege was under way around him that would in the end suffocate and kill him. He shook his head, expelling his thoughts, but he decided against his specimen-gathering trip. He yanked the rope of the motor, regained the channel, and headed for the ramp at the Market, from which he had departed a quarter of an hour before, but he didn't feel calm even after he pulled up to the mooring and leapt onto the dock.

Still pursued by acute distress, with the heat increasing and the beer tasting like medicine, he became impatient when two small boys sought him out to display a lizard with two tails, which they carried in a shoe box. He had to restrain himself mentally to avoid rudely shooing them away, which he felt like doing, and he sighed as he saw the lizard. Normally he would feign great interest at the find and make up stories about lizards to whom he would give people's names and surnames and attribute virtues and shortcomings, but he surprised himself by speaking in a professorial manner, in a condescending monotone, even frowning when one of the boys, a bit disappointed at the tenor of the conversation, tried to find the humor in what he was saying. He picked up the lizard by the neck and said that there was nothing unusual about it, as many lizards could rid themselves of their tails; it was a way of frustrating predators like the boys themselves, and besides that, the fact that the tail continued wiggling after being separated served to distract or disconcert the predator because it became like another small animal, independent, shaking, and reacting to touch for quite some time. When the severing is incomplete, he added, pointing out the planes in the vertebrae of the old tail where the separation could occur, the old tail remains after the new one emerges; there may even be three. The boy asked what that long word he'd used meant; he became irritated and answered sourly: "It's a cut, a cut!" And, with maniacal compulsion, he continued to discourse about reptiles in general and lizards in particular as if he had memorized a lesson. Only after he had talked for more than ten minutes, ignoring the boys' perplexed expressions and waving the lizard in his right hand like a baton, when he heard the expression "amniotic egg," did he come to his senses and begin to laugh. Startled at first, because they had been forbidden to laugh before, the boys joined in, and they spent a long time like that, until the younger one pointed to the lizard and asked if it wasn't laughing too. Animals don't laugh, the man replied, now in a better mood, and ordered two soft drinks. Affecting the intonation of a radio commentator, he said that lizards were awfully dumb animals. The only invention of the reptiles was that of which he had spoken, among the many other words the boys hadn't understood, the amniotic egg. The amniotic egg wasn't anything complicated; it was just an egg, like a hen's egg. So the reptiles invented the amniotic egg, which works better than laying and fertilizing eggs in the water, like the majority of fishes and amphibians. But that's as far as they went, awfully dumb animals, who didn't even take advantage of the scores of millions of years that they dominated the entire world. Nonsense; no animal laughs, much less a lizard. In that, they lost out to us, the mammals. Even their most perfected relatives, the chickens—what do we do with them? We raise and eat them! You want to know what the mammals invented, that is even better than an egg that's buried in the earth or laid in the nest? Well, the mammals . . .

Now, so long afterward, for no reason João Pedroso recalls that strange day as he walks down Direita Street, at dawn, to open his fish market. The day that was beginning showed no signs of a heat front like that other one, for the north wind exhaled its humid breath over the city and the waves of high tide broke over the docks. He was happy, looking forward to the time when, along with the fishmongers Nascimento and Boa Morte, he would begin removing the fish from the freezers to lay them out on the counter; he imagined taking off his sandals and rolling up his pants to enter the water and greet the canoe men and boatmen pulling up to the beach with mackerel caught during the new moon. He felt happy about being the owner of a fish market and almost thanked fate for having brought him, albeit by the most tortuous means, to this situation. Much better a fishmonger than a biologist, he thought, turning into the side street to the Market. And perhaps he was about to laugh, recalling his talk about reptiles, when he heard a rustling of dry leaves on top of the wall around the elementary school, and a lizard, of the same species as the one with two tails, but much larger, raised its neck before him, its body half-buried in the leaves, and appeared to stare at him, its small eyes abnormally prominent in the upper part of its head. João Pedroso was slightly startled at first, but he quickly stopped to admire the animal, which now moved its head up and down rhythmically. To his great surprise, he saw it was smiling. He squinted, straightened his glasses, but still wasn't sure if what he was seeing was something distorted or imaginary. The lizard did in fact seem enveloped in an atmosphere of laughter; something suggested that it really was smiling. It was not, however, an agreeable sight, because there was a bit, perhaps a lot, of mockery in the smile, almost hostility. Trying not to frighten the animal, he took two cautious steps toward it, but it quickly stirred the leaves with its hind legs and reared its trunk in a stance of alert. Two more steps and the animal, in an abrupt sequence of moves, turned its body to flee and was motionless for the briefest instant, the disconcerting aura of laughter remaining; it turned sideways, allowing a glimpse of its two well-defined tails, one coming from its body in a straight line, and the other, slightly smaller, set at a grotesque angle. João Pedroso was startled and attempted to get even closer, but it plunged noisily into the leaves and disappeared.

Of course, it was obviously all a coincidence, but a very strange coincidence, fitting together too well, overly complete. But still a coincidence, perhaps even one easily exaggerated. Yes, he repeated to himself, nothing more than a coincidence, and he would surely have turned his mind to something else if, as he raised his eyes to the choppy sea that revealed itself from the side street, he hadn't found himself engulfed by the same disquieting sensation that had assailed him that other day, to the point that he shuddered. No, no, it was all merely an impression—but once again he felt his heart tighten, his head throbbing, and a distressing fear, a fear that attacked him from every side.

Far from there, the secretary of health, Dr. Ângelo Marcos Barreto, finally came out of the bathroom after nearly an hour, as was his custom. Despite having hemorrhoids for some time now, he had never been to a doctor from fear he would recommend surgery, and so he would stick in a glycerin suppository or two and wait five minutes, standing as if at attention, smoking and contracting his buttocks until the urgency became unbearable. Only then, sweating heavily despite the breeze that always came through the jalousie windows, would he sit down on the toilet, sometimes managing to read a newspaper and sometimes moaning and invoking the saints at the lacerating sensation; then after a long time he'd move to the bidet, where he allowed a jet of water to cool at length his blazing nether parts. He went on afterward to execute a meticulous routine that he had not observed when younger but, after an uninterrupted succession of swindles, diversion of funds, kickbacks on public works and purchases, bribes, land grabbing, and various kinds of payments for administrative advocacy, during a public life of slightly more than twenty years, he had become a millionaire and, in reading and consulting under false names the etiquette and fashion sections of men's magazines, had learned above all how the modern man should act. Over the years he had elaborated a complex toilette, which began before the full-length mirror with a weigh-in and evaluation of muscle tone and skin, went on through shampoos, name-brand rinses, and soaps of exotic colors tied to small ropes, ending with a body lotion, a cologne *pour l'homme*, and drying his hair with an American hot comb.

Remembering the good old days of student politics, when he almost led the leftist ticket to victory in the elections for student government, without recourse to anything beyond his already recognized political talent and the power of his oratory, he recited, his voice modulated as he had been taught in the diction courses he'd taken, phrases from the speech he would make at the inauguration of the new hospital facilities on the island. The speech would be read, because he couldn't risk leaving out certain observations that he needed to make, but even so he had practically memorized it—his was a prodigious memory, a gift that had always distinguished him, now fortified by the American vitamins that he was in the habit of bringing by the trunkful when he came back from New York. He looked at himself again in the mirror. That slim youth with the fiery eyes, the enormous and rebellious head of hair falling over his eyes, the inspired word, for whom so many professors predicted a future of glory and dedication to public causes, had not disappointed the soothsayers. The post of secretary of health, which had never been one of the best platforms for rising to the top in politics, had in his hands been transformed into a magical instrument that he wielded with ever greater skill. A medical clinic in each municipal district was his goal and his war horse. A goal with great political-electoral potential, made possible, perfectly possible, by the recently obtained financing from the World Bank, to the point that the works had already begun in several districts, in the hands of the construction firm belonging to his cousin Rubem Barreto Chaves, with whom he maintained close commercial and personal ties. Ângelo Marcos thought about the slogan he had been secretly creating to suggest to the agency handling the publicity for his campaign. He pictured it resplendent at the bottom of a stunning list of accomplishments throughout the state: the Secretary of the Century. No, no; it doesn't sound right. The other version is better: the Administrator of the Century. Better, much better. Something along those lines. It had to be "century," he insisted on that, because it was true in many respects, including the dynamism. And besides, Goebbels, the great Goebbels—or Hitler, one or the other—had recommended that type of bombast. It worked; it was capable of exciting the masses. It was indispensable to think big and talk big.

"Whether it's medical attention, technological capabilities, or the qualifications of personnel," he declaimed before the mirror, his cupped hand fluttering in the steamy air of the bathroom, "we can state that we are at this time providing this long-suffering region with one of the best public hospitals in the North or Northeast, capable of delivering to the entire population out-patient, obstetrical, and general care of the highest order. The agreement which, through great effort and in the face of the severest, most underhanded, and most unpatriotic criticisms, we signed with the Lloyd Gunther Foundation and Loechs-Stroheim Laboratories today results in this magnificent complex, worthy of the most advanced centers of this country where even scientific research, under the terms of exchange also effected by the agreement, enjoys a prominent role, with diverse programs of great importance already underway even before the new installations are complete. This is the most eloquent and resounding answer we can offer to the critics of our administration. Democracy does not penalize the citizen in the name of xenophobic, reactionary prejudices. Democracy is not synonymous with backwardness, as the outmoded left seems to wish. Where it is in Brazil's interests, we want international cooperation, and, yes, we have the courage to openly proclaim this patriotic stance in defense of the well-being of our people, even if such a position is unpalatable to the demagogues who label themselves of the left but are nothing more than the perverse embodiment of immobilism and reaction—disguised, masked, covered by a tenuous and fragile shell of pseudonationalist and pseudoprogressive bravado and untruths! We don't just talk; we act! We don't just speak; we do! We don't just promise; we deliver!"

He brought under control the exaltation that overcame him, breathed hard for a moment, ran his hand through his hair, and smiled. Really, it was a curious thing; it must be what old Abreu Godinho called civic spirit: If the topic was the people, the great masses of Bahians and Brazilians in general, he was unable to contain an emotion of rapture, which left him in ecstasy and speaking as if a transcendental voice possessed him. That might someday work to his disadvantage, as had in fact already happened occasionally, but it was at the same time a source of pride, the pride of being a sincere politician, committed in his heart to the defense of the legitimate interests of the people, in a calling that could not be denied. If he had anything to drink before the speech, he knew for sure that he'd cry. It had always been that way, and even his antagonists knew it. When he joined the government's Arena party, back in the days when the Brazilian Democratic Movement was still known as Modebrás, some saw in it a betrayal of his principles. What betrayal, and of what principles? He was still a visceral democrat as before, maybe more so, but tempered now by the level-headedness of middle age. Politics, something those guys pretend not to understand and only understand in relation to their own interests, is pragmatism, feet on the ground, realism. His ethical position during that entire period is conveniently forgotten in favor of a mere question of form, a simple party affiliation, a circumstantial matter devoid of any real importance. No one recalls that, despite his ties to certain sectors of the armed forces, through officers with whom he had established friendships at the time of Reserve Officers Training and during the two tours he had done, he had never informed on anyone whatsoever, just the opposite—he helped a lot of good people out there who got off light thanks to his influence. Many of those big shots, who today are back with avowedly communist organizations and who feel free to shoot off their yaps and come down hard on him, were saved by his intercession, when Operation Bandeirantes almost had its hands on them. In other words, it would be no exaggeration to say that lots of people owe him their lives, or at least their health, since most of them were never even beaten, which is the least they could expect in prison. All that in addition to the help he'd given scores of people who'd lost their political rights, though not members of the underground, of course; there are limits that can't be crossed. But none of that was remembered. No one even remembered the crystal-clear truth that without people like him, working within the system, even today redemocratization might be nothing but a dream. All that was remembered was the supposedly negative things. The human being's capacity for envy and destructiveness is appalling; no wonder people like him so often end up dominated by an overpowering disbelief in humanity. And, ironically, after he joined that fabled BDM, would it have made any difference to them? But let them say what they would; the dogs bark and the caravan passes.

He opened the bathroom door, which faced onto a suite with a veranda and was decorated in shades of orange, with a wall of mirrors opposite the huge round bed with a shiny bronze headboard, two large built-in stereo speakers over the marble-covered night tables, a thirty-six-inch television set on a small table with wheels, and a kind of small sitting room next to the veranda, comprising an oval table, four chairs of undefined style, and two low-slung leather armchairs, amid ferns and anthuriums. Passing through, with an irritated gesture he ripped a leaf from the fern and crushed it between his fingers. How, in that period, could he *not* have joined Arena? he asked himself, annoyed as always when he came up against baseless arguments. He wanted a political career; everyone knew that. He had ideals that could only be realized through power. In politics, anyone who's not in power is just making noise. There's no such thing as politics without power. And what had been his great passport, his great springboard to access to power? The backing of old Abreu Godinho, of course. The old man's only son, his classmate, didn't even want to hear about politics; he lived ensconced in a laboratory, chasing endocrinological deliriums, and worked at a clinic only to have an income besides what he earned as a university professor, which wasn't even enough for him to eat decently. So, in a perfectly understandable process, the old man had adopted his son's best friend as his political heir, and almost as a son as well.

The options were clear: a) join Modebrás and bang his head against a wall, fall out of favor with the old man, run the risk of compromising himself once and for all, become poor for good, get maybe a thousand votes if he was lucky, and do absolutely nothing other than complain; b) join Arena with his election guaranteed by the old man's votes in the São Francisco region, take a seat as state representative and have the means to actually accomplish something. Only a mental defective could conceive of a choice different from the one he had made; it was a question of conscience. He was convinced that his ideas and his way of looking at the world hadn't changed. He had merely made a tactical-strategic decision of a pragmatic nature, that and nothing more, just as the debacle of the Social Democratic Party had led him to join the BDM—a basic question of political survival. Those idiots have good things to say only if you screw up and fall on your face. Politics can't be conducted on the basis of unproductive and merely headstrong passions, and many people refuse to understand that, or pretend not to understand.

All right, time to pick out what to wear. A light suit, because of the island's heat. But a coat and tie, none of that populist tackiness that's so in fashion nowadays, low-class Workers Party stuff. He recalled his inclusion on the list of the ten best-dressed politicians—"a spontaneous and casual elegance, always discreetly in step with fashion" the columnist had written in the caption to his photograph, which he had spent the whole morning contemplating. Of course, of course. Things like that count; it's a matter of image. A vest? No, no vest; that would be overdoing it, reverse tackiness. The beige linen suit, with its wrinkled charm, and a burgundy tie. Or the light blue? He regretted that Ana Clara wasn't there to give an opinion. They didn't see each other even in the mornings anymore, ever since she came up with that idea of opening a fitness center above the garages and began spending her time from 7:00 A.M. on ordering a battalion of women in leotards to spread their legs and jump up and down to the sound of eight loudspeakers going at full blast. Nonato had been right, at the time of the separation from Regininha, that shitty business that was public knowledge, when he told him, as they were getting plastered at the Méridien: "Changing wives is just changing headaches. One's a miser, the other's a spendthrift. One puts horns on you, the other watches over your very shadow. One talks her head off, the other can't keep a conversation going. One spends two years' cacao income on clothes, trinkets, and face lifts, while the other lets herself go like a tapir with lordosis. And so it goes. It's foolish to change; the only reason it makes any sense is to break the monotony." Well, to give Ana Clara her due, at least she didn't hassle him like Regininha. The day she suddenly came into his office, caught him hastily removing his hand from under Telminha's skirt and that awkward atmosphere set in, she didn't raise the slightest fuss, didn't say a thing, and was absolutely unflappable. Now that he was thinking of it, it wouldn't cost anything to give her a call in the middle of the day and say something pleasant. After all, she *was* his wife, a good wife, honest, pretty, and relatively cultured, though maybe a bit flighty, a little too unambitious, even in intellectual terms—something of a princess, to tell the truth, but in a nice way, harmless, with the ability to carry on a conversation and not be an embarrassment at cocktail parties. His wife, in short. And another separation, at this stage, was out of the question—politically and economically it would be a disaster, and he still had veritable paroxysms of hatred whenever he recalled how Regininha had set out to take him for everything he was worth during the proceedings and how he had to grease more palms than the entire population of Maceió to get a better settlement—no, grease wasn't the word: anoint, anoint, swab! Jackson Florêncio, Esq., there in court with that face of an upright and honorable soul, that sonofabitch, that corrupt scoundrel: The more assets he saw her add to the inventory in the trial, the more he wanted to grab. Today he was an appeals court judge. It's enough to kill anyone's hopes of a better future for the country. Well, the thing to do is forget it: What's done is done and there's no point in rehashing it.

Yes, he decided, he'd give her a call, considering whether to send some flowers as well. In the beginning he would say good-bye to her right there in the fitness center, but perhaps because he couldn't help being mesmerized by those enchanting fannies, in those no-need-to-move-it's-already-enough-to-kill positions, she finally told him she didn't want him coming by: It could cause talk, and the some of the women's husbands might not like it. He preferred not to argue, and now he went straight down to the small area next to the pantry, where he was served breakfast. As always happened with him, when he saw the attractively set table, white napkins almost glowing in their silver rings, cheerful and delicately colored porcelain, sparkling crystal glasses, the slim and graceful cutlery, he felt resentment at being forbidden to eat what he would like and as he would like. That table was like a city with perfect architecture, but absolutely deserted, without any kind of life, not even a plant. Never again fried eggs with bacon, never again an omelet like those they served in first class on international flights, never again tiny fried sausage with pancakes, never again slice after slice of toast drenched in melted butter. He sat down, feeling rather melancholy, and drank more grapefruit juice with sweetener than he had originally intended. He looked with displeasure at the *compotier* where the cereal had been placed, opened it, took out a handful of brownish flakes, sprinkled them in a kind of small bowl, and poured a little skim milk on top, starting to chew like one forced to eat dead leaves. With small, furtive gestures he glanced at the pantry door to see if there was some servant who might catch him in flagrante delicto, then sprinkled two spoonfuls of sugar on the cereal, with a small childish laugh of satisfaction.

By the second cup of coffee, accompanied by a low-tar cigarette, he felt less discouraged, although he also knew he had to give up smoking, as he had already tried to do several times. Hell, you're pushing fifty and can't do anything anymore: It's triglyceride here, cholesterol there, carcinogen somewhere else. Everything's bad for you, even taking care of yourself: It causes stress. Nobody lives forever, we're all going to die, he thought, upsetting himself so much at the idea that he had to leave the dining room as if in flight. When a guy is young he's immortal: It's only other people who die. But suddenly people of our own time start dying, and it seems that every day another one cashes in his chips. Unbidden, there came to his mind the ghastly purple corpse of his friend Macedinho, who had been with him just the other day, very much alive, and—ironically—at a funeral. His health wasn't good, but neither was it all that bad, and hell, forty-seven isn't old. But he died. He died suddenly, shortly after arriving at his ranch, according to his relatives, a horrible death, clutching the sheets for lack of air and snorting horrifyingly. "Edematous laryngitis," Gomes de Melo had explained. "A textbook case: His epiglottis became a worm. That's not your case, because he had kidney problems and a lot of other things that contributed to it, but it's plain to see that his level of risk increased greatly because he always had a cigarette in his mouth. Your case is much simpler, of course, but don't forget you're the same age he was. Yours is a bad case of smoker's tracheitis, which has affected your voice. If you don't quit smoking, C.A. Leave it to me. I'm good at radical tracheotomies: There's nothing to it." He didn't even like to look at Gomes de Melo, who had a face that belonged on a county urologist in a red-light district and not a prestigious otolaryngologist. Besides which he thinks he's funny, because no one can make a prognosis that way: It's a matter of statistics. Macedinho's face, a plum-colored island in a sea of sad flowers, insisted on being remembered. Yes, he would quit smoking, except that today, especially because of the upcoming trip, he needed that cigarette. Smoking after breakfast sometimes made him feel like going to the bathroom again, and he panicked at the idea of needing to do that on a trip, so he had to take precautions.

The half-smoked cigarette still in his hand, he went to the patio beside the kennels. It'd be one more chance for the dogs to get to know him. Despite having raised them from puppies and requisitioning an army sergeant to train them, he couldn't convince himself that those ferocious animals were trustworthy. Hadn't they almost eaten a gardener, a man they seemed to be used to and who'd never threatened them? The three mastiffs were lying at the rear of the kennels but got up and pressed their muzzles against the wire fence when he approached.

"Well, Winston?" he said, bending down and clapping his hands. "Well, boy?"

Winston did not move and continued to stare at him with a kind of disdainful attention, one eye bloodshot and showing a yellowish secretion. Ângelo Marcos thought of patting his head, as among all of them this was the one he feared least, but he didn't like the look directed at his hand and withdrew it. Maybe the left hand. No, that was stupid. He wasn't about to risk having his hand, left or not, reduced to hamburger in the mouth of a pachyderm like that. OK, it would be enough to stay here a bit longer, while they got a little more used to their owner's scent. What was the command for "sit"?

"*Sit!*" he ordered in English, suddenly remembering, but none of them sat. "*Sit!*"

After appearing to reflect on the order, only Winston, with a yawn in which his mouth replaced his entire face, decided to sit, looking ahead indifferently. The others remained as they were. A bit annoyed, Ângelo Marcos threw away his cigarette butt, called a security guard to recommend he have someone put drops in Winston's eyes, and came to the conclusion that he wouldn't need to go to the bathroom after all; there was no sign of the feared recurrence. He resolved once again that next week he'd get his courage up and schedule the operation; the problem was becoming quite unpleasant, and even a long plane trip was torture while he held out to go to the bathroom only at the hotel. The security man went to call for the car, which stopped beside him a few seconds later. To set an example he used his own car, driven by a state employee, whose salary he supplemented with a small bonus. If a secretary has the means to use his own car, in this case one of five, why put wear and tear on a state good? This was merely one facet of his personality, his aversion to luxury at taxpayers' expense. He got in the back seat, muttered a greeting to the driver and, as was his habit, found the car not very roomy, a cramped and clumsy matchbox, a piece of Brazilian crap; there's not a one of them that's any good. Right, but he couldn't have the Volvo of his dreams, the one that sent him into reveries when he saw the ads in foreign magazines. He couldn't have one of those gorgeous cars because it would call too much attention to itself, even if he could show, with tons of proof, the legitimacy of everything that was in his name. But the comments that he knew already circulated were enough, the same way they circulated about every public man in Brazil; it comes from our low level of political education. It might not seem like a great sacrifice, but it is—one more great sacrifice among many, many others. Yes, it might not seem that way, but a person who likes cars understands, he thought, telling the driver to stop first at the home of the American consul, who was his guest and was going to the island with them.

At 5:00 P.M., after spending the morning with the workout classes, swimming in the pool, lunching by herself, and taking a nap, Ana Clara decided she would smoke a huge joint in the company of Bebel, to let her know she'd finally made the decision to find a boyfriend, maybe even two or three. The number didn't really matter; strictly speaking she hadn't decided to find a boyfriend—she'd decided to make love, generically. Make love, make love, make love, she thought, almost twirling around like the heroines in American musicals in moments of ecstasy. She stood before the large drawer in the back of which, behind a disarray of cloths and purses, she kept the small can of marijuana, and she let out a little laugh, a kind of mocking *ho-ho-ho* that surprised her. She enjoyed the laugh and repeated it in front of the mirror, throwing her head back and finding herself very pretty. Make love! Systematically. Routinely. A new philosophy of life, Ana Clara in a new phase. Enough of half-measures, as Bebel herself had proclaimed the day of the biriba game when, without raising her eyes from the cards, she said, "I don't think. I've *done* it," when the question arose whether any of the four had ever thought about going to bed with another man since getting married. Marcinha, who had never lost her Minas Gerais accent or her habit of turning beet red and twitching with laughter whenever something made her nervous, dropped her cards on the table and had to leave her chair, nearly choking, until she managed to drink half a glass of water and the attack of laughter and coughing stopped.

"And I still do," Bebel added, this time raising her eyes. "What's with her—did she make a natural canasta?"

She joined in the general laughter and helped Ana Clara slap Marcinha on the back.

"Don't say anything else just yet, Bebel," Marcinha said, coughing and drying her eyes. "Let me recover."

But Bebel spoke right away, because no one was interested any longer in anything except hearing what she recounted with a half-twisted smile—the game now abandoned and forgotten and dry martinis ordered for everyone but Marcinha. She began by explaining that when she said "I still do," she hadn't meant she was doing so at the moment because, honestly, she didn't have anything going with anyone away from home. She had merely expressed a general attitude, an approach to life, a philosophical position—with its playful side, of course, but the playful side was part of that philosophy. Because, in all sincerity, at the moment there really wasn't anybody, and it wasn't as easy to find a man as people thought.

"And even if there was, I wouldn't name him because of my upbringing and I think it's vulgar to talk about the men I screw," she said with mock solemnity, as Marcinha had another fit of laughter, though less severe this time.

As absolute silence established itself in the large glassed-in veranda, as packed with plants as a solarium, Bebel, at times looking for a telling phrase or other, and perhaps gesturing in exaggerated fashion, laid out her philosophical position. She was by no means a loose woman, and she even thought of herself as a serious and prudent woman who hated, absolutely hated the idea of hopping from bed to bed with anything that wore pants. She just didn't consider herself dead because she was married, and she knew that her husband didn't consider himself dead either. So, from time to time an experiment was permitted. Using good judgment, with balance, and—might as well say it—upbringing, upbringing. Yessir, upbringing is much more important, in everything, than you imagine; coarseness and insensitivity are horrible. She was an adult, sensible, well-bred, she had a sense of propriety; she wasn't crazy enough to put her husband in jeopardy by having affairs with second-class men and committing foolish acts. Still, she couldn't give up that playful aspect, that thing that was so innocent in reality but which we invest with such a bad image and so much negativity, that beautiful thing that is lovemaking, the joy of a new affair free of guilt. So, when the opportunity arose and no one would be hurt by it, absolutely no one, oh yes, you can bet on it! Nando, of course, knew all about it. Of course he did; she'd been carrying on with Nando long before she separated from Tavinho. Nando knows what she thinks, and contrary to how it might seem, their marriage—their love, rather—is strengthened by it; it's a solid marriage, free of repression, in which nothing needs to be hidden and everything can be discussed. Only, naturally, she didn't tell him the details, nor did she want to know the details of what he did, because she considered that sordid, degenerate; the only thing worse was those contemptible perverts who pay to see their wife get it on with someone else. It's necessary to keep respect and good manners in any love relationship, and she adored Nando, couldn't stand the thought of being without him, didn't even like to consider the possibility. But she didn't believe in that business of putting out just to cuckold the man, as a kind of revenge; never—that takes away the playfulness of it and puts a bad tone on everything, which comes back to the person in the form of negative energy. When she suspected that a guy, it could even be some Italian hunk straight from the shower, wrapped in a towel, was after her because he wanted to cuckold Nando—forget it, nothing could make her go for it. Not even Tavinho, not even Tavinho! Was anything better, for both parties, than a rendezvous with one's ex, after being separated for a time, without any fighting or resentment, in a playful and affectionate encounter? Everybody agreed there wasn't, you could ask anybody. She'd even considered it in relation to Tavinho. Tavinho wasn't a bad person, just the opposite—he was funny and pleasant; he just wasn't the kind to marry. And things were already half under way when, during one of Nando's trips, they ran into one another at a party, from which they could perhaps slip away without major difficulties, and she realized—you know those flashes that come out of nowhere, you can't say why, but you're certain of it?—that Tavinho wanted to get back at Nando by countercuckolding him; that was his motivation. Things cooled off instantly, but instantly! Not only was that sort of thing unworthy of her, who after all would merely be serving as an instrument for the self-affirmation of an airhead who, as a man, wasn't good enough to lick Nando's boots, but also she would never allow anyone to do something like that to her husband, to offend his honor and dignity—no, never.

"But I think it's kind of brassy of you to pretend you didn't know," she concluded after speaking twenty minutes without interruption. "I'm sure it's been whispered around, or even said out loud, because after all I've never tried to hide it. I don't go around flaunting it to the four winds but I don't attempt to hide it either. I detest hypocrisy."

"I thought it was in Tavinho's day. In Tavinho's day, fine, with those weeklong parties in the country and all those people there and the television actors and those crazy foreigners . . ."

"Well, in Tavinho's day there wasn't any alternative; it was practically compulsory, wasn't it? Snorting the way he did. Tavinho—"

"Does Tavinho have a breathing problem? Snorting, I mean. Like a deviated septum?"

"Marcinha, there has to be a limit to your stupidity! A deviated septum?"

"Uh, Bebel said—"

"Cocaine, cocaine, Marcinha, cocaine! You've heard of cocaine, haven't you? Is there a living soul who doesn't know that Tavinho's always snorting powder? I don't know by what miracle he still has a nose left. Don't you remember that day he came to your house freaking out and wanted to do a few lines with you and Afrísio and you ran and locked yourself in the bedroom, paralyzed with fright, and Afrísio almost got into a fight with him?"

"And I'd lock myself in again. I can't stand those things. I don't know how you all can take such things so naturally; I don't even like to think about that day."

"Fine, Marcinha, but there's no cocaine here, nobody here is even sniffing glue. Let Bebel answer the question; you were the one who asked about Tavinho's time. You were saying, Bebel, that in Tavinho's day there wasn't any alternative."

"There wasn't; you'd have to be a mummy to stay out of it. Everybody stoned out of their minds, him included, all that unbridled snorting—it was inevitable that something would come along. And he even encouraged it. When he snorts a lot he can't get it up. It's no secret; he goes around advertising it, and it's true. He goes totally limp, with that little thing hanging there like a boiled peanut, one of the shriveled-up ones at the bottom of the bowl. But in his head, sweetie, he's turned on like crazy, all he thinks about and talks about is sex. Just let him get a line of coke in his gray matter and he wants to screw everybody, his wife screws everybody, everybody screws everybody; he even talks about screwing the women in his family. You've seen him revved up like that, Aninha, you know how he gets."

"Yes, but he's also funny at those times, talkative, witty."

"To you, because even when he's snorting he's never had the courage to hit on you, not only because you don't do coke and therefore don't encourage him, but also because he's afraid of Ângelo Marcos. But trust me, I've seen his tricks thousands of times. He's not easy."

"And he encouraged you to—"

"Encouraged? He practically threw me! And at the time I was still quite naive, crazy about him, thinking that coke was the greatest thing in the world, I ended up going along with it, in a big way. Until, of course, it got to be a drag and I discovered I wasn't cut out for that type of life."

"Didn't that ever bother him?"

"When things got rough, until the next line. When he woke up crazy and hung over, and decided to eat, drink milk and take vitamins and minerals for several days to recuperate from the battle, he'd usually get real somber, wouldn't say much. He wouldn't want to talk about the night before and would lock himself in his studio for hours. He was always saying he was going to take a long break, go six months without snorting coke, that sort of thing. But you know how he gets his coke, don't you? It's usually free. Can you believe it—free coke, even though he's rich? I mean, the guy who gets him the coke is always borrowing money and never pays it back, things like that, but basically it's free. Straight from the police, the highest quality, which the police always get. The one who gets hold of it is that guy, a cousin of his that he grew up with and who's also a heavy-duty user; I never can remember his name. Alcíades—what a name. Anyway, Alcíades never fails, and with all that coke in the house it'd be ten at night and Tavinho, after devouring warm raw eggs like a raccoon all day—it was the only thing he managed to eat at such times, besides drinking the milk of forty cows—and saying that he felt well fed, would decide on a boost. Just a boost, you know what I mean, a tiny boost. You can imagine what kind of boost. When he would raise his head from the warming tray, with his eyes flashing and his mouth puckered up and give that little snort, wiping the side of his nose, you could have screwed a two-hundred-watt bulb in his mouth and it would've lit up. And then everything would be back to normal, everything natural, everybody should screw everybody, et cetera, et cetera—the same old business."

"And now, with Nando, it's different."

"Completely! It's not even close, and Nando and I don't snort anymore, except socially, once in a blue moon when some friend offers some, but even then not always. No, none of that stuff. Nowadays it's a healthy thing, honest, open, something normal, without any of that craziness. It's like I said before, a solid, peaceful, serious philosophy of life."

In the months following that conversation, which Ana Clara came to consider historic, Bebel and she grew even closer, and now there was no doubt that each was the other's best friend. Absolutely certain, beyond a doubt. A real gift from heaven, Nando's return to Bahia, after such a long time in Rio. Intelligent, brave, loyal, and with a sense of humor always well honed, always; as she herself said, in extremely high spirits, Bebel had literally subverted Ana Clara's life, had effected a total revolution; that's the truth. I'm a different woman, Ana Clara thought, opening the drawer and having some difficulty finding the canister, which she finally located, wrapped in an old scarf. American cigarette paper, extra-large size, the best brand, with a little built-in wire so you can smoke the joint down to the very tip. Grass of the highest quality, obtained by Bebel herself, who seemed to know every dealer and pothead on the planet and had the brass to get out of the car late at night to buy a couple of joints from the hand of dealers at the fruit stalls at the Model Market, in plain sight of the police, right next to their building. Everything right on the money, everything perfect. Ana Clara, with the canister in her skirt pocket, went down to the living room where they were to watch a videotape that Ângelo Marcos had brought from Miami.

But they didn't succeed in paying much attention to the film, not only because it was the third time they'd seen it, but also because Ana Clara became impatient, even before they were through, to smoke the joint, and, her head spinning and with a sly smile, she told Bebel she had something important, very important, to say, something that could only be told to a friend like her. Bebel slid across to the edge of the easy chair and turned to her with a wide-eyed expression.

"It's this, Bebel," Ana Clara said, pushing a button on the remote control to turn off the set. "I've decided to get a boyfriend, maybe two or three. I decided that from now on I'm going to make love. Systematically. As a philosophy of life. A new Ana Clara."

Bebel threw herself backwards in the chair and shook her legs in the air. What? What were her eyes seeing, her ears hearing? It was almost too much to believe! Was it really true? Of course it was true, and Ana Clara proceeded to recount in detail how she'd been thinking for weeks and weeks and how that conversation with Bebel and others that had followed were important, especially because she had learned to reason objectively, to see things rationally, just like Bebel. And there was only one answer to the question that she couldn't help repeating constantly: In exchange for what was she faithful? Love? No, because in reality she no longer felt any love for Ângelo Marcos, who to tell the truth was little needed at home, where he was rarely to be found, except to sleep. In exchange for security? No, because he would never get a separation anyway; he himself said she was part of his political patrimony, and besides that, he had a terrible fear of being forced to part with any of his goods, much less his money, even the tiniest part of it. Nor did she want a separation; it was stupidity, an act devoid of rationality, and from this moment on—now hear this!—she was the queen of rationality. Without rationality there was no salvation. Separation would only cause problems and endless hassles, among other reasons because she herself had no stomach for fighting over alimony, beach houses, apartments, percentages, and whatever. So should she remain faithful at least to protect someone? No, because she had no children; she had nothing and no one to lose. In exchange for reciprocity? Patently not, for she had already caught Ângelo Marcos in the act with his hand under the skirt of one Telminha, who worked in his office, and she knew perfectly well that he fancied himself God's gift to women and was constantly spouting vulgarities about how every woman deserved to get laid at least once, or that his motto was "If it moves I'll screw it," and so forth. And you couldn't count on your fingers the times he'd given visible evidence of having been with another woman before coming home; there wasn't one classic indicator that she hadn't caught at least once, from scandalous perfumes on his shirt to purple-edged lips standing out in relief on his very white skin. She had even discovered a pair of undershorts with lipstick stains in front, and had said absolutely nothing. The answer then was obvious: She was faithful in exchange for nothing. No, not for nothing; in exchange for living in boredom, for never having experienced the least of her fantasies, for seeing her youth go by too quickly without anyone flattering her, praising her, esteeming her as a woman, a female, sexy—the way she had always thought of herself and had never again heard from anyone, not even him. Who was she hurting? Herself, and him too in a way. So she had adapted Bebel's philosophy to her own situation. With one basic difference: Although, like Bebel, she didn't want to hurt anyone, nor expose her husband, it never entered her head to tell Ângelo Marcos anything. If he found out through somebody else, which she would prefer not to happen but might happen, too bad; she would flatly deny it. But she would never tell him about it; her situation was very different from Bebel's.

It *was* different, and Bebel, unable to keep still from so much excitement, agreed that it was a very healthy attitude, even one of survival—it was sure to be the best therapy! Otherwise, Ana Clara would go on hemmed in by her frustrations and end up withering away and a sick and unbearable bore—repression like that leads to horrible things! What a fantastic decision, what an existential about-face!

"It's as if I had opened a new life for myself, a new path, understand?" Ana Clara said, her eyes glowing, and Bebel answered that she understood, of course she understood.

They first thought of making a toast with white wine. Ângelo Marcos had bought about ten cases of German wine, that glorious Rhine wine with names as long as a train, from a yacht owner who anchored on the island with tons of contraband; there should be several bottles in the bar's refrigerator. Naturally Bebel was game; how could they not toast it? And besides that, the greatest high of all the great highs she had experienced was marijuana followed by a superior wine. But Ana Clara suddenly decided that German wine wouldn't do; she was going to open a bottle of champagne, no less. Which they proceeded to do quite noisily, while Bebel began a hilarious dissertation about men and lovers that made Ana Clara laugh till she fell off the sofa and practically rolled on the floor, spilling champagne on her head.

Much later, alone in the second-floor living room, she attempted to walk to the balcony but felt dizzy, tripped over the furniture twice, and preferred to sit facing the sea on the large white-leather lounge, though the sea could only be heard and not seen, beyond an endless darkness. She tried to recall Bebel's talk and advice but couldn't, and then she noticed her face was taut. Why, when she should be laughing? She relaxed her facial muscles and smiled. Ana Clara's new life. But none of her thoughts seemed to have continuity, countlessly piling on top of one another in disorder like a kaleidoscope that wouldn't stop turning. Men, bedrooms, beds, kisses, entwinings, sensations, memories of orgasms. Her eyes closed; for the briefest moment she was possessed deeply by an undefined man and she felt an unbearable fullness that made her open her eyes in anxiety and draw in a deep breath. I'm pregnant, she thought, but she didn't laugh as she expected she would. To the contrary, she clutched her hands tightly in her lap and sighed a bit apprehensively, as she saw with fright that the idea of becoming pregnant, which previously had intimated a degree of repugnance, now took over her entire body and conveyed a strange, unfamiliar eagerness into which, despite her fear, she desired to plunge ever further.

She spent a long time lying ponderously on the lounge, not knowing just what she was thinking or even whether she *was* thinking, until the darkness outside seemed to be howling like an animal and she, leaping up suddenly and not looking back, descended the stairs toward the kitchen, turning on every light in her path. So hungry that she had stomach cramps, she opened the refrigerator and ate for half an hour, unable to stop, until she felt drowsy and made her way into bed without changing clothes. She fell asleep instantly and had nightmares until morning.

Sitting with their heads lowered and wearing hats but shirtless, the three crew members of the mullet-fishing lighter had just located the fish and begun maneuvering to cast the net, unfurling it in a precise and graceful circle completed by the boat itself. As sure-footed as if on land rather than a swaying piece of wood, one of the men, as soon as the circle was complete, rose and began to beat the water with a pole so the frightened fish would become entangled in the mesh and unable to escape by leaping over the floats, as a few had succeeded in doing.

"Admirable," said Dr. Lúcio Nemésio, who had stopped near the fort, accompanied by João Pedroso, to watch the fishing. "A truly admirable spectacle."

"Yes, it is. Especially at dusk like that, with those red and gold reflections in the water, it's a very lovely sight; it looks like an impressionist painting. And they were lucky today. There are fewer and fewer fish around here, fewer and fewer. The other day I decided to go by the point in that same spot and the water was very yellowish and at an extremely high temperature, such as I've never before seen in these parts. I even thought about measuring the temperature, but I stopped by the square to have a drink and forgot."

Lúcio Nemésio appeared not to be listening and kept his eyes fixed on the fishing. "Admirable," he repeated, and turned suddenly to João Pedroso, waving a cardboard file folder in the air.

"Sometime soon I'll tell you all about this," he said, speaking louder than before. "It's fantastic. But first let me say I wasn't admiring the scene from an aesthetic point of view, nor was I surprised because they've managed to catch some fish. When I said 'admirable,' I was thinking of something completely different; I was thinking about how resistant those fellows are. They're veritable walking zoos, every one of them—every type of nematode, platyhelminth, protozoan, those animals that you're more familiar with than I am; whatever you can think of, it's here. Schistosomiasis, you say? You don't have to be a Hippocrates, who taught how to tell from his face a guy with one foot in the grave, to look at them and see that their livers and spleens are the size of a watermelon. Filariasis, you say? I'll see that and raise you trypanosomiasis, ascaridiasis, amoebiasis, and every other type of infestation by assorted insects from lice to chiggers. Maybe you say chiggers are the least bad because they give you that pleasant itch and you remove them with the point of a pin. Well, let me tell you something: We amputated a foot—no, not a foot, a leg—because of chiggers. I'm not lying; it was a girl from the other side of the island with an infection and parasitology chart that would be enough for a World Health Organization conference just by itself. And on top of everything else, a diabetic, like so many people here, perhaps for some genetic reason, reinforced by that semi-incestuous endogamy that you see so often around the Recôncavo area. Her foot didn't even look like a foot; I don't know what it did look like, maybe an ulcerated jackfruit. Of course the problem is basic sanitation, education in hygiene, et cetera, et cetera. Everybody knows the litany by heart—but in the meantime we can't stop treating those wretches and doing something to improve their situation. That's why in my speech I came down so hard on the point of parasitology. I didn't study hospital administration, but I can't resign myself, given our conditions, to this business of the parasitology division, in addition to having no equipment, being under the supervision of some third-rate hematologist and entrusted to two newly graduated turd-pushers whose only experience in the area was breaking up fecalomas when they interned in Emergency. But, besides the speech, I also spoke in private with Ângelo Marcos, who was my student and respects me a great deal. I know that politically he's worthless, and morally as well, but what interests me is my hospital, and I'll go to the bitter end in that struggle. And I also spoke to reporters. I hope something will be published; I was as emphatic as I could be, because this is truly scandalous."

"Lúcio, haven't you ever been asked why a man in your situation, with a distinguished and solid career, well established and with no problems, able to take things easy for the rest of his life, came here to the island and hid away in that hospital? I know you and I think I know the reason, but didn't they ever ask you that?"

"They ask all right, and I have my answer ready. It's not to get to heaven, because I don't believe in God, unlike you, who I suspect would like to be a saint. Now that you mention it, I'd ask you the same question. How is it a man like you, with your scientific background, a biologist who today could be doing whatever he wanted to and doesn't do so because he's crazy and prefers to sell fish—"

"I'm not a biologist. Biologists are those types who do molecular biology and lots of other things that I don't understand in the least. At most I became a naturalist, as they used to say. But forget about that; we can talk about it some other time. Tell me what answer you give."

"The answer I give is 'I wanted to be a doctor,' just that. A doctor in the broad sense of the word, free to do what I like and as I like, to treat people who need treatment. I feel good when I succeed in curing someone of a disease; I feel very good. I'm very close to the poor people of the Recôncavo, for one reason because I myself wasn't exactly born with a silver spoon in my mouth. I was poor too, though not as poor as them. I wanted to be a doctor, a doctor of the kind I always desired to be. This hospital satisfies me and fulfills me and I must confess that I've come to like Americans and Germans for the help they gave us and continue to give, because if it weren't for that everything would be falling apart, as always happens."

"Just what do the gringos do there? Don't they have some kind of separate building?"

"No, just an annex in the gynecology/obstetrics wing, a couple of labs and some offices. A large part of their work isn't strictly medical, it's socioeconomic. They collect data about birth rates, family structure, labor relations, that kind of thing. I can't be very precise. And there's also the personnel who work with fertility, conception, et cetera. Plus the interns and visiting staff, who work with us in the hospital. All allies of mine in the parasitology struggle, which we're going to win. And speaking of parasitology, I want to show you this new thing here, which with all this talk I was almost forgetting. Prepare yourself for a shock. It may not even be anything new to you, but I doubt if you've ever seen an actual case. It's the kind of thing we think only exists in science fiction, not in reality. What a case! Do you know what a hydatid cyst is?"

"Huh? Yes, it must have something to do with the eggs of cestoids, doesn't it? I was good at worms in college."

"Not good at worms, good at everything. I know. To this day I don't underst— Never mind. Anyway, I hadn't heard about it myself until less than a year ago; I had the devil's own time getting all the research together. You got it right away, except that it's not eggs, it's larvae."

"Yes, of course. Larvae. A small round sac, a little ball."

"Not a little ball, my friend, veritable ping-pong balls. We've taken them from the liver and the lungs. In the latter case, the guy had three in his right lung: two marbles and one ping-pong ball."

"But was there some generalized outbreak of infection around here? I never heard—"

"Well, I don't know what you mean by generalized, but three cases in less than a year of something that had never been heard of here . . . Not to mention that the guy can have one of those cysts and not feel a thing, at least not for a long time."

"What kind of taenia is it? They have some peculiar cycles, some specialties. Are you already familiar with the vectors?"

"I know everything. I researched everything. The name of the disease is echinococcus. I know it's nothing to laugh about, but I had an attack of hysterical laughter that almost split my diaphragm when I read the name, which gives the impression that the subject contracted the disease from eating so much horse manure."

"Echinococcus, of course. I remember it. *Echinococcus* what?"

"I don't remember; multi-something-or-other, something with 'multi.'"

"I don't remember either. But of course it has nothing to do with horses. Of course you know that; the prefix is the same as in 'echinoderm,' which means—"

"There you can't teach me anything, doctor, because I had a real course with Tosta Filho, who knows more about parasite worms than the Pope knows about Mass, and I know everything. He even gave me a couple of monographs. Intermediate host: ruminants, especially sheep, which there are practically none of here. And people, of course, as in those three cases. Definitive host: dogs, which there are plenty of here, though I haven't heard of any southern dog in these parts, because Tosta told me that where it's found is in the South, and in fact one of the monographs is by a professor from Porto Alegre and the other by a Uruguayan. All of it, naturally, as always in such cases, involving shit, because the adult parasite lives in the intestines of dogs—and around here shit is also in great abundance. But none of the three guys has a dog, much less a sheep, although the third one, a young boy, likes to play with dogs, just any dog from the street. Which means there's some detective work there, and who's my Scotland Yard? Do I have a decent sanitarian, one who knows how to put together a small but accurate research project? No, I have two turd-thumpers and that pitiful hematologist who sit there with their idiotic faces and limit themselves to correcting me like a professor when I call a taenia a worm and who don't solve a thing. It isn't, of course, nor do I think it will become, a significant public health problem, but it has a kind of symbolic significance for me, a great symbolic significance."

"Hydatids? Echinococcus? I don't understand."

"You will. This here—"

"Is it the x-ray of a hydatid cyst?"

"No, take a look. It's the report and the graph of an electroencephalogram. You don't understand anything about encephalograms, do you? Neither do I, but I do know the rudiments; a surgeon needs to know at least the rudiments. An EEG doesn't allow you to be sure about anything, in this case. But the kid who does the EEGs, a jaundiced little guy from Sergipe who studies like a maniac, is very good and has some ideas; he explained everything to me and I haven't any doubt. These waves here, look, these thicker ones here that flatten out slightly here, form what they call the delta rhythm. In reality it's a tumor in the encephalic mass, clearly inoperable. If it were trauma in the cephalic truncus as was first thought, because he began to complain of head pains following a fall, the wave would probably be different; it would also be somewhat broad, but smaller—the theta rhythm. This is a tumor, no doubt about it; the guy from Sergipe is willing to bet his fish knife on it, and I'll bet anything myself, because of course I'm not banking on just the EEG. On the very first day he went to the hospital, the boy was already a classic textbook of symptoms, from the head pains to vomiting and neurological manifestations—subtle but quite unmistakable. Well, up to this point nothing unusual. Now and then somebody shows up with a brain tumor; it's part of life. But would you like me to tell what I think that tumor is? It's just what you're thinking; I'm almost certain it's a hydatid cyst, for one reason because he also has one in the lung. I had a hunch and ordered x-rays taken of everything. There was the little white ball—left lung, basal lobe, clear as day. So I phoned Tosta, who's very interested in the case and who hasn't been here yet only because he never has any time, and managed to get the boy admitted to the Clinic, attended by Tosta and other neurologists, neurosurgeons, CAT-scan specialists, sawbones, and all that crowd from the University. They're going to enjoy it; it's what can be called a beautiful case. The boy's going to die, of course, even if those perverts cut away half his parietals to relieve the pressure in the dura mater. This is where the symbolic aspect comes in, the symbolic aspect I mentioned to you."

"Yes, you're going to have to explain, since I see no symbolic aspect whatever."

"It's this, my dear Dr. João Pedroso," said Lúcio Nemésio, adjusting his hat on his head and preparing to start for home. "As a doctor and a Brazilian, I'm ashamed to know that now in Brazil you can die of brain worms. There's something symbolic in that, isn't there? I suspect there is, among other reasons because worms are usually associated with shit."

He laughed in a rather unpleasant tone, his large pendulous cheeks appearing even more sagging than usual. "We'll see each tonight," he told João Pedroso with a vague gesture. Carrying the folder in his hands, crossed behind his back, he took Largo da Glória and slowly disappeared down Patos street. João Pedroso once again felt admiration for the old man. Civic spirit, fighting spirit, competence, unselfishness, courage. All I have is civic spirit, and not much of that, he thought, recalling that during the old man's interview with the press he'd had the opportunity to talk to reporters about the destruction of the island and other things that he was always thinking of censuring and fighting against, but he hadn't managed to say a thing; he'd stood there like an imbecile, fearfully, strangling on his words in a corner of the room. He took a deep breath, rubbing the nape of his neck forcefully as if in reality he wanted to crush it. Yes, there was no excuse; he was going to change his attitude, do something. Of course he was; there was much that lay within his capacity. He felt a sudden anxiety as he thought about this, almost nausea, and walked quickly toward the square, as he badly needed something to drink.

2

Killing himself was Ângelo Marcos's first thought as he returned home after hearing the news. He even took out the .38 from the small built-in cabinet where he kept it hidden beneath a false bottom. Balancing it in his hand for several minutes until, with a contraction of his shoulders that nearly knocked him over, he began weeping in breathless sobs, falling face down on the bed and burying his head in the pillow. Only much later did the convulsive sobbing subside, and he got up, tears still streaming from his swollen eyes, the revolver in his right hand. He examined it up close, read aloud the words engraved in English on the barrel, read the numbers, also in English. He tried to find some amusement in it but didn't even manage to smile, then felt once again the impulse to break into tears, but this time he bit his lower lip and took control of himself. Moving very slowly and sniffling with his head bowed, he went back to the cabinet, opened the false bottom and replaced the revolver in its customary spot.

Afterward, in an act that he himself later would not remember clearly, he found himself turning on the air conditioners in his office, sitting down in the large revolving armchair, and resting his heels on the desk, in the direction of the silver picture frame that held a photograph of his and Ana Clara's wedding. He nudged the frame with the tip of his shoe until he could reach it without great effort, held it in his lap, and after staring at it for a long time, decided he looked ugly and had a stupid expression on his face. A joke, a big joke, life is a meaningless joke. He raised his eyes and looked about him, the bound volumes that he had never read appearing even more remote and absurd than they had always secretly appeared, the bookcases nothing more than tyrannical pieces of furniture, the curtains ridiculous. Yes, not only the portrait seemed different; everything was different, sketched in lackluster colors and distant, as if he were not in this world. He breathed deeply and laid the picture frame down on the table without looking at it again. Tremulously at first, then in a resolute way, he assumed a firm countenance, exactly the one he intended to display the first time he broached the subject to Ana Clara, and began talking to himself. All things considered, the worst was past, the doubt was behind him, the anxiety, the anguish of uncertainty. No longer; now it was a reality. A hard reality, no denying that, but perfectly tangible and therefore capable of being faced—and not only being faced, but defeated. And Deraldo had been clear, even emphatic. "You'll make it this time, don't worry; we'll be able to contain it," he had said, with that look of a composed owl that ever since Medical School had undergirded his reputation for competence. Sure, sure; everything was understood. Deraldo wasn't leading him on, everything was under control, there was no reason to panic, no reason at all, just the opposite—there was even some cause for relief.

Yes, but crying hadn't necessarily been a bad thing, and perhaps if he hadn't cried he might actually have put a bullet in his head. No, no, he wouldn't have; that had been more than anything a gesture of protest against God, a kind of blasphemy without uttering the words he lacked the courage to say. The questions could not avoid coming up, the same questions always come up, and it's infuriating to see that, from so much use and repetition during an entire lifetime, they fail to have the desired effect, do not cause the revulsion and puzzlement they should cause. Why him? Why so early, at such a productive age, facing the perspective of full maturity, which would finally, after a lifetime of such great effort, repay him for his struggle? Why, why? Yes, crying had been a good thing, for he had practically bottled everything up all these days longer than months and more agonizing than a season in hell, in which his shoulders and neck turned to granite, his stomach became a wrinkled pillowcase, and any phone call might be the herald of death—ever since that terrifying moment when, returning late at night from a trip, he went to the bathroom after much resistance and, as he raised his hips a bit to throw a cigarette butt in the toilet, saw coming from his body like a leaky faucet a continuous flow of blood that had transformed everything below into a crimson puddle. He got to his feet, confused and a bit dizzy; a sprinkling of thick drops of blood formed a semicircle around his feet and at once a small, hot, viscous stream ran down to his ankles. What kind of crazy hemorrhage was this, he was going to go into shock, he would die, how much blood must he have lost in the now black depths of the toilet, could that be the cause of the dizziness he had felt? Moving cautiously, his legs clamped together and barely lifting his feet from the floor, he sat down on the bidet—his heart straining against his ribs and sweat burning his eyes—staring at the red spurt that continued initially as vivid as before; then the cleansing water caused it to fade little by little until it became completely clear. He looked around; it seemed as if someone had slit a chicken's throat and then slung it about the bathroom. Raising his body very carefully, he remembered other times that he had cleaned up small drops of blood from the space between toilet and bidet, because he didn't want Ana Clara to see them and insist he have an operation. But they were just small drops, drops to which he customarily paid no attention, nothing like this which he began to remove with toilet paper and a towel that he wet at intervals, this sea of blood about whose eruption he spoke nervously in Deraldo's office at nine the next morning.

"You must be anemic," Deraldo commented. "Well, let's take a look at it," he added, rising and indicating the small adjoining room.

"Do you think I'll need an operation?"

"That depends. Without having a look, how can I tell?"

He had a look, and then came the initial blow, because he wasn't satisfied with an examination, and, after a series of procedures that Ângelo Marcos found humiliating and made him feel compelled to serve up a string of jokes that appeared to go unheard, Deraldo made prolonged use of the rectal speculum, finally announcing that he was going to take some specimens for biopsy.

"It doesn't hurt a bit," he explained, without raising his eyes from some notes he had made. "It's nothing, and I'll even use Novocain. Wait right there, I won't be long."

"Biopsy? What the hell do I want with a biopsy? Ever since Med School I've always believed that biopsies cause cancer. No sir, you don't have to be that meticulous and follow the ass-doctor's manual to the letter. I know I have hemorrhoids. I'm afraid of operations. I don't trust hospitals, but I'm willing to be operated on. I don't want a biopsy, I don't see any reason to do a biopsy."

"Well," Deraldo said, without altering his voice, his eyes nearly closed behind his glasses, "I can't remove material from your body without your authorization, but my professional duty is to emphasize that you need to have this biopsy done. You have a tumor in the anal canal, it's easily visible, perhaps two centimeters at its greatest diameter. You can't hide the obvious; the best thing is to have the biopsy. May I get the forceps?"

"Deraldo, how can you look me in the face so calmly and tell me I have cancer of the ass?"

"I'm not saying you have cancer, I'm saying you need to do a biopsy."

"It's the same thing! You already know I've got cancer; the biopsy's just to confirm it. And you say that with complete indifference, as if I were just another case."

"Mamaco, what do you want me to say? How do you want me to talk to you? I—"

As he unexpectedly used the nickname from high school days, when they had also been classmates, and he saw Ângelo Marcos cowering like a terrified child, Deraldo relented. He sat down, removed his glasses for a moment to rub his eyes, sighed, asked Ângelo Marcos to pull himself together for a few minutes, and, rolling a pen between his fingers, paused before he began to speak. Yes, there was a type of ulceration in the anal canal, a tumorous formation. He breathed deeply a second time, ill at ease, dropped his pen on the note pad. Yes, he said, his eyes on an indeterminate point in front of him, he thought it was a carcinoma, an epidermoid carcinoma. Epidermoid carcinoma of the anal canal, he recited, emphasizing each syllable and exaggerating the final *l*'s. But there was no need to rush headlong into things; they must wait for the test results, especially the biopsy. Normally he wouldn't have done that, considering it to some degree irresponsible, or even frivolous; but because Ângelo Marcos was also a doctor, he could foresee things to some extent. He believed it was a relatively recent tumor, which as everyone knows improves chances for treatment. And the treatment he would most likely choose had been showing rather encouraging results—besides which, in Ângelo Marcos's case, there was further the distinct statistical advantage that patients with these carcinomas were almost always decrepit old men and not men who were still young and strong like Ângelo Marcos, despite his almost certain anemia.

"If many of them achieve what can only be considered an extraordinary survival rate, just think of you—" he said, then immediately appeared to have second thoughts. "No, no," he added with a smile that gave the impression of being hindered by tiny spasms, which increased Ângelo Marcos's uneasiness. "No, no; you'll walk away from this one, don't worry. We'll be able to stop it."

"What about the treatment? I mean, the likelihood is I'll have to have an operation, won't I, to get rid of the thing? Well, maybe it's better that way. Sooner or later I was going to have to have my ass operated on anyhow, isn't that right?"

"No, no, I wasn't referring to surgical treatment. That is, in my opinion we're not going to opt for surgery. In this case it's not the best solution."

He averted his eyes again, leafed through his notes, frowning, reluctant to answer the question about why surgery wasn't the best solution. Radiotherapy and chemotherapy, he muttered finally, tearing from the pad the sheets on which he had made notes and gesturing with them like someone who must deal with a more important matter and has no time to waste. But something in Ângelo Marcos's almost belligerent look must have bothered him; folding his arms and adopting an impassive expression, he said, radiation therapy, cobalt, chemotherapy, *fluo-ro-ura-cillll*, *mi-to-my-cin-C*. High rate of effectiveness, low percentage of recidivation. We're not going to operate.

Standing up abruptly in his office and burning with hatred that was both diffuse yet so intense that he felt it as something solid inside his body, Ângelo Marcos remembers Deraldo returning to his earlier statue-like posture immediately after declaiming the names of the drugs with that morbid delight. And with such indifference to death—death, an amorphous and horrifying nightmare, amid blood-soaked sheets, exposed viscera, excruciating pains and nocturnal terrors, the vision that at the time overwhelmed Ângelo Marcos, faced with that preposterous announcement in that equally preposterous office—all of this was really happening, wasn't it? And what drugs were those? Weren't they the kind of drugs that caused uncontrollable nausea, made you want to die all day long, a martyrdom almost as unbearable as the disease itself? Yes, Deraldo had replied with that same stony face, and they usually cause hair loss as well, although I think you're indulging in certain poetic overstatements; you always did have a bit of the Castro Alves in you.

"Why not surgery, then? Why all that suffering, the nausea, the loss of hair, leukopenia, agranulocytosis, whatever else, everything the treatment causes—why not surgery?" Deraldo answered that the hair would grow back. The hair, yes. And what about the nausea and the suffering and the horrible examinations and punctures in the sternum and agonizing waits and life itself and all the rest? Better than surgery, Deraldo said, after once again taking a long time to speak. But why, why? And Deraldo, at whom he became so infuriated that he had a flash of delirious fantasy in which he flayed him with a blowtorch, didn't limit himself to the objective answer that his responses up to that moment led Ângelo Marcos to expect, but instead, his face again transmogrified into a paving stone, asked rhetorically whether Ângelo Marcos recalled any of his Anatomy, anything from the classes of old Robério Caldas, or whether his concerns as a great politician had made him absentminded. He had mentioned the anal canal, "*analll canaaalll*." Anal canal, therefore . . . Therefore what?

"Therefore," he said, this time looking Ângelo Marcos straight in the eye, "if the solution were surgical, you wouldn't have a sphincter. And if you don't have a sphincter—" he continued, as if beginning a class, but Ângelo Marcos, almost shouting, drowned him out, although he then fell into a tense silence for a few seconds, until he asked in a small voice if that would mean (of course it would) he'd live with a bag permanently hanging from his stomach, threaded onto a repulsive little tube—and he felt a chill when he saw Deraldo, now back to his earlier restraint, nod his head.

"Epidermoid carcinoma of the anal canal," Ângelo Marcos repeated in his office, imitating Deraldo's way of speaking. Placing his hands behind his back, he began pacing in front of the bookcases, as if he were inspecting the books. All of them unfamiliar, cold, indifferent. Everything indifferent—loneliness, loneliness! He stopped abruptly before the large gilt-edged Bible with the sides of its leather cover hanging like the brim of a hat, enclosed in its carved wooden holder and suddenly radiating a magical aura. The Bible, yes, the Bible; it was more than merely an interesting coincidence that he had stopped in front of the Bible. The Bible, yes, the Bible; how often had he thought of opening it at random to take from it some word of guidance, hope, or consolation, as so many others did? He crossed himself with a contrite expression, and, his hands shaking, opened the enormous book and avidly read the first passage his eyes fell upon: "The Genealogy of Ezra," said the heading. "Now after these things, in the reign of Artaxerxes, king of the Persians, Ezra the son of Seraiah, the son of Azariah, the son of Hilkiah, the son of Shallum, the son of Zadok, the son of Ahitub . . ." The text went on in an endless succession of names that meant nothing to him, no message, no friendly word. The Bible was indifferent too, everything was indifferent, there was nothing. He thought about making another attempt, but decided not to. It no longer had any validity, could no longer convince, and he almost slammed the book shut.

Even so, perhaps he could still pray. Wasn't there such a thing as the infinite mercy of God? Infinite, infinite; one must focus on that word. Infinite. Didn't such mercy exist? It did, it really did. It was true that he had prayed so much, before the result of the biopsy had arrived, had prayed so much that once he'd felt himself almost levitate after spending ten minutes kneeling in fervent prayer in his office at the Ministry, and then got to his feet convinced that the report would be negative. For some hours he reflected confidently about how it had all been nothing but a scare, a way of shaking him and forcing him to take a new tack in his life, to observe certain things, take a fresh look at certain habits and practices. After all, there was truly great wisdom in the saying that God writes straight with crooked lines; life really is the only great school, and God is good. For that very reason he almost cursed God and all the saints when he saw, in a book whose cover was embossed with a horrible crab transfixed by a dagger, the macabre words that continued to pursue him like some funereal verse, written by a computer printer: EPIDERMOID CARCINOMA OF THE ANAL CANAL.

No, he wouldn't pray again. Deraldo had told him not to drink; there were several preparatory measures that must be taken before beginning the treatment, and one of them was to stop drinking. Well, he'd stop tomorrow, not today. Today they'd just have to be patient; a guy who's just been told he has cancer has the right to tie one on. Pray again, no. Besides which, he needed to think about certain important questions, among them how to tell Ana Clara the whole story. Now the distance that was becoming ever greater between them was unacceptable, a waste, senseless, something preposterous. Yes, he had to do a self-criticism in relation to his marital behavior; he would do that self-criticism and make a clean breast with her, in total sincerity and the greatest humility. And he needed to examine other things as well, extremely serious matters, such as the leave he would have to take, the political repercussions of his absence and of his illness, many other things.

With far greater pleasure than he expected he could feel, he opened the small refrigerator and took from the freezer compartment a sealed bottle of Polish vodka and a short glass frosted with a fine layer of ice. He put two ice cubes in the glass and watched with delight as the vodka tricked out viscously until it almost overflowed. A little more than twenty minutes later he was drunk and had taken some notes, which he now made a final copy of for the third time and which he no longer quite understood. An hour and a half later he had finished the bottle and fell asleep with his head plopped on the desk between piles of crumpled papers, his hand on his pen and a sheet of paper where he had written "Philosophy of Cancer" and, underneath, the words "It has been said that cancer is a revolt of the cells, a rebellion that utilizes the organism's own forces against it, and my thesis is that—" followed by a winding line that trailed to the bottom of the sheet.

The Molly Bloom type, thought Ana Clara, lying in bed on her stomach and supporting herself on her elbows. No, the Lady Chatterley type—what was the name of her lover's dick? John Thomas. Of course, John Thomas; she even had three or four references that mentioned John Thomas—torrid delirium, apocalyptic masturbation as in imagination she screwed Lady Chatterley's lover day after day, hour after hour, doing everything possible and fantasizable in the realm of depravity, in those wonderful English places: forests, moors, greenhouses, barns, attics, and scary lawns and gardens, that sort of thing, which here in Brazil exist only in news stories about the interior of Santa Catarina. John Thomas here, John Thomas there; and by the way, how funny that the French called a man's balls *les valseuses*. Bebel knows the darnedest things. Funny, John Thomas always invoked for Ana Clara the image of a cock medium or less in size, with an appearance that didn't really inspire enthusiasm, kind of whitish and rosy and a bit fragile, among pubic hair of a wishy-washy color. But it still gets you hot, perhaps because it got Lady Chatterley hot. No, not Lady Chatterley—how would it be possible to find an employee like that in the midst of so many toothless blacks? No, no, the Molly Bloom type, even a pale copy, of course without a millionth of Molly's experience; the only thing she had in common with her was lying here stretched out on a bed thinking the craziest things a mile a minute, but with better punctuation and paragraphs and wildly drawn-out like that boring and pretentious book, which she'd read only to do the culture bit, in the words of Bebel, who was acting as a kind of intellectual stimulus.

Well, it didn't do much good, she said in a low voice, appraising with displeasure the notebooks and pads of papers lying about. Everything in life is easy till you try it. Including writing—and how! A person has a lot to say and thinks she's going to say it and then fails; nothing comes out the way she meant it, and it ends up making her unhappy. And structure, how difficult structure is! The words always elusive, always leaving the impression that there's a better one hidden away in some corner of your mind. What a crazy thing, this writing idea! She didn't even know for certain what she wanted to write, whether it was some kind of study, or a testimony, a diary, a novel, articles—at any given moment each seemed the best choice, and then, suddenly, everything fell apart and confusion reigned once again. All she knew was the subject matter: the observations she made and the theses she formulated during the months she had dedicated to what Bebel and she were in the habit of calling the Experiment. Which is to say, her love affairs. Much easier said than done, dear! Great thing, the Experiment—though it was ridiculous to use that word with all its pomp. She laughed as she opened a notebook to the first page and came upon the pseudonym she had made up in Bebel's company, scratched out capriciously with a felt-tip pen: Suzanna Fleischman. God only knows why. Neither of them knew; it just popped up suddenly, and Bebel had the abominable taste to suggest it was because of a yeast that was around when they were girls—didn't there used to be a Fleischmann's Yeast?—Well, since yeast is supposed to make things rise, the name was a great symbol of Ana Clara's growth as a person, someone now transformed into . . . a true philosopher, why not? That's it! "What a horrible explanation," Ana Clara had said, "but I like the name and I'm going to use it."

Suzanna Fleischman, however, seemed destined to remain as frustrated as Ana Clara, if not more, because after all she depended only on herself. An ironic fate for one who had been born with the mission of neutralizing, or at least mitigating, an earlier frustration, that Experiment. Since she hadn't succeeded in doing to her satisfaction what she had set out to do, she would write about it, a kind of feminine venting of steam, because even in such things men have the better of it; they have a much larger field of action, and everybody thinks it normal for men to go out and hit on women. There's no such thing as a female cuckold, only male. But do they really hit on them? Questionable, questionable. There's even a line of reasoning, postulated by Suzanna Fleischman and seconded by Bebel with only a few reservations, that deep down men only like other men. Interesting thoughts, clever reasoning, curious observations. Bebel was absolutely sure it would make for an international best-seller. But how? To have a best-seller you've got to have a book. Well, maybe now, with this enforced stay on the island, Suzanna Fleischman can get her thoughts together and put them on paper in a way that's at least passably organized. Things change from one day to the next. If it had been a month ago that Ângelo Marcos made the decision to continue his treatment and convalescence on the island, she would have received the news very poorly, although she probably wouldn't have refused to go with him—wifely duty, it wouldn't look good, et cetera and so forth. But not now; now it's extremely welcome, even a gift from heaven. The off-season, nobody on the island, beaches, tranquillity—and above all no chance that Eduardinho would show up, and even if he did there'd be an excellent excuse stopping him from being a pain: On the island it's impossible; everybody would know about it in less than twelve hours.

She frowned and closed her eyes slowly. Monster. Monster. Beast in human form. A real monster. She found it hard even to feign alarm over Ângelo Marcos's illness, much less actually feel anything. She did pretend, of course, and had had the patience to listen to the constant repetition of the sickly-sweet monotonous rigmarole with which he reapproached her after confirmation of the diagnosis, conversations patently motivated by his being shit-scared and nothing else. A good cancer in the asshole can work wonders. Anyway, as he himself had said, he was looking death in the face and maybe because of that there was some sincerity in his sudden transformation into an affectionate, attentive, and supportive husband. But there wasn't any, none in the least; it was all temporary, only as long as the carcinoma didn't go into remission, his hair failed to grow back, and the terror persisted. His hair, eh? He was mortified about his hair and had had several photos taken from every conceivable angle so he could order toupees with the look of his natural hair. Poor thing, so much shampoo and creme rinse, so much massaging and brushing—she even felt a little bit sorry about that, funny how things are.

Well, maybe her indifference was due to Deraldo's conviction that he would be cured. Deraldo is obviously a degenerate of great talent and competence who would rather die than sully his reputation with an incorrect prognosis. He gives the impression that if he predicts the death of a patient and the patient doesn't die, he'll show up with a revolver and take care of the matter personally. He must be a furious lover, one of those who go into semicataleptic trances and suck toes, howling with their eyes shut. She herself hadn't ever had any such experiences but knew of them and many others, each one more unpleasant than the last, and Deraldo had all the signs of being that type. Yeah, he'd never make a prediction he wasn't sure of; that must be why she wasn't affected. No, that wasn't why. Let's admit it: The idea of Ângelo Marcos dying didn't upset her in the least. If he died, fine, he died. She had dedicated hours to imagining what it would be like if he died, had visualized every type of scene—farewells, last words, final sighs, intensive care units, terminal wards, unpleasant visits, would-be philosophical talks, the coffin descending into the ground, people wearing dark glasses and looks of sympathy, everything, everything, everything—and had been cold as a Popsicle. She felt nothing, only a certain bother, when she foresaw pantomimes of the inconsolable widow, excruciatingly boring Masses and sermons, idiotic ceremonies, inventories, and other death-related nuisances. Yeah, better for him to stay alive; it's a lot less trouble. How horrible! Monster. Tyrannosaur. But what else could she do if that was honestly what was happening, what else could she do? At least she had been abashed when she confessed it to Bebel, who thank God will always be Bebel and wasn't shocked.

Yeah. Yeah. Honesty. Objectivity. Rationality. The trip to the house on the island—almost a change in residence, for the plan was to stay six months—she now saw from two main angles: opportunity to give poor Suzanna Fleischman, rather spaced out by now, a bit of breathing room, and to get rid of Eduardinho, a feat she hadn't managed to pull off completely in Salvador because he was a pest who didn't give up. Poor thing, he's not a bad person, but he's impossible. It's impossible with him; you feel like laughing out loud, which in fact happened once, and it hurt his feelings and he couldn't get it up the rest of the evening despite all the rubbing and heavy breathing that she submitted to and the stories about how this had never happened to him and all the times she had to say that it didn't matter and him going into about a thousand acrobatics and frenetic stroking because he took it to be a matter of honor that she wouldn't leave there before she came, when what she really wanted was to go home and take a shower and then she made a guttural semi-grotesque sound that she'd come up with by chance and that seemed to cause him great satisfaction and she moaned like *sssffff uhhhn-uhhhn* did you come darling yes forced murmurs you're killing me my love *ahhh-hh sssfff sssfff* how do you write those and other bed sounds Suzanna Fleischman jots down that the sound track of amorous encounters admits frightful variations and the rattling produced by certain endless screwings especially when you've already had it up to here for the day it's positively nauseating genital cacophony as Bebel suggested in any case Eduardinho thought I'd come and he'd saved the sexual reputation that for some reason he thinks he has he left me alone I smoked three cigarettes while I got dressed just to have them lighted in my mouth and he couldn't come around with those unpleasant little postcoital kisses of his and I went home I took a shower rubbing myself with the rough glove I had another attack of laughter like the one I had with him while I was fixing something to eat and I knocked over the toaster and there were only three besides the four or five flirtations that went nowhere how difficult it was I practically had to climb into Serginho's lap after riding next to him in that small car with my leg across the gear shift and every time he shifted gears he had to put his hand on my thighs but he didn't notice he danced with me with a hard-on without saying a word as if he couldn't care less like those guys they used to have in the movie theaters who'd rub their knees against mine looking straight ahead while I let them in the theater where I went to cut the private English class I was fourteen but looked eighteen everybody said and when I put on makeup I could get into adult-only films by paying full admission I felt his hand on my knee I didn't even think of moving my knee I had seen him in the lobby much older than I was and he had a mustache and everything but I didn't think he was a special turn-on just regular an older man normal screwable but at the time I opened my legs let him stroke my thighs and grab me right in the middle underneath my panties and when he put my hand on his fly I squeezed squeezed squeezed without taking my eyes off the screen and he took out that thing thick and soft and good to grab I had only touched two before and even then one on top of the clothes and I thought they were all the same thickness but this one filled my hand more and I had an uncontrollable urge to do what I'd seen in the dirty comic books that Débora stole from her brothers by the dozens and took to school to show me all the women in the stories dying with pleasure from sucking those enormous things and I don't know to this day why I didn't I should have done it like Suzanna Fleischman says we only regret what we don't do I think it was because I couldn't bend over in the theater the wildest thing I ever felt in my life I haven't forgot I go wild when I remember I should have gone ahead it'd be a great beginning I don't forgive myself for it we do a lot of stupid things in life he shuddered and stretched out his legs when he came I said I was going to the bathroom to wash my hands in spite of him lending me his handkerchief and I went and diddled myself I remember I came so hard I slipped and almost fell on the floor and I disappeared and never set eyes on him again and I had the balls to confess everything to Father Anselmo who I thought I was going to seduce and he didn't even bat an eye he gave me a chewing-out and a zillion penitences that I never did he wasn't like Molly Bloom's Father Corrigan who used to touch her in those days that's all I thought about. Maybe I'm losing it but I'm not I can't be because it hasn't been all that long that I danced with Serginho that way almost half an hour rubbing and rubbing against him I felt almost like that day in the movie theater and I came close to grabbing him right there I took him to the terrace and grabbed him and raised my skirt leaning against the railing like when I was a girl he came as soon as his body touched mine he was embarrassed and started pacing back and forth and said if there were time of course his cock would rise again I said of course of course but there wasn't time they might miss us despite everybody going crazy at the party and Ângelo Marcos as busy as could be thinking he was going to succeed in screwing Sílvia Regina crawling all over her and before I went back in I gave him a few kisses just to feel the pleasure of lightly biting his beautiful mouth and sticking my tongue in but he wasn't in the mood I smiled and said come on come and we went back inside and a few days later I found out that his premature ejaculation was a sure candidate for the Guinness he should be studied by medical science he must have made those two children with Veroca without her even noticing it sometimes he didn't even have to touch me it got up again and went down again the same way so I wanted to give him the treatment I read about in Masters and Johnson but it's so awkward that I'll never know if it works out because I didn't get it right the first two or three times I tried it I'm a failure as a sex therapist and I stopped seeing him and by all indications he got better and I got better really better as Suzanna Fleischman says fantasy is better fantasized than lived and without moralism without any moralism whatever none none none the truth is that without love it's no good it becomes just two people sweating and panting and twisting themselves into comic positions that's why I had that fit of laughter with Eduardinho because maybe if I loved him I could enjoy those would-be sexy expressions of his and his manner how shall I put it impetuous and virile turning the person over abruptly and making those lunges that seemed more like a goat butting and made me feel like a medieval fortress besieged by Vikings with a battering ram and calling me every dirty name in the book including some horrible ones in his Rio Grande dialect which I thought unspeakably gross it was like that with all of them one way or another it's no good that way watching the clock weird habits disappointing bodies unexpected odors sentimentality and hassles ludicrous subterfuges poorly timed intimacies oligophrenic rivalries it's not worth it no I'm not losing it and if I am I don't care monster tyrannosaurus humanity is really backward and like animals just like animals and in many ways never left and never will leave the Stone Age but I'm not losing it I'm just right I don't know what I do know is there's nothing wrong with me horses horses also thinking about posing nude like Molly horses Mellors horses mares John Thomas me lying on the flowery grass with him between my hands and receiving him gently to live everything to live everything ideally in your head from so many sides wanting but always saying No.

"Did you stuff these fish yourself?" Father Monteirinho asked, standing before one of the display cases that held fishes of several types, very shiny, that hung from nylon strands. "This snook here is perfect; it makes one feel like taking it home and having it cooked."

"These fish aren't stuffed," João Pedroso said. "Everything there is fake, except for the shape of the fish, of course. In the old days they used to stuff fish but it never really worked. No way, these are models. Even the scales are artificial; it's a polymer they invented that looks a lot better than the natural scale. The guy makes a mold of the fish and goes from there. And I wasn't the one who did it; it was a friend of mine who also restores antiques and has a real knack for such things. It was in the period when I was studying the motion of fish. Won't you have some more? Your glass is dry. There's no ice left. I'll—"

"No. Are you crazy? I'm not a blotter like you, and besides that it's getting late. I'm leaving soon."

"It's true, isn't it? I *am* a blotter. I'm going to be honest with you about that, Monteirinho. If you weren't my friend I wouldn't tell you, but you are my friend. Aren't you my friend?"

"Of course I'm your friend. But even so you had never shown me this museum of yours. Impressive. The fish, the shells, the insects—"

"The arthropods! Not only the class of insects but every type of arthropod. All that and almost the entire right side of the room is arthropods, including the card file. I was fascinated by them; they're great competitors of ours. They have nothing to do with us, you know; it's a different phylum, a different logic, a different strategy. See the large blue crab over there? That crab has a wonderful scientific name; it's called *Callinectes exasperatus*. Isn't that funny? Because not only is it a really a good swimmer but also it's really exasperated, it's— I'm going to pour you just one more, none of that stuff about leaving now; I'm an old bachelor myself and I don't even have the company of the church women like you. Tomorrow Father Coriolano can perfectly well say the seven o'clock Mass instead of you; you can claim you have another migraine."

"Well, just one more, but let me pour it myself. Otherwise you'll put half a liter into the glass. Yes, I was going to ask why you don't open up this museum; you could even charge admission. This is a real museum here, three enormous rooms—"

Feeling suddenly much drunker than before, João Pedroso walked unsteadily back to the small table where he had gone to get the ice bucket and didn't drop it only because the priest jumped up to help him. He declined the suggestion to sit down, preferring to lean for a time against a bookcase until he could steady himself.

"I'll tell you why, my dear friend Father Olavo Bento da Costa

Monteiro," he said, assuming a dramatic expression, chest half-expanded, mouth twisted in a exaggeratedly embittered rictus, eyes roaming aimlessly about the bookcases. "I'll tell you why. It's because, my esteemed and illustrious friend, this isn't a museum. Or rather, it *is* a museum, but not the kind you think. It's not a zoological museum, or one of natural history, not at all. There aren't even any collections here; no decent collector would call this jumble of rubbish collections. A museum all right, but a museum of failure, an inventory of incompetence, dispersiveness, and frustration. The rubble of an irresolute soul, my dear fellow, witnesses to a path of defeat, withdrawal, weakness, and incapacity. And cowardice, my dear fellow. And most sordid abjection, if you will permit me to besmirch your sainted ears with the description of my vileness. It's a very personal museum, my good reverend, and that's why only now have I been moved to show it to you. It's an act more radical than confession, much more radical. I'm confessing, Monteirinho, put on your confessor's face. I told you a while ago I'd explain that business about being a blotter, but I ended up not explaining it. It's a very simple explanation, nothing new about it: I'm a blotter—no, not a blotter; blotter is one of your delicate ways of putting things. A drunk, boozer, a real souse—in confession you ought to call things by their right names. I'm a drunk for the classic reasons; I'm not even original. I drink to forget. And I drink because I can't face things unless I have a buzz on. If I don't have something here in my thinker I get crying fits and attacks of melancholy. Everything seems absurd and impossible to bear. It's true, it's true. It isn't some fabricated explanation of convenience, it's true, it's true, I know it's true. And I haven't ended up in the gutter yet because I wasn't man enough, but one day I'll disappear and turn up there; it's the only culmination worthy of a guy like me. At least that; at least one day I'll have the dignity to carry things to their natural conclusion and wind up in the gutter. My ideal in life is Marmeladov; now and then I pick up *Crime and Punishment* just to read the parts where he appears. I'm telling you the truth, Monteirinho. I'm telling the truth as I never did before; you may think I'm joking or talking like this because I'm soused, but you can be sure that's not the case. This is a confession, and you should have on your confessor's face now.

"It's a complete confession; confessions are only good if they're complete. Fish . . . You remember asking about fish? Well, *voici* a mackerel, *Scomberomus regalis*, member of the tuna family, et cetera, et cetera, like all his relatives a great predator; you don't want to be a mullet around a tuna. Impressed? Scientific names always impress, they give the idea the guy knows something. They're the best way of faking knowledge, which is exactly what's happening at this very moment. Observe its sides and back, fleshy like those of all members of the tuna family, a pure muscular mass. The myotome is this muscle here. When it's as developed as this it indicates, along with other morphological, anatomical, and physiological characteristics, that the fish is good at acceleration and especially at sustained swimming. Extremely well supplied with blood vessels, highly oxygenated—that's why the meat of many of them is red, sometimes black like the blood of Homer's heroes. Many fish are specialized; some can dive quickly, others have stamina, others maneuver like mad, such as this spadefish from these parts; it's interesting. Anything else about fish? All about fish with Professor Pedrosonsky!

"There are lots of other pompous things I could say about the subject," he added, walking about the room as if swimming, bending over and holding onto the furniture in his path to maintain his balance. "After all, I own a fish shop and a couple of fishing boats and have the background to give pedantic names to everything that the other fishmongers and fishermen already know. Various things. It'd probably be enough for a short class at the high school level. Yeah. Slow learners, maybe. Because in reality I don't know anything about fish except that rote stuff that anybody can read in the encyclopedia, plus some bull picked up here and there. That's the reality."

"But what about that study of fish you mentioned? I don't understand. You said before—"

"Yes, the study of fish. Well, there wasn't any study of fish. There was supposed to have been, but it didn't come about. But there was a research project about fish. I was invited to participate and accepted. It was an excellent project, very well financed, with two or three ichthyologists from Cal Tech, a computer, a small ship, everything. I accepted, my dear Father Monteirinho, but just ask if I went. Go ahead, ask me if I went."

"You didn't go."

"You guessed it. I got sick with my kidneys just before time to leave, but today I know I'd get sick with some other thing, because I recall very well the fear and the insomnia that would hit me before the briefings. I only took part in two; at the third one I got sick. But I also know I could have studied. I'd sit down to study and wouldn't study. I preferred to sit there like a zombie and stare out the window, drinking wine—in those days I was in my wine phase. The fish I helped to make—my help was very little—are a kind of memento of the project, like everything in this museum something for me to look at and reaffirm just what I am, which is a piece of shit. They came back after the project. I picked up the paperwork they'd left with me, thought about it, saw that it would've been fascinating work for me, work that—Anyway, that's neither here nor there. Look at these dozens of things scattered around here that I was going to do but didn't, things I was going to build but didn't. See that over there? That's from my arthropod period. Two colleagues and I were going to study the chemical communications among *saúva* ants and among leaf-cutting ants, genus *Atta*—don't be impressed by the scientific names; they're in the *Young People's Illustrated Guide to Science*. It was from reading it that I got the idea for the project. The idea was to discover some way to ball up the chemical exchange of information among the ants and thereby ball up their lives without the use of pesticides. Many of the compounds they use to communicate are known; others aren't. Ask if I went through with it. Go ahead, ask! That over there, those little boxes of glass and those small tubes, was for an artificial anthill I designed, more or less lifted from an American design, and was going to build but didn't. No, my dear fellow, I have no wish to deny my pusillanimous and defeated state, for I know it better than anyone else and absolutely refuse to deceive myself. Do you mind if I get myself another drink, my good man? Believe me, just one more won't make any difference in my degradation, or even an entire bottle, my good reverend."

"João, stop talking nonsense. I don't believe a word you've said; things must have happened differently. I know you. I do believe that you may have suffered some disillusionment, some trauma that has undermined your work, but I can't believe that you have such a low opinion of yourself, that you're the human remnant you make yourself out to be. And you haven't convinced me of your incompetence either. It's clear that you still have command of your science, even when you try to ridicule yourself. Admit that you're dramatizing a bit, even to the point of speaking like Marmeladov, with that servile 'my dear fellow' right and left; you're playing a part. A man like you can't really be in such a state. I think that by tomorrow you'll be over the liquor and back to normal. You're just drunk. Speaking of which, everyone's had enough for today. I'm leaving; we'll see each other tomorrow."

"A moment, just a moment. One little moment. Monteirinho, I have to say what I'm about to say. Everybody's always talking to me about that business of 'a man like you.' It's like a cabalistic phrase. Just the other day it was Lúcio Nemésio who came out with it. That's a mistake; people think I'm different from what I am. Must be something about my face; do I maybe have blue eyes? The evidence couldn't be clearer—it leaps out at you, but still everybody thinks I'm different from what the evidence shows. It's crazy. There's no disillusionment or trauma involved, Monteirinho. You're right, I may have been dramatizing a little just now, but you're used to it; it's just a way I've found to face myself, like some kind of survival exercise. I don't know exactly how, but I'm sure that's what it is. I'm just what I told you—no more, no less. Or rather, I'm worse, I'm worse, I know I'm much worse, so much worse that I don't even want to go into detail about it. And even worse than that because of lack of hope; today I have no hope about anything. I find my individual destiny and our collective destiny as discouraging as can possibly be. In general I can't stand to hear what's going on, I can't hear about what's happening without going out of my mind and feeling like screaming. It's un-Christian to be without hope; it's as if it were a damnation. Maybe someone else would think I'm being melodramatic, but you know I'm a religious man, despite not accepting the teachings of the Holy Mother and hating those footnotes in the Catholic Bibles. You know I'm not being melodramatic when I say in all sincerity that I feel myself damned for betraying my gift, because it's the greatest sin against God and evolution, the greatest sin, understand? You can't betray evolution, which is the work of God and which is in the direction of intelligence and harmony, and everything to the contrary is the work of evil and the opposite of life. And, still I sink, I sink. I do nothing but sink further down. I haven't even had any children. I've done nothing! Look at me: almost fifty, degeneracy incarnate, an animal that has betrayed the species, a child of God betraying intelligence and light; it's the greatest of sins, the greatest sin, understand? It's true; I see it with dazzling clarity. I studied at a school run by priests, and they taught me Lucifer's motto. You know: *non serviam*, I shall not serve—exactly my case. So I know I'm damned. I feel the evil, I'm sure of it. God in heaven, Monteirinho, am I responsible for evil? I mean, does this evil that surrounds me come from within? Monteirinho, does the devil exist? Eh? There's a lizard that smiles, even if I don't know what connection one thing has with the other. But I have the sensation that some connection exists, and that frightens me even more. I don't know how to explain it to you. Yes, a lizard that smiles, maybe two, maybe more, always with two tails. It's not a smile like a human smile, it has a kind of aura about it that gives the impression that he's mocking something, or serving as some kind of symbol for my own ridiculousness. It's not a friendly smile. And it's not good, it's not good to see that lizard; it makes me feel like running away. I've been experiencing a kind of strange fear, a kind of sinister apprehension. Do you think I'm going crazy? It's not impossible; at times I'm convinced that's what it is. What can you tell me about Satan? You have to teach me about Satan; all I know is that his name means 'adversary.' It's a lot, I know. I'm aware that it's a lot, but I need to know more!"

Much later, before going to sleep, feeling his bed rock like a small boat on a heavy sea, João Pedroso remembered that, despite the drunkenness, he had managed to be coherent under the grave, concentrated, and attentive eye of Monteirinho. No, Monteirinho hadn't doubted anything; he had acted as if he took all of it quite seriously, had said he was going to study and give the matter some thought. One thing was sure, he had said: The Enemy exists. Evil exists. Hadn't he? João Pedroso couldn't muster the strength to recall precisely, because his eyes were already closing with sleep, and at that instant he sensed that, framed by the door to the living room, a presence that was not quite a body was delineated in imprecise and menacing outlines, its malevolent character manifest by something emanating from it. He was afraid. He didn't want to go on looking, and he decided he was having hallucinations. He pulled the sheet over his head and closed his eyes resolutely, telling himself over and over that he was drunk, very drunk, drunker than he had ever been.

This, however, did not occur with Father Monteirinho, who, still unable to sleep, got out of bed and in his nightshirt walked down the halls of the large old colonial house in search of a book to read until he could fall asleep. Among the dark recesses of the large bookcases and the cabinets of black wood carved with figures of angels, leaves, and fantastic animals, in the dim light of two bulbs, he ran his hands along a shelf and pulled out one of the old French volumes bound in leather. A curious collection, texts by eighteenth century prelates on philosophical, theological, and esoteric matters. He had never brought himself to actually read any of them, limiting himself to now and then opening one at random, leafing through it briefly, and smelling at close hand the odor that rose from the ancient pages. All right, he'd take one of them. But, despite having thought that he would find the reading amusing, he soon became disturbed and set the book aside, picked up his chaplet, and fell asleep praying. He had come across a text by a certain Abbot Fiard, who in his time must have been a very influential man, about the existence of devils. Man is assailed by *légions sans nombre d'esprits méchants*, the abbot said, before describing with distressing eloquence the troops of demons that everywhere besiege man, and Father Monteirinho recalled his conversation with João Pedroso. No, no, João Pedroso wasn't being pursued by Satan; what a silly situation, but even so, Father Monteirinho put the book aside and picked up his rosary.

The ones that stroke their own legs aren't too common but are perhaps the most irritating. He angrily remembered seeing on another occasion a young man having lunch at a table there in the Largo da Quitanda who, as he saw the dishes being laid out before him, took on an air of anxious and unsatisfied gluttony and never lifted his eyes from the food even while talking nonstop, constantly putting down the silverware to stroke his own thighs, his eyes turned upward and his breathing anguished. Although that day, after weeks of uninterrupted work, Lúcio Nemésio had decided to devote some time to himself and could stay until quite a bit later, reading and sipping English gin from the bottle that he had kept behind the bar for his private use, the young man's behavior had irritated him so much that he had to leave, suddenly fearful that he might not be able to contain himself and might commit an aggressive act and put an end to that intolerable behavior by insults and shoves. When he rose unexpectedly, ignoring the surprised chatter of Luiz the Waiter, he became even more incensed when he saw out of the corner of his eye that the detestable young man was eating from three dishes simultaneously, spearing slices of tomato, wolfing down chunks of barbecue, and, with lunges of his fork as rapid as the pecking of a chicken, ingurgitating a mixture of rice and some undefined substance—and not letting more than a few seconds go by without stroking his thighs. No, he couldn't stand it; it was too much, he had to get out of there, making an effort to avoid a further look at that objectionable scene.

And how could he not recall the self-caressing young man when another irritating type, though of a different genus, had just sat down?

The genus that spends hours obsessively combing his food with a knife until it's transformed into an unrecognizable mortar and then, after putting an outsized forkful in his mouth and beginning to chew in earnest, loads his fork again, holding it eight inches above the plate and sits there glassy-eyed staring at the next mouthful as if he has to keep watch over it lest it disappear. Unbearable, unbearable. He looks like a dog. Not as bad as the man with the thigh strokes, but still unbearable. Anger, real rage, fantasies of putting those guys and their entire families in a Vietnamese reeducation camp for at least twenty-five years, antagonism, true antagonism. All of them: the one who cuts his meat into little pieces before he starts to eat, the one who demands seared beef and picks off the condiments, the one who bends over his plate like a Muslim in prayer, the one who looks uneasy because he hasn't yet had a chance to sample all the dishes at a buffet, the one who smacks his tongue and sucks his teeth, the one who sticks his fingers in his mouth to push in the food—all, all, all of them. Unbearable! Right, but he couldn't let such people tyrannize him; today he wouldn't leave like the other time. He would, however, change tables. It was impossible to stay at that one, despite its being his favorite. Yes, he would change tables and turn his back on everyone, looking at the street and the sea beyond. It was the only solution.

"Anything wrong with your table, Dr. Nemésio?" Luiz the Waiter asked when he saw him change places.

"No, no. Take this piece of shit away and have them put in some gin, more ice, and three fingers of tonic water, and do me a favor. Run over to the post office and see if anything's arrived for me. If it has, bring it."

It wasn't intolerance at all, merely standards. He had the right to be irritated by patently offensive behavior. Humanity is still crap, an extremely backward specimen, the Brazilians most backward of all, and Bahians the most backward of the Brazilians. Yes, but he'd think about that later; right now he wasn't going to get upset about absolutely anything. The day was pleasant after a heavy rain, the calm sea reflecting the few clouds, both newspapers still untouched, Luiz bringing the copy of *Nature* that had arrived at the post office, the gin at precisely the correct measure, a sparkling glass, no obligations the entire day. The off-season, the city lethargic, just two or three gringos with their incredibly white legs, accompanied by blond catarrhal children. No, in reality, getting upset would be stupid. And he leaned his head back and opened the magazine.

The day had begun in a decidedly negative fashion because, walking with steps as tiny as the man himself, Dr. Sinval Penafiel, at first seemingly just passing through on his way home, caught sight of him, stopped in his tracks like a turkey, twirled about as if he were pecking in litter, and headed toward the table, his arms and face raised happily. Shit! Lúcio Nemésio attempted to bury his brow in his hat and hide his face behind the magazine, but to no avail. He was going to have to put up with another beginner's talk, a nice enough new young doctor but the most boring company this side of a logarithm table. And worse still: genteel, dedicated, studious and helpful, impossible to treat badly—what a drag! And even if he were to treat him badly, the other would think it normal, something that the venerated senior physician was entitled to do with the younger man. And he's going to talk about the hospital and about patients and he's going to ask questions and pile up a mountain of inexcusable appetizers on the table—truly, life has its cruel moments. No, worse than cruel: perverse. Worse than cruel and perverse: terrifying, crushing, for lo and behold, to complete the makeup of the table, which was now verging on a massive invasion, a silver station wagon was pulling up, and getting out of it, yelling and waving at Sinval, were the two doctors married to each other, Carminha and Antônio Mário Fontana! A roundtable, debate, seminar, what a drag! And what a seminar! The little guy wasn't so bad; one could tolerate him for fifteen minutes or so without serious neurological damage. An abdominal surgeon with a future of mediocre promise, industrious stupidity confined within reliable limits. So much so that he had made great progress in the few months since that day when, performing his first appendectomy at the hospital, he began the procedure with a medical school reference to McBurney's point then probably had McBurney doing cartwheels in his tomb when he opened an incision in the poor devil's belly big enough for a complete exploration of the abdominal cavity. And did he manage to find the cecum, despite the size of the hole he'd dug? No, he didn't, and you could see his jaw trembling beneath the mask, his hands looking as if they were afraid of the forceps. The one who located it was Lúcio Nemésio, who took pity on the intestinal ansae of the suffering patient and removed the forceps from the neophyte doctor's hands without a word, with the intention of finishing the operation himself if the appendix wasn't intact. But it wasn't even perforated, and the young doctor was able to proceed with his initiation. And he even did well from that point on, although Lúcio Nemésio thought it prudent to remain in the operating room until the belly had been properly stapled and decorated with a scar that would make everyone think the patient had had a run-in with Jack the Ripper.

But the other two, no. The other two lack the semisolid virtues of the first one; they're yuppie doctors, so to speak, or else in training to be. Even the chichi Rio accent that they affect, with definite articles in front of people's names, indecently dragged-out vowels and all the rest—that habit of Rio-like speech that snobbish Bahians have. And all the time dropping names of friends they consider important and wearing cutesy clothing covered with slogans, and exhibiting their cutesy ways of doing things, cutesy slang and an extremely annoying sense of humor—especially him. He laughs at anything he doesn't understand, which is to say practically everything he hears. The only way to get him to stop reacting to the world with those brays of his is to chew him out. And you still have to pretend you believe it when, with that saintly face of his that gives you the creeps because it's so obviously hypocritical, he speaks of his intention to help the low-income disfigured, when it's obvious that he's just getting experience and building a résumé to prettify rich noses and breasts worth their weight in gold, which in fact he already began doing in Salvador, backed up by notes in the society columns and little newspaper articles in badly edited jargon. He should have started with his own wife's ample schnoz. She's not really ugly, but she's not pretty either, and she's the type of woman who incessantly plays with her hair over colossal earrings and runs her eyes over every corner of the place. She must find herself quite interesting and sexy. Fontana had better watch out. She says she's a pediatrician. Standard treatment: antibiotics. Principal procedure: looking at throats and talking of the need for education about hygiene. Basic bibliography: the instruction sheet accompanying the medicine. Only a reader of instruction sheets says things like "hepatic parenchyma" and calls a nosebleed an "epistaxis"; no serious doctor talks like that. Well, close the magazine, fold the newspapers, put your elbows on the table, resign yourself. What about his expression? It didn't really matter if he looked bored or ill-humored, since he'd never been Mr. Nice in any case, and the older he got, the less patience he had, not only with boring and stupid people but also with everything that struck him as irrelevant. On second thought, they must be used to it by now. There are certain rewards to being known as an old fogy. Here comes Sinval leading the way, with his ornithoid gestures that recalled a worried seedeater. Following the handshakes, the pats on the shoulder—why the devil do people have to greet one another with a ritual of pats, clasps, strokes, shakes, and other forms of touch like dogs that meet and start sniffing each other?—and kisses on each cheek from Dr. Carminha, Sinval, who doesn't even read English and hasn't the faintest idea of what *Nature* publishes, is going to grab the magazine without asking permission and say, with a familiar air, "Is that the latest *Nay-toory?*"

"Is that the latest *Nay-toory?*" Sinval asked, thumbing through the pages, as soon as all of them were settled.

"Yes," Lúcio Nemésio said, and something in his way of speaking led Sinval to put the magazine down, as if it were an object that had suddenly become quite hot.

"It really rained today, didn't it?" Fontana said, as he summoned Luiz the Waiter with his hand. "Geez, I never saw so much rain, geez. Did you see how it rained? Geez!"

"Yes," Lúcio Nemésio replied, almost snarling, and Fontana cut off midway the smile he had essayed, pretending to pay great attention to Luiz's arrival.

An uncomfortable silence, and Carminha shook her earrings as if trying to achieve flight. Fontana, laughing at what he himself was saying, although there was no apparent reason for doing so, placed an order for drinks with Luiz and attempted to prolong the conversation by asking to hear stories about the island, but Luiz was very busy and left at once, after which silence again descended, broken only by the clinking of Carminha's earrings and by Sinval's fingernails drumming on the table. Lúcio Nemésio shifted in his chair, tapped the newspapers several times, and for a few seconds harbored the hope that they would cancel the beers they had ordered and leave, for he was a bit ill at ease acting in such an openly rude manner, even if a type of perverse obstinacy prevented him from changing his attitude. He might even have wanted to, but he didn't. As he knew it would be, he quickly saw the hope was in vain, because Sinval got up, went to the Bahian street vendor whose place of business was under the large chestnut tree and returned with an elephantine helping of fried bean-cakes, beans with pepper and palm oil, animal spleens, boiled peanuts, and unidentifiable tidbits wrapped in banana leaves. Lúcio Nemésio sighed. To him, appetizers always seemed a gross abuse; there ought to be a law against them. Drinking is one thing, eating is another. A man must be regarded with suspicion who sits down to drink and right away orders something to chew; there's something wrong with him. But he was really beginning to feel somewhat bad at being unable to go beyond monosyllables and grunts at a gathering in which he should at least be cordial, so he would therefore ignore as much as possible the feeding frenzy about to ensue, though it wouldn't be easy. And, after all, maybe he should say something, because if he didn't, they would take the initiative and bring up elementary topics, asking dumb questions and expressing childish opinions, not to mention Fontana's asinine braying. But talk about what?

He didn't know, and, partially not to have to look at anyone, or at the appetizers which by now were scattered in confusion around the table, he turned his eyes upward. Among the four or five birds perched on the wires across the street, chestnut-colored swarms of flying ants made the air seem alive and tremulous. Where do those insects come from in such numbers, just after a heavy rain? One day he had decided to counterattack when his house was invaded by thousands of them, and he had doused them with insecticide. The next day the servants filled a bucket with their dead bodies.

"To me it's spontaneous generation," he said suddenly. "To me it's spontaneous generation," he repeated, feeling pleasure at hearing his own voice and a light intoxication that couldn't be attributed to the gin and tonic but must be because of the power that he possessed and knew how to exercise, a power that now made him feel different. "To me it's spontaneous generation," he said again, pointing with his chin to the flying ants and resolving to amuse himself with his own talk, since he had in mind interesting things that he now felt like saying, and that way this trio of microcephaloids would have no chance to try his patience.

"Yes, spontaneous generation," he intoned, with enjoyment at making his deep voice thunder. "All you need is one of these April rains, a downpour like today, and they appear out of nothing. If the swallows and flycatchers had a Bible too, it would be written there that it's a gift from heaven, God raining food from the firmament as he did with the Hebrews in the desert. As we don't eat flying ants, we don't recognize the miracle. It's the same thing with those haunted frogs that meow like cats all winter and then vanish: spontaneous generation. My friend João Pedroso, who's crazy and whom you probably know as a fish vendor but who is one of the greatest scientific talents of my acquaintance and knows more zoology than all of us put together know medicine, would probably have a logical and well grounded explanation, but I would continue to argue for spontaneous generation. Certain convictions are non-negotiable. I am a materialist and can therefore perfectly well formulate the hypothesis that certain physico-chemical reactions, after rain, provoke the sudden appearance of that form of life. A form of life in fact better than our own in at least one respect, because there is no individuality in it. They don't function as individuals; there's none of this disorderly, chaotic, undisciplined, tense thing that we've created. Uniformity is as elegant as a beautiful mathematical formulation, don't you agree? And that's why I don't believe in God; I can't believe in an intelligence that would intentionally disorganize itself. Don't you believe that entropy, understood as the tendency toward disorder, is proof of the nonexistence of a supreme being? Any Cartesian here who'd like to quibble to the contrary? Those verbal proofs, based on logic that in the final analysis is arbitrary, aren't scientific, they're sophisms—ingenious sophisms and worse, wishful thinking. It's not because it's that way, it's that way because one wants it to be. Repeat the Cartesian proof of the existence of God so I can refute it. St. Thomas, Locke, whoever you want. Does the soul exist? They thought it does. Come on, state your case. I know you're like everyone else, unreconciled to being mortal and unresigned to the indifference and transitory nature of the universe."

Now in a very good humor, reinforced by the conviction that his audience didn't understand what it was hearing, he gave an intentionally hollow laugh and stared at each of them for an instant, feigning to await the answer he knew would not be forthcoming. Fontana joined him in laughter but Lúcio Nemésio stopped abruptly and Fontana was unable to continue by himself. Carminha shook her earrings and ran her hand over the back of her neck, beneath her hair. Sinval thought the best thing to do was to nod his head repeatedly.

"Do animals have souls?" Lúcio Nemésio burst out again, in the same sudden way. "*Anima*, animal—everybody knows that. So, do they have only an etymological soul, or do they have a real soul? Well, what about it—do they? If they do, they're immortal, aren't they? Look at that pack of dogs playing over there. Dogs play; why do dogs play? They amuse themselves; why do they need to amuse themselves? If they amuse themselves and need to amuse themselves, they must have a soul like us. Does a crab have a soul? A crab is alive, but I don't think it amuses itself, exclusive of some sensory pleasure or other, if we can call it such in a rudimentary neurological structure. Do fish have souls? It's hard to believe fish have souls. Is the soul a privilege of animals with greater organic complexity? Is the soul unique to the higher mammals? To primates? Lemurs, those hairy animals that remind you of startled opossums and that we see only in television films about Asian fauna, are primates. Even my friend João Pedroso, who inexplicably believes in a soul and in God and is the one who teaches me such things about biology, told me there's serious speculation that if the dinosaurs hadn't become extinct through some monumental catastrophe around the end of the Mesozoic, their encephalization index and related phenomena would have led one or more species of those large lizards to intelligence, just like us. Truthfully, he told me, a bit sheepishly because of his irrational belief in God, it's thought that the tendency of intelligence, universally, if life evolved along similar paths to those it took here on earth, would be to develop itself into reptiles. The earth would be an exception with this business of mammals. Primates, men—it's all random, fortuitous, an accident. Even comic books grasped that long ago; extraterrestrials are always tremendous huge lizards. If it weren't for the catastrophe, large lizards would be talking here today, philosophizing and believing in an Absolute Lizard and in their own immortality. And we, the primates and hominids, if we accept the doubtful hypothesis that we would even emerge, would probably be raised for slaughter, since our evolution would long since have been directed by the lizards, through selection mechanisms like those we apply to cattle, so we'd be plump, docile, and as intelligent as an average-IQ jackass. Does only the human being have a soul? What is a human being? Phylum chordates, subphylum vertebrates, class mammals, order primates, family hominids, genus *Homo*, species *sapiens sapiens*. Each cell contains forty-six chromosomes. Its specificity depends on those forty-six chromosomes; it's a very delicate thing. So I can say, indeed I must say, that man is an animal with forty-six chromosomes. Very well, as Dr. Maria do Carmo could explain much better, but I'm also a studious chap, carriers of Down's syndrome, the mongoloids, have an aberrant triplicate twenty-first chromosome. In other words, a total of forty-seven chromosomes. So they don't fit the definition of a human being, and a computer programmed with rigorous criteria would not recognize them as such. Therefore they have no soul? Who has a soul? What has a soul? Many of the atrocities committed against black slaves sprang from the generalized and then well-established doubt over whether they had souls. Does a lizard have a soul? Does a turtle have a soul? Ah, my dear colleagues, how backward we are. Consider the brain-damaged percussion sounds coming from Zé's there on the corner. It's not because they make that disrespectful din that I say they're primitive, for that's cultural; every Bahian thinks that others want to listen to what he's listening to, at the volume that he favors. Yes, he's primitive, but peculiar to Bahia. But music in itself, any kind of music, from that mindless cacophony to Beethoven, is in reality a universal psychotropic drug, thus its mysterious effects even on people's physiology. Not only on people, on animals in general. Everyone's read some piece of nonsense about the influence of music on the well-being of cows and hens. There are several medical references in classical antiquity about music and health; there was even one guy who swore that flute music cured snakebites. A snakebite in his head maybe, nowhere else. But other effects aren't so mysterious to me, because if the body has various unconscious natural rhythms it's conceivable that exposure to periodic sounds, combined with the emotional associations that we learn to make with music, may produce certain effects on those rhythms. An animal instinct. What is music? What is dance? I sympathize greatly with Plato on that point. His gnoseology strikes me as addled; shadows in the cave and all that crap. But not his politics; the Republic strikes me as attractive. He was right in not wanting to have anything to do with musicians. Primitives, irrational and basic primitives. Consider: What is music? What's this thing of not being able to resist moving the body, or some part of it, upon hearing certain sounds? Yes, backward, backward, very backward. I'm going to tell you a few things, but first I must provide some preliminary information. Do you know how the fishermen in these parts fish at night? Naked. They fish naked. In the type of fishing known as casting-net fishing, which is done with two canoes, one of them, who's called the net-lowerer . . ."

He turned to the others with an expression that would have been affectionate had it been less ironic, and went on talking as if he would never stop, still feeling the same pleasure at hearing his own voice, saying whatever came into his head and happy at knowing himself to be better than the others and able to prove it in various ways.

3

It may have been his first turtle, an important turtle to a boy of twelve, but in any case João Pedroso blinked more than usual when he saw the expression of pleasure and the shining eyes with which the son of the fisherman Bededéu climbed onto the back of the turtle, which had been wounded by nets and gaffs, held it by the head, and cut its throat with a fish knife, using a sawing motion until the head was held by only a leathery string, which took a long time to cut because the turtle thrashed after it was decapitated, making the boy lose his balance. But, under the gaze of his father, observing him from the canoe as he rolled a black cigar in his mouth, the boy demonstrated that he took his mission seriously, and, a bit angrily, turned the animal on its back and finished cutting off its head, which he threw to one side, and stuck the knife into the base of the neck, while its legs fanned the air as if it were trying to run. The viscera and muscles were then exposed as the boy carved up the animal with quick strokes, unhampered by the organs and flesh that contracted and shuddered the entire time.

"How horrible!" said a woman behind João Pedroso. "And isn't it illegal to kill turtles?"

A stranger's voice, a tourist's voice, lightly affected but not unpleasant. He turned around, raising the brim of his hat slightly, and saw a woman a little past thirty, wearing loose bermudas, a blouse knotted at the waist, a large straw hat, and enormous dark glasses. Next to her, his elbow on the counter of the fish market, was a man with a drawn and fatigued appearance who was also wearing large dark glasses and was dressed in a type of sailing outfit with short pants and short sleeves. Perhaps they were the owners of the white boat that had shown up this morning docked alongside the ramp, almost a yacht. Yeah, they had the appearance of rich people. And now the two of them were looking in his direction, as if the woman's question had been meant for him.

"Did you ask me something?" he said finally.

"Yes, I did," she said, sounding a bit authoritarian. "I asked if the killing of turtles isn't prohibited. What a horrible spectacle. Are you the one who's going to sell it?"

"No. I even tried to buy it to let it loose. I always do that, though everyone around here says I'm crazy. But the fishermen hate turtles; they say they foul their nets and that they're cheap meat, so Bededéu wouldn't sell it to me and ordered his son to kill the animal."

"Oh, you buy them to set them free? He buys them to set them free, Marquinhos. If I could, I'd buy them too. Have you already let many of them go?"

"Some; about ten or twelve. The fishermen say it doesn't do the least bit of good since once they've been caught in a net for long they die anyway."

"But in any case it's prohibited, and you're the only one who obeys the law, and you even pay."

"I don't know if it's actually prohibited; I never inquired. It must be, because I believe most species are in danger of extinction. But it's also because I feel sorry for them. Maybe I was a turtle in another incarnation."

"Ha-ha. Who knows? I may have been one myself, because it's the same way with me. I don't feel sorry for fish, but for turtles I do. Don't you think turtles are nice animals, Marquinhos?"

She took off her glasses and hat as she said this, shaking her head to arrange her hair, and João Pedroso, with something close to shock, realized he had never seen such a beautiful woman. A very full head of blond hair, eyes of a lively color that seemed to change with the light, a clear and open smile, a very attractive mouth—and something about her, something impossible to describe. He felt his ears turning red, feared he was blushing, gave a tiny smile, and averted his gaze, not knowing where to look. But he couldn't stop himself and looked again in her direction. Hat and glasses in her hands, she was chatting with her husband.

"Speaking of fishing," she said, glancing at her watch, "it's already after seven. What time are we leaving? Serious fishing can't start late."

"I don't know," her husband replied, his voice as tired as his appearance. "Joaquim is out there, waiting for the guide. Without a guide there's no point in leaving here; the crew on the boat isn't familiar with the fishing places in these parts. And Bebel hasn't shown up yet; aren't you going to wait for her?"

She clicked her tongue in disdain, looked at João Pedroso, and smiled. Yes, he was blushing; this time he was sure he was blushing, though he hoped that in the faint light inside the Market no one could see it. Why didn't he get out of there? Why didn't he plunge into the rear of the fish market and pretend he was doing something with the frozen goods, why did he insist on standing there with his ears burning and his Adam's apple bobbing up and down and his heart racing so fast that his sternum seemed to be throbbing? It wasn't because he was trying to overcome his fear, for on the occasions that something like this had happened to him, if never so intensely, he had always tried unsuccessfully to dominate his fear and, in one way or another, had ended up fleeing. He didn't leave now because he was rooted to the spot, his feet glued to the ground and refusing to move, his eyes fixed on her face despite the actual physical feeling of discomfort that it evoked in him. He couldn't bring himself to return her smile, though he would have liked to, and instead—silently cursing himself—made only a vague gesture with his head, which he hoped would be interpreted as a sign of courtesy.

"Oh yes, Bebel," she said, turning again to her husband, and João Pedroso, now sweating slightly, would have liked very much for her to be wearing a low-cut blouse so he could see her back. "You think she's coming? She hates to get up early, but she promised she'd be here at six-thirty. Her and Nando."

"I have my doubts about Nando. He once told me he didn't close a deal in which he was going to make over three hundred thousand dollars, just so he wouldn't have to get up early in the morning. And early for him is anything before eleven, preferably before noon."

"You're right," said a very tall woman with a jovial face who burst on the scene beside them, having come from the other end of the Market without their noticing her. "It was because of him that I'm late. He swore he'd wake up; I believed him and spent the better part of half an hour trying, but there was no way to get him out of bed. Fishing for him is a nighttime activity."

Very different from the other woman, João Pedroso observed, though not unattractive, perhaps even pretty, a type of beauty emphasized by a certain showiness, but still beauty. She was wearing an extremely short skirt, slit at the sides, as well as a short blouse that showed her navel, a colored kerchief on her head, glasses on her forehead, and carried a large yellow straw bag with a red sun at its center. With sprightly steps, she kissed both her friends, then placed the bag on the counter to straighten up.

"I thought Marquinhos would be terribly angry with me by now because of the delay. I thought I'd spoiled everything; everybody says fishing is only good in the early morning."

"Not at all, love; you didn't miss a thing. In fact it was better that way because you didn't witness the murder of a turtle here by a boy I won't even let wash my car, a horrible spectacle with the animal squirming around after it was dead. Horrifying."

"Spare me. I can't stand to see anything dying; it's awful! Let's drop the subject and think about fishing. So where's the fishing? So then, Captain, you make me get up at an ungodly hour, I show up here fully equipped and ready for anything, and what happened to the fishing?"

"I don't know if there's going to be any fishing. The guide still hasn't arrived; the people in these parts say one thing and do another. Without a guide there's no point in even starting out because we won't catch anything, we'll just be bathing worms. There must be someone who knows the places where there are fish."

"What about the people here? Can't we hire somebody else?" And she looked at João Pedroso as if expecting him to introduce himself. "These people know everything around here; why not get one of them?"

"It's not that easy. Few people are good guides, and many of those who are don't know certain fishing spots. It has to be a guy with experience like that fellow I hired. I've been out with him before; he's very good, but he's a boozer and must have tied one on last night. Probably still isn't awake. Well, we can always go out for a cruise. We'll leave the bait shrimp and squid in the refrigerator and make a lunch of it later. You know how well Cornélio cooks from the days when he was chef at the ministry and I requisitioned him for my office, so he could work on the yacht and there at the house without time problems. Now he's taken some course or other for gourmets, which I paid for, and is even better. We can take a spin around the bay, Cornélio will prepare a nice dish of shrimp and squid. . . . What do you say, Bebel?"

"Oh, I don't know. Ana Clara and I have made so many plans. What'd you think, Aninha?"

"If it's just to wander around, the best thing is to go to the beach. I already know everything here backwards and forwards," Ana Clara said, again looking at João Pedroso as if seeking corroboration for what she was about to say. "We might even try fishing, take a chance, stop somewhere and drop in our lines. There are fish everywhere; all you need is a bit of luck."

"I think it's idiotic, but you're as stubborn as they come," Ângelo Marcos said with a yawn. "Whatever you like. For my part, I think I'm going to take a nap on the boat. These days, what with the nausea medicine, all I do is sleep."

Why was she still looking at João Pedroso that way? She could have left as quickly as the other woman, who went at once to the edge of the ramp to await the gig, accompanied at a distance by the man. But she took her time, picking up a bag and a package with a handle after first leisurely adjusting her hat and blouse and sticking the arm of her glasses down her neckline. Would she stop, after turning her back and starting to move away? Yes, she did stop, turned partially and, with the same smile that he already found almost unbearable, said "Ciao" and left, walking slowly away.

"See you later," João Pedroso said, his throat tight.

No, he couldn't do it. He'd never manage; it would be embarrassing. He'd never make it halfway there, never get out a single word. But he strode quickly toward the ramp, overtaking the group waiting for the gig. He tapped the shoulder of Ana Clara, who'd had her back to him and turned around with a slight start.

"Excuse me," João Pedroso said, staring at the sea as if watching the progress of the gig. "If you'd like, I can be your guide."

At first Ana Clara didn't understand, but then she uttered a small cry, and it seemed for a tiny instant that she would embrace him. "Really? You will? You will?"

"Marquinhos!" she said, grabbing her husband by the arm. "We have a guide! This gentleman—What's your name?"

"João Pedroso."

"Glad to meet you, Mr. João Pedroso. Ana Clara Barreto. This is my husband. Dr. Ângelo Marcos, and this is our friend, Bebel Magalhães. Marquinhos, isn't it fantastic? A miracle: A guide showed up at just the right moment!"

"How much do you charge, Mr. João?" Ângelo Marcos asked. "You people around here are shrewd. When you know somebody has money you gouge."

"No, no. I won't charge anything. I don't do this professionally. I have a fish counter over there and—"

"Oh no, Mr. João, you're not going to work for nothing. You have to give us a price."

"Let it be, Aninha. If João says he doesn't want to charge anything it's because he doesn't want to. Right, João?"

"Of course, of course."

"He'll take part in the fishing and the cruise with us. You *are* going to dip a line, aren't you, João?"

"Yeah, maybe. I just have to tell Boa Morte, who works with me in the fish market. I'll be right back."

He still didn't know how it had all happened when the crew prepared the boat to weigh anchor and he made himself comfortable beside the first mate, his mouth dry and his heart again beating rapidly. He wanted to ask for water but felt he was still too nervous and frightened to confront the difficulty of drinking a glass of water under her gaze. She was sitting in the stern, in a kind of living room, close to the others.

"You're giving the orders," she said unexpectedly, behind him. "Rubinho here will put this boat wherever you like. Won't you, Rubinho?"

"Just say where."

João Pedroso turned. She had removed the blouse and was wearing a bikini top. Quite nervous, he managed to talk and, although he was fearful of looking her in the eye and spoke as if he needed to inspect endlessly every corner of the boat, he found the courage to ask if he could have a glass of water, which she herself brought a short time later. Did she notice that their fingers brushed when she handed him the glass? He decided he was delirious and perhaps at risk of going out of his mind for good, since he'd never acted this way in his life and therefore wasn't himself. He must see if he could control this craziness to some extent, at least till he could calm down. Light-headed and disordered, he turned to Rubinho and told him to steer north, crossing the channel and passing outside the buoys.

Impossible. Maybe, yes, no, of course, yes. No. Yes. No! Enough! Well, no sooner had they dropped anchor at the first fishing site, after magic passes by this man, who merely squinted in the direction of vague spots along the shore and murmured instructions to the first mate and the bowman—what a really, really beautiful thing! They had no sooner stopped when Ângelo Marcos, stuffed with nausea medicine and worried about the marine performance of his American toupee, fell asleep in the suite of the boat. She had already noticed that the man was more than a fishmonger, of course he was much more than a simple fishmonger, and had confirmed this in his eyes, despite their evasiveness, at the moment Ângelo Marcos spoke to him with that condescending familiarity. And she had confirmed it a second time when, as her husband snored and Bebel was more interested in getting a tan and reading than in fishing, she had talked with him for a good part of the morning, while they amused themselves with locating the fishing spots and the fish. At first it was difficult to get more than a short sentence or two out of him, and there were times when it seemed as if he wanted to go on talking but choked midway through, bit his tongue, averted his eyes, and essayed a series of awkward gestures which in the beginning came close to making her laugh but soon instilled in her a certain tenderness, almost affection. Attractive? No, you couldn't say so just like that, in an objective sense, despite there being something very solid in him and his face invoking in her indefinable memories. Yes, attractive, yes. Why not? Certainly.

"Fishmonger, wino, ex-biologist," he had answered after becoming more at ease and after they had laughed a great deal when, instead of the expected snappers at one of the fishing spots they caught only puffers, one after the other. Impressed by his explanations of puffers and of fish in general, she had commented that he seemed like a biologist and very erudite.

Criticizing herself for creating what might be excessive intimacy, which could even bring problems in the future, she was unable to control the impulse to ask questions about the half-morbid emphasis he had given to the word "wino," as if attempting to display indifference, or even pride, but in reality concealing great shame. She told him this, trying to sound the least psychoanalytical and meddlesome as possible, and for the first time he showed his teeth as he smiled.

"Could be," he said. "Anything is possible."

"Avoidance," she said, immediately feeling rash and a boor. "I'm sorry; it's none of my business. I'm sorry. Let's change the subject."

And she wanted so badly to change the subject that she rose from the side of the boat and decided to go below for a few moments, pretending to be taking care of something. But as she turned to go to the passageway, her eyes met his and they looked at each other perhaps a bit longer than they should have; no, not perhaps—they definitely looked at each other, and she blushed, as did he, something she didn't know could still happen to her.

Jealous of Bebel; that's a good one. Well, not really jealous—a small crisis of possessiveness. After twice changing books, in a manner that Ana Clara wouldn't have noticed before but which now struck her as somewhat blatant, Bebel, who in all fairness still has the same great body as when she was in her early twenties, paraded conspicuously along the deck, consumed by a sudden interest in fishing and in João. Ana Clara felt uncomfortable thinking of him only by his first name. Too much closeness, threatening to some degree. But what nonsense; she couldn't go on referring to him as "that man." All this was exaggerated defensiveness, neurotic fear. Stop it. Yes, but how innocent Bebel's face was, swinging her hips around the boat in a flawless embodiment of the bombshell, a perfect mulatto dancing at a barbecue joint if she weren't so white, pretending to be unaware that the eyes of every man there, with the natural exception of Cornélio, were glued onto her. Yeah, childish, based on possessiveness, as if Bebel weren't Bebel, the queen of the hedonists. As if João Pedroso were her plaything and Bebel wanted him too, that's what it was. But she had to acknowledge that she had gotten irritated when, with João seated at the rail with a line in his hand, Bebel had practically rubbed the front of her bikini in his nose. She doesn't shave anywhere, so it must have tickled his face.

She had felt like leaving in a huff but instead went below to the suite, where Ângelo Marcos was still sleeping in his toupee and beret. She looked at herself in the mirror angrily, noting the horrible pair of bermudas that recalled those gym shorts that girls used to wear in Catholic schools. She undid the cord impatiently, leapt out of the bermudas, and evaluated her stomach and hips. Shape for shape, I can hold my own with anyone, she thought rather irritably. But she wouldn't go up in this bikini. She'd go up in the yellow one whose cut showed off her hips better and wasn't the classical type she was wearing now—too much good taste can get in the way sometimes. Making no noise, so Ângelo Marcos wouldn't wake up and want to grope her if he saw her nude, she changed bikinis, quickly straightened herself, and returned topside, where she emerged glowingly before João Pedroso, and upon approaching him stopped and let down her hair, and remained for a long time with arms raised as she arranged it behind her head.

Ridiculous but true. Of course that night, as they walked along the deserted Boulevard while the men played poker at home, they laughed themselves breathless over what had happened on the boat, both of them like those women who flaunt their fannies at Carnival dances. Back and forth, pouts, wiggles, brazen strutting, and posturing. Marine madness, that's all it could be, one of those things that suddenly attacks anyone who exposes himself to too much ocean air. The great Miss Fish Market pageant, Bebel said, having to hold on to a tamarind tree till she managed to stop laughing. The poor guy's face when they sat down, one on each side of him; he looked like he'd swallowed a spider. Yes, but during the contest it was serious business, and poor João must think he came across two ravenous perverts and that next time they'll be on him like a pair of barracudas. Bebel, in a way, had come out ahead, because Ângelo Marcos, though still groggy and looking as if he would vomit on the next person he spoke to, woke up and decided to fish also. With someone watching, the competition naturally became impossible. Even so, there were moments when she and João could look at each other again, and each time she thought she had seen in his face that she was the winner.

No, of course Bebel hadn't come out ahead. How foolish. She *had* come out ahead at the end of the fishing, but even then she didn't know what kind of man João was. She still thought he was nothing but a simple fishmonger. Not Ana Clara; she had enjoyed herself with him, had learned things, had laughed a lot. She laughed especially because, once he stopped acting like a cabbage, he became very funny and cheerful.

Highly cultured. Impressive. And not only in biology. In everything; he seems to have read everything. And he's not one of those bor-ring affected types who only talk in polysyllables and look down their noses at everything other people enjoy. He's a man of great simplicity, one who deems himself ignorant but you can see it's not affectation. The man is a mystery. Fishmonger. Wino. What fine company! And when they said good-bye she was also the winner, for he looked at no one but her and blushed again when she shook his hand, saying that she was greatly pleased with the fishing and with him and hoped there would be other pleasant days like that one. Could she invite him again? Yes, yes, and he ran his hand along his face for a long time as soon as she released it.

Suzanna Fleischman, who was working on a collection of observations in an admittedly confused but quite prolific phase, might have pricked up her ears. She had written a veritable monograph on smiles between men and women, concluding that a lot of unbridled laughter was a sure sign of some kind of hanky-panky brewing. Too much on the same wavelength, too much charm. Danger, danger. And what couldn't be denied was that they had laughed a great deal; there had never been a more delightful fishing trip. Now that she thought about it, she hadn't done anything so enjoyable for a long time. Danger, danger. Suzanna Fleischman would probably come up with some sardonic comment, and she'd be absolutely right. Besides which, since Eduardinho—who incidentally must detest the island, since fortunately he'd stopped making those adolescent phone calls with all their whispers and secret codes—this business of affairs had been canceled, for reasons both practical and rational. Suzanna Fleischman, implacably objective and logical, with her latest working hypotheses: having a lover, as amply corroborated by experience, means love or fooling around; fooling around is no good and gets you nowhere. Love is hard; it's for those who can swing it. Those who can't swing it do their own bit and end up as ecologists or some such thing. The rest is neurosis.

It's a matter of rationality. Rationality demands that these ideas about João Pedroso, vague, imprecise, and hesitant, but vivid enough, be quickly digested and forgotten. In the first place, it's true she is in a vulnerable and difficult phase in general. What a situation! Ângelo Marcos like a plucked chick, nauseated all the time, dying from self-pity, more dependent than a kitten and falling into abysmal depressions at every turn. She—a total monster, a tyrannosaur—went on forcing herself to simulate worry that she didn't feel, if it could even be called feeling and not indifference. No, indifference wasn't the word. It was horrible to recognize: a certain disgust. An undefined, diffuse disgust that made her imagine in him nonexistent repulsive odors and find him viscous to the touch. What a sacrifice to have to endure—and she was enduring it gallantly; in that respect she was being truly heroic—the periodic bouts of virility, horniness, and passion that beset him, days and days of huffing priapism and grandiloquent declarations. Therefore, it's patently clear that she's at the right point for latching onto the first more or less suitable man who comes along, and that's what rationality doesn't allow. Let's not be stupid and inimical to our own self-interest. In the second place, what does she know about João Pedroso? Nothing. The way he said "wino," right at the start, really exposed something, almost certainly something unpleasant, much more than just taking a drink now and then. Although he doesn't have the puffy look of the professional toper, he could be one of those I-became-an-alcoholic cases, which would explain why a guy so apparently competent would prefer selling fish in that poor, dirty market. Maybe he was trying to give a warning, or to defend himself beforehand. Suzanna Fleischman, who claims to hate proverbs but is a real Sancho Panza when it comes to using them, would immediately chime in with something about where there's smoke there's fire, or something equally malicious but sound. If experience proved that, despite appearances and despite mythology, a good man really *is* hard to find, even in the places where you'd expect to find a reasonable percentage of them, what's this man—into middle age but in good shape, single, very interesting, and convenient as can be—doing here just waiting to be grabbed up?

Something was wrong, of course. Wrong, all wrong. Rationality.

But, on the other hand, there was no need for involvement just to spend time with him. After all, he's one of the few stimulating people on the island. Socially, of course. Spend time socially. That's not irrational, especially if you know how to look out for yourself. Not only on the fishing trips—there was already one set for Saturday, when the boat came back from being overhauled—but also on other occasions, even for lunch or dinner, a little get-together to break the monotony. If you play with fire you get burned, Suzanna Fleischman would say straightaway, and Ana Clara clicked her tongue. Better safe than sorry, don't poke a tiger with a short stick, experience is the best teacher, fools rush in where angels fear to tread, Suzanna insisted irritatingly. What rubbish, he's just a nice man with whom they could all be friends, nothing beyond that, nothing at all. It was being blown out of proportion and she didn't want to think about it anymore. But yes. No. Why not? Yes, maybe. If you play with fire . . . No. No. No. Impossible. Enough!

Adversity anneals the spirit. It was the truth, an ineluctable truth that Ângelo Marcos now felt in his flesh. At first, standing before the mirror when he tried on toupees, he almost wept at the sight of the glabrous ball that shone like a gloomy moon under the light of the bathroom cabinet. Not a hair, not a single one. Terrifying, how a man's face changes when he loses his hair, especially if the baldness is total like this and previously he had a bushy head of hair. Yes, Deraldo said the hair would grow back. Grow back? And if it did, would it grow back the way it was before, with the same health, the same beauty? In the first few days, he had agonized so much over these questions that he suffered attacks of fury even against the plants in the front garden, in one instance pinching a jasmine bush so hard that the caretaker put the blame on leaf-cutting ants. It was horrible, unbearably horrible to go into the shower and, running your hand over your head, feel that smooth skin that couldn't be yours, the water pouring down your face in a way you'd never experienced before. Taking a bath the day after the attack on the jasmine, he advanced, naked, upon the bottles and tubes of shampoo lined up on the shelves and methodically destroyed them all, leaving a panel of blues, greens, and pale yellows on the tiles. In the mirror he was an extraterrestrial, some kind of exotic creature. His eyes had become larger as his eyebrows grew more and more sparse. Would his chest hair fall out too? What kind of animal would he turn into? There are also toupees for the chest. The macho American movie stars use them; he'd been told of it. A chest toupee! My God! How strange, how ugly, almost repulsive, was the skin on the head, full of wrinkles and weird moles. What a confusion of raging sentiments, what a desire to disappear, to have never existed, to awaken from the nightmare.

But not now, honestly. He had learned a great deal, had discovered unsuspected strengths, was proud of the bravery with which lately he had been confronting the disease, the treatment, the practical consequences of his condition. These, in fact, in a political sense, were having precisely the opposite result of what he had feared earlier: His withdrawal, instead of harming him, was working to his advantage, because gradually he was losing identification with a government tending toward a decline in prestige, as was already beginning to happen. Better, much better to continue like this, waiting for things to take clear shape, in order to form a strategy. Looking at it objectively, he could even say it was a good thing. After all, for one who not long ago was literally reduced to a psychological tatter, his condition was exceptional. Even the toupees proved to be a source of entertainment and had turned into a hobby. With great effort and the help of the hairdresser Lucius, whom he had called in Salvador and practically rented for a month, he had learned to put on the extremely complicated, but perfect, Japanese toupee, made of brown hair identical to what he used to have, which was now his favorite. One of the American models, also excellent in appearance and much simpler, had been shunted aside except for the occasional daytime wear, outdoors—a sport toupee, so to speak. It might be that no one noticed, but he did and suffered hours of anguish when he wore it to a meeting of the Friends of the City at the Library. By chance passing a mirror, he was horrified to see that under the fluorescent light his hair had taken on a phantasmagorical green tone, with a luminescent aura that gave the impression that the toupee would soon take flight like a spaceship. He managed to pry himself away from the mirror, and, pale, sweating, and smiling wanly, was inattentive and ill at ease for the rest of the meeting, smoothing his hair at frequent intervals. The Japanese toupee, however, was perfect, an extraordinary engineering feat which he at first was unable to assemble properly. Assemble was the term, because the sidepieces were separate from the top, in a combination that looked easy to adjust but wasn't, for any slight dislocation gave the head a different appearance, especially on the days when the sidepieces were switched around to simulate growth or a haircut. By now he could consider himself an expert on the subject and had acquired complete confidence in it. He was natural and was certain that many people didn't even suspect he was bald. He resisted a bit at first and was very nervous when he surfaced after his first dive wearing the toupee, but now diving was no problem, though he wasn't fond of swimming in the ocean anyway. And finally, the last threat in this area of hairiness, the terrifying hypothesis that his eyebrows would also fall out, was now under control. Lucius had taken the measurements and would handle things; he's also an excellent artisan, even if everything he sells and does costs an arm and a leg. This toupee thing, totaling up all the expenses, must cost over twenty thousand dollars, at a conservative estimate. But of course you don't think about controlling costs at a time like this. Without the toupees he would be in a state akin to madness, incapable of maintaining the attitude of positive resignation that he had so laboriously managed to achieve; without hair it was impossible.

A healthy life, no smoking, no drinking, lots of fresh air. Nature and relaxation, following a more or less bland diet because of the chemotherapy's assault on the liver—isn't there a paradox here? Yes, there is, because in a routine whose delivery he had rehearsed thoroughly and all his friends found amusing, he had been declaring that cancer had given him back his perfect health. Even his sexual vigor had returned with a drive unexperienced since he was twenty, after the low point of the discovery of the disease, to the point that if Ana Clara weren't the fiery woman that he had somewhat forgotten she was, he'd have gone out looking for some black girl on the island, one of those who for pocket change you lay on the porch of some empty summer house—a fantastic experience, by the way, one he hadn't had the pleasure of for a long time, since the days of dry humping. He should really think about doing it again one of these days. Strange, very strange, enough to make you believe in the hand of God. The cancer breathed new life into even that: A marriage on the wane and practically without sex, or even communication, was now solid once again, more solid than it had ever been, he could say with great happiness. Ana Clara, who had her justifiable reasons for complaint, had proved to be a woman of unshakable support, concerned but optimistic, at all times encouraging, affectionate, tender, a firm and courageous companion. Life's like that; it was necessary for a tragedy to nearly happen for him to take notice of something that was always there. A new love, rekindled in both of them, a breath of hope and confidence, the opening to a beautiful future. The island had been good for Ana Clara. True, now and then she had to put together some political luncheons, host boring people for dinner or even for a weekend, the sort of thing she didn't have to do very often in Salvador, but she faced everything with grace and good humor; nothing to criticize there. She no longer worked out regularly, but she didn't need to; everything around here is exercise, sun, and clean air, and her beauty had blossomed again in full splendor, to such an extent that if it weren't for the reassuring fact of there not being any man nearby who could interest her or have the guts to come on to her, he might be jealous. A bit abashed, he remembered thinking of asking her not to wear certain bikinis from her endless collection, the most daring ones. No, that would be ridiculous, and besides, the relationship had to be based on trust, a trust that absolutely could not be begrudged her, a trust that was totally deserved.

So everything was perfect, or at least as good as it could be. But happiness is never complete, and the nausea problem is a nuisance, the most unpleasant sensation there is; at times you think you'd prefer to die. And there's a synergistic relation to the psychological state, plain to see. From time to time a vicious cycle forms: The guy gets depressed because he's all the time on the edge of vomiting up his guts, amid bouts of nausea of seismic proportions, and the queasiness gets worse because he's depressed. And, except for the sleepiness they cause, which is sometimes a blessing, the nausea medicines end up having no effect. He had complained to Deraldo, who, after some fatalistic comments about differences in individuals' systems, had recommended marijuana.

"Seriously. This is no put-on. Marijuana is good for nausea. I've never even put a candy cigarette in my mouth, but there are studies proving it; it's been common knowledge for some time in the United States. There they even have THC pills, tetrahydrocannabinol, you know, which is the main active component of the infamous weed. But you don't have to go looking for some pill in the United States; everyone says that Bahian marijuana is of the highest quality. I suppose, if we really wanted to, I could prescribe it for you formally, but I don't think that's a good idea; it might be a nuisance and cause a lot of talk. You must be on good terms with the police—through them you can get it easily, by way of some friend of yours. Or else one of our contemporaries; lots of people used to smoke in our time and probably still do."

In point of fact it really does help a lot, Ângelo Marcos thought, sitting on the large veranda and resting on his lap the book he was leafing through without reading. It doesn't go away completely, but it helps a lot, and it gives you that sensation of torpid light-headedness. He had run into some difficulty getting the marijuana because he felt shy about discussing the subject and had even told Deraldo that he preferred not to pursuit that line of treatment. He regretted not having experienced, even peripherally, the hippie era, not having some old acquaintance from bygone days to whom he could go without embarrassment. Not even Tavinho, Bebel's ex-husband, despite their friendship. Not only did he not want to give him the satisfaction, after having censured him so often for using drugs, but also in all likelihood he probably didn't know anything about marijuana. His thing, as he himself said, was "bright"—*brilho*, as he called it, with that semidegenerate little smile of his. And he had once proclaimed his distaste for marijuana, dirty, smelly stuff, something for poor people, a blacks' and Indians' thing. No, no, it was necessary to find someone else. Finally Ângelo Marcos remembered a flaky architect with whom he'd spent time during his student politics days and later at the Ministry, who had declared publicly, at a restaurant, his preference for marijuana over alcoholic beverages. And, Ângelo Marcos recalled clearly, he had offered him a puff—a toke, man, he'd said with his hand outstretched, as if offering a potato chip—the day they were visiting work sites in a jeep he was driving. Of course he had refused, with an ill-disguised sense of scandal, and had spent the rest of the visit fearful that the degenerate would go teetotally crazy and send the jeep crashing down a ravine, thinking he was on a sled in the Alps or some such thing. But it was different now; for one thing, there was the medical reason, which he could mention. It took some time for him to make certain of the name: Victor, Victor Almadino. He must be in the phone book, because as Ângelo Marcos knew firsthand, besides being an architect and pothead, he was a very successful crook. Therefore he should have not one but several telephones.

It also took some time to gather the courage, but he finally called, and Victor was quite solicitous. Not to worry; just keep one thing in mind: Take out the bottom of the can. Ângelo Marcos didn't understand, and Victor merely repeated: the bottom of the can. Three days later a very securely wrapped package came by mail, containing a can of talcum powder. After a nervous inspection, Ângelo Marcos discovered that the can's bottom was false. When he succeeded in removing it, a dark wad wrapped in transparent plastic fell out amid a cloud of talc, as well as a tiny envelope full of cigarette papers. He felt happy, but he became frightened and made a botch of trying to clean up and brush away the spilled talc with his hands, until he recovered his calm and, stuffing the small packages in his pocket, without explanation ordered a maid to run the vacuum cleaner over the living room floor.

Choosing the time and place where he would do the first experiment was not easy. It had to be hidden from Ana Clara for several reasons, including the fact that he felt a certain degree of shame to be seen smoking that stuff—what if he started talking nonsense or making inconvenient confessions? And there was the chance she might want to experiment too. Never. Liberalism has its limits and it was his duty to protect his wife from the risks of that sort of thing. She would never find out that he had smoked marijuana and he would still have the moral suasion to continue voicing the same vigorous objections as before, against any type of drug. Yes, he would smoke in hiding, when she was at the beach, for example. And he would smoke in the glassed-in room in the attic, where the servants were authorized to go only after calling on the intercom and where he could open the windows so the wind could dissipate the smoke.

As he had done once again, some forty minutes earlier, then come downstairs intoxicated, carrying one of the American books whose subject had interested him, all of them about roads to success and self-affirmation. "Be Yourself and Be a Winner," the cover announced in large red letters. He lay down on the old chaise longue on the large veranda, put on his glasses, and opened the book, but his thoughts quickly began to wander, and he saw he was turning the pages without paying attention. No problem; he wasn't in a rush for anything. There was nothing he had to do; he could stay there as long as he liked, looking at the large crescent of brown sand unfolding before him, the herons wagging their necks and walking as if in frisky fear of stepping on something dangerous, the shellfish gatherers silhouetted against the blue of the sea, graceful sails, snowy plump clouds, a cool northeast wind fanning the leaves of the mango trees—everything was fine, just fine. Yes, the stay on the island was turning out much better than anticipated. Even socially, to his surprise as much as to Ana Clara's, for they had put together an interesting circle, people of their own level, even refined people like João Pedroso, now a companion for fishing and conversation, and old Lúcio Nemésio.

Speaking of whom, as he always does on the rare occasions he decides to have lunch at home, Lúcio Nemésio has just gotten out of the hospital station wagon, will pass through the market and immediately walk down the street opposite and stop for an instant to greet Ângelo Marcos and complain about something. He will refuse the invitation to come in but will discourse at the gate for a few moments, so Ângelo Marcos took from his pocket a vial of eyewash and dripped two drops into each eye because if they were red Lúcio might suspect something. The old man knew everything and could probably spot a pothead's eyes at a hundred yards. Five minutes later, his mind once again on other matters, he was about to respond to the booming "good morning" of Lúcio Nemésio, who had suddenly materialized at the gate and cut him off, going directly to the subject that was now incensing him.

"English sparrows!" he bellowed. "English sparrows! And imbeciles! Imbeciles!"

Ângelo Marcos ran down the three steps leading to the patio and opened the gate.

"How are you, Professor? Come in! This time you must come in, have something to drink."

"English sparrows!" Lúcio Nemésio repeated in the same tone of voice. "There were no English sparrows in Brazil; there were Brazilian sparrows, which have a slight resemblance to them but are far from being the same scourge. Some half-wit with a colonial mentality, no doubt envious of the squares in Europe where every day it rains tons of sparrow and pigeon droppings, decided to import this pest to Rio de Janeiro, and from there it spread to the whole of Brazil. And even after that there were no English sparrows on the island—they lack the sustained flight to cross the bay even from the closest points on the mainland; they're like flies. But another cretinous delinquent had the idea of bringing a few pairs here. And now, after they preyed upon and expelled most of the other birds, here there are nothing but English sparrows, sparrows everywhere, an inferno of sparrows!"

"Yes, it's really like that. An ugly animal that doesn't sing but just chirps, and does expel other birds. I remember it used to be full of canaries around here, redbirds, seedeaters, and a host of others, but now they've almost all disappeared."

"They lay eggs twice a year; the others, only once. And they're among the most aggressive animals in all of nature. If they were a little bit larger they'd attack people. They only live near man; they're incapable of surviving by their own resources—in a forest, for example. They even like to build their nests inside houses, thus expending the least amount of effort. They only know how to live around here, skipping from garbage to people's food and plantings. They don't even like to eat insects, only as a last resort. A scourge, a behaviorally unacceptable animal that ought to be extinct; evolution shouldn't be allowed to reward bad traits. Their success is obtained through processes that we shouldn't permit."

As frequently happened when he talked to Lúcio Nemésio, Ângelo Marcos was unsure whether the old man was speaking seriously; you never knew. But, fortunately for those who could find no reply to his comments, he rarely expected a response. He did give the impression of speaking seriously, his enormous jowls shaking and his extremely thick eyebrows rising and falling to the rhythm of his voice.

"And there's that cretinous mentality, ignorant and maudlin, absolutely devoid of any rational basis! That mentality!"

"That mentality? The mentality—"

"Yes, that mentality," he said, as if offended because Ângelo Marcos didn't know what he was talking about. "That backward mentality that I can never accustom myself to. Right now, in the Market, an old woman who says hello to me hereabouts but whom I neither know nor like, came up and questioned me because I was telling João Pedroso that I might even establish a reward of a Popsicle or soft drink for every sparrow killed and send the kids into action. Which, now that I think about it, is an excellent idea, and one day I'm going to put it into effect."

"Yes, it is. Not a sparrow would be left."

"But the old bag was indignant and you can't imagine the litany I had to suffer through about nature, as if nature were a being and a moral being at that, and about the poor creature, and even something that made me want to strangle the old woman: a symphony of sparrows. She used that expression: symphony of sparrows. But I didn't argue. I can't argue with ignorance; I can only become exasperated and leave at the first opportunity. What the devil does she know about nature and life? What life—that which she annihilates by the millions when she pours bleach on the floor? That which she destroys to eat? What does it mean? It means nothing; it's all a primitive mythology. As if man weren't part of nature, man and all he creates and that accompanies him. Why is a nest, a beaver dam, or a beehive part of nature and a house isn't? Man is part of nature and it is his place to eat any animal he wants to, to change the course of rivers, and to extinguish cockroaches, rats, or English sparrows. If I were speaking of bats, I doubt she'd have been so worked up, although in general bats aren't a species that shouldn't be tolerated, like sparrows. But there are no bat symphonies and she no doubt sees Dracula films and thinks of vampire bats and also forgets that, for hematophages, drinking blood is natural and that if they could think, they'd consider it one of their basic rights. I can't stand stupidity, and still less emotional and presumptuous stupidity. What does she know about this life business? If she had AIDS—and it's too bad she probably doesn't—what would she think about it being very natural that to a virus she's only an environment for it to grow and reproduce in until it destroys that environment? And that's to a virus, mind you, an infinitesimal particle that lacks subjectivity—or does it? Does it? What is subjectivity? What use is such a woman? Is she of use to herself or to the virus? Which is the correct point of view, in keeping with nature? What use are her cells? Who knows if in her totality she's not a function of a viral system, a testing grounds for reverse transcriptase? Who must decide how things are, and why they exist, is we ourselves, not the English sparrows, the rhinoceroses, or the alligators. To hell with those people. What do they know? Nobody knows anything, nobody studies, nobody thinks. Everybody takes delight in repeating the nonsense that best satisfies their neuroses and insecurities. Sparrows! Unspeakable animals! A Popsicle or soft drink for every sparrow killed—a lovely idea. How much do you think I'd be spending?"

Suddenly peaceful, he smiled affably, as if he had not just been speaking in that vehement manner. In contrast with before, it now all appeared to have been a joke, and Ângelo Marcos, not knowing what to think, returned the smile and repeated his invitation to come in. But the other man gave him a warm wave of the hand and promised that one of these days he would come in, but now he had to rush home, as he'd come to lunch only because he needed to consult some papers.

"Fine, Professor, I'll hold you to that visit; you've never given us the pleasure of your company. In the meantime, I'll see if I can kill a few sparrows for you. I'm going to get an air rifle."

Lúcio Nemésio laughed, waved again, and took off hurriedly down the street. Ângelo Marcos turned, laughing also, and went back to the veranda, but he was already frowning on the first step and sat down in the chaise longue with a scowl on his face. English sparrows: Kill English sparrows. Kill English sparrows. The memory that this had conjured up in him—the most secret, unconfessable, and disturbing memory, a memory he would give anything to forget—would not leave him today and might even persist for many days yet. There it was, as sharp as a scene in a film and throbbing like something alive, as if it had all been yesterday and would come again tomorrow. And, what was worse, there was a part of him that wanted to go on remembering and did go on remembering—and he clenched his fists forcefully, bit his lips, and squirmed uncomfortably in the chaise longue.

He always officiated at the seven o'clock Mass, but that was not the reason Father Monteirinho rose very early, even when he had gone to bed late the night before; it was because he had an affinity for the morning. He tossed in bed from four o'clock on and by four-thirty at the latest would fold the white nightshirt in which he'd been in the habit of sleeping since he was small, and, after ten minutes in the bathroom, put on his cleric garb and leave for a walk along the seawalls, whatever the weather, even in the severest of storms. In reality, he actually liked storms and thunder, and, wrapped in a blue raincoat and wearing a plastic cap, his umbrella pointed into the wind, he was always to be seen at that time, observing and thinking unknown thoughts, above the quay of the Market and in the midst of the billows that washed over the street. At first, people found it strange and commented that he must have some kind of obsession, perhaps some secret kinship with the sea, but soon everyone got used to it and began visiting him, fearing he was ill, if by any chance he failed to show up on a given morning.

That, however, was quite rare, because when he missed his walk, he considered the day marred and without purpose, which made him unsuccessful in carrying out anything he had planned. For some time before he came to the island it was not like that; it was just the opposite. The many occasions on which, in stony solitude, he had felt sorry for himself, close to despair, all took place in the morning hours, mornings of melancholy perspectives; colorless Wednesdays, Thursdays as monotonous as incessant dirges. He felt great shame about this weakness, which he considered the gravest sin of impoverishment of faith, forcing him to pray continually, eyes shut, before the main altar. And, despite this effort and suffering, God apparently wished to put that vacillating faith permanently to the test, and again, again, again, suddenly, in the early hours, the same feeling engulfed his soul and, painfully, it would all begin once more.

On his first morning on the island, dwarfed by the large two-story parish house and still disoriented in it, he awoke at four o'clock, excited and unable to remain in bed. He pulled the old Bakelite knob attached to the wrought-iron headboard. Now lighted, the very high ceiling became cavernous and menacing, and he was afraid those same feelings would come back to him, perhaps even worse, and maybe for the rest of his life without surcease. And his fear grew when, carrying a flashlight to inspect those dark garrets, corridors with creaking boards, staircases behind great double doors, and furniture from antique engravings, he thought he had suddenly returned to his grandfather's house, and he felt dizzy. In a small, unexpected room facing a staircase, furnished with four austere cane chairs, a small, circular hardwood table, and a hat rack with a round mirror that looked like an eye, the dizziness increased, and he had to sit down. Had he been in that room before? Yes, in a way, in the large old house where he had lived with his grandfather and which no longer existed, just as no one any longer existed—grandfather, grandmother, father, mother, the brother he never had. No one, he thought, looking at the darkness at the top of the staircase and imagining that if he shined the flashlight in that direction he would see one of their ghosts up there. He pointed the beam of light and made out only a balcony and two wide doors leading to the drawing room of the floor above.

Alone, completely alone. If not for his faith, more alone than anyone could be. This time, however, as the dizziness passed, he noticed that the usual uneasiness had not overtaken him and that in its place was a sense of peace and serenity, and his fear vanished. He became aware of the sound of the sea for the first time; he opened a shutter and stood looking out at the brightness of the moon cutting a tremulous wake through the water. Had it really been a punishment, an exile, his being sent to this small, impoverished, decadent parish, which evidenced only a bit more life in the summer? Yes, that had been the intent, but the result might be otherwise. Something told him it would be, that the solitude would be eclipsed by freedom, as he noticed already, smiling at the prospect of this unknown life, yet a life so serene that he smiled buoyantly and took a deep breath, with great pleasure. Without resentment, he recalled Father Rabelo. By nature and by conviction, he forgot everything and found a way to forgive, but now he was going beyond that. Now he was beginning to think his former professor at the seminary, and his confessor for a time, had done him a favor when he withdrew his confidence in him. Monteirinho had expected understanding, and had found none. He had also expected protection for the strength he was finding to resist temptation and all it entailed, but neither had he found protection.

"You should be ashamed!" Father Rabelo had told him, very pale and repeatedly starting to sit down, without succeeding. "Your cynicism amazes me! You must immerse yourself in repentance and contrition! You are on the path to absolute perdition!"

But that was the only time he had weakened, and even so he hadn't weakened totally because he hadn't given in, but had merely felt like giving in. He hadn't given in, he hadn't, despite the loneliness into which he had plunged after the death of his father, his last relative. He had distanced himself from everything that might lead to contact with her, and he went to see her for the last time one afternoon in Campo Grande. As they walked side by side, but well apart, he explained to her forcefully that he was a priest and would continue to be a priest and chaste, for if he violated those vows he would never again know peace and might even die of anguish. But the sublime feeling of redemption that he had waited for did not come after he said good-bye with the same firmness with which he had spoken and left without looking back and without even thinking about the expression of hopelessness on her face. Instead, what he felt was sadness and loneliness, an enormous and tearful self-pity, pursuing him like a swarm of mosquitoes, especially in the early hours of morning. And along with that, her image, the memory that he had once held and caressed her hands, the wish to go further than that, the thoughts that inflamed his entire body and made him pray aloud, clutching his head in his hands. It was then that he decided to speak with Father Rabelo, to tell him with total honesty of his suffering. And the priest did not limit himself to rebuking him harshly but also made a point of showing that he did not believe nothing physical had taken place, beyond that brief episode of the hands, between Monteirinho and the woman who had almost changed his life. I don't believe it, I don't believe it, he had said several times, and Monteirinho even considered falling to his knees to protest his innocence and sincerity, but he finally stood up, nodded good-bye, and left.

Yes, punishment, reproof, penitence, retreats, spiritual exercises, almost opprobrium. To cap it all, exile. Exile, he said in a low voice, looking around and, contrary to what he had expected, experiencing not bitterness but tranquillity, perhaps happiness, surely happiness. What exile, in front of this liberating window, in a house with an atmosphere so fundamentally linked to his own history, in a cool, lively breeze—what exile, this victory? He had chosen to be a priest, he had chosen to be a priest, he had chosen this special solitude. He had been tempted, he had been betrayed, he had overcome all. He had triumphed; he was fully a priest and had resisted the terrible force that had almost made him cease to be one. Enveloped by a wave of faith and love of God that spread through his body, he fell to his knees, his moist eyes looking into space beyond the window, and said, in a loud voice that must have echoed through the walls of the neighboring houses: "*Petrus, tu es petrus et super hanc petram aedificabo Ecclesiam meam!*" Upon this rock, upon this rock, he repeated transfigured, his heart gripped by the same strangely prideful humility he had felt when he was ordained and which that night had not permitted him to sleep for thinking of God's work and the duties of men.

That same day he began his morning walks, immediately establishing a route that he was loath to vary, which always started and ended at the ramp of the Market with conversations with the fishermen and fishmongers until shortly before the sounding of the bells at the main church summoning to Mass. He had convinced himself that varying his routine was rashness, an act that could be called frivolous, because that way one learned nothing, and there was already too much to learn even in a single unchanging route. For the events and things of morning, though always repeated, also always differ from what one saw the previous day. Not only is it never entirely identical to before, but neither are the schedules and textures of the tides, the combination of light and reflection, the wind, the waves and the boats, the outcome of the fishing trips, the dangers of the sea and its victims, which were more frequent than he had thought they'd be in the days before he lived among people of the sea. He felt a shiver as he recalled the day when he first perceived how much he had to learn from that intimacy, the day he postponed Mass to take the fisherman Coló da Misericórdia to the hospital in his ancient jeep. Coló was today covered with facial cuts and calloused scars, but alive. Monteirinho had experienced a scare when, surrounded by the screams and moans that had suddenly transfigured the scene, he arrived at the ramp and saw the hasty docking of the canoe *Sua Mãe*, which had come to the aid of Coló, who was transformed into a fountain of blood, entangled in the thousand fishhooks and lines of a dragnet aboard his towed lighter. The ray fishermen on *Sua Mãe* had cut the main line, in which a manta ray weighing hundreds of pounds was hooked and was no longer struggling, the floats bobbing only with the waves. But after Coló, distracted as one in his profession should never be, had hauled in over half the line on the side opposite the animal, it suddenly lurched away, its wings open like an airplane's, dragging the barge out to sea and rapidly enveloping Coló in a bramble of deadly fishhooks. Luckily, the *Sua Mãe*, which was tacking nearby, came quickly to his rescue, and some of the hooks dug into the barge's side, preventing that fish, more powerful than a tractor, from dragging Coló to a horrible death, perhaps to be eaten alive by the sharks that patrolled the anchorages around the island. Even so, he was close to death from loss of blood and from his frightful wounds—and Monteirinho again recalled his surprise at learning that such things were relatively common, and how it had brought crushingly home to him how much he didn't know, how it had helped him to get closer to a people he had come to care about greatly and whom he felt he understood and loved so unequivocally, to the point that when he gave his sermon on feast days and spoke of those who gazed at him from the pews of the church, at times he had to pause so his voice would not betray his emotion.

It was his custom to leave through his front door and walk up Direita Street, past the main church and the small chapel of São Lourenço, sometimes sitting on the wooden bench beside the house and waiting for the thrush in the oiti tree to begin its song. He preferred the colder, more dewy mornings, perhaps because of the intense brightness on the cobblestones and foliage. He might remain there for a long time, watching the light establish itself, but normally he continued on his stroll, turning at the corner of the Largo da Quitanda to go to the Market, where at that hour there were only three or four fishmongers and the usual layabouts, sometimes shrimpers or mullet fishermen stretched out on the sidewalk beneath tarpaulins and grimy canvas. From there, after discussing the weather for a few moments, listening to everyone's complaints and the stories of the older men, chatting with João Pedroso, and sipping half a cup of coffee, he would leave on his fixed route. Each day, the same black kitten, in an attitude of wary vigilance, watching his passage through the rear of the bar, would leap over the iron gate of the house next door, never allowing him to get as close as he would like. And each day, the same rooster by the yellow house loudly flapped its wings before crowing; there was the same chestnut tree with fruit bats fluttering around before quickly resettling into the copious crown; the same jasmine bush spilling over the wall of the green-and-white house, its perfume announcing itself little by little from the street corner; the same ancient fort, the same ficus trees and acacias, the same pounding surf, the same smell of the sea, the same pumpkin-colored sun rising behind the hills of the oceanfront district before him. But, despite this, there were so many new things and so many thoughts; he'd experience a spiraled reverie that sometimes found him regaining awareness someplace where he had arrived without his knowledge. From time to time, perhaps he felt guilty about this happiness, as it surely depended on his isolation, which allowed him to feel as if the island were not part of this frightening country that daily astonished him with news he did not want to believe and horrors about which he refused to think. Yes, perhaps, but the island also had its sufferers, many of them, the majority—and he did what he could, more than he could, from the miraculously supported school to the associations and the tenants', fishermen's, and craftsmen's cooperatives he had organized from the ground up and to which he still provided guidance and protection. No, he had no reason to feel guilty; it was his parish, it was where God wanted his labor, and if he found happiness in it, it was the happiness of carrying out his ministry honorably and taking joy in the blessing of faith and the priesthood.

But now, as he left the parish house, with reddish clouds framing its roof and a cool breeze forcing him to reposition his beret, he looked about without his customary enthusiasm and even thought of going back inside. Once again he was not going to take his route, did not want to go by the Market, neither at the beginning nor at the end of his stroll. All because of João Pedroso. Yes, but because of himself as well, for he had wished to avoid the conversation that, sooner or later, he must have with him. Besides which, the situation was already a reality, and therefore the longer he postponed the talk, the worse everything might become. Women, women. Interesting that he'd had a serious problem because of a woman and now the same thing was happening to the one to whom he was perhaps the only close friend—and vice versa, now that he thought about it. That crazy hermit, who seemed to have a peach pit stuck in his throat when he spoke to any woman he was interested in and who, more than once, drinking like a fish, had described in melodramatic tones his ignominious shyness. "I'm afraid. I'm afraid; that's the truth. I'm afraid of them. I always have been!" he would say, his eyes bulging in a genuine show of fear. "What shame I've gone through, my dear sir, what great shame, what unspeakable mortification, what indescribable humiliation, the nadir of abjection! What opinion could a chaste priest have about impotence caused by panic? Ah, my dear sir, my fine priest, even if it were an excellent opinion and even better advice, it would do me no good. It does me no good; my fate is that of the most obscure of worms. I am a worm, my dear sir!"

Monteirinho wrinkled his brow as he remembered João Pedroso's Marmeladov-like tirades, always an intriguing mixture of histrionics and sincere desperation. Perhaps all of it was the truth, a grotesque truth but in any case the truth, because in fact he did always give the impression of fleeing or being ready to flee. Now, however . . . He sighed, once more adjusting his beret and starting to walk in the direction of the fountain. Why did it have to be his problem too? Yes, it was an adultery about to happen, but you can't go around preventing adultery; all you can do is speak out against it. Yes, but in this case it was an adultery close to him, of which he had direct knowledge through one of the parties to it. Yes, yes, he couldn't refrain from speaking; couldn't remain indifferent; after all, a priest is a priest. But wouldn't he merely be a meddler, a spoilsport? Would it do any good to speak, now that by the look of things it would happen anyway? No, that should never be the criterion. But it was possible he might lose his friend, or win his eternal enmity, by such meddling. Why couldn't he be a normal friend of João Pedroso's, knowing that such things happen all the time and are even looked upon by many as something natural, and in a certain way are trivial? Priest or friend? What right did he have to interfere in the life of a friend who for the first time was truly in love and apparently was loved in return, who for the first time had managed to conquer his shyness? Middle-aged, solitary, and complicated, so in need of a woman—and who could say, she might be the right woman for him at this stage of life. Of course, she might be the right woman for him; nothing stood in the way of her separating from her husband like so many others and going to live with João Pedroso. But how? In a state of adultery? Great God in heaven, what kind of thoughts are these, Father Monteirinho?

He stopped, anxiously, at the corner of Patos Street. Would he find a way, would he find a way, God in heaven, to sound sincere when he asked João Pedroso to give up that affair with Ângelo Marcos's wife, an affair by now visible in gestures, glances, and furtive contact—at least to one who, like him, was aware of it? Or would he let it show that part of him—perhaps, from a certain point of view, the greater part—had no real objections and was even rooting for things to turn out well for his friend in this adventure that to almost everyone else was so commonplace? Ordeals, worldly ordeals. Why must this horrible dilemma confront him now, when everything was going so well? Why hadn't João Pedroso found some other woman? Why did it have to be one in her situation? But he wasn't to blame. No one has control over such things; the woman simply came into his life. It's true, it's true. Priest or friend?

Priest, priest, priest, he thought stubbornly, stamping his foot on the sidewalk and slowly resuming his walk. Priest. Above all, his obligations as a priest. He would rehearse what he would say; he wouldn't allow his dilemma to even enter into it. He would act as it was his duty to act, even if it meant losing his friend and his company, so enriching, so enjoyable, so spontaneously fraternal. He would do everything to keep that from happening. He would be as clever and eloquent as he could be, but he must take the chance; there was no choice. Priest first, friend second. He muttered something almost rancorously, thought a curse word, and, a bit startled by what was happening in his head, prayed silently all the way to the fountain.

4

Shortly before going downstairs to offer some last-minute tips on the Great Luncheon, wearing a light-blue matching outfit trimmed in white, with a wide ribbon providing the finishing touch to a young-looking hairdo with bangs, Ana Clara went through her bedroom several times, gathering up Suzanna Fleischman's notebooks. A truly vast output, she thought, depositing a pile of them on the dresser and leafing through the one on top, a compilation of ideas about the difference between the sexes that she considered particularly felicitous. The article in which, after some rather stilted considerations about how the female chooses the male—surely influenced by the conversations on biology between Ana Clara and João Pedroso, into whose personal affairs she had avidly pried during the fishing trips, almost to the point of taking notes—Suzanna Fleischman had risen up in devastating prose against what she called "bestial naturalness," stupidity, and degeneracy, which brutally assaulted the prerogatives of the human female. Bestial naturalness, she said, consists in thinking that if something is natural, one should act in relation to it like any animal. Breasts, fannies, and pubic hairs are natural, so let's run around naked. Crapping is normal too, so let's not only run around naked but also crap in the street in front of everybody. You don't have to be a genius to get the idea that what's human, and therefore natural, is to wear clothes, do certain things in private, and not go around coupling in public like a pair of dogs. Nowadays everyone lets everything show and sex has been reduced to a single fulcral point. A clitoro-vulvar, phallo-scrotal generation. They were the only points, if one leaves out the gynecological position assumed by women who pose for magazines, clearly demonstrating that if you have enough money they'll show you what you want—do for one, do for anyone. Nobody can stand to look at a naked woman these days; everything in excess becomes a bore. Suppose you're crazy about peanut brittle. Then they offer you one peanut brittle, two peanut brittles, three peanut brittles, six peanut brittles, eight peanut brittles; you get to the ninth peanut brittle and can't stand the sight of peanut brittle. Then they force you to eat twenty more peanut brittles (note: check whether the plural of p.b. is actually peanut brittles; only the aberrant know the pl. of compounds), and you have indigestion and nightmares in which a sorceress with foul breath imprisons you in a house out of Hansel and Gretel and gives you nothing to eat but a cauldron full of peanut brittle and you vomit just at the mention of the words peanut brittle. It's the same thing. Besides the feeling of embarrassment that sweeps over dignified men and women when they see those cows in G-strings on TV tossing their vaulted asses back and forth—great embarrassment. There's something biologically wrong in that. I'm going to investigate; I have access to sources.

Brilliant, Ana Clara decided, caressing the notebook cover, which she closed reluctantly, because all of this was extremely interesting, more of a gas than she'd ever imagined. Suzaninha was writing better and better; it was a pity she couldn't put it all together, because she was always starting new projects and abandoning old ones. We must do something about that, Ana Clara promised herself, but then she felt it was a secondary priority, very secondary, not even a priority, what with her head spinning from the speed with which she was getting involved with that once inconceivable man; a crazy life, a thousand-mile-an-hour merry-go-round, and desire like an ocean, an ocean, a flood. That drivel about rationality—you only live once, as Suzanna herself, previously so full of restrictions and suspicions, had reminded her. Besides which, there was nothing they could do about it; it was real passion, serious business, the kind that causes your heart to race, makes it hard to breathe, leaves you not knowing what to say, the limpid-eyes-tango-in-the-moonlight kind, unabashed adolescence, won-der-ful. Sighs, hands on her breasts, day-dreams, runaway pelvic contractions, everything, oh, everything!

Yes, she needed to see how the lunch was going. After all, there had to be food, although food was a mere detail at the Great Luncheon. True, it would be nothing more than a formal visit to the kitchen, as everything was already taken care of, and in absurdly exaggerated quantities, since Bebel, the culinary coordinator, accomplice in so many romantic plots, and collaborator with Suzanna Fleischman, had stated that it was an atavistic issue, ancestral trauma, because the starving side of her Northeastern origins obliged her on such occasions to want to see enough food on the table to feed Biloxi for a year. Truckloads of fish simmered in oil and pepper, truckloads of risottos with clams and lobster and shrimp, zillions of tidbits, breaded crab legs, huge oysters quivering in their shells, celestial omelets, an epic fish stew. Bebel had clapped her hands in excitement: "I won't do the heavy labor, sweetie, but give me four good black women like my granny had on the plantation and leave everything to me; I'll put together a superproduction." Four good black women was impossible, because things were a lot different from old Detinha's day, but there are two strong black women right here on the island and there's Cornélio, who must be worth five black women and is a wonderful and impeccably clean fag and has to be one of the best cooks in the state civil service, maybe in all of Bahia. He'll only go back to the Ministry over my dead body, Ana Clara thought. I hope he finds a boyfriend here on the island, one of those big black studs in tiny trunks with heavy-duty equipment, and gets so well serviced that he never wants to leave. I'm going to ask Bebel to suggest it; she's got the brass to actually do it.

Check the mirror; everything in keeping with Suzanna Fleischman's standards. The modern woman is opposed to bestial naturalness, that throwback to caveman days. A discreet bermuda, not too short, sleeveless blouse with a high rounded neckline, a light jacket that she planned to take off later, at the moment that inspiration struck her. Braless, yes, but not to show anything, just to hint delicately through the medium-gauge mesh weave of the blouse. Leather sandals with two copper decorations on each side, ankles secured by straps, toenails painted in a red the tiniest bit dramatic to establish a possibly intriguing contrast with the simplicity of the outfit, a fine silvery anklet around the left leg. He might go for feet; it's unbelievable the number of men who break out in Niagara-like salivation at the mere thought of a woman's foot. If so—Bebel thought he met the profile of a foot fetishist, but sometimes Bebel was too smart for her own good—fine and dandy, her feet were in shape. He might like knees and legs also. Knees and legs in good shape, smooth skin, zero cellulite, front, sides, and rear. That stuff about a little bit of cellulite having its place was just bunk from a scoundrel husband. Zero cellulite, like a nude goddess. Nothing shaven, a golden peach fuzz that could only be seen in the sunlight, charming. Hands: It could be he liked hands. Funny, she felt that she knew him so well and yet she knew nothing about him. How many times had they spoken to each other? Relatively few, even on the fishing trips, because there were usually people around. How many times had they touched? Him touching her, none to speak of. Her touching him, four or five times, out of pure nerve, a few quick squeezes of the arm, some rubbing of the shoulders with fake sporting camaraderie, and that time when she slipped on the boat, a slip that began legitimately enough but which she rather took advantage of, when she grabbed on to him so hard that she practically had her nose in his chest as she lifted herself while leaning against him. Not practically; she did have her nose in his chest, and she liked the smell, an intimate, secret smell that made her think of his groin and caused her pelvic region to contract. He did nothing, merely held her awkwardly by the wrist for a brief instant and stood there like a pillar, red as a beet. Charming. Well, in any case, her hands were in good shape: the nails not too long, the same unusual polish as on her toes, the wedding band and two other rings. She leaned forward to examine her face closely, arranged the edge of her bangs, touched up her lipstick, adjusted one of the wings of the mirror to see herself from the rear, and, in a final inspection, rehearsed again the combination of a smile and a wave of the head that she had discovered accidentally and planned to turn into a kind of trademark. She searched for any overlooked notebook but found none, put them all in the large drawer in the dresser, locked it, and went down to the pantry two steps at a time, feeling as sprightly as a grasshopper.

"Turn around, turn around!" Bebel said, almost running into her at the kitchen door, then taking two steps backward, her arms wide and an exuberant expression on her face. "Stunning, girl! Not a single detail wrong. Turn around, turn around! That outfit's really nice; from the moment you showed it to me, I thought it'd look great on you, and it does! Your hair . . . Hmm . . . An impeccable combat uniform, stunning, really stunning!"

"Don't exaggerate, Bebel. As a matter of fact, I'm not trying for stunning today; it's not the right effect for today."

"Of course. But that's why it's perfect; that's what stunning is. Perfect, perfect—beauty, purity, innocence, freshness, and fragility! I know the objective, sweetie, are you forgetting? If you showed up looking deliberately stunning, you wouldn't be stunning. You have to be very careful with these men who are afraid of women; they scare easily and run for cover like squirrels. Perfect, a true masterpiece!"

"You really think he's that scared of women?"

"Terrified. At first I was suspicious. He doesn't have a limp wrist, but a guy over forty—"

"Forty-six."

"He doesn't look it; he looks younger. But anyway, a guy pushing fifty, no wife, no children, no anything, buried away in a sinister old house . . . My grandmother Detinha always used to say, 'Every confirmed bachelor is either crazy or false to his own body.'"

"Yeah. I do think he's half crazy, but a wonderful kind of crazy. A fag he isn't, that I'm sure of. If you talk to him—"

"I already did, but he always seems to be close to a nervous breakdown. He bites his tongue, looks away, and sometimes even quivers."

"That's at first. At first he was like that with me too. Later he got a lot better. He's practically normal, especially if he has a couple of whiskeys. A little shy, but I like it. The day I declared myself, as the boat was coming in, he wasn't a bit surprised, just nervous. He got nervous and turned very red and waved his hands in the air as if he were trying to hold onto an invisible fish, but he wasn't scared—to the point that he answered that he liked me too, without stuttering, without a tremor in his voice, without anything. I already told you about it."

"Every time you tell me about that declaration of yours I feel sick. You had to do it someplace where there could be a follow-through, a physical follow-through, where you could grab him and kiss him on the mouth, or whatever. You've got to have a follow-through to these things. Gab, then grab; otherwise it's no use."

"But how, if I was never going to get a chance to be alone with him before we talked? Now that we've laid our cards on the table, it's different. But I'm not sure I'll have the courage to grab him. I don't think I will; he disarms me."

"You have to, hon. After all, there's no great mystery to it. I'd grab him, I'd've already found some way to grab him. If you don't make the first move, I doubt he'll take the initiative. I'd bet any amount of money he's the type that has to be grabbed. Unless you want to do the Camille number and faint in his arms, but I find that fainting business a real drag, besides which it might not work. He might put you on the sofa and go for a glass of water and medicine for low blood pressure, you never can tell. Maybe the best thing is for you to ask if he knows mouth-to-mouth resuscitation and when says yes, jump off the boat and drown yourself a little. It's either that or grabbing; I don't see any other way."

"I'm going to set up a meeting with him the first chance I get. Tuesday. Ângelo Marcos is going to Salvador and won't be back till Friday night. A medical checkup with Deraldo, business, politics, I don't know what all. I was going to go along, but not anymore; I made up a bunch of things I have to do in the house."

"Aninha, you weren't this determined even at the time of the Experiment! Look, I have to hold my chin to keep it from dropping. What a change!"

"Are you against it?"

"Against it, me? How could I be, when I've been encouraging it all along? I'm just surprised by your rapid progress; you're getting better all the time. I think it's great. Honestly. I'm even learning something. I think it's fantastic; there's something very playful in it, a highly positive energy. I think it's fantastic. Where's the meeting going to be?"

"Well, I'm not quite sure yet. I mean, I haven't really given it any thought. I thought maybe he might have a suggestion. It's really a problem; it's very difficult around here."

"I don't think it's at all difficult. You're crazy to leave a matter of this importance in the hands of a man like him. He'll get all balled up, he'll stop to think, he'll want to disappear, and it's going to be a disappointment."

"Oh, Bebel, you're exaggerating. It's not all that bad."

"OK, but I still don't see any reason to take chances. I think it's a lot safer if you have a plan ready. Do this: Invite him to your house."

"Are you crazy? Here, in the house? I'd have to be crazy. I—"

"Why not? Ângelo Marcos will be away, won't he, and only the servants will be here, right? And I won't go back tomorrow with Nando as planned. I'll decide to stay a few days with you and help with those things around the house. Now that I mention it, I'd like to putter around in your garden. It looks kind of sad with nothing but leaves—no colorful flowers. Flowers—"

"Bebel, I don't understand a thing. Stop talking about flowers and explain. I don't understand the first thing."

"Sometimes you astound me, girl. First you're clever as can be, then you act like a retard. It's obvious, isn't it, that with me here no one's going to think you're meeting your boyfriend in your house? You invite him here and I'll act as cover for you. Don't worry about it; nobody will suspect a thing. For example, the three of us go upstairs together. You turn to the right and into the large suite, I turn to the left and go to the small room by the veranda, you nestle away with him there, and I'll watch videotapes or read until you call, with secret knocks on the door and everything. To all intents and purposes, the three of us are together, and I don't think the black folks are going to think we're having an orgy in the living room with a fishmonger."

"I get nervous just thinking about it, Bebel. I'll never be able to do it, never!"

"Of course you will. And it's actually the most sensible solution because if you go out somewhere with him, it'll be a lot easier for someone to suspect or see something. You don't have to tell him anything; just invite him to come over. That way he won't get scared. Look, the more I think about this solution the more it seems like a stroke of genius, excuse the immodesty, total genius. It solves all the problems, including the possibility that he wouldn't go along with meeting you, because it won't be an invitation for a tryst, just for a meeting. He has no reason to be frightened, and there's nothing he has to take care of—and the rest is up to you."

"Now I'm the one who has to hold her chin. Bebel, look me in the eye: Are you serious?"

"Of course I am! You don't kid around about such things. I couldn't be more serious."

"But do you think it'll work? I—"

"Certainly it will. What probably wouldn't work would be for you go up to him and whisper, 'Find a motel where we can get it on.' He'd get all flustered, that I guarantee. And even if he didn't, it'd be a major production, with all sorts of complications and problems galore. No, the more I think about it, the more I find it a thing of genius. Here, here in complete tranquillity; it's so perfect it hurts!"

"I don't know. It scares me. I really don't know."

"Of course you know, girl," Bebel laughed, placing her hand on the other woman's shoulder and leading her to the kitchen, where, in a kind of anteroom, surrounded by indescribable seasonings and shining in every color, were arranged various tureens, platters, and trays of food, dominated by the solar brilliance of the colossal bowl of *vatapá* sitting in the middle. But Ana Clara, still dazed by the suggestion, which now struck her as better and better and increased her state of excitement, could not pay any attention to what seemed to her merely a conglomeration of gold-and-purple hues floating before her, and came out of her reverie only when Cornélio, wearing a crisply starched chef's hat and a lilac apron printed with recipes in English, came up to her, weeping, and commented that he had overshot the critical moment of the ambrosia dessert; it was all the fault of that stupid, irresponsible mulatto woman who had been watching the pot while he took care of the green papaya compote. Over a gallon of milk, I don't know how many eggs, and Dr. Ângelo Marcos's favorite dessert was ruined; it looked like a lumpy, coarse pile of mush, nothing at all like the delicacy to which he had become accustomed. Oh, to think of his sweet boss, his chief, his father, the man he looked to on earth as he did to God in heaven, being disappointed like this! But Bebel consoled him by pouring out effusive praise and reminding him of the coconut custard, the *baba-de-moça*, the light and dark coconut bars, the *queijadinhas* and even the green papaya compote and so many other desserts that were available, most of which he himself had made with his incomparable skill—had he forgotten? Cornélio heard her, was overcome with emotion, and tried to reply, but he could only move his lips tremulously, then cover his mouth in a surge of feeling and dart back inside. After a great deal of laughter, she glanced at her watch and looked startled: It's late, people will be arriving soon and here I am looking like I just got back from some honky-tonk! I want to be a knockout too, she said, and in the bad sense of the word. And in fact, laughing and slapping her legs, Ana Clara confirmed that she was precisely that when she reappeared, sparkling in a short brick-colored pongee jacket over a translucent chemisette printed in light colors and very short tan culottes. Her hair, very dark and wavy, was pinned on top of her head in an arrangement that left strands free around her face and made her appear taller.

"Everything under control," she said, sitting down and crossing her legs flamboyantly, after a small promenade for Ana Clara's benefit, on the second floor terrace. "We're ready to face this luncheon. Any interesting men around, besides both yours and mine?"

"We're monsters," Ana Clara said.

"*Goga*," explained Father Monteirinho, after paying for Gumercindo's eggs and the star fruit, "is the same thing as *maria-lígia*, a funny name that, isn't it, *maria-lígia*? I don't know why it has that name. It's also called *jacuba* and other names that I forget; it's a very widespread thing. You take manioc flour, put it into coffee, stir vigorously a few times, and swallow the whole thing quickly, while the flour is still in solution. It fools the children's stomachs. Except that now they can no longer afford coffee or refined sugar, so they use barley and sweeten it with raw sugar. Gumercindo was telling the truth when he said his family has been subsisting on *goga*. When that happens, he goes out and steals a few eggs and some fruit and gets the small amount of money needed to buy a couple of mullets, squash, gherkins, cabbage, and bananas—the main meal of the week. You know that's commonplace around here; these eggs and star fruit are stolen, but I can't make accusations without proof, and I do feel sorry for him. He's a kind of honest thief, so to speak, who only steals what is absolutely necessary to keep his family from starving to death, and when he finds work he doesn't steal. And if they arrest him they beat him at the police station. He's been beaten several times: the hand-paddle, the belt, blows to the face. No, God will understand; I don't stop buying eggs from him and I pretend I believe they're really his, though conscience dictates that afterward I give everything to the sisters' orphanage. Will you help me carry these eggs and star fruit home? Take the eggs; I'm very clumsy and this horrible wrapping will come apart at any moment."

I've known Gumercindo since boyhood and I'm sick and tired of knowing what *goga* is, João Pedroso was about to reply, but decided to say nothing and merely took the package of eggs. He wasn't exactly irritated with Monteirinho, although he had lost some of his patience during that impossible-to-interrupt logorrhea. He had already seen that it was useless to change the subject, or even to try to answer, because Monteirinho continued to speak about what he wished, in the manner he wished. And João Pedroso had opted to resign himself; after all, Monteirinho was a fine friend who was visibly upset, and one must show some understanding. Only, unable to think of anything other than Ana Clara, João Pedroso could no longer rule his head and finally spoke out in spite of himself.

"What other news do you have for me, Monteirinho?" he asked, with obvious intent at irony, but Monteirinho once again acted as if he were deaf.

"Star fruit is excellent for high blood pressure," he said, picking up the fruits. "The leaves also make a good tea. My grandfather got along very well and attributed his longevity to it. It also makes a compote, an excellent compote. And dried fruit; it makes dried fruit, superb dried fruit. I hope Sister Bernadete, the sister in charge of the pantry, is better of her rheumatism and makes some star fruit candy. She's a first-rate candymaker."

Right. It did no good, and João Pedroso resigned himself again, even regretting having spoken as he had. Monteirinho was upset—more than that, disturbed. After disappearing from his mornings at the Market and making up all sorts of excuses to avoid talking with him, suddenly he had showed up at the ramp before five o'clock, in this state of excitement, answering questions about his absence with smiles and vague hand gestures. He also seemed quite anxious, but João Pedroso pretended not to notice anything, as if nothing unusual had happened, and merely asked if he had decided to vary his famous itinerary, the object of so many learned and philosophical discussions in times past. But Monteirinho merely said "Temporarily, temporarily," without looking at João Pedroso, and began wandering aimlessly from one side of the Market to the other, not even pausing for his cup of coffee, which he drank as he walked down the center aisle. Until, as if suddenly remembering something, he stopped at the counter and began rattling away in that funny style of his, lapsing into silence only after an abrupt change of expression, when they had already left the Market and arrived at the door of the parish house.

"Very well then," Monteirinho said, coming to a halt in military fashion at the threshold. "For some time I was thinking about whether I would ask you in. But of course I will. In the first place, you're my friend and it wouldn't be right for me not to ask you in. In the second place, it's silly to continue trying to avoid the inevitable. I'm going to have to talk with you sooner or later, and it's no good trying to put it off. That just makes things worse, at least from my point of view. Let's go in. I don't have much time; Mass begins soon."

"Monteirinho, you don't know what a pleasant surprise this is for me. I was sure you had a screw loose. That was the first lecture I ever heard about star fruit. First you disappear, then you jabber away like a fishwife and—"

"Yes. I wanted to avoid a conversation; I didn't really know yet how to say what I'm about to say. Perhaps I still don't. All I know is *what* I'm going to say, that I'm certain of, but I'm uncertain as to how. Go on in."

He took a long time arranging the eggs one by one in a fruit bowl; when João Pedroso tried to interrupt him with a question, he said he was praying a silent prayer and asked him to kindly give him a few moments.

"You present me with theological problems," he began finally, speaking with his hands folded on his chest. "But I'll not speak of them. They're sufficiently disturbing to be aired; I don't even like to think about them, though I do. And you also present me with problems of conscience. About these I can speak; although I may not want to, I must. It may be that, as a priest and as a friend, it's wrong for me to admit this, but I would prefer—prefer with all my heart—never to have learned of that problem of yours with that lady, that problem of which you spoke to me."

"But, Monteirinho, who else was I going to talk to? You yourself said so at the time."

"I know. I said it, I said it. It's true; you couldn't talk to anyone else. But that obliges me to do what I'm going to do, and I would prefer not to be in this situation. Because, looking at things honestly, I know that if I weren't a priest my attitude would be different, and that nearly drives me mad. It's a far more serious and graver matter than it may appear at first glance: It's a duality, an execrable ambivalence that couldn't exist. As a priest, I feel I shouldn't see that possibility of acting differently, shouldn't even think about it, and that disturbs me, because I'm a serious priest; I aspire to be both a serious priest and a saintly one, and I know you respect that. At the same time, can I lie? Am I to blame that it's the way it is, that this ambivalence exists? I must have it, I must, of course, but in a more subtle form, embedded in my imperfection. I shouldn't interfere; it's your life, and I'm aware that you're like a new man, since . . . since this passion. I shouldn't involve myself in that. I shouldn't interfere in your life. For, despite being a priest, I live in the world like you and I'm used to seeing this sort of thing happen and be regarded as normal. I'm a modern man like you and I know I shouldn't interfere. But—"

"What's this? You're my friend; you have every right to interfere in my life."

"That's another complication. Have I really? I see it as more obligation than a right. I'm going to break the promise I made to myself, not to say what I'm about to say—which, in a way, I've already said: If I weren't a priest I wouldn't meddle. But a priest isn't like a judge; he can't disqualify himself. I have to meddle. The first duty of a priest is to his priesthood, not to friendship. That's the truth, that's the truth."

"Monteirinho, I think you're confusing things royally. I don't even know what you're driving at. I know perfectly well that, under the circumstances, you have to be against it. Naturally you have to be; that doesn't offend me in the least. That was the very reason I didn't ask your opinion, so as not to oblige you to say what you think. But if you want to—"

"I *am* obliged to speak! Moreover, I'm obliged to urge you to give it up. I can't be told anything about it. I can't talk with you about it without voicing my permanent opposition. I can't approve anything. I can't risk the slightest complicity. I have the duty to point out that your behavior is indefensible from every point of view."

"Fine. You've made your point. I understand. I understand perfectly. Do you have anything to drink around here?"

"Yes, but I'm not going to give it to you. It won't be here that you get drunk at six in the morning."

"I'm not going to get drunk; it's just a swallow. Your tone is so apocalyptic, I thought it'd lighten things up a little."

"Don't change the subject. I too find this a disagreeable duty, certainly far more disagreeable for me than for you, but I have to insist. I'm not being apocalyptic. I'm just being serious. You're going to promise me that you'll forget about this clandestine affair, forget the whole thing, find some normal girlfriend like everybody else, change your thinking. I can't stand by with folded arms and watch what you're doing. It's not right."

"But you're exaggerating, man. It's me who's sinning, not you. And isn't it your place, like the Lord, to live among sinners, to understand and forgive them?"

"But not to be an accomplice. I can't pretend I don't know, especially since it was you yourself who told me, directly. You told me that you and she are about to do something that I condemn in others. Should I condemn it in others and encourage it in you, even by omission, which in this case would be strong encouragement? Because you're the priest's friend do you have the right to an exception? Because I know of the personal circumstances of your life, know you well and like you, should I be especially permissive? For me to know about all this, to in one way or another share the lives of you both, is to be an accomplice. I can't; this is much more serious than you think!"

"Monteirinho, you sound like a fanatic. Do you mean that because of this business you can't be on familiar terms with me anymore? Is that what you mean?"

"No. I can be on familiar terms, but I can't be your friend, which pains me, pains me greatly, pains me deeply. I can't—not by my own will, for in my heart I shall always be your friend—but because, to continue as your friend in the full sense of the word, as we have always been, I would have to live a situation untenable for a priest. And for a friend too, in eternal opposition to that which you think will bring you happiness. How could I honestly stand beside you in a crisis, when you face the problems that this affair is sure to engender, if the demands of friendship conflicted with those of the priesthood? How will I be able to avoid everyone's thinking that, given our intimacy, you calmly confide in me things that I could not hear without protesting? You may even object that what worries me is the opinion of others. Well, it does; it does, not so much for myself as for the institution of priesthood, the Church, which I represent. The priest must set an example for the community. He owes it the maintenance of a position above any suspicion; he must be absolutely impartial in matters of principle, because only then can he exercise his ministry. At the core everything comes down to a single issue. That issue is: A priest is a person, yes, but he is a priest. I'm not being a fanatic, nor am I being rigorous. It would be rigorous if I were trying to preserve something beyond the fundamental, but all I'm trying to preserve is the fundamental. If I didn't act this way, I wouldn't be a priest, and being a priest is, to me, fundamental. It's how I see my humanity and my spirit. If I don't preserve this, my life loses its meaning. I'm not even going to that luncheon; I'll make up some excuse. And not only because I find those ostentatious banquets indecent in the midst of so much hunger. It's also because, although I know that lots of people are going and that officially it'll be a simple social occasion, I also know what's going on between you and the lady of the house, and if I go, I'll feel like an accomplice. So I can't go. You've told me many times that you didn't sustain your vocation, that you betrayed your gift. I don't want to feel that way in relation to my vocation and my duty. I cannot bow before the Adversary."

"What adversary—Satan?"

"Yes, if you want to think in those terms, although that word always calls to mind those devils in the drawings, with horns, goatees, and pointed tails. I prefer to use the word 'Adversary' because, besides being the original meaning of the word 'Satan,' it better expresses a set of—"

"You think I'm Satan incarnate? Or rather, you think that, for you at this moment, I represent in material form Satan's intentions for you, threatening to drag you into an untenable situation, bringing you closer, if only a tiny bit, to the precipice of self-betrayal and damnation? You think I'm your Satan? That's interesting. I—"

"Don't be a fool, João, it's nothing like that. Don't twist what I said—which, in fact, is a good way to run away from the problem that began this entire conversation."

"Look here, Monteirinho, I don't understand anything about Satan, or sin, or evil, at least not one one-thousandth of what you understand from professional duty. But I do understand enough to see clearly that you're right. You didn't say everything, but from what you did say I can draw inferences. Logical, precise inferences, the pure truth. I'm not the incarnation of anything, of course, but in one way I am. I'm the arm of Satan attempting to pull you in. But you'll resist; it's not all that hard to resist Satan, or the exogenous sin. Endogenous sin is what's hard, because it's not sin induced by Satan, but by one's own temptation of self."

"João, you're delirious, you—"

"I'm not delirious, I'm thinking. And more clearly all the time. I'm not delirious at all. Why doesn't God redeem Satan? Why is the Fall irreversible?"

"Well . . . Look, this isn't the time to discuss a matter of this sort. Our conversation is simpler; our conversation is about the situation you're creating for yourself and for others, including me."

"No, no sir. This is the time, exactly the time! Why doesn't God redeem Satan? Because it's impossible to redeem one who sins by himself, from his own spiritual degradation, one who had the light, the knowledge, the opportunity, and, on his own, plunged into sin, into enmity with God, and consequently with Good. God can do anything and could transform Satan into a benevolent spirit. But then he would be a different entity, not one resulting from the spontaneous and voluntary transformation of a formerly evil entity. It's no good that way, obviously; it's a logical impossibility. If there were no possibility of sinning and doing evil, doing good would have no meaning. It's self-evident—more than self-evident. You can't fool me like that; I've read the Scriptures too and know perfectly well what I'm talking about. Satan's sin was different from Adam's sin. For Adam's sin there will be mercy, because he was deceived by Temptation, by the Enemy. For Satan's sin there can be no mercy; it's a logical impossibility, as I already said."

"I can even agree, but in this case your sin is that of Adam, as a man, which you are."

"No, my sin is the sin of Satan! What is my sin, in your opinion? But you already know what my sin is, you're sick of knowing it and must have tried to distance yourself from me before, without the necessity of that silly little sin that you're making into the Himalayas. For that sin, there can be mercy. Murderers, thieves, and slanderers can find mercy. But one who sins like Satan can find no mercy. It's quite true that Satan was originally an angelic being, but I am made in the image and likeness of Him! Of Him, of God! And I—"

"Calm down, João, you're not making sense. I didn't know you were so upset. Calm down!"

"I'm not upset! A little excited, maybe, but not upset. I mean, I am. I am but I'm not. It's more because it hurts me as much as it does you the fact that we can't go on as friends. But now I see it was inevitable, sooner or later, because my presence would always pull you away from the straight and narrow. And sin makes man the servant of sin; that's in St. John, also in St. Paul—I've read the Scriptures too, so you can't trip me up. I don't want to be the instrument of your perdition. Let Satan look for somebody else. My own damnation is enough for me, I don't need him."

"You needn't be sarcastic. I still insist the problem is much more simple; you're letting yourself be carried away by one of those delirious oratorical raptures of yours. Have you had anything to drink today?"

"No, I haven't had anything. And I most definitely am not being sarcastic; I was never more sincere in my life. And I'm going to continue not resisting that woman, I don't know how, I don't know anything, I don't know what's going to happen, but she said she loves me, she said it unmistakably, and I managed to tell her I love her too. I'm feeling lots of things I never felt before and I like what I'm feeling. That has no importance as a sin in itself; it's a fifth-rate sin. Abraham had a lover too, not to mention Solomon. And David's behavior with Uriah was really shitty, a total lack of character. It's as I told you and always tell you: I've read the Good Book too; you can't dupe me. This peccadillo is only the spur for our separation, a separation that's for your own good, because my sin is basic and would always find ways to entangle you."

"João, I repeat: You're upset. This argument is complete delirium. Go calm down; we can talk later."

"No. We won't talk later. We're not going to talk anymore; that's the least I can do for you, and you know I'm being sincere, totally sincere. If you don't know, I hope you'll find out someday, somehow. I was merely reasoning about your initial argument, which was perfect, except for the nature of my sin. My sin, as you know because you yourself spoke of it, is the sin of betraying my gift, doing none of what I can and ought to do, not playing my role in life and in evolution, betraying the Creator and Creation. And it's not the fruit of temptation, but from within myself. I was born here, went away, studied, lost my courage, inherited a few things, came back, perished. I want nothing. I'm capable of nothing. I do nothing. You could tell me: Plant a tree; write a book; have a child. But I wasn't born to plant trees or write books, and I'm practically a virgin—rather, I'm a militant virgin, a jack-off. I was born to study, to research, discover, interpret. But I do none of those things, which is surely the reason I feel Evil surrounding me; it's very clear now. I'm being quite sincere. I have great affection for you and, in a certain way, will always be your friend, but that's how things are."

Much later, alone in the sacristy, Father Monteirinho wished he were merely having a nightmare, and came to see that such it was, for only in a nightmare could all this, which struck him as so absurd, take place. But he didn't awake from this nightmare, and the memory of João Pedroso leaving the large old house, in all certainty never to set foot in it again, remained with him. Suddenly, everything changed: It was another city, another life, another time. With immense sadness, he kneeled at the altar of Our Lady of Perpetual Help and prayed at length, asking her to intercede for the salvation of João Pedroso and for the friendship which he already missed so much.

Unexplainable things, something a guy does as if he were on autopilot. During a short stay in Salvador, where Deraldo gave him excellent news about the progress of the treatment, Ângelo Marcos called a store chosen at random in the phone book and asked if they had good air rifles. The man said they did, and he wanted to know if the rifles killed sparrows. "They take 'em apart," the man said, apparently laughing at the other end of the line. Then Ângelo Marcos, neither able to nor wishing to think about the reason he was doing it, put on dark glasses and a hat whose floppy brim came down over his eyes, donned an old pair of heavy cotton pants that he wore in the country, stopped at an automatic teller to withdraw money, and went to the store. As it was little more than a hole in the wall, hard to find among the darkened passageways of an old building in the Sete Portas district, he was forced to remove the glasses, but the man behind the counter, who barely glanced at his face and concentrated on chewing his bubble gum and massaging it with his tongue, gave no sign of recognizing him.

"I'm the one who phoned a little while ago," Ângelo Marcos said. "About the air rifle."

The clerk did not reply and turned to a cabinet with a glass front, from which he took out four different air rifles, one of them with the appearance of an assault rifle with retractable butt.

"Is that an AK-47?" Ângelo Marcos asked, trying to be funny, and the clerk said "Uhn-uh" behind his wad of gum, as if hearing the joke for the tenth time the same day.

"A repeating rifle," he said. "See here? This tube here is like a clip that takes twenty-five of these pellets. You load the clip, break it here, and it cocks and loads automatically. This other one's good, but it's the conventional type and you got that nuisance of putting lead in your mouth and reloading one at a time. I've killed a lot of sparrows myself with the repeater. Sparrows are fast; they don't stay in one place very long. The weapon's gotta have velocity and accuracy."

"You used to kill sparrows?"

"Not used to; still do. I live in a house full of ventilation ducts and they get in and shit all over the place; they've even shit in the plates and pans. So I kill 'em and feed 'em to the dogs. I got one of these at home. It's real good. The only ones better are the American CO_2 models, but they're practically machine guns, and the lead is round, not pointed like this."

"Do you have ammunition for it?"

"Are you taking a hundred boxes? If you want a hundred . . ."

He didn't take a hundred, but he did take two dozen—six thousand pellets in small, round boxes, which, upon returning to his house on the island, he stacked carefully in the masonry bookcase at the head of the stairs. Except for one box, which he put in his pocket to take outside with the rifle the next day. He awoke excited, much earlier than usual. He skipped breakfast and went to the yard by the side door of the kitchen, without answering Cornélio's greeting. Two English sparrows were pecking near the garbage cans. Rather nervously, he loaded the rifle and fired, but the sparrows flew away and the pellet pierced a caladium leaf at the other end of the yard. A couple of inches to the left, at least. A bit high too. The sight must be off. That's all it could be; he'd always been a good shot. And he spent the better part of the morning turning the gun-sight controls back and forth until, around eleven o'clock, he'd hit dozens of tin cans, matchboxes, and plastic wrappings, but no sparrows. Not only did they not stay in one place, as the man in the store had said, but also, after hours of shooting, they seemed to recognize the rifle and became skittish as soon as he raised the barrel in their direction.

Close to noon, having had to stop to make some important phone calls and take a second look at the balance sheets of the cacao plantation, he cut short in irritation the advice offered him by Cornélio at the door to his office. Better to exterminate those little pests with poisoned rice and bread, Cornélio opined, volunteering to take full charge. It was a simple matter, and he had experience. Or else bread crumbs soaked in rum, which leaves the birds drunk and staggering all over the place, very easy to kill, even with a broom.

"Cornélio, I don't want to poison sparrows, or kill drunken sparrows. I want to kill normal sparrows, with my air rifle!" Ângelo Marcos said gruffly and slammed the door.

"Balance Sheet and Quarterly Report," read the heading of the four or five sheets from an American printout, which made for difficult reading because of the lack of Portuguese diacritical markings. But that was not the reason that, after spending a few minutes reading the report, his lips sometimes moving, he pushed it to the front of the table and rose impatiently. He couldn't concentrate on any of it. Camilo could send in his report late, as in fact he always did. Were there any sparrows in the trees visible from the window, or in the patio downstairs? There were, there were, and on the telephone lines between two poles in front of the house several of them perched like notes on a musical staff. Too far to shoot from here; the wind would take the pellet off target. But if they remained on the wires, it could be a wonderful opportunity; he could fire from below, next to the wall, maybe as close as ten yards from them. Without bothering to place a paperweight on the report, and without closing the window or door, he ran to the case where the air rifle and ammunition were. Not very many pellets in the clip. To tell the truth, he probably wouldn't need more than one, since after the first shot all the sparrows would disappear for several minutes. But he wanted a full clip, so, with sweat dripping from his brow, he loaded the pellets into the tube, ignoring the large number that fell to the floor. Because his hands weren't steady, he had problems getting the clip in place and had to pause for a moment, resuming the task only after a few deep breaths. The clip in place, he cocked the rifle as slowly and silently as possible, because his several hours of practice had convinced him that the animals could hear the click when he cocked it, even inside the house, and hid on the roof or camouflaged themselves among the heavy tree branches. Holding the weapon with its barrel up, as he had learned from television, he carefully opened the patio door closest to the telephone poles and anxiously confirmed that the sparrows were still on the wires. He could try from there, avoiding the risk of frightening them off as he approached. But no, no. He wanted very much to hit one this time; it wasn't possible for him not to hit one. He had to get as close as he could. Almost leaning against the wall, he rested the butt on his shoulder and slowly lowered the barrel, aiming at the large, plump sparrow perched on the lowest wire. Squeeze, don't jerk, he thought, remembering his shooting lessons, and pulled the trigger firmly. A different sound than normal came from the weapon, and the sparrows, including the big one, scattered. Why did the controls of the sights work with targets even smaller than sparrows and never with the sparrows? Annoyed, he cocked the rifle again and pointed it at an empty pellet box that he had used for practice. He fired; the same muffled sound was heard, and nothing happened to the small box. Of course: Something was wrong with the rifle. He discovered that in his haste he had put some of the pellets upside down in the clip and the rifle had jammed. He tried to empty the clip, but the deformed pellets were wedged in, impossible to remove by hand. He used a small knife; the pellets had compressed against one another, giving the impression they would never come out. Barely containing his exasperation, he finally thought to make use of one of the dozens of tools he had bought during the phase when he had decided to smoke a pipe, and after much effort managed to remove the obstruction and reload the clip, this time inspecting the position of each pellet.

The sparrows, however, had disappeared for longer than he expected, and by lunchtime he had found no others in a good position, though he shot at every one he saw, causing them to take flight and roost in some inaccessible spot from which their chirps sounded like catcalls. He put the rifle back in the bookcase, told himself he was making too much of it, and went down to lunch. But he had no appetite and forced himself to eat a bit of grilled snook only because he had asked Cornélio to make it and didn't want him to start pouting and get all weepy, as he probably already was to some extent because of the recent dressing-down. Well, he could take a look at the report now; he didn't feel like putting up with an upsetting call from Camilo, lying about the tax and loan deadlines, and dealing with a thousand other equally unpleasant topics. And there was also a string of other problems to be examined, so he had to get some work done.

But he couldn't work, despite sitting at his office table with the report in his hands, exactly like the first time. And, exactly like the first time, he saw sparrows perched on the wires and grabbed the rifle. But the sparrows didn't wait for him to go downstairs, and throughout the afternoon he alternated between shots at distant birds, which might not even be sparrows, and plinking at cans, buckets, pans, and even full beer bottles stored in one of the rooms off the yard. Finally, he put away the rifle and thought about going back to his office, but he had barely entered it, before he left again to ambush sparrows only minutes after his decision to quit. He even thought about taking the rifle to explore new territory, but he hated the idea of having curious kids and busybodies around him, and he felt embarrassed at the idea of being seen shooting birds. The sly laughter that must be coming from the black servants there inside was enough. Finally he developed the strategy of sitting by one of the patio doors with the rifle cocked, waiting for a sparrow to light near the garbage cans. He shot at several and had the impression that one of them had been hit, but the bird merely hesitated for an instant and then took off, along with three others.

At five o'clock, with a desire to smoke unlike anything he had felt since he gave up cigarettes, he decided on impulse to get closer to the sparrows around the garbage, because it was clear he would never hit them. He got up, the air rifle held high, and slowly approached the cans, but as he was readying his shot the birds took flight. Two of them, however, did not go far and limited themselves to climbing to the crosspiece of one of the telephone poles, well beyond the wall against which the cans stood. Without attempting to get closer, he aimed, shot, and, not believing his eyes, saw the sparrow droop and fall to the ground behind the wall with a clearly audible thud. For a few moments he didn't know what to do and wandered about the yard, making it to the gate twice and both times coming back inside. He left the rifle leaning against the wall and returned to the gate, but as soon as he opened the padlock, he decided to get it. And he left with it in the direction of the telephone pole where the fallen sparrow had been, but he spent some time without finding the bird and was beginning to think there had been a mistake, when he spotted it, camouflaged by the black and white of the Portuguese sidewalk tiles, in a place much farther from the pole than he had estimated. He didn't expect to become nervous when he saw the animal up close, but he did, his muscles tense, his legs not very firm, and his mouth suddenly full of saliva, which he swallowed in displeasure. The sparrow must have dragged itself this far, because it was still alive, though it couldn't move any further. Lying on its side, its beak open, it breathed with difficulty, and one of its legs, above which were a spot of blood and shattered feathers, twitched spasmodically from time to time. His mouth still filled with saliva, almost drooling, Ângelo Marcos cocked the rifle and shot the dying sparrow from about a foot away. The animal's body shuddered and it gave a death rattle, but its chest continued to rise and fall with a heaving rhythm. Ângelo Marcos, his arms so weakened that he had to recock the rifle in three steps, this time rested the mouth of the barrel against the sparrow's head and fired another shot, closing his eyes as he pulled the trigger. When he opened his eyes, there was a hole in the bird's neck. It finally died, and until nightfall Ângelo Marcos kept entering and leaving the house to see the cadaver again. From that day on, he killed many and wounded countless, who at times returned, some horribly mutilated, with open wounds even in the head. But he was interested only in those he killed, because, as he knew but told no one, it was not from hatred that he wanted to kill them.

After noon, with an enormous sun pouring an excess of light over the island and obliging everyone to squint, the stones of the sidewalks hot as burning coals, and prostrate old men waiting on the benches at the square for the ocean wind, the guests began to arrive. One of the three policemen provided by the lieutenant and compensated by Ângelo Marcos took his place on the sidewalk, shooing away the children and vagrants trying to wait at the gates to ask for food.

"Five o'clock, five o'clock," he repeated, idly waving his baton and smiling with bonhomie. "Five o'clock, at the rear gate, the food left over from the party will be distributed. Everybody bring their own container. Five o'clock, the rear gate. Now move along, five o'clock, the rear gate."

Another policeman, who had remained in front of the house, came to ask if he needed help.

"No," he answered, with the same smile. "You don't know these folks yet. They're all good people. And there's nobody hungry there either; they just want to try some different food. They know that at this party there's a lot of different foods. They feel like eating little meat pies, codfish, that kind of thing."

The other man looked uneasily at the small multitude.

"Well, you know best," he said after a time, and went back to his post, looking back three times on the way. It wasn't his problem, at least for now, and in any case the hosts of the party were charitable people who were going to give away the leftover food—he just hoped they wouldn't forget him. And he wanted to go on enjoying the action at the party, the waiters, their sparkling trays and their snow-white gloves, dancing their way between small tables shaded by parasols with colorful designs, the tables of food glimpsed there inside, the men standing around talking with glasses in their hands, the women wearing cheery and daring clothes, like those two before him, especially the pale one with the dark hair, with her thighs showing and her breasts jumping out of her blouse.

"A success," Bebel told Ana Clara, standing at the doorway facing the entrance to the patio. "I mean, not entirely. I was speaking just of the luncheon, because he hasn't arrived yet, has he?"

"No. You think he's not coming? Now I'm afraid he won't come. It's quite possible, he's so odd, though he did promise. I was looking him right in the eyes when he promised."

"Of course he's coming. Don't even think otherwise. Think positive. And it's still very early. The only ones who've arrived are those yokels from the island, who're used to polishing off an ox hoof with beer at 7:00 A.M. and skipped the meal and saved their appetite today and by now must be starving to death; just look how they're scarfing down the appetizers. Good thing we ordered about five tons of all that crap, thank God. The life of a politician's wife isn't easy. Say, has that doctor with jowls like a bulldog, what's his name, has he arrived?"

"Dr. Lúcio Nemésio? No."

"Well then? I'm almost certain they're coming together. They're friends and João is probably afraid of coming by himself."

"No way, Bebel. It's not that bad. He can stand on his own two feet."

"But he's afraid to come alone. Either he'll come with Dr. Lúcio Nemésio or he'll come with the priest. He's a friend of the priest's too, isn't he?"

"Huh? The priest? Yes, he is. I think so, yes, he is."

"You're spaced out, girl. Calm down. I'll get us something to drink. What do you want?"

"A martini. American style, dry with lots of gin."

"I thought the gal was game. Don't worry, I'll use my famous recipe: I show the martini bottle to the glass and fill it with gin. Leave it to me; stay here and greet the guests. I'll be back soon; don't want to miss a thing."

Oh, Ana Clara, how surreal this all is; it seems like those English films about India. No, Jamaica, Jamaica because of the blacks and mulattoes, the English giving their garden parties and pretending that they socialize with the Creole aristocracy. There goes Bebel, plunging headlong into the house, swinging her hips more than ever, and stopping to chat with a small group. That martini is going to take some time. A drink is good for the nerves. Nerves, my God? Yes, nerves—that's right, nerves. From time to time the melancholy sensation that none of this craziness will work out; really all an act of craziness. Here come more people, what's the name of that idiotic Dr. Fontana's wife? The type of woman who goes on the Ethiopian Diet, loses weight and ends up with skinny legs and a drooping butt, without ever losing her chubby face; the face is always chubby. Even more so with those earrings cut from shackles, which she continually shakes like a cowbell. Carminha, Maria do Carmo. Carminha. Here comes the pushy vulgarian with his kisses. Suzanna Fleischman is right as rain when she lambastes this kissy-kissy habit of everybody's, rubbing your skin and mouth against unacceptable skins. A T-shirt cut out at the armpits. Keep away from him when it's time to eat, with that underarm odor of his and that bear-sized back. Not to mention that he can't form two sentences without saying "geez" and is going to insist on talking about Formula I racing, which he watches on TV with an expression like an australopithecus, according to his own wife. Thank you, thank you, you look lovely yourself. Impressive, those print pants laced at the shins. Must be the Queen of Damascus costume she modeled at the Portuguese Club, which she's now wearing socially. All that's missing is the cloak, decorated all over with sequined scimitars, but those glittering shoes with their spike heels were beyond a doubt part of it. God, what lack of patience with people! It's nerves. Isn't he coming? It's true it's fun to relive adolescence, but sometimes it's a drag. Things could very well be a lot simpler. Would she be able to go up to him, with the greatest of gall, and say "Drop by the house on such-and-such a day, at this or that hour"? Dr. Sinval Penafiel and his bucktoothed mouse of a wife, Helliete—just like that, with *H* and double-*l* and an Ipirá accent. Hello, Liete, why didn't you bring the kids? Thank God she didn't, of course; it's enough with Stephanie, the more annoying of Ângelo Marcos's two pain-in-the-tail daughters by Regininha, and her boyfriend Caio Túlio, a couple of scrawny stammerers who fortunately preferred to go off somewhere and grope each other rather than stay around there saying "Right on" every time anyone addressed them. Bebel, of course, has already said good-bye to that group a couple of hundred times and returned a couple of hundred more; better to get the martini herself. The mayor and the mayor's wife; what's the mayor's name? Nothing comes to mind but Aricanor, of course it's not Aricanor, even if here in Bahia any name is possible. Ariflinor? Abriginoel? Why doesn't Ângelo Marcos show up? After all, the entire crowd is here because of him. The only one not coming because of him is João.

But Ângelo Marcos did show up, at the very moment that the mayor was extending his hand to Ana Clara and she had already decided she would say "Mr. Mayor!" or some such thing. And he showed up looking very elegant, in a French shirt of naval cut, American bermudas, and Italian deck shoes, smiling with the corners of his mouth turned lightly downward. He had just finished smoking a marijuana cigarette in the attic and was anticipating with enormous delight the glass of wine that, Deraldo or no Deraldo, he had decided to drink—and it was Deraldo himself who told him that according to the tests his liver was in surprisingly good shape.

"Arionaldo, a great pleasure to have you here," he said, shaking the mayor's hand as Ana Clara exchanged kisses with his wife. "Dona Salete, how are you? A beautiful day, eh, a beautiful day—this sun, this breeze cooling our side of the island. You really might say that you're the First Lady of a paradise. Ana Clara and I have been seriously thinking of settling here permanently. Isn't that right, Aninha?"

Lots of people, aren't there? His head very light and in a great state of good humor, Ângelo Marcos ran his eyes over the patio. Prestige, prestige, even if officially out of power. And all these women; where do so many women hide themselves here on the island, some of them downright fantastic? No, not some—many. Many, like that brunette with an incredible complexion and an extraordinary ass who keeps looking over here every five seconds. Bebel herself, whom he'd seen in there, was smashing in those culottes. He could swear she wasn't wearing anything under them. No, not Bebel. Bebel wouldn't do. Although, when she drinks she becomes another person; there's something in her eyes, the way she leans up against you. These things aren't all that simple; sometimes it's a question of opportunity. Well, in any case he'd be able to circulate and take a few soundings during the luncheon. But obviously everything must be handled discreetly, and Ângelo Marcos, after a friendly squeeze of the mayor's arm and a peck for Ana Clara, excused himself to greet other guests, with a generic smile and quick waves of his hand to all sides.

"Cancer gave me back my perfect health, ha-ha!" he was telling a group of three couples, when, as he paused to enjoy their laughter, he glanced suddenly to the side and saw Lúcio Nemésio, accompanied by his wife and by João Pedroso, just coming through the gate.

"Didn't I tell you I'd be here to lay into some of that manioc mush?" Lúcio Nemésio said, after Ângelo Marcos hastily abandoned the three couples to go to greet the recent arrivals.

"That's true, that's true. It's a great pleasure, professor. Dona Rosário, how are you? Looking better all the time, that I can assure you! And our João Pedroso, king of the seas and of fishery!"

João Pedroso smiled, tried to say something witty but managed only "king of the seas, right?" and continued to smile, not knowing what else to do, as he accompanied the others to a vacant table at the far side of the patio. Very strange, very strange all of this, especially after that obsessive conversation he'd had with Monteirinho. He was going crazy for good, of course. It was all one big insanity, with reality manifesting itself more and more in unconnected fragments. True enough, to overcome his anxiety and even a certain fear that Ana Clara's luncheon caused him, he had lunged with frightful lack of ceremony for the portable bar in Lúcio Nemésio's living room and served himself two strong doses of straight whisky while they waited for Rosário to get ready. But he wasn't drunk, not even close, and therefore it was for another reason that everything seemed different and semiabsurd, even the air, even the texture of the coconut palm fronds, which now appeared as metallic blades, polished sabers. Even people, often distant and with incorporeal voices like in a badly dubbed film. And he hadn't thought about the husband until this moment; interesting how he hadn't thought about the husband at all. Now he was being forced to think about him, after being welcomed with such courtesy, even with affection. Although rather simple, he made an effort to be pleasant and no doubt had some good qualities; after all, he was a rich and influential man. There he is, two steps away, the husband. Funny thing, no remorse, no pang of conscience. Maybe after something happens, if it happens. No, he won't feel anything. Perhaps because he knows nothing is really going to happen; it's all a kind of game, a fleeting madness. It would be very good to have someone to talk with about the matter. But there isn't anyone. Where can she be? The luncheon is for you, she'd said, looking at him in a manner so full of intimidating insinuations and at the same time unbearably exciting that he blushed as he became aware of a persistent erection brought on by the memory.

"Did you know that the animal closest to man is the black?" Ângelo Marcos told one of the waiters, a husky black man of about twenty who responded with an embarrassed smile. "You shame me, boy. Seems like you have goat crap not just on the outside of your head but inside as well. Didn't I tell you not to put ice in the wine like you see on that tray? What kind of crudeness is this, boy? You're really one dumb black. What your father has of intelligence—no, not intelligence, knowledge, because a black has knowledge, not intelligence, like people around here say—what your father has of knowledge you have of thickheadedness."

"It was because they asks for it."

"Ah, they asks for it. . . . They asks for it, does they? They asks for it, the waiters brings it. You're right about that; you haves to bring what the customer ask for, ha-ha! All right, but bring me a glass of white wine, one of those glasses from here. Listen, pay attention, Einstein, you black rocket scientist—a glass of white wine without any ice in it. Ask Cornélio; he knows which wine."

They were sitting at a table in a corner of the patio, where Ângelo Marcos, after pulling out Rosário's chair and waiting for the others to sit down, had told the waiter to serve them anything they wanted and had leaned back with his legs extended and his hands behind his head. He looked at his audience the entire time he spoke with the waiter, but the jovial tone he attempted to give to his words made no one laugh, and he was a bit disconcerted.

"That urchin is my godson," he explained, pointing his chin toward the youth. "I always kid around with him like that; I feel a certain affection for him. I've helped his father a great deal, and my father helped his father, who was the family's black handyman for a long time when I was a child and we summered here on the island. He's a conscientious black, knowledgeable, who has a small pension, though he never ceases to complain. I arranged a scholarship for that one there and hired him as a clerk in the Ministry and—"

"A clerk? Does he have the background to be a clerk?"

"I put him at the service of my Department. The salary's a lot better than if he were a custodian; it's a way of helping out his family. I'm not ashamed to say that I give that kind of help whenever I can. There's little enough we can do for these people, so every time I can do so, I help out. His father has some minor landholdings, a small house or two, but even so it's a difficult struggle, on top of which he has two families, each with I don't know how many children. The boy wasn't doing much of anything; he washed my car, brought the goods from the grocery and the street markets, little things like that. But he didn't want anything to do with studying and he got homesick for this place—imagine. And he ran away from our home, actually ran away; one fine night he failed to return home from school and came here, abandoning his job, giving up everything. It's a question of upbringing, or of mentality. Instead of taking advantage of the chance to be something in life, he prefers to come back to bum around on the island. His father told me the only reason he doesn't use those greasy hairstyles so in fashion with black people these days is that he knows he'll be thrown out of the house the day he shows up with dreadlocks on his head. But he's not going to amount to anything; all he cares about is afro music, and now they tell me he's even taken up smoking marijuana, which means he won't amount to anything. A guy who smokes marijuana loses initiative and ambition; research proves it. But even so, I like him and go on helping him. I find a few small jobs for him, give him clothes, bring him to eat here, that sort of thing. At heart he's a good kid and we like him."

He stopped suddenly, realizing that he was overexplaining, giving excessive importance to a run-of-the-mill incident; after all, he'd just been kidding around with a black boy from his household, practically a member of the family. He'd seen rougher joking between cousins and even brothers. Yeah, it's in style now to make sanctimonious faces every time someone says anything perfectly common about blacks. It's like the Jews. If you won't lend your toothbrush to a Jew they call you an anti-Semite. There's a true story to that effect. Nowadays everything's racial prejudice; even recognizing that a guy is black is racial prejudice. What stupidity—facing reality isn't prejudice; it's just objectivity. For example, it's an objective truth, which anyone can prove for himself, that blacks are closer to gorillas or chimpanzees than they are to us—an incontrovertible truth, and it does no good to try to hide the factual evidence. Just take a look at a white man, then a black man, then a monkey. Blackmail, that's what this business of racial prejudice is. Blackmail—hypocrisy, pure hypocrisy.

"Dr. Nemésio," he said, running his tongue along the inside of his cheeks, his mouth half open, to give an air of challenge to what he was about to say, "don't you think there's an element of exaggeration in this matter of racial prejudice? Race relations were always much more easygoing in Brazil than in other countries, though I admit prejudice does exist, despite the fact that I personally have none. But now they're hardening; it's a type of Americanization. You can't say anything, you can't make a joke, nothing. You can make jokes about the Portuguese, Arabs,

Jews, Italians, Japanese, but you can't make jokes about blacks—that's prejudice. And even when it's not a joke but an objective and undeniable reality, free of value judgments—that's prejudice too, if the blacks don't like it. For example, you see Edsonil there, coming back with the tray. Is it a joke to say he looks more like a monkey than any one of us? That doesn't mean he's a monkey, but he looks like one. That's plain to see. They may not like it, but it's true and they recognize it themselves, you can be sure. But to recognize that fact, without any value judgment, is considered prejudice, and that's what I can't accept."

"João," Lúcio Nemésio said, "you could very well give one of your talks now. Have a couple more to loosen your tongue. What you said is interesting, Ângelo, and it's a good thing you don't consider it pejorative to say that somebody looks like a monkey, because I'm sure the opinion of Dr. João Pedroso, here beside us, is exactly the opposite of yours. Mine also, but I learn these things from him. Even though I understand very little about monkeys, I am curious about the subject. Speak, João, present your counterarguments. I'm sure Ângelo will find it interesting."

"I will. I'll find it quite interesting. You must be kidding, or else engaging in sophism. I'm familiar with your intelligence and shrewdness."

"No, I'm not joking, nor am I all that intelligent. It's true: My opinion is exactly the opposite of yours. Explain it, João; you talk well, go ahead."

"I didn't hear clearly what Ângelo said."

"Of course you did. Stop playing hard to get. He said that blacks look like monkeys and I know you believe that in general it's whites who look more like monkeys. You can— Ah! Ah, Dona Ana Clara, a vision of beauty, and here I am between a couple of overgrown louts and Rosário, who doesn't count because your wife doesn't count, but how lovely you look, younger all the time! Come closer! How are you? It's obvious that you're fine! You're just in time to hear a lecture about man and monkey that Dr. João Pedroso is going to deliver as soon as all that kissy-kissy is out of the way. I'm the only one here who has the right to kiss you, because I'm old and the others are buttinskies. How are things, my dear?"

"João's going to give a lecture? Are you going to give a lecture, João?"

"No, no. It's just a joke of his."

"Yes, he is."

"No, I'm not. No. You have more of a background than I do, and you're the one who brought up the subject."

"What subject is that?"

"It's about men and monkeys, my dear, as I said. Or rather, about whites, blacks, and monkeys. Your husband here says that blacks look like monkeys and João and I support the opposite view. We contend that whites, in a certain way, are much more like monkeys than are blacks. Explain it, João. You once told me about it in brilliant fashion."

"Oh no, you explain it. You understand more about it than I do."

"You know I even agree with you? But only certain aspects; others you know far better, because I don't have a general background. I just sample things here and there. Go ahead, man, explain it. It could be an interesting debate."

"Explain it, João. You've explained fish to me so well."

"No, not me. No, no. Lúcio understands such things better and he also talks better than I do. I hate debates; I don't have the necessary bellicosity. Not me; you go ahead, Lúcio."

"You're a real drag, a wet blanket! He must have been in a strange mood when he explained those fish, Dona Ana; this guy here is a full-blown lunatic. All right, I'll handle this. Leave it to me. Let's get on with it, Dr. Ângelo Marcos. I'd even like you to offer me elements to the contrary; I really am curious about the matter. But I doubt if you have those elements, because I've given this a lot of thought. In the first place, the difference between you, or me, and a chimpanzee are two small linked chromosomes, the so-called chromosome 2, in man. A matter of one percent. A minuscule difference, though of course not insignificant. So, unless you think blacks are not human beings, in which case Dr.

Sinval, because he is a mulatto, wouldn't exist under normal circumstances, all of us must resemble chimpanzees in one form or other. It's just that we're selective in what we see; we make the choices that are advantageous to us—which, incidentally, has very interesting practical implications that I cannot, and should not, discuss here. So the eye of the white, which is the dominant eye even for blacks, sees only the similarities that are, so to speak, advantageous. And it's blind to others; it's an old gnoseological tradition, especially for you religious types, immortalists et cetera. For example, the monkey is hairy; blacks aren't hairy, whites are. The white, in this sense, is closer to the monkey. The black's hair is curly; the white's is straight like the monkey's. Monkeys have thin lips; blacks have thick lips. The platyrrhiny and cranial conformation of blacks, if one can generalize and I know one can't, is another question. Platyrrhiny, to begin with—"

"Dr. Lúcio is sharp," Ana Clara whispered to João Pedroso, wishing she could rest her legs against his under the table but keeping her ankles crossed beside the legs of her own chair. "I admire intelligence," she continued, grasping his arm as if the subject demanded this gesture. "I think it's cool. You're like that"—she said, taking advantage of Ângelo Marcos's being blocked by Lúcio Nemésio's extremely broad shoulders to prolong the contact a few moments—"You're good looking," and João Pedroso felt his pants bursting and the veins in his neck throbbing.

Neither of them took notice of how much time passed since Lúcio Nemésio had bombarded Ângelo Marcos with an unanswerable argument, and the latter was now trying to change the subject, amid compliments toward the other man, lavish but reluctant. And they didn't know just what they had done until they sat face to face when the hot meal was served, with Bebel supervising everything, because although she dissimulated from time to time and had spent close to half an hour walking arm in arm with Ângelo Marcos, Ana Clara wasn't paying attention to anything. Before the meal, neither of them thought they'd be hungry, with their stomachs tight and their hearts beating uncertainly, but they ended up filling two generous plates and sat down facing each other, at a different table from Ângelo Marcos, Lúcio Nemésio, and Rosário, who were now surrounded by lots of people eating from plates held in their hands and listening to the conversation. Lúcio Nemésio was no longer talking about monkeys; he was talking about something to do with democracy, which he classified as an illusion fated to disappear because of its impracticability. But, although his voice made its way to Ana Clara and João Pedroso, interweaving with the murmur of the party, the words couldn't be easily distinguished and they heard nothing of what was being said around them, to the point that Bebel had to tap Ana Clara on the shoulder to get her attention.

"Aninha, could you come to the kitchen with me for a minute? It's quick, a problem Cornélio came up with that I don't know how to solve. Then you can come right back. You'll excuse us, João."

Ana Clara got up, continuing to look at João and holding the napkin that had been in her lap.

"Are you going to take the napkin?"

"Huh?"

"You have a napkin in your hand. That's not a purse, it's a napkin."

"Oh, so it is. I was distracted. A problem with Cornélio?"

"I'm not quite sure. He's in tears back there, but I think it can be solved. Let's go see."

"I'm on my way. I'll just be an instant, João."

They hadn't gotten to the door when Bebel took Ana Clara by the elbow and asked into her ear if she'd by any chance drunk a whole bottle of something. No, she hadn't, of course not, just that one martini and later a small glass of beer. Why?

"You remember that film *Tom Jones*, where there's a scene of him eating, sitting across from a woman, that was practically screwing? You remember, they ate with their hands and got food all over themselves and kept exchanging those looks and those sly little expressions. Well, between you and João all that's missing is the food-smearing part, because you two are attacking that *vatapá* like some erotic mush. You're not even looking at your plates; you're screwing each other with your eyes. It's as plain as the nose on your face, girl, anybody can see it. Marquinhos hasn't noticed it yet because the crowd there is hyper, although Lúcio Nemésio asked about you and I said you must be taking care of the luncheon things, and João must be off in a corner somewhere with a glass in his hand. But Marquinhos *will* notice before too long; I think a lot of people may already have noticed. The two of you practically haven't let daylight between you."

"Is that true? I thought I had disguised it pretty well. I walked around with Marquinhos, talked to lots of people; I didn't have the slightest idea about it. I mean, it's true we were over there looking at each other, but there wasn't anyone at the table, so I didn't think . . . We didn't go to Marquinhos's table because it's packed with people; there's nowhere to even put a plate."

"Sure, sure, but I had to warn you. You can't go putting on a show like that; you have to cool it a little or you're going to ruin everything and there'll be hell to pay. Marquinhos is such a male chauvinist and—"

"You're right. I'm going to pay more attention. I do have to be careful."

"Have you spoken to him about coming here?"

"I haven't had a chance. I came close once, but I haven't been able to yet; it looks easier than it is. The only time I started to talk about it, that pest Fontana latched onto us to talk about Formula I's. I got as far as saying 'We have to get together,' and he replied with an expression that made me feel like grabbing him on the spot. Oh, Bebel, it's really something. I'm so excited you can hardly imagine. I'm so hot that I can't describe it. It's like I have an animal in the middle of my body. It almost hurts, and makes me so impatient that I feel like jumping around. I swear to you, it's really strange!"

"Yes, but you've got to stay calm. You can't be like this."

"Yes, I'm going to try. I'm going to be calm, I'll manage. Of course. After all, it's not as if I were some out-of-control pervert."

No, she wasn't an out-of-control pervert and therefore she didn't go back to the table where she had been talking with João. She'd return in passing, much later, apologize, explain that several problems had kept her, and, if there was an opportunity, mention the meeting. In the end, it was a matter of luck. She had to count on a bit of luck and not push things. Once more, Bebel was right on the money. Right on the money, she thought again, feeling the intense fire she had described to Bebel become even more intense, while she quickly ascended the living room stairs, hoping the few people nearby would think she was going to touch up her makeup or take care of some domestic task. On the money, she repeated, entering the suite, where she went straight to the chest of drawers and got a ring with the keys to some of the downstairs doors, which had been shut to keep anyone from going where they shouldn't be. All identical, but fortunately the key to the second door to the powder room, which opened onto the vestibule in front of the smaller stairs, was easily recognizable because it had always had a slightly darker color than the others. She moved toward the kitchen light to be sure she was taking the right key, separated it from the others, stuck it in the pocket of her bermudas, and left, as hurried and nervous as when she had entered. Now to find Bebel quickly, before things changed.

She spoke more loudly than she should, when she found Bebel after an agitated search that seemed endless. The people around her were surprised and some laughed, including Bebel, who asked if the house was on fire. Ana Clara came to her senses, joined the laughter, and apologized. It's just that this thing of giving a luncheon always has its unforeseen aspects and she was having a problem back there that had made her nervous, though it was just a trifle, but that's how she was, exaggerating any little trifle that she couldn't fix—perhaps Bebel, without whom she would be lost, could excuse herself from her friends and pop into the pantry with her?

"Cornélio is in tears," she added. "Shall we?"

"Cornélio has really been crying up a storm today, hasn't he, honey?" Bebel said after they began moving away from the others. "What happened? Did you speak to João?"

"No, I didn't. But I decided I'm going to. I'm not going to wait for things to happen. I'll create the circumstances myself and talk to him. I can't stand it anymore."

"Fine, but don't take any chances. You're beginning to worry me. I didn't think things had gotten to this point."

"Me neither. But you're right, right as rain. There's no need for me to take chances. That's why I want to ask you a favor. Only you can do it for me."

"It depends. If I think it's madness I won't do it. I think you're a little too hot to trot. Stay calm!"

"I *am* calm, I promise you, I'm calm. Turned on, but calm. What I want from you is very simple. You know the powder room for the living room to the left as you go out? Sure you do. Here's the key to the far door, which leads to the small staircase. I had it put aside so that no one using the powder room could go into the private part of the house. I'm going to the powder room to put the key in place. Then I'll go up to Ângelo Marcos's office, which is the best place because there's no bed for us to lose control and do something crazy and because he hates going there when he's not working; he says an atmosphere like that doesn't go with the peacefulness of the island."

"Aninha, I see where you're heading. You're really crazy."

"Not in the least. I'm not going to do anything; I'm just going to speak with him about the meeting. I know I can't take long so we won't be missed. It's just to talk. And maybe I'll give some physical follow-through, just some tiny follow-through."

"You're nuts, nuts. Don't you see it can cause a horrible free-for-all?"

"There's not going to be a free-for-all. Bebel, are you going to let me down at a time like this, when I'm even following your advice—a playful thing, physical follow-through, and all that?"

"You want me to tell João to casually go into the powder room, open the other door, go up the small staircase, and meet you in the office."

"Exactly. I like you because you're intelligent. It saves lots of talking. Well?"

"I don't know. I'm worried. I think it's hasty on your part. Wouldn't it be better to give it some thought?"

"Tell him not to leave the key in the door, to take the key and lock the door from outside."

"Aninha . . ."

"I'm going now to leave the key. Tell him I can only wait ten minutes and only be with him for two or three."

"Think he'll show up?"

"He will, he will. He's just like me. I feel it. I'm sure of it. That's it, Bebel, that's it. Let me go now. I don't know what I'd do without you. I really don't. Later I'll tell you all about it."

She still remembered the way Bebel looked, standing open-mouthed at the door to the pantry, one hand on her hip, and she was about to draw the curtain aside a little to peek at Ângelo Marcos down there, seated next to a dark-skinned woman with a firm behind and talking excitedly, when the door opened and João Pedroso came in.

"I wanted to talk to you for just an instant; we don't have much time," she said, approaching him, and both extended their arms and embraced each other with such force that they didn't fall only because she supported her back against the desk. Neither releasing the other, she pulled him by the neck to rest against her, feeling him hard and voluminous on her thigh. She moved her hips to the right, to fit into him. She only planned to stay like that for a time, then move her head so he could kiss her as she wanted, just one kiss. But he moved forward when he felt her lean against him, and a shiver ran up her back. She suddenly freed herself from him, gently pushed him away, and, her face agitated, her eyes fixed on him, and her teeth clenched behind half-opened lips, she placed her thumbs beneath her bermudas and panties and began lowering them until they were at her ankles and she raised one leg, leaving the other still clinging to the clothes. And it wasn't necessary for her to do anything but lean, half-sitting, against the desk, because he acted exactly as she had anticipated, opening his pants without taking his eyes from her and without speaking, advancing slowly toward her and penetrating her with two or three impatient movements until he entered deeply and gently, as if his place were there and he had never left there. Lifting her pelvis forward as if in a spasm, she heard him groan and felt the large member that filled her so powerfully and smoothly begin to pulsate inside her, and then she pulled herself toward him with all her strength and came deeper than she had imagined she could ever come, and she stifled a cry that she wanted to scream as loud as possible, with her mouth pressed against his shoulder.

She hadn't expected that they would both be so calm, immediately afterward and for the rest of the party, which didn't end until five-something, when she said a smiling good-bye to João and Lúcio Nemésio at the main gate, then returning in high spirits, hands in pockets and her eyes happy, she helped Ângelo Marcos solve the problem of the soldiers, servants, and waiters wanting to keep all the food for themselves while the kids and beggars complained outside.

5

An owl began to hoot, always a few yards ahead of them, and Little Hand 3 crossed himself, thanking God he was in the company of a priest, and told himself he didn't believe in such things. But for as long as he could remember, everybody had said that important apparitions took place there, to the point that the spot's reputation had spread throughout the globe. Tremendous apparitions of all sorts and in keeping with every belief, even—begging the father's forgiveness—even with the beliefs of the Holy Roman Apostolic Mother itself, since there were more than a few stories of the Church's saints descending here with all their traditional paraments, many of them bearing swords of fire to punish the ever more insolent sins of humankind. That owl could just as well have gone off hunting in another direction, but it insisted on anticipating their route and waiting for them at frequent intervals in the trees, with those somber hoots. The owl, Little Hand 3 explained, isn't a bad omen in itself; it's just that since earliest times it's been held to be the eyes of spirits and beings both good and bad. And therefore, where there are owls there are surely spirits watching in the darkness, with who knows what designs—not that he believed in such things, he was just talking to be talking. The day he had first come to see the saint—not the saint, sorry, the healer and sorcerer Bará da Misericórdia—it was right about here, just a little further on, where the owl is hooting now, beside the largest of the *ingá* trees, that he had felt the most terrible of the phantom itches, which drove him crazy and made him want to tear off the stump of his right arm. His brothers had to hold him back so he wouldn't go running off madly through the woods banging into trees and squealing like a stuck pig.

"I don't even like to think about it," he said, waving his arm stump forcefully. "But Bará explained I shouldn't be afraid of the memory and that when it showed up I should face it."

A family of crazy people, that's what they'd become, all of them mad, mad, mad, waking up in the middle of the night amid blood-curdling screams, throwing themselves against doors and walls and making life hell for their wives, who were beaten for what they did and for what they didn't do. Little Hand 1, Little Hand 2, Little Hand 3, Little Hand 4, 5, and on it went. It was bad enough that none of them any longer had a name, since the baleful days of their ill-fated emigration to the sisal plantations, whose machines ate, one by one, the right arm of every man in the family, even Geminiano, who was only fourteen when he lost his arm almost to the elbow. They lost their names too; no one, not even members of the family, used their names any longer—except to their face, and then only after protests, but never when their back was turned. And on top of that, to which they learned to resign themselves—since it's well known that God marks certain families and God's will isn't to be questioned—came those diabolical itches, which began with Little Hand 5 and then attacked the rest, one after the other, like scabies on a dog. They all immediately started trying to scratch nonexistent forearms and hands, and some became so desperate in their anxiety that they even made their stumps bleed, futilely rubbing them against tree trunks and rough objects. The priest remembered it, of course he remembered it—hadn't he been sought out by them and their wives and daughters in an effort to alleviate the suffering through prayers, holy water, candles burned at the feet of saints? But neither prayers nor holy water nor candles had had any effect, and the priest had been candid: better for them to look for a doctor; he was no saint to broker miracles. The doctors, however, were of little help; they prescribed pills that left the brothers lethargic and didn't get rid of the itching.

"For a long time we hid it from you," Little Hand 3 said, looking ahead of him as if he were ashamed of facing the priest. "Until just a while back the women didn't want us to give you Bará's message. They thought you might get mad and maybe excommunicate the whole family. Everybody retired on account of disability, everybody crippled, everybody on edge, and then excommunicated besides?"

"I don't excommunicate anyone, Florisvaldo. I just don't approve of such things. I can't approve."

"I know you don't approve, sure you don't approve. We don't approve neither. We're all Catholics, thank God; you know that. But, out of desperation from the itching—"

"Florisvaldo, are you really sure you were cured of the itching because of that man's treatment? How much money did he get from you?"

"None. He didn't ask for money. He asked us, if we could, to replace the sheep he used in our case, and we give him two sheep and some money, but it was 'cause we wanted to."

"And he used a sheep?"

"He always uses a sheep in cases like ours. The sheep has the ability to suffer in silence. And the sheep's like all the animals in the manger—the mule, the rooster, and the others—that the devil can't take on their shape. He didn't tell me so, but I know it; everybody knows it."

The owl hooted again and Little Hand 3 crossed himself once more. Was the priest afraid? There was only a short way to go on that trail and then the climb up the small hill to the home of the saint—no, not the saint, the healer. There was no reason for apprehension; it wasn't possible for that owl to make a tight curve and follow them up the hill.

"No, I'm not afraid. You're the one who appears to be afraid. The only thing that frightens me is all of you referring to that man as 'the saint.' How can a man who lives in low spiritualism, a healer, a sorcerer, be a saint?"

"It's the custom, Father Monteirinho. That's what people call him. People have picked up the custom."

"Yes, but they can't. He's a sorcerer, a witch doctor, a voodoo person, never a saint. That is a grave error; it's like confusing good and evil."

"But he does nothing but good; he's never done harm to nobody."

"His very existence does harm," the priest said in a tone that discouraged any response from Little Hand 3, who busied himself moving his flashlight from one side to the other along the path in front of him, pretending to be trying to reveal something ahead. "His very existence!" he repeated almost with rage and perhaps with regret at having agreed to make this strange visit, through these dense woods, in the company of a good but somewhat unstable lad—like, for that matter, most of his family, phantom itch or not. Yes, they had been cured of the itching, that was undeniable, but there was nothing surprising about the cure—a psychological problem solved by the applied psychology of that voodoo man with his hand passes and sacrificing of sheep. Did Monteirinho really have a good reason for accepting that very strange invitation? He had to admit that curiosity, plain and simple, was one of his principal motives. Well, perhaps not so plain and simple because, after all, this man was very important throughout the region. People came from all over to see him, and there was no denying he was an obstacle, a major obstacle, to the pastoral work. The flock was pulled one way by the evangelicals and another by the voodoo spiritualists, a difficult pastorate, a complicated mission. Saint, saint—why that persistence on everyone's part in calling him saint? And what about those marvels and cures of which they spoke, and the unselfishness they always mentioned? Yes, he was curious to meet such a person. He'd always heard stories about people like that; in one form or another they were part of day-to-day life on the island. But it was also undeniable that this was an expedition to get to know the enemy face to face and thus have more authority and concrete arguments with which to neutralize him, or at least to diminish his influence more and more; naturally, naturally—and thus, Father Monteirinho placated his conscience, which had been disturbed ever since he had accepted the invitation and had been weighing on him throughout the journey.

And there was also the mysterious nature of the invitation—more than an invitation, practically an appeal, a very odd appeal consisting of a spoken message from two of the Little Hands and a letter in oblique language, in old-fashioned handwriting but grammatically impeccable, despite a certain pedantry. The letter did not limit itself to repeating the invitation but also launched into a kind of treatise about how Father Monteirinho's work and dedication—known and admired by all humble people—attested to the existence of men of good will and love for their neighbor and, consequently, the author of the letter felt he could make a request of that good will. He would have sought out the priest personally, but unfortunately, besides being lame and able to move about only with difficulty, he couldn't go to the city without a crowd gathering around him, including those who, against his will, insisted on considering him a saint. He knew that if he sought the priest in good faith, the priest, as a man of God, would receive and hear him. And, as he could not go to the priest, he begged that the opposite be done, that the priest come to him, for it was not a matter of his personal interest but a matter, he believed, that concerned not only everyone in the priest's parish but all of mankind. There was little he could do, especially because he was held in low esteem by the powerful and learned and was without a hearing from anyone other than the poor and ignorant who came to seek him out. He was certain that when the priest learned whereof he spoke, he would see that it was truly a terrible issue and that it was necessary to do something. What, he did not know, but it was necessary.

"The light of the body is the eye," the letter ended, just above an illegible signature that seemed to have been made by another hand, not the one that had written the text. A quotation from St. Matthew? Why a quotation from the Gospels? Why exactly that one, which seemed not to have much to do with the message? Did he know it was a quotation, or was he merely repeating a phrase he'd heard somewhere? What did he mean by it? But the priest had no time to continue with these thoughts, because he was brought back to himself by a tug on his coat sleeve by Little Hand 3, who pointed with his chin to a kind of stairway carved into the mud that wound its way to the top of a small hillock.

"Is this it?"

"This is it, this is it. Just past that jackfruit tree, right past the jackfruit tree up yonder."

When they finished the climb, both the priest and Little Hand 3 raised the beams of their flashlights from the last step of the stairway and, pointing them ahead, illuminated a portion of the front wall of a house partially hidden by the enormous trunk of the jackfruit tree. A dim light came from the arch of the porch before which they found themselves as soon as they passed beyond the tree. Behind the arch were two doors, the one on the right closed, the one on the left ajar. Beside the latter, extending as far as they could see, was a patio or yard surrounded by poorly constructed cubicles and pens for animals. Its compacted clay floor reflected the moonlight in ferrous tones, the air above it swarmed with fireflies, and from time to time a light wind passing through the crown of the trees could be heard in the otherwise motionless silence. Father Monteirinho felt relief when he saw that, apparently at least, the sorcerer had kept his promise to have none of his clientele around during the visit. But, despite the half-open door, there was no one to invite them in, and he was about to ask Little Hand 3 how to proceed, when a dark form lunged toward him and he raised his arms to defend himself against the large, black dog that suddenly burst from the darkness and stopped a few steps away, its eyes fixed on him and its enormous tongue dripping.

"He doesn't bite," said a voice from inside the house, and another light went on, while the left door opened fully and a man with a cane appeared on the porch. "Lie down, Cherub."

He approached more quickly than would be expected from someone who had a withered and almost useless leg. He extended his hand to the priest with a smile in which his tiny eyes wrinkled and disappeared. Speaking always with the same odd and flutelike intonation that caught the priest's attention from the first sentence, he apologized for not being on the porch waiting for such an ennobling visit, but he had been running somewhat behind because he had been obliged to attend to more people that afternoon than usual, to keep the promise. There were some people in the cubicles nearby, but they had already turned in or were occupied with other matters.

"My dogs alone are here," he said, motioning them to enter before him. "I truly appreciate animals, most notably dogs."

Several pedestal lamps and a small round desk lamp on the table made the living room very bright, contrary to the priest's expectations. And, also contrary to what he had anticipated, there was no object of cabalistic appearance, no image, no print or painting of saints or pagan entities—a living room like that of any spacious middle class house. There were two areas separated by a masonry cabinet the height of a counter, with a passageway in the middle, which housed dishes and other objects. The sitting area was laid out symmetrically, with two armchairs, a sofa, a low table, and a lounge chair with cushions.

"Make yourselves comfortable, and please forgive the appearance of the living room," the man said, pointing to a spot on the sofa where the upholstery was worn. "I am ever planning to redo it, but conditions are difficult to the utmost. Where would you like to sit, Reverend Father? I believe this armchair will not be entirely uncomfortable. It is the one I deem to be the least vexing to the spinal column. Make yourself comfortable, my dear Florisvaldo."

Father Monteirinho sat down and found himself not knowing what to say, and he examined the man with interest. A dark mulatto, well dressed, of undefined age—he could as easily be forty as over fifty. His gestures were a bit effeminate; he had a jovial manner, although somewhat tense. His speech was very strange, not only in his almost singsong tone but also in his words, which sounded as if he had memorized everything he said and was repeating it without pauses or hesitation, giving the impression that he didn't need to breathe. Who was this man; where did he come from; what secrets did he actually know?

"But, what discourtesy on my part," the man said, leaning forward and supporting himself on the cane with both hands. "I have not even had the affability to introduce myself formally; after all, this is the first time the Reverend Father has honored me with a visit. I am aware that I am known by the nickname Bará and such practice does not perturb me, for, like the poet, I see naught that is special in names, as these confer neither dignity nor opprobrium, save pejorative epithets, which is not the case in point. But it is, after all, not in keeping with good breeding to introduce oneself by a sobriquet, and thus I inform you that my legal name is Sebastião Boanerges da Conceição. At your service."

"But you are also known as 'saint,' " Father Monteirinho said, a bit nervously and ending with a hesitant smile as if wishing to avoid being overly aggressive.

"Not to my face, for I acerbically reprove such an appellation," he replied, closing his eyes. "I ask you, in the name of charity and of the Christian spirit that orients you, that you not harbor preconceived thoughts about me. Believe me, Reverend Father, that I speak the most ardent truth. I too merit charity, because I know nothing and what I do, I do because I do not know how not to do it. I am fully conscious that I do not convince you, just as for that matter the majority of people impute no veracity to me when I tell them I know nothing and lay claim to nothing. I have merely accustomed myself to whatever befalls me—or rather, resigned myself. A great deal of time passed before I realized the futility of resisting such occurrences, but I was obliged to capitulate to the inexorability of fate, or however one may term that appeal to which, were it not for the unexampled pretension contained in such a paraphrase, I would react with the selfsame phrase of the Master: Take this cup from me. Do not believe, Reverend Father, that I have ever sought the condition in which I live, nor can I even consider myself a religious man. I believe in God, yes, because I believe in Good. But I also believe in Evil, and let them not ask me for the answer to the most vexing theological question, in my view that which inquires whether God, the Good, having created everything, also created Evil? And why, as is written in the sacred books, is the Enemy also a child of God? Do not ask me, for I merely sense the existence of the contrary force, the tremendous opposition that frowns upon the Good and repels it, and I know nothing about it other than that it exists and is as tangible as the water and the air. I do not know how to address such a question, I do not know how to respond to anything, Reverend Father, and that is the pure and crystalline truth. I am not a saint and have no pretensions to such even in dreams, which I no longer have, and am solely carried along, as I asseverated, by events. All that I do, I can only do. Difficult it may be to understand what I am saying, but, aside from the immense and unshakable respect I have for the Reverend Father, I must underline, even emphasize, that I do not nurture, knowing it to be in vain, the intention of convincing you of what I have just told you and of my essential innocence. I long ago desisted from doing so and merely accepted my fate, for I have no choice, as was proven with plenitude and painfully all the years of my life when I tried, to no avail, to flee from it. I do not even believe in saints, and even if I believed, I judge that saintliness would exist through force of free will where there was an express, conscious, and active volition on the part of the one who covets it, and the effecting of good works and thoughts by design. But such is not applicable to me, because, as I have already explained to the Reverend Father, I do what I do without having a choice; I have not been vouchsafed governance over certain events of my life. The Reverend Father may ask: Does he receive spirits? Is he a necromancer? I answer, my heart in my hands, I do not know, but this is what they relate to me. As for me, I have no knowledge of what a spirit is in fact, and it follows logically that I cannot postulate the existence or nonexistence of something that I know not what it is. But I am told that I receive all sorts of spirits and they attribute to them characteristics, habits, and names that I do not ordinarily recall, with the exception of some that I consider picturesque—Master Carlos, Xaramúndi, Anabar, Faustina, and so many others that often make me smile, like now, and inquire of myself whether it's not because they want and need that they hear that which they want and need. I do not know; I do not know; I do not wish to know. If once I wanted this, I no longer want it.

To me, at best, it's like sleeping, although frequently I awake overcome by great weariness. That is all I know. Many people seek me, furthermore, who profess to be vehicles for spirits, and I have oftentimes observed the occurrence of what appears to manifestations of the aforementioned spirits. But I understand nothing about the matter. I have never studied it; I do not wish to know; I desire to prove nothing. I do what I do, forgive the reiteration, merely because I have no choice. Consequently, it is with the utmost good faith and no less sincerity that I affirm that I seek to prove nothing to the Reverend Father or to any other person, convince him of anything, persuade him of anything, except for the fact that motivated my appeal—for it is not an allegation but a fact, and a fact that has absolutely nothing to do with my activities or my supposed beliefs. I know that I bear the reputation, more than unjust, of being a sorcerer and that this introduces . . ."

Father Monteirinho gave up attempting to interrupt with a gesture, as he had been trying to do for some time, because the man was speaking with his eyes closed. But he did insist on breaking in because, the longer Bará went on in that astounding long-winded speech like someone reciting, the more the other two felt themselves drowning in a sea of words, and Father Monteirinho feared that if no one interrupted him he would never stop.

"But you can't deny that your practices—" the priest interjected. "In the case of the family of Florisvaldo here," he began again, "you ordered a sheep sacrificed in one of these rituals. And, by every indication you plan to go on killing more sheep, because you demanded another sheep from them to replace the one sacrificed. And in fact I know you received two."

"It is not my wont to deny my practices. I have even just alluded to them in some detail. What I contest is being a sorcerer, as I understand nothing of sorcery, nor have I ever had the wish to become a sorcerer or the like. They sacrificed a sheep, yes, it is said at my instructions. I do not know, but I do not take them to be liars. The sheep, nonetheless, is merely an irrational animal, subject to slaughter like so many others, and if its sacrifice resulted, God knows how, in alleviating the inenarrable suffering that they endured, what evil there could be escapes my ken. I even believe that a sacrifice of the type mentioned is not altogether foreign to the Christian tradition—although in this I make no claim to legitimacy and seek only to offer an example and spark a recollection—for, if a memory dimmed by the years does not fail me, there are abundant references to the same in the Scriptures and—the Reverend Father will correct me if I labor under a delusion—I recall that the beginning of Leviticus establishes rules for the sacrifices dictated by God, and even specifically mentions sheep. And I did in fact solicit from them another sheep, given that the one they slaughtered here belonged to one of the poor families who lives in the vicinity of this hill and they were greatly in need of it. When they brought the two sheep, I gladly accepted them and gave them to that same family. But, as I have already told the Reverend Father, I have no intention of proving anything, and the Reverend Father will see, after learning what I have to relate to him, that whether or not I am a sorcerer has no relevance, in this case. It distresses me that you judge me a sorcerer, but I am fully aware of that circumstance and can do nothing to alter it."

"Yes, nothing. It's necessary to make quite clear the reason for my visit here. I came exclusively in response to an appeal, one in which I judge to be fulfilling a duty as a priest, in part because of your physical condition. I would have a problem of conscience if I did not come. I don't know what the subject is that's worrying you, but I wouldn't like to suspect that I could help solve some human drama and did not. But I insist on making it patently evident that I will collaborate with you only if that collaboration, in my judgment, coincides with the goals, spirit, and laws of the Church. You will excuse my frankness, but I doubt very much that this is the case."

"You will see, I am sure."

"That depends. It may also be that I don't want to see anything. If it's your intention to have me participate, even as a simple observer, in a . . . in one of your ceremonies, that is absolutely out of the question. Don't even think of it, as they say."

"No, no, Reverend Father. It would never occur to me to disrespect your convictions. I merely intend to speak with you, tell you of something that I have seen."

Bará smiled again, breathed deeply, raised his eyes to the ceiling, and, after remaining silently in that position for a time, observed with exquisite courtesy that the matter was of such gravity that he had never confided it to anyone and he needed the opinion of another, such as the priest, before taking action. For a reason that the priest would later come to understand, he had first thought of speaking with the student of animals João Pedroso, at the end of the island, and had gone so far as to dispatch a letter to him similar to the one he had sent the priest, but he had never gotten an answer. Now he felt that everything had gone as it should; it was better not to have spoken with João Pedroso. And, as the priest squirmed uncomfortably in the armchair, he added that he didn't want anyone else to know of it for now, so he begged the forgiveness of his friend Florisvaldo, but he needed to speak with the priest alone, and would he please wait a bit on the porch, or go inside and have some coffee, or some other thing. And in his incessant flutelike voice he began recounting the story as soon as Little Hand 3 left.

"Gray snapper, muttonfish, red snapper, shark, ray, threadfish, cobia, cod, even barracuda, which people here call *goivuçu*," said João Pedroso, assessing with approval the contents of a wicker creel filled with shrimp, squid, and mullet, after Ângelo Marcos asked which large fish they could fish for in those spots of Jereba's. "I've yet to see Jereba come back without fish, even if they're four- or six-pound spot snappers, some nice mojarras, some jacks—he always comes back with something."

"Speaking of which, where is he? When people around here disappear I smell a rat right away."

"He went to get his lines at the Market. He'll be right back; no need to worry. He needs the money."

Ângelo Marcos looked toward the Market with his hand on the

visor of his cap, clicked his tongue disdainfully and sat down on a piling at the edge of the dock. They were near the ramp of the Largo da Quitanda, waiting for the skiff to be lowered from the larger boat and come for them. Only the men were there, since Ana Clara, fearing that João Pedroso might give himself away in that first meeting since the day of the luncheon and not wanting to awaken suspicion by showing an excessive interest in fishing, preferred to go to the beach with Bebel and take the opportunity to talk about the latest events. Besides João Pedroso and Ângelo Marcos, now occupied in transmitting orders to the crew in military jargon on a walkie-talkie—"affirmative," "negative," "over"—there were Nando and Tavinho, the former adjusting an American fishing vest whose dangles and shiny insignias gave him the appearance of an overly decorated sailor, the latter rubbing the side of his nose with his index finger, while not ceasing for an instant to pace rapidly back and forth between two trees.

"For God's sake, you're not going to snort now, are you?" Nando asked. "It's not possible. You were up practically the whole night."

"No, no, it's just a pick-me-up to tide me over. Is there any whiskey on the boat? Without whiskey to get you through, it's impossible. If there isn't any, I'm not going."

"Of course there is, but you might as well run up a flag drinking whiskey at this hour of the morning."

"Oh yeah? Around here people kick off the morning with rum and chase it with beer all day long; they think it's normal. Marquinhos thinks the world of me and considers everything I do very chic, you know? And, last but not least"—the phrase was in English—"the women aren't here to keep us in line. All women are repressive; it's a typically feminine characteristic. And there's another reason I think it's good that Ana Clara didn't come along, 'cause when I snort I get the hots for her like crazy, and the worst part is that I feel—I really do, no crap!—that she has a thing for me too. If I could get it up when I snort, I'm sure that, after she did a line or two with me, I'd—Bebel too, Bebel too. I really get turned on by Bebel. I won't try to hide that from you; you screwed her when she was still married to me, so I have every right to talk this way. I'm talking this way because it's a normal thing and you're like a brother to me. Who's my closest friend? No, really, answer!"

"It's OK, Tavinho."

"It's all normal, man, all normal. Human beings have to stop living with these medieval sentiments. I wouldn't think anything wrong if I screwed Bebel, just like I wouldn't think anything about it if you'd screwed her. I—"

"OK, but I still think you ought to give it a rest. Drink some whiskey, let the hangover pass, take one of those pills, go to sleep in the suite on the boat, and that's it. You don't need to snort, and I'm sure you're going to flaunt it, and there's João, the crew, the fisherman who's going to guide us to the fishing spot; it'll be a drag. After the effect of that shit wears off you have a moral hangover and get totally depressed. I know you."

"Don't give me that. Don't lay that negative shit on me. What're you trying to pull, man? Flaunt it! Nandinho, stop being repressive too, goddamnit! There won't be any flaunting. I brought the vial with the coke spoon; the powder's made up; all systems go. I just have to get away in a corner somewhere and hit it. I've got *savoir-faire*; I've done coke in the great hall of the Commercial Association in the middle of the installation of the board of directors and nobody caught on to a thing. You know about that—you know me, and you've said so yourself. Especially among these yokels here. If you doubt it, that fag who cooks for Marquinhos snorts too. Did you ever have a homosexual experience? I did. I'm going to the john in the bar to take a whiz and when I come back I'll tell you about it."

"Look at those landlubbers," Ângelo Marcos said to João Pedroso, after the skiff had been lowered. "I'm sorry I called them. Nando hates getting up early, and Tavinho must have seen the sun at most once or twice in his life."

"Right," answered João Pedroso with a distracted smile, because he'd barely heard what the other man had said. He'd had his eyes fixed on Ângelo Marcos the entire time he was using the walkie-talkie and aiming a huge pair of binoculars at the boat, but he couldn't pinpoint what he had thought about; he'd thought about many disjointed things. Confused things, confused feelings, everything confused. Could he be this man's friend, as Ângelo Marcos was obviously desirous of having happen? A horrible situation. And did he suspect anything? Was this closeness some kind of tactic on his part? Had Ana Clara given herself away, however subtly? Could Bebel really be trusted? And what about this sensation of triumph, of exuberant joy, that almost made him tell her husband everything, like someone telling friends in confidence about his great passion? And what about these gloomy and worried feelings that came all mixed together? And this disorder to everything, this anxiety, this discomfort?

"Of the fish you mentioned, is the barracuda the hardest to play?"

"No, it's the hardest to find around here," João Pedroso said, relieved because he had brought up the subject of fish again, for now he could reply at length and in so doing change the course of his thoughts. "Most of them aren't really barracudas; they're bicudas. Same family, same genus, but a different species. And generally people catch bicudas with a net, along with whatever fishes they're eating at the time—needlefish, mojarra, snook, that sort of thing. No, not barracuda; it's easier to catch by diving, even though it's a fish that attacks the diver; it's not stupid like the spotted jewfish that just hangs around doing nothing, waiting to take a harpoon in the middle of its forehead. A difficult fish, especially when it's large, is the spotted eagle ray. If it's too large, it's better to cut the line at once, because it's hard to boat one of those monsters. Butterfly rays are also a nuisance, because if you let them, they hug the bottom and getting them out is difficult. Sharks not so much, because they tire faster, though sometimes they bury their snout in the sand at the bottom and it's almost impossible to bring them up. The fish I usually have the most trouble bringing in is the gray snapper. With large bait like mullet and squid, if you hook a good-sized gray snapper, say, ninety pounds, you'll know it right away, because he doesn't give up, and lots of good fishermen, after hours of struggle, end up losing the catch. He raises hell down here; he—"

"João, what you don't know about fish isn't worth knowing, either in theory or in practice, huh? You could recite the scientific name of every one of those fish. You know everything, don't you?"

"Some of them, but that doesn't mean a thing. People get overly impressed with that business of scientific names. It really doesn't mean a thing. Anybody can pick up a book and memorize the names."

"Of course it does! You could be rich, putting your knowledge to work. You could even run a fishing industry. Didn't you ever think about that?"

"No, you're mistaken. God forbid! My business is different."

"That's because no one ever prodded you, never called your attention to a good opportunity. But look, I always liked the idea of a fishing industry; I was always fascinated by it. Maybe we could plan something together. There couldn't be a better partner than you. No, no, I'm not joking. We could be partners! Have you thought about it? A tremendous partnership. I provide the capital and you provide the talent!"

João Pedroso thought he was blushing, and, avoiding Ângelo Marcos's eyes and not knowing what to say, he took advantage of the skiff's arrival at the ramp to pretend he wanted to say something to Rubinho, the harbor pilot, and help him with docking. After securing the poop to an iron rod, Rubinho examined the group and voiced the opinion that, with a bit of squeezing, they'd all fit in a single trip.

"This piece of shit is gonna sink. This piece of shit is gonna sink!" Tavinho shouted with genuine fear when the skiff, dipping below the waterline like a shy baby whale, began to pitch as it headed for the boat, its eight-horsepower motor almost submerging amid its own wake.

"Don't worry," João Pedroso said. "At this distance we can swim to shore or to the boat with one arm tied behind us. It wouldn't be a major shipwreck."

"That's what you think," Tavinho replied, patting the shirt pocket with the vial of cocaine, while the skiff went around the unlighted buoy in front of the boat to come alongside the rope ladder.

Now on the main deck, Ângelo Marcos, without abandoning his walkie-talkie or his binoculars, adjusted his kepi and started giving instructions to the crew with a martial tone and gestures. After watching the hoisting and securing of the skiff with a scowl, he went to the bridge, where he turned on various devices including the electronic monitor of the instruments and on-board systems, examining digital dials and panels of small colored lights.

"OK, all systems operational, all set to weigh anchor and shove off," he said to himself in English, with the expression of one carrying out a routine task in a professional manner.

"Aye-aye, sir!" answered Tavinho, saluting and humming "Anchors Away." He continued, in English: "All hands on deck, skipper! *Tennn-shun*! *Feee-eeee-eeee*! Captain to the bridge, captain to the bridge! Now hear this, now hear this, all men to their battle stations! Dive, dive! *Weee*! *Weee*!"

Though he did not appear to find this amusing, Ângelo Marcos smiled, clapped Tavinho on the shoulder and immediately resumed his absorbed air, looking ahead as if he were observing something very important on the horizon.

"An admiral's sea, a brigadier's sky. I think I'll steer today. Where are we going, João?"

"I don't know exactly; he's choosing the spot. I'm not familiar with it, I just know it's out there. Where are we going, Jereba?"

"Well sir, the tide here'll stop going out soon, but out there it's still going out a lot more. The current's a nuisance, there's a heavy tide, and no sinker will hold the bottom. Wouldn't it be better for us to go out to a small fishing spot around here until the sea settles down and we can head further out?"

"What do you think, Marquinhos?"

"Fine with me, fine. I insist on not giving up going to that spot, but it can be any time; we can go a week without leaving the boat.

Cornélio loaded the refrigerator and larder. All you have to do is say where it is and I'll get us there."

"Jereba, what can you tell me about the anchorage behind the Limo crest, the one that Miroró locates by the Petrobrás poles and the radio antenna?"

"It's rock there, it's good. You practically always catch snapper, and Miroró filled it with tree limbs and old tires. It's a good fishing spot. But I don't really know the direction; I was only there once."

"I'll show the way. Let's go. Marquinhos, head that way, as if you were going to follow the Dourado shoreline. Straight ahead, you can't go wrong. When we get close I'll let you know."

"South by southwest," Ângelo Marcos said, preparing to start the motors. "Weigh anchor. Air motors. All hands ready for departure. Attention, helmsman. Verify for presence of small craft on collision course to starboard; visibility from this vantage incomplete. Course south by southwest, cruising speed."

"All present and accounted for, skipper," Tavinho said in English, with another salute, but this time Ângelo Marcos neither smiled nor looked to the side as, thoroughly intent, he engaged the motors and maneuvered through the channel with an abrupt turn of the rudder that made the boat list, causing Tavinho to spill his whiskey and ask where the life jackets were stored.

A few minutes later, with the boat anchored at the fishing spot, Ângelo Marcos commented that he'd like to sit beside the professor and installed himself in the stern with João Pedroso and an equipment box of anodized metal which, open with its dozens of small shelves and drawers, recalled the window of a tackle shop. João Pedroso selected the lines and hooks, adjusted the gear, and suggested dropping the line close to the hull because they were right at the edge of the spot and the fish should be coming soon.

"They didn't take long at all!" Ângelo Marcos shouted, making a wry face and grabbing his line with both hands when a foot-long snapper appeared at the end of the line. "A good catch, a good catch!"

Tavinho ran from the bow to see. "You got it that time, didn't you, sucker?" he said. "Just look at the bastard's face; he must be shitting a brick inside his scales. What's that swollen white thing inside him?"

"That's his stomach, sir," Jereba explained, pointing to the same thing in the snapper he had just landed. "When you pull on the line fast, the stomach swells up."

"It's the decompression," João Pedroso said. "It's a bit deep here and so when he comes up too fast there's no time for his flotation and pressure system to function properly."

"Poor thing. It takes a hook in the mouth and on top of that gets pulled up by force. Don't you feel sorry for him? I eat them but I think it's a dirty trick."

"You get used to it," Ângelo Marcos said. "I myself once scaled a small spotted jewfish, alive and still jumping around. I didn't feel the least bit of pity."

"Yes, they really give fish a hard time," João Pedroso said. "Kids scratch the belly of puffers so they'll swell and then stomp them to see the animal explode. I'm a little ashamed to say it, but I've done it myself."

"Right, it's the habit."

"I also have the impression there's another factor. Fish aren't like mammals, for example. Mammals care for their young, have families, some live in groups, they demonstrate social solidarity in many cases, and so on. But not fish. Natural death is practically nonexistent in the sea; it's unbridled eat-or-be-eaten, and parents eat their children and vice versa. Everybody eats everybody."

"It ought to be like that on land too. I'm in favor of everybody eating everybody!"

"Hold on, Tavinho, lay off the clowning and let me hear the lecture."

"No, it's not a lecture, not a lecture at all, just reasoning, conjecturing. We don't feel sorry for the fish because it doesn't feel sorry for itself. But a whale, accompanied by its young, makes us feel sorry, even though there are those who kill it anyway, of course."

"It's an interesting idea, but I still go along with the thesis of habit.

You yourself just said people feel sorry for a whale with its young but kill it all the same."

"Yes. Right here in the Recôncavo there was the practice of wounding the whale pup so it would cry out and the large whale would come to help it and get killed."

"Right, lower than snake shit, but there were those who did it. The first time, the guy might have felt pity, but he'd get used to it and wind up doing it without blinking an eye. I know an interesting case that illustrates this. My grandfather Zenão told me. He was a rancher at the time of the colonels and bandit gangs and he had hired gunmen himself and was called Colonel by lots of people. He told me that one of the worst triggermen he ever met, perhaps the coldest and most pitiless, who'd kill a stranger in front of his small children like you kill a dog, started out as a young man from an excellent family, who even went to seminary, what they call a jewel of a person, incapable of stepping on a cockroach, much less killing a man. Respectful, religious, a good son, et cetera, et cetera. Then someone took a vivarium full of sparrows to his land, with the idea that they'd eat insects and brighten up the small town, but what happened was they thrived too well and turned into a scourge. And then this fellow, outraged because the creatures were eating even the green fruit from his orchard and forcing out the other birds, decided to kill sparrows. In the beginning he felt bad if the animal didn't die from the first shot, and when he saw the first one he killed he almost vomited. But later on he started liking it and lost any pity. Then he discovered that the tanagers, birds he had really liked before, had destroyed the flowers on the papaya trees on the plantation and he started shooting at tanagers too. And at bemtevis, lizards, doves, any small animal that he took a dislike to or that came into his sight when he felt like killing. Until one day, without the slightest trace of anger but with an uncontrollable morbid curiosity, he fired point-blank at his pet talking parrot. My grandfather said that he spoke softly, and when he remembered that part he commented that he had thought about his freedom. He said that at the time he thought about his own freedom. Who rules me—myself or the parrot? And then he shot the parrot. And he used to say that after killing the parrot he felt he could kill people with the same ease and indifference, and that it could be a worthy and lucrative profession, as in fact it turned out to be. He told me—he didn't tell me, of course; he told my grandfather—that after accepting an assignment to kill he would change entirely and no longer be the same person until he completed the mission. He would change, speak differently, walk differently, eat different food than he was used to, not even listen to the same kind of music. And he started out by killing sparrows. Sparrows. That's why I say it's habit; a guy gets used to anything. He began by killing sparrows."

"What a crazy story. What a strange man."

"Extremely strange. My grandfather himself told me he didn't want to have anything to do with him. Not only because he was a professional killer but also because in that respect my grandfather was just like me: He couldn't stand fags."

"The gunman was a fag?"

"Yes. The worst kind. For me, what nowadays they call AC-DC, a closet faggot, one of those who do it with women and men, is the most disgusting kind there is. I'm an open-minded man—you could hardly find a more liberal guy than me—but I can't accept that faggotry stuff. I just can't accept it. It's something instinctive, something I can't control. It's true rage. When I think of a guy spreading his cheeks or, even worse, sucking off another man—I have to spit; it nauseates me to think about it—when I think of it, it revolts me. I try to get hold of myself but I can't. Besides, all queers are no good."

"But isn't Cornélio a trusted employee of yours? And Cornélio's up front; he doesn't try to fool anybody."

"And he's also no damned good. Don't think I have any illusions about him. But he needs me; he's never had it so easy in his life, so he doesn't give me any trouble. And Aninha adores him because he solves all sorts of problems for her so she doesn't have to think about a thing inside the house. So he stays, but I don't have the least bit of confidence in him. Above all else he's a faggot, and you can believe that's a determining factor."

And Ângelo Marcos went on talking that way for the rest of the fishing trip, until Jereba felt that the tide had changed further out and it was time to weigh anchor. Ângelo Marcos didn't want to steer this time and briefly left João Pedroso's company to settle a dispute that had broken out between Tavinho and Nando, because Nando wasn't interested in Tavinho's experiment, which consisted of inserting a small spoonful of cocaine into the mouth of a live puffer, cutting off the end of its tail so it would have no rudder, and then releasing the frenzied animal.

"The circumstances are irrelevant," Father Monteirinho was saying, when one of the doors to the front opened with a violent shove. A sturdy black woman, her hair in disarray, her feet bare, wearing a full skirt down to her ankles and numerous gilded jewels hanging from her neck and wrists, entered and, placing her hands on her hips, stood before Bará, who twisted his mouth in anger as the hand resting on the head of his cane trembled.

"Please," he said as if barely containing his impatience. "Excuse me, but you are imposing. I am having a conversation of a very private nature and your presence is inadmissible."

"You have to believe him," she told the priest in an accent tinged with Spanish. "It's necessary that you believe him. It's the purest truth."

"Who is this lady?"

"A thousand pardons, Reverend. I assure you that I have nothing to do with this visit, as impertinent as it is unexpected. Please, Calim Carmen, be so good as to retire. We have nothing to talk about at present."

"I came to convince him," she said. "I came to help convince him."

"You're not helping in the least, just the opposite. Please retire. Please!"

"Who is this lady?"

"She—Well, she calls herself Carmen. She also enjoys being called

Puridai—according to her an honorific title, or something of that ilk. But, Reverend, believe me when I say this is completely unforeseen and that I am utterly desolated by this unacceptable interruption. I beg you accept my protestations that I am as irate as are you."

"What do you want? Why are you so interested in my believing what Mr. Sebastião is going to tell me, something I haven't a hint of what it may be? What do you have to do with this?"

"Reverend, I assure you that nothing she might say can help in the least, just the opposite. Please, Calim Carmen, please!"

"Yes, all righ', I'll leave, but if he doesn't believe, I'll smash the Virgin of Triana with a hammer and throw her away."

"Yes, yes, do whatever you like, but enough now. You've already caused sufficient disturbance. Go, go at once, go to your quarters, retire."

"Yes, all righ', I'm going."

"Reverend, be so kind as to once again accept my humblest apologies for this most deplorable episode. I pledge my solemn word that she will not return."

"Mr. Sebastião, I believe I was quite clear when I said I would not in any way participate in any of your practices, or sessions, or rites, or whatever it be. What does this mean? What's going on? And what's this story of smashing the Virgin with a hammer and then throwing her away? What act of sacrilege have you practically just authorized? Is that the custom here, one of your practices?"

"Please, Reverend, be calm, please. As I told you, I would be incapable of showing you any disrespect; nothing could be further from my intent. It was a fortuitous and lamentable incident, one not of my planning. I am not a man to go back on my word; believe me when I say that everything was the workings of chance. She intruded upon us; under no circumstances was she summoned. A thousand pardons, in all innocence."

"Very well, but I want some explanations. I think I'm entitled. No, I don't think so: I *am* entitled."

"I would prefer not having to give them. Nonetheless, I recognize your right."

"You would prefer not to give explanations? You would prefer to hide something from me? Is there something serious to hide? This is becoming more and more nebulous, more and more suspicious. If you do not provide me with full particulars I shall leave immediately."

"It's not really that I have anything to hide; I have nothing to hide, as you will see. But I fear for the outcome of our conversation, following those explanations."

"You will agree that this is none of my concern, as I did not bring about this situation. In absolutely no way can I dispense with those clarifications."

"Very well then. What clarifications does the Reverend desire? You may direct at me all the questions you wish to formulate and I shall respond to the fullest extent of my knowledge of the matter, concealing or withholding nothing."

"First, this mystery about the Virgin. Just what Virgin was she referring to?"

"An image of the Virgin of Triana, a religious tradition of Seville, if I am not mistaken."

"And why did she speak of smashing it with a hammer and throwing it away? Is it some kind of satanic ritual?"

"It's a gypsy custom, to the best of my knowledge. Gypsies beat upon the images, punish them in various ways and cast them out, when they are dissatisfied with the performance that they attribute to them. But I have nothing to do with such practice; it is merely beyond my power to prevent it."

"What a barbaric custom, what an inconceivable act. You should attempt to dissuade the woman."

"I can try. But I surmise that my efforts would be to no avail, for gypsies are fervently steadfast to their customs, which they have preserved even during the centuries-old persecution they have suffered."

"But you would not have me believe that woman is actually a gypsy. She may dress like a gypsy and affect an accent, but I do not believe there are any black gypsies. I have never heard of such."

"Nor have I, but this is what she says."

"Does she live here? You told her to retire to her quarters. I'm also certain that gypsies do not live in such manner, at least around here."

"Well, Reverend, again I fulfill a promise made to you, in this instance that according to which I would conceal or withhold nothing from you. As I said before, I would prefer not to give this explanation, but I shall do so."

"Please."

"She resides here because in her, shall we say, normal state she is the caretaker's wife and carries out domestic tasks, not only for her own family but for me as well. She—"

"In her normal state? Are you telling me that she was, as they say, channeling? Is that how it's said?"

"Yes, it is said thus and in other ways. I myself have scant acquaintance with that vocabulary."

"And you want me to believe this is true?"

"By no means. I do not know if it's true and therefore do not undertake to convince you of anything. As I affirmed before and now reaffirm, I do not foster the most tenuous intention of persuading you of anything whatever, through any means whatever, directly or indirectly. I wish to persuade you merely of one concrete fact that occurred concretely, in the selfsame manner that this awkward visitor unequivocally appeared, whoever we may judge her to be. Just as the visit witnessed by the Reverend was a concrete event and was also witnessed, it was a fact that truly occurred and is occurring."

"You're saying that you don't know if it's true, but you treat her like a gypsy. What did you call her?"

"Calim Carmen. That is in fact her gypsy name, according to her. And also that epithet, the significance of which I am unaware, Puridai. But I have no other recourse. If while she is in that state I call her by her, shall we say, real name of Bernadette, she protests and pays me no mind, not even responding to what I say to her and turning a deaf ear to me. As I told you, I do not know if it's true, but I act in a practical manner."

"That means that by treating her like a gypsy you are at a minimum taking part in a farce and are the accomplice to a farce."

"Assume, worthy Reverend, that the lady in question is mad, or that she goes through periods of mental imbalance, a hypothesis that I am in no way qualified to judge, both because I lack the specialized background and because life and experience have taught me that madness is the most relative of all our states. Be that as it may, is one an accomplice to madness when one treats a mad person in the way that he understands and accepts? An immensely rich question this, I am sure the Reverend will agree. My answer, for several and diverse reasons, would be no. I must differ, *data venia*, with the Reverend's position, assuming I properly understand it. I address people as they wish to be addressed; it's practical, it's sensible, and it's civil."

"Well, in any case that's irrelevant, though I confess I have my doubts about your sincerity, because I see contradictions in what you say. What is her interest in this story? I remember perfectly well that you said you had never confided the matter to anyone. Evidently you withheld the truth from me when you said that."

"No, Reverend, I did not withhold it. I harbor the anxious hope that later you will come to perceive that mendacity is not among my countless defects. For in reality it was she who confided the matter to me in the first place, not I to her."

"She confided it to you? You mean then that you called me here to pass along a revelation—a pseudorevelation, rather—of that, that impostor, that—What do you think I am?"

"No, Reverend, please sit back down. Please have the goodness to listen to me. Until now you have not listened to me. If I recognize the Reverend's right to explanations because of his suspicions of me, he should recognize my right to be heard, all the more so because I seek to impose nothing."

"But—All this is very, very strange. I can't be anything but suspicious."

"I ask your good will, Reverend, only your good will, only your good will; it is not too much to ask of a priest. I did not invite you to hear a revelation of hers. I repeat what I told you before and I shall repeat it as often as necessary in the name of truth, candor, and once again, good will. I repeat that I invited you to hear the narration of a fact, a grave fact of which I am witness and which I shall relate to the Reverend, if I am permitted, in the exact form in which I witnessed it. I ask nothing of the Reverend except the good will to hear me out. Let the Reverend think, should it so appear to his judicious discernment, that I am a sorcerer. Let him think whatever his perception dictates; none of that is given to me to redress. But let him think, please, in the name of good will, that I am also a man and there must be another man's ear for that which I have to say. I hope, in the name of Good and Truth, to convince the Reverend that what I shall say has nothing to do with my being a sorcerer or unwilling saint. I know nothing about such things and it is not about them that I wish to speak. I ask your good will."

"You're a strange man"— and Father Monteirinho intertwined his fingers, not knowing what to decide.

"Yes, I am afraid so, and nothing is greater than my ignorance, ever more extensive," said the other man with a sad smile. Then, closing his eyes again he thanked the priest for listening to him and asked permission to tell everything at once, not leaving anything in doubt. If there were any questions to be asked afterward, let them be asked and he would answer all those he could answer. The Reverend had the right to know everything; it was better for him to know everything, although at the risk of not understanding—but then, what in this life is really understood? It had not been part of his original plan to speak of the gypsy woman because if it were simply her story he would never call the priest. He would have heard what she had to say and kept everything to himself, as he had kept so many other things, so many that he had forgotten most of them. She had appeared suddenly, sought him out for reasons he did not know, as in fact was what always happened. She said she had a mission because in life, despite that title of Puridai in which she seemed to take such pride, she had not committed a certain act entitled "*rocanebaro*" or something of the sort—he had tried to find out how it was written, but because she was illiterate she couldn't say—an act fundamental to gypsies like her, for some reason he didn't know. Thus she had decided to return in that form, to complete what she judged to be her mission, surely to expiate the feeling of guilt she had because of that *rocanebaro* thing and, perhaps, because of a certain adventurous spirit that was a more than intimate part of her essence. Thus she had told him, and thus he told the Reverend.

"As I have already explained, it is not my wont to argue about these occurrences. I have had to habituate myself to them, to accept them as the ineluctable burden of my life," Bará said, opening his eyes and staring intensely at the priest. And, continuing to speak with the same fixed and disquieting gaze, he said that his memory was vivid of the occasion when she had appeared suddenly one evening, more or less as she had tonight, but much more nervous and having difficulty speaking and breathing. He had attempted to help her with a tranquilizer but she refused it and merely repeated distressed phrases in her language, admixed with "I'm very afraid. I'm very afraid. I'm terribly afraid," covering her eyes with the palms of her hands and stamping on the ground. Finally, after crying and saying dozens of times that she felt a fear greater than she had ever thought anyone could feel, a fear superior to that which all the dragons and monsters of the universe could instill, she told what terrified her so.

"She related that she was far from here, on the other side of the island, when she became thirsty as she approached four small, isolated houses at the edge of a salt marsh," he said, leaning forward with his hand tightly clutching the handle of his cane, maintaining a disconcerting gaze and stopping for a brief pause, the only one that would punctuate his speech the entire night. He then resumed his monologue with the same uninterrupted fluency and said that, when she went up to one of the houses to ask for a glass of water, the gypsy encountered three beings never before seen, three beings like children, but which she was certain were not people. She asked the woman in the house about them and the woman replied that one of them was her child and the others, a boy and a girl, were the children of two neighbor women. The gypsy pretended she didn't understand and asked if they had actually come from their bellies, and the woman said they had, and with a weary look anticipated what she knew would be asked and said they were in fact different children. They were their children but they were a little different, so different that their mothers usually hid them; everyone around there hid for a thousand reasons. The gypsy then tried to talk to them and approached the children, who were naked and huddled together so closely that they recalled a bunch of bananas. And it was then that the inexplicable terror came upon her, a frightful shuddering, her hair standing on end, her skin crawling, her heart racing, the air trapped in her lungs, because when her eyes met theirs she saw they were not human. They were the fruit of something diabolical, they were people and they were not, they were like unfinished souls, and perhaps no soul at all dwelled within them, and their eyes, their eyes, their eyes!

"She related that she didn't run away in terror only because her feet were rooted to the earth and her legs, suddenly trembling, would not obey her," he said, looking at a spot on the ground in front of him, while Father Monteirinho crossed and uncrossed his ankles. Finally, he continued, she freed herself of that terrible paralysis and succeeded in turning around. And now she knew, she knew, and she spoke to him and attested to having seen a thing of great evil. But he, as was his habit, had listened, neither doubting nor affirming, merely listening. Until she, showing up frequently, always nervous and out of breath, convinced him to accompany her to the place where she had seen the creatures, despite the enormous fear this caused her, to the point of having prayed in every language from start to finish on the journey. Arriving there, he saw it was not a lie, not exaggeration. It was this that he wanted to tell the priest, only this: He had seen the creatures and they were just as the gypsy had described them. They really existed, and there was in them something greatly evil and terrifying, perhaps not in them but around them. It was not possible to describe their eyes.

"I also had a sensation of terror and felt just as she did and couldn't bear to look into those beings' eyes because I felt such great fear and every other emotion at the same time. I cannot describe it. I cannot describe it," he said, his voice a bit more high-pitched. He hadn't seen them for long because another woman was there besides the one who had spoken with the gypsy. This woman, also mother of one of the creatures, refused to talk to them, admonished the first woman, and denied the existence of the children. But because the shacks had no doors, Bará took advantage of the argument to go into one of them, precisely where the children were, two of them crouching in a corner and the third sitting on the floor appearing to be playing with a piece of wood in its strangely bony hand. Despite the fear that invaded him, despite his leaping heart, Bará managed to take a couple of steps toward the closest of the creatures and, confronting with effort the unbearable discomfort its gaze caused him, tried to speak to it. But he did not even succeed in opening his mouth, for as that gaze was becoming impossible to stand, the creature showed its teeth. In a hoarse voice, much deeper than would be expected for its size, it said something he did not understand but which froze his blood in fear and made him turn and flee as quickly as he could—and it was unnecessary for the second woman, over whom he stumbled at the entrance, to repeat the screams with which she expelled them, because he greatly wanted to leave, and he returned home as rapidly as the donkey he was riding would carry him, sensing the air about him charged with malevolence. It was not that the creatures were monstrous, properly speaking, but they were not human. They were not human. Animals? No, that wasn't the right word, and the woman had said they had given birth to them, that they were their children by blood.

"In my opinion, Reverend, they are not creatures of God. I know how singular, audacious, and apparently presumptuous this assertion is, even more so stemming from a person such as I, who does not deem himself qualified to issue judgments of this nature. But if they are human, they are a different kind of human. If they are animals, they are a different kind of animal. And if you saw them perhaps you would not feel the same fear that we felt, but if they were taken to you to be baptized, I believe you would not baptize them."

"But what are you saying? Are they from another planet or some such thing? Do you see flying saucers?"

"No, Reverend. I believe what the woman said. They are their children, from their wombs. And they acted like mothers; they seemed like mothers. I can't explain why, but they *were* mothers."

"You must admit that this story is exceedingly strange. To be sincere with you, I'm having trouble believing it. Where are these creatures? Can one go there and see them?"

"No, one cannot, and that is terrible. Calim Carmen told me they had abandoned their huts and disappeared into that region of mangroves and sparse population. And in fact I went there to verify this information in person, and it's true. There is no sign of them, except for the deserted shacks."

"You will agree with me that this makes it more difficult to believe the story."

"I know, and that too is terrible. But consider, Reverend, why would I make up such a story? Why would I call you to relate it, unless I knew you have always protected the poor among our people and can perhaps do something to restrain the appalling phenomenon that I am certain is taking place? And unless it's because I fear that some unknown person, or thing, is effecting this frightening act among these people? And note that the second woman seemed nervous. Perhaps in fear of being discovered, in fear of someone or something, she acted like one pursued. So much so that all three of them disappeared from there."

"Perhaps because they were never there. I have no idea as to your reasons, Mr. Sebastião, which might well be to get closer to me, to take advantage, to legitimize yourself, gain publicity, et cetera, et cetera. I don't want to make judgments about you, but to believe that fanciful story I would need proof, and beyond that, proof like St. Thomas's—seeing is believing. And according to what you tell me, that's impossible."

"If I find further elements, may I send them to you? Believe me, Reverend, I am sure that there is a threat in this, a threat to humanity. I am sure. There is something terrible in those creatures' eyes. This is the work of Evil."

"Yes, yes, I understand. Well, do as you wish, as long as you don't waste my time—as in fact, you will pardon my saying so, seems to have been the case today, unfortunately. If I knew I was coming here to listen to this—pardon me, but I must be frank—this tiresome discourse, I wouldn't have rushed away from my tasks."

"Yes, I know I must offer proof. But if we always waited for proof, without doing anything, without taking a stance—"

"All right, Mr. Sebastião, what can't be cured must be endured. I'm on my way, but I'll tell you what you can do. Look for me when you find those children with the unsettling eyes. Have them come to me for baptism and I'll decide then if you're right. Beyond that, I think we have nothing further to discuss."

"I have done my duty. I hope the Reverend has the opportunity to do his," said Bará in a low voice, rising with difficulty to follow the priest, who didn't hear him because he had already gone out, leaving in the company of Little Hand 3 and becoming irritated when the latter said thank God the owl was no longer hooting.

In the middle of a dunghill delimited by the droppings of the donkeys that had been chewing on cardboard boxes, a sparrow stuck its neck into an eggshell half full of moldy manioc flour and took on the appearance of a small, gray cylinder, hammering away like a piston. Ângelo Marcos turned the corner carrying his twenty-five-pound threadfish by the tail and upon seeing the sparrow pecking at the egg amid dozens of others like flies in garbage, tried to look in a different direction but didn't succeed. He dropped the fish and leaned forward to vomit a copious stream followed by spasms that caused him to stagger with his head practically between his legs.

"Tremendously colorful yawn," Tavinho said while Nando and João Pedroso picked up the fish and he tended to Ângelo Marcos. "Feel any better? Generally, after you vomit you feel better. And you were doing so well in the bar, man."

"It's over; it's over. I shouldn't've had that beer," Ângelo Marcos said, though he knew it was a lie. "You're right; I was doing well. Today was such a great day, but in a little while everything's going to be OK again; I already got rid of the beer."

Yes, it had been a good day, with the boat barreling through a sea that looked like the surface of a great precious stone, a cool breeze blowing from all sides, no chance of anything bad happening, anything bad at all, and their arriving for some glorious fishing, the most beautiful fishing anyone could ever desire. Guided by Jereba's whispers as he stood by Rufino's ear, the boat put in along Friars Isle and dropped anchor off the stern, the bow pointing listlessly into the current at the end of ebb tide until the boat stopped completely and nestled its white belly in the water like a fat aquatic bird in repose. The precise spot, #90 nylon, eight-ounce sinker, hooks 5 and 6, steel gear, a lot of line with which to play the fish, mullet and squid for bait, a silence as tense as that of parachutists just before the jump, Tavinho intensely concentrating and gravely examining his hooks, Nando sweating under the skeptical eye of Jereba unsuccessfully trying to attach an American artificial plug to his gear, and João Pedroso removing spools of line from an old wicker creel. For a long time no one said anything, and Ângelo Marcos was beginning to have poetic fantasies, gazing at the blue of the water with the line between his legs, when Jereba said "Um-um" and, with his face creased and both hands on the line, began to pull, landing two elegantly shaped fish with yellowish coloration, each about four or five pounds. "A nice little yellow jack," Jereba said, removing the fish from the hooks and throwing them into the cooler, where Ângelo Marcos went enviously to admire them while they were still thrashing about.

A short time later, though Ângelo Marcos said nothing, he had become sad, much sadder than might be expected solely for the reason that everyone was catching fish except him. He had already changed places four or five times and even exchanged lines with João Pedroso without getting more than a light nibble from time to time. Even Nando's American plug, a multicolored cigar-shaped thing, festooned with a dazzling profusion of hooks and cast from a rod and reel, was snapped up on the surface of the water by a good-sized Spanish mackerel that could only be landed with the aid of a gaff after it was played with João Pedroso's help.

"Is only Dr. Ângelo going home empty-handed today?" asked Jereba after Tavinho landed several yellow jacks and a small grouper amid great clamor and trips back and forth to the bathroom, from which he invariably returned sniffing.

"The real fisherman around here is me," Tavinho said, shaking in Ângelo Marcos's face the grouper, still hanging from the line. "Just the tail of this devil's bigger than that quarter-pound snapper you caught a century ago. Where's the fish, Angelocildes?"

"Fuck off, Tavinho," Ângelo Marcos was about to say, but the spool of his line spun on the floor of the bridge and he barely had time to catch it before a violent tug could carry it off. "Hey! C'mere, you sonofabitch!"

"Give him some line; give him some line, give him a bit of slack, and then tighten up and pull in. Don't let him command the line."

"Damnit, I can't hold on. He'll cut my hands to ribbons with the line."

"Let me have it. I'll take him. Give him more line and let me have it. If it's a grouper he'll fight till you can pull him closer to the top. Then he'll fill his air bladder and give up. Give it to me; he's running to the inside. It's a shark or gray snapper."

"Threadfish, sir. That's one of their moves. Here it comes!"

"Let me have it; let me have it. Don't let him take the line and light out. He could turn and run under the boat and complicate things."

"No, no, leave it to me. This is mine. This fish is mine. He's coming; he's coming. I've got the sonofabitch!"

"You can hold tight; the line's strong. Set the hook hard and the sucker'll die. Set it deep!"

"It's coming; it's coming; it's coming!"

A beautiful struggle lasting over ten minutes, yielding a beautiful threadfish weighing more than twenty-two pounds, glittering handsomely and metallically alongside the boat. Panting, his fingers bloodstained, Ângelo Marcos had a scare that nearly stopped his heart when the fish, just as it was almost aboard, flailed on the line and it appeared it would drop back into the sea. But it didn't, and it was thrown resplendently on top of the other fish in the cooler, beside which, still breathing as if gasping for air, Ângelo Marcos stood for several minutes, from time to time patting the animal's flanks. Only when he noticed that the fish's back was stained with blood did he remember his fingers cut by the nylon. He opened the first-aid chest and took out a small bottle of antiseptic and a box of bandages with which he treated his cuts. When João Pedroso, examining his hands from a distance, asked if he would still be able to fish, he answered with a smile, said that fishing is necessary, living is optional, and cut a large squid in half to rebait the hooks. He had to wrap his hand in a flannel cloth when another threadfish took the hook and darted sideways, without his managing to check it. But in the end he succeeding in bringing it in also—another beautiful fish, slightly larger than the first and much larger than the third, the fourth, the fifth, and the sixth, with which, in dizzied euphoria and laughing heartily when Jereba called him the threadfish king, he declared the fishing ended and, without leaving his place beside the cooler, ordered the craft back to the island, where they arrived at eleven o'clock.

Close to 450 pounds of fish, weighed on João Pedroso's large scale and divided among João, Jereba, and the crew, because none of the others wanted to keep any of it, except Ângelo Marcos, who insisted on taking home the twenty-five-pound threadfish. But he refused to leave it in the fish market's freezer when they went to the Largo da Quitanda to celebrate; he decided to carry it with him despite the weight, affecting great nonchalance and even indifference when passersby stopped to admire the fish and congratulate him on the catch. He couldn't remember when he'd felt as happy as this, truly blessed by God. God liked him; he had a star that shined on everything he did; life was beautiful. He didn't think twice, while Tavinho and João Pedroso were drinking whiskey from a bottle brought from the boat, about asking for a glass and having some of Nando's beer. He placed the fish next to the chair's legs and, still patting it from time to time, gave several speeches about friendship, brotherhood, comradeship, a healthy life in contact with nature, and his new childhood friend whom he'd had the good fortune to meet on the island, our great João Pedroso, who, just wait and see, would one of these days be his partner. Finally, after more than an hour in the square, he decided he'd have a monumental fish stew made at home from that threadfish; they would leave immediately. When João Pedroso appeared reluctant, he said he would be gravely offended by a refusal, really offended, seriously, as would Ana Clara, when she found out, because she also thought a lot of him. "She thinks a lot of you," he repeated with his hand on the shoulder of the other man, who smiled abashedly, averted his eyes, and took a large swallow of straight whiskey.

If it weren't for vomiting in the street and especially for the memories that sparrow had suddenly unleashed, the fish stew would have been much more enjoyable. Nando was what they call a happy drunk; Tavinho was extremely funny recounting his sex life and the thousand times he couldn't get it up; João Pedroso, half in the bag, laughed at everything he heard and would begin speeches he never finished; and Cornélio, in high gear, swished all over the place as he supervised the cleaning and cutting of the fish, carried out by Edsonil.

"Roe, she's got roe!" he crooned when Edsonil took a yellowish mass from the fish's belly. "What lovely roe. Dr. Ângelo Marcos adores roe; I'll ask him how he wants it. Don't touch that roe, you creature, and watch out so the cats don't eat it. If the cats eat it I'll skin you alive. I never liked black men anyway. They're only good for one thing, and you're not even good for that."

But Ângelo Marcos wasn't interested in the roe; he said his stomach was upset, and he lapsed into a deep melancholy, to the point that even the servants noticed that Ana Clara had become rather nervous, surely from worry about his condition. He was indifferent to the fish stew with its bright thick slices arranged beside a mountain of greens, white rice, and manioc mush, though he forced himself to eat a small piece of fish. He tried to take an interest in the conversation, laughed at Nando's and Bebel's jokes, and managed to remain at the table, before an almost untouched plate, while the others were eating. But he couldn't withstand the sad and numbing lassitude that each moment permeated him more and more. Excusing himself, he explained that he was feeling slightly uncomfortable and accepted the suggestion of Ana Clara, who was now somewhat less nervous, to go rest a bit. But they shouldn't be concerned, no need at all for concern, make yourselves at home, he'd be down later to join the party.

He went up to the large suite with slow steps, thinking about his lies. Yes, he had lied, had lied a lot, when he told João Pedroso the story of the sparrows. He ought not to have said anything, of course; there was no reason to open his mouth and say more than he should, but it was an impulse he was unable to silence because, despite knowing it did no good, he greatly wanted the lie to be the truth. But it isn't, it isn't, it isn't, he thought, nearly having another attack of nausea, but also feeling an uncontrollable arousal that made him stick his hand inside his bermudas and massage himself convulsively. He quickly appeared to have second thoughts, withdrew his hand and lowered himself into the suite's large armchair, his eyes closed and that fiery remembrance sundering his brain. Why, why remember if he wanted not to remember, if he detested remembering, if he felt horrible when he remembered? But he did remember, and again such arousal came upon him that he forcibly clasped his hands to his thighs. He remembered all the times they had been together, remembered voluptuously how he had kissed him on the mouth at their first meeting, with a naturalness as unexpected as it was delicious, and how they kissed each other afterward, kissed many times. He remembered every one of their meetings, all the times they, barely containing their anxiety and ardor, grabbed each other and impatiently tore off their clothes as soon as they were alone, and he remembered, remembered how nice he thought it was that he, as if seeking something vital without which he would die, had eagerly lowered his undershorts and, even before his feet were out of them, come tremulously to stick his nose in his pubis and sucked him, purring softly with his eyes closed, one hand affectionately cupping his balls and the other caressing his rear, his fingertips gliding along the hair between his buttocks and lightly touching his deepest intimacy.

No, no, no, he thought with revulsion, trying to rise and expel these feelings once and for all. But he didn't get up, nor did he remove his hand from his swollen fly. His breath more rapid than before, he bit his lips as he relived the afternoon they'd had just for the two of them in a hotel room where they bathed together and afterward sucked each other endlessly until, in that unforgettable way, he got on all fours and asked to be penetrated. He recalled in unbearable detail how he came so intensely that day, inside him as far as he could go and biting his neck and asking him to turn his face to be kissed and lying on top of him without coming out of him and masturbating him with such synchrony that they came together, crying and moaning, neither wanting to separate from the other. And how he also came so exquisitely, so overpoweringly, when he lay with his back to him, a pillow beneath his stomach to better offer himself, he moistened his glans with a prolonged, wet kiss and waited, in pleasure and expectation ever more breathless, for him to finish kissing him, licking him, and sticking his tongue into him, to brush him with that large, soft, and delicate head, until he aimed at the right spot, hesitated adorably, and, slowly but with resolve and avidity, entered and filled him and gave him inexpressible pleasure as he moved backward, opening himself with his hands until he felt against his buttocks the other man's hairs and balls—and then, with his help, he came in that way never before tried, that visceral coming, long, draining. He took pride in this, the fact that because of it they were complete lovers instead of, as he earlier thought would happen, his never being possessed—and it hadn't even hurt as he had feared.

No, no, none of that, and he finally succeeded in getting up, intent on occupying himself with something else. He might have gone out to kill sparrows if it weren't for the visitors downstairs. Yes, but why all this anyway? After all, who was Boaventura? Today, just a professional killer, a gunman living in Goiás, nothing more than a remote memory, an event from the past that no one else knew about. There was no reason for this obsession, this sensation of guilt, this carnival of contradictory feelings. But then, why, after never having seen each other for so many years, had the thing repeated itself when they met again for the first time? Staggering, although he wasn't dizzy, he sank onto the couch, the same excitement returning to him, this time stronger than ever. No, no, he was merely a professional killer, nothing important.

He had seen him again unexpectedly when, after an endless fight with encroachers and squatters on his holdings in Una, he had come to the conclusion, on advice from his uncle Thales, that the solution would be to hire a gunman to get rid of Zenóbio Parente, lawyer and leader of the squatters, a man whose arrogance, effrontery, and gall dictated that recourse, as undesirable as it might be. The old folks were right: Some things could only be settled with bullets, by getting rid of a bastard here, another one there. And the blame, after all was said and done, was his alone, for he had even turned down an extremely generous financial offer to leave the area. So it was either him or the lands. Uncle Thales made the contact and they set up a meeting in the Arataca countryside, where Ângelo Marcos expected to deal with a man called José Honório and couldn't believe his eyes when he saw that José Honório was Boaventura.

He hesitated in admitting that he knew him, but the other man took the initiative by telling Uncle Thales that they came from the same area, had been friends for a long time, and then their lives had taken separate paths. No, his name wasn't José Honório, of course, he couldn't hide anything from his friend Marquito—how good to see him again. He'd had many other names in the exercise of his profession—no, not profession, almost a hobby these days. He just did a special service or two now and then, because he dedicated practically all his time to the ranch he'd bought near Anápolis. He was going to send someone in his place, but when he heard about the party in question, he'd insisted on coming in person. And after casually settling details about the assassination of Zenóbio Parente, which in fact took place without any problem a week later, he invited him to spend the night at the ranch, despite Uncle Thales having to return to Una before dusk.

As night fell they drank together, asked each other numerous questions about how life was going, spoke about their marriages, laughed at situations in which both had found themselves. "I started by killing sparrows," Boaventura commented when Ângelo Marcos asked him how he'd become a gunman. And he spoke about the sparrows, the tanagers, the other birds, the parrot, the first men he killed. Ângelo Marcos looked at him intently, as if he didn't know him well. And, thinking about it, he didn't know him—this was a killer before him, the first killer with whom he had ever spoken. In reality he was a stranger, or had become a stranger.

But no, he wasn't a stranger, because, after they undressed to sleep, without having said or mentioned anything intimate, Ângelo Marcos lay down but remained as excited and restless as if he'd taken amphetamines. He tossed from side to side; a shudder ran through his body. He could stand it no longer and knocked on the door of Boaventura's room. The other man, stark naked, opened it, embraced him, and, without releasing the embrace, they fell onto the bed. No, no, he didn't want to remember, but he remembered, inflamed, how they slept not at all that night, how they could not quench the lack that each had felt for the other, so repressed and so much greater than they had thought. He lowered his hand to his fly, opened the zipper. No, not just the zipper; he would take off the bermudas and his shorts. He removed his shirt also and masturbated, imagining an everlasting erection in which they came in every hole and every part of each other's body, but he could not hold back the orgasm as he desired, and he gushed with such force that a few drops almost reached his chin.

He opened his eyes, ran his hands over the sticky sperm on his chest, and was seized by enormous displeasure, enormous disgust, enormous shame that made him run to the bathroom and take a fifteen-minute shower, during which he thought once more that someday he would find the courage to kill Boaventura, because that was what came to his mind when he felt he would never be able to resist his power.

6

João Pedroso may well have been drunk, as he'd already had his fifth shot of whiskey, but he didn't feel the least bit drunk when, sitting in a bar whose sole occupant was a dog curled up by the door, he saw Monteirinho pass by, got up, and went to him.

"We can talk in a bar, can't we? I struck up a conversation with the dog there, but he doesn't answer, and Zoinho the Barman has a vocabulary smaller than any dog's."

Monteirinho smiled and extended his hand. In the entire square, poorly illuminated by a series of mostly unlighted street lamps, no one was to be seen but a group of shirtless youths playing dominoes on the bench in front of the old two-story house, and two elderly men in hats who were watching them. It looked as if it would rain, judging by the clouds beginning to pile heavily above the towers of the church of São Lourenço and by the warm gelatinous mass into which the air was gradually being transformed. In a cage hung beside the rum brews, a black hawk, as if suddenly awakening with anxious eyes, started bounding from side to side.

"The only thing moving around here is that hyperkinetic bird," João Pedroso said. "I'm grateful for it, but sometimes it's monotonous. I preferred the days when Waldemar had a station on the pier and we'd go there to watch the gasoline pump work."

"It's true. I'm feeling the need of a good talk myself. How are you?"

"Sit down, sit down. I promise to stick to purely public matters."

Pretending not to understand, Monteirinho sat down, still smiling. He commented that the city was a real desert, even more than usual for that time of year, and ordered coffee in a glass.

"Have you ever eaten cat?" João Pedroso asked.

"Cat? You mean catfish?"

"No. Cat, a real cat, meow-meow, *Felis catus*, domestic variety."

"No, heaven forbid, only if it was a mistake. Why? Have you eaten it?"

"Yes. I had one for lunch today and I can't say it was bad."

"You had a cat for lunch?"

"Yes. Two cats, to be exact. Barbecued, with pepper sauce, tomato and onion, rice, beans, and manioc, in the company of Little Hand 4, just the two of us because his wife doesn't eat cat. He'd been insisting for a long time that I go there and have cat with him, so today I decided to go. When a cat wanders into his house it can ready its last meow because he gives no quarter; he grabs it by the tail and crushes its skull against the wall in the back yard."

"How horrible."

"It is, but I've seen you buy pork chops, and you know how they kill pigs around here. The cat's fate is less bad. It's more or less like a guillotine; it doesn't have time to know what's happening. But I didn't take part in that ceremony. When I arrived, the cats were already marinating; they'd been seasoned overnight."

"You have to have a pretty strong stomach. I wouldn't have the courage."

"Yes, I know you're rather fussy about what you eat. Not me; I'll try anything. I've eaten snakes, toads, turtles—"

"Right. As my grandfather used to say, I'm not that versatile. You must hold some kind of record."

"Hardly. I read in an almanac that a certain Dr. Buckland, who lived near the London zoo in the last century, prided himself on having sampled practically the entire animal kingdom. When an animal died at the zoo, he would go there and get a piece to eat. They say that once a leopard died and was buried while he was away on a trip and when he got back he went there, dug up the animal, and cut off a piece to try it. I don't know if he ever ate a human, but he said that one of the worst things he ever ate in his life was a mole, though a blowfly was even worse. He was an exceptional man, of course. I wouldn't choose leopard *faisandé* or accept a blowfly appetizer."

"Well, St. John the Baptist ate locust. They say it's like freshwater shrimp."

"You're right. In this world people eat everything. You can't imagine what folks around here are capable of eating. Skunk is a delicacy compared to some of the other things they cook and eat. If you knew those woods out there the way I do, the habits and practices of these people—"

"It's true; every day we discover something new around here. You mentioned Little Hand 4; Wednesday of last week I had an interesting experience, though not exactly a pleasant one, in the company of one of his brothers, Florisvaldo, Little Hand 3. Have you heard of Bará, that sorcerer from Misericórdia?"

"Of course. Everybody's heard of him. People call him a saint and say he performs miracles."

"Yes, I know, but naturally it's all a hoax. However, that doesn't keep him from being an interesting man and a very curious figure."

"He came to see you?"

"No, actually I went to see him. He sent me a letter asking me to visit him concerning a matter of utmost gravity, which he did not specify. I wanted nothing to do with the fellow—just the opposite, as he's a terrible influence on my parish—but the letter aroused my curiosity, so I went there with Florisvaldo, at night. A very strange man. You have to hear how he talks; he sounds like a recording, never fumbling for words, never hesitating. He talks as if he had everything memorized in his head, and all this in a stilted language full of 'inordinately' and 'incomparably' and such."

"So what did he want?"

"It's a long story, with a gypsy woman in the middle. Later I'll tell you about the gypsy. Bará wanted, in fact, to talk to you; he said he sent a message and you never answered."

"True, he sent one, but I didn't have the patience to go there, and I felt it was to ask me how to get closer to you, or something along those lines. And that must have been it, because now he sought you out directly."

"Yes, it's possible, because his story is unconvincing."

"What *is* his story?"

"Well, he says that, led by that gypsy—who, to begin with, is a black woman who's not a gypsy at all but who says that a gypsy woman descends into her, just imagine—led by her, he went to some shacks at the edge of a salt marsh and discovered there some women and their children. Except that the children, according to him, weren't people but neither were they animals, exactly. And they had a strange way of speaking, and, more than anything else, a look that struck terror in both him and the gypsy."

"A crazy story! Couldn't it have been some kind of monkey he saw?"

"No. He said that the women swore they were the children of their own bellies."

"Did he describe their appearance?"

"No, he just spoke of their look and the bony hands of one of them."

"And where are they? Did he show them to you?"

"That's the problem. It's always that way with these things. It's like flying saucers and extraterrestrials. The photographs that turn up are always indistinguishable blurs in which no one but believers—because this flying saucer business is a kind of religion—recognize the disks. He said that despite his fear he went back but didn't find anyone; both the women and the children had disappeared."

"Why do you suppose he wanted to speak to me too?"

"I have no idea. Most likely because of what you suspected, to get closer, put up a false front, acquire respectability, whatever. He imagined that, because you're a biologist, you'd be interested in the things he made up. I don't believe him at all. Not him, not the gypsy, not anything about the whole affair. What did he imagine I'd think? Maybe that I'd believe they were the women's children by some interplanetary visitor, because I'm not illiterate enough to believe those women could, for example, have had relations with some animal and produced offspring. To me, relations with an animal is inconceivable and revolting—I'm not so innocent as to think it doesn't happen—but offspring? Of course not. Otherwise this island would be full of centaurs and, shall we say, donkey-people."

"Some years ago, you would have been absolutely right, but not now. Since about the seventeenth century it's been considered that two individuals belong to the same species when their mating produces fertile descendants, capable in turn of engendering progeny. But now the growing tendency is to reformulate this, and I'm sorry to disappoint you, but in a way it can already be said that the means will be created to produce that centaur."

"The child of a man and a mare? What kind of craziness is this, João?"

"Well, not the child of a man and a mare in the strict sense, but a transgenic being that would incorporate a man's genes in a horse. Though with many limitations, this is already perfectly possible and there are lots of guys around the world doing something along these lines."

"Do you mean bringing together human spermatozoa and the ova of a mare?"

"No, that doesn't work, at least not yet. But I don't discount anything. There's a lot of dough in this business and lots of high-powered brains looking to win the Nobel Prize. For now, that type of fertilization is only possible in very restricted instances, with closely related species like donkey and horse, man and chimpanzee. And to tell the truth, my dear friend, this latter case is already a reality, at least up to a certain point."

"What? There are hybrids of people and monkeys?"

"At least embryos have been attained, in vitro. But as far as I know, they were destroyed. And I also don't know whether they would be viable if the gestation had been carried to term, whether they would survive after birth, and so forth."

"But that's barbaric, monstrous."

"My noble Father Olavo Bento Monteiro, you're behind the times. Prepare yourself for what I'm about to tell you. Less than a week ago I read a report about some nuts in Pennsylvania and Maryland who've produced pigs with the gene for human growth hormone, which in other words is nothing less than a kind of crossing of people with pigs. The pigs didn't grow as they hoped and many were born with problems, including with the libido. But they're going ahead; they're clever and they're going to end up with something. You can't deny that it's another very strong link between humanity and swinity, besides those that already exist because we get essential amino acids from pork and many other things from them."

"I can't believe that. It can't be true."

"Believe it, because it's really true. And it's less complicated than might appear. In the old days they needed more sophisticated equipment. To centrifuge ova, for example, because the cytoplasm of the ova of many mammals is practically opaque and doesn't allow the guy to see the pronuclei, but now there are techniques and microscopy materials that permit flawless pinpointing of the pronuclei. Plus the following: Shortly after the ovule becomes an ovum—that is, after fertilization—the chromosomes, which previously were, so to speak, packed together, disperse and come to reside in small bodies called pronuclei. Then the guy takes a couple of pipettes, a slightly larger one to hold the ovum by suction and another very delicate one to inject DNA sequences, meaning genes, into a pronucleus. It requires a jeweler's touch but it's done relatively easily. And it's also possible, if you're not dealing with a gene too large for it, to use a partially crippled retrovirus, one whose capacity to replicate itself has been inhibited, to transport that gene to any of the cells like a ferryboat or a raft. It's more complicated, because the retrovirus can't penetrate the *zona pellucida*, the covering of the embryo. But they find a way; they partially remove the covering. All that, plus other procedures, combined with progress in embryological techniques, makes it perfectly possible, viable, and in certain cases, desirable for them to do things of that sort."

"Desirable? How can it be desirable?"

"If we can locate, for example, what could be called the nitrogenic gene in plants, the problem of hunger would be solved, at least from a technical standpoint. There are already experiments, for example, to produce transgenic sheep with more wool. And speaking of sheep, it's not just pigs that are being crossed with people, no sir. At least in Scotland, I know for a fact that they've manufactured a sheep with a human gene, to produce blood coagulation factors in the teats. In the teats, mind you, and not in the liver, which is where such factors are normally produced. That's because they directed the gene to the teat cells so the milk could be used for extraction of the factors. So human blood will no longer be used to obtain these factors. A good thing for hemophiliacs, who won't have to pay so dearly for their medicine and will run less risk of getting AIDS. The production of a humongous number of organic substances, which today are very expensive, could be greatly facilitated, or handled completely, by the creation of such transgenic animals. It's a tiny bit complicated, but I more or less get it; if you'd like, I can explain it. The possibilities for the future are so astounding that I sometimes get confused."

"No, you've explained enough already. I don't want to know any more about this business; it makes my skin crawl."

"What would be the name of the hybrid of chimpanzee and man? *Chimpomem* or *homenzé*—what do you think? No, it'd be in English, of course—*manchimp*, *manape*, something like that. What do you think?"

"I don't think anything. I find it terrible. It can't happen; there has to be a limit to these things. Why would anyone want to make a hybrid of chimpanzee and man?"

"Ah, the uses are endless, even for target practice. You never know what some rich guy might want to do. They might serve as organ banks for transplants. Or as guinea pigs. Or they could be used for heavy or unpleasant work, they could serve as shock troops for dictatorships, guides for the blind and attendants for invalids, a source of animal protein, whatever. I only know that the embryos would have to be implanted in female chimps and not in human females because, in addition to it being difficult to find a woman willing to give birth to a monkey, or half-monkey, there's still the problem that, if the animal came from the womb of a citizen it would have the right to a birth certificate, and what would happen then?"

"Horrible, horrible! Can it be humanity will come to such a point? What a horrid thing! And it's interesting that he told me that if I saw those children I would refuse to baptize them. Have you stopped to analyze the monstrosity of this whole thing?"

"More or less. I also have a certain hang-up and don't like to think about it. But there's no need to worry; I doubt very much that your sorcerer saw any such animal. It's all bull. Everything I've said is very much in its infancy, with the major part of the problems still to be solved, so don't worry. It'll still be some time before they can produce an animal like that, and even if they'd already done so it wouldn't be here on the island."

"Yes, you're right, but I don't know. I keep thinking about that strange fellow, surrounded by his sinister dogs, sacrificing sheep—"

"Sheep? He sacrifices sheep?"

"He says he thinks he's sleeping when he orders sheep sacrificed. No doubt it's to make people believe he's in a trance. But the fact is that he orders the sacrifices and then the people kill sheep and do other things that I don't even care to know about."

"Interesting what you're saying, interesting. Dogs and sheep—interesting."

"What's interesting about dogs and sheep? Are you about to tell me another story, this time about a cross between a goat and a German shepherd?"

"No, nothing like that. It's because of a discussion I had with Lúcio Nemésio some time ago. Are there many dogs?"

"Judging by what he said, yes. But I only saw one."

"What does he do with the sacrificed sheep?"

"I haven't the slightest idea. Nor do I care to find out, for that matter. I don't want any further contact, direct or indirect, with that man."

He asked for another drop in his coffee glass, said that this was the last swallow because he had to leave, but he didn't get up. He remembered that Bará and the gypsy woman had said something about whether the beings had a soul. Unfinished souls, she had said—he remembered that very well. And *did* they? If someday one of those hybrids of man were to be created, with the gift of speech and a certain intelligence, would it have a soul? My God! His head shook. He said he felt afraid that perhaps he had the same fearful apprehension described sometime earlier by João Pedroso, the sensation that something evil lay around them, he didn't know what. The two men fell silent, the priest finished his coffee and said good-bye. He was going to get up earlier than was his custom, because he'd made plans to go fishing with Eduardinho. He hadn't been fishing for a long time; Father Coriolano was going to say Mass in his place. He rose, made a final gesture by touching the visor of his cap, and took Direita Street to go home.

João Pedroso now felt that the drink was rising to his head, but he decided that even so he'd have one more double, at least one more, before Zoinho got sleepy and decided to close up. Bad news, this business of a halfway friendship, never again like it used to be. He was envious of the fishing trip on Eduardinho's boat; in the old days they'd have invited him, but in all likelihood Monteirinho no longer wanted him as a fishing companion. And he's right, João Pedroso thought, downing in a gulp the whiskey remaining in the glass and holding it out for Zoinho to refill.

Two hours later, he staggered out of the bar and almost fell as he stepped from the curb to cross the Largo da Quitanda. He wanted there to be someone in the street, anybody with whom he could talk. No, better that there wasn't anyone, as in fact there was not. He had been on the verge of telling Zoinho all about Ana Clara and had opened his mouth to begin. Damn, not being able to tell anyone was as if the whole thing only partially existed. Monteirinho was right to avoid him, as had been proven once again. If he'd remained in the bar he'd have ended up hearing everything. Or he would have left, covering his ears. João Pedroso stumbled again, and again came close to falling, amid faltering steps. He gave up trying to avoid the puddles left by the rain and walked through them, wetting his shoes and his pants cuffs. Rotten booze. What if she saw him like this? She'd already seen him half lit, but never drunk this way, really pie-eyed, nearly without motor control and knowing that if he spoke, his words would come out botched, an unquenchable torrent gushing forth grandiloquent drivel which he frequently tried to contain without success. What had she seen in him? Boredom, a rich woman's boredom, wasn't that it? Boredom. No one on the island and she wanted to have a little fun. It might not seem like it, but it must be the truth. It had to be the truth. Well, at least he hadn't failed to get it up, as he'd expected—the miracle of a little whiskey beforehand, no doubt. But he'd eventually not get it up, wouldn't he? Always like that, always a defeatist outlook. Although it was only an outlook, because, for the moment, he seemed triumphant. She said he drove her crazy in bed, and she did in fact appear crazy; they both did. Where was all this going to lead? It would last till she tired of him, of course, as would inevitably happen. They screwed and screwed, almost without talking, without speaking. Of course, of course, of course—she must be used to that sort of thing. She was amusing herself and afterward she'd get fed up and discard him.

He stopped at the corner of Glória Street, rested against the wall of a small two-story house, and breathed deeply. Often, right there, drunk or not, he had been forced almost to pray in order to believe that life had meaning and in order not to nourish the fantasy, vague but real, of killing himself. And did life now have meaning? Could he deliver himself to this passion, which dominated him completely, but which he was ashamed to confess, a passion destined to do him harm, perhaps in a humiliating manner, perhaps destroying him in the end? As had already happened many times, he saw before him a replica of himself, looking at him with severity and a certain contempt and giving him a sermon. Yes, that was it, everything was within his reach, all he had to do was react against this very real masochism of his, do something constructive. He didn't have to be a piece of shit his entire life. It was a matter of choice; he didn't have to be a piece of shit. Of course, of course, everything was in his hands, so why see the world through an unchanging prism of defeat and depression? That's it, he thought, sticking out his chest as far as he could and raising his head. Naturally he knew, but liked to pretend he didn't, that the next day everything would go back to being the same, or he would even forget what now seemed so definite in his mind. Yes, a new life tomorrow, new paths, he said several times, clenching his fists and resuming his journey home.

She got all wet just thinking about it. She noticed it because she wasn't wearing panties and, as she spun around for the simple pleasure of making her full skirt whirl, she saw a tiny mark on it. She touched herself; she was dripping. Well, no cause for surprise, since she had been in an indescribable state of excitement, sitting with her thighs together and on the point of coming by thinking about him. She didn't want to change the dress; it had to be this dress and without panties, so she could enjoy the lovely expression he was sure to display, a kind of amazed shock, a kind of divine moue, when he stuck his hand under her skirt and she revealed herself before the expected moment, ready for him, ready! Or, why shouldn't she wait for him already nude? Nude, with a sheet over her. Nude, standing by the door. Or wrapped in a towel. Nude, why not? *Aaai*! No, that's foolishness. The dress is more appealing; the detail of the panties is sufficient to provide the adequate touch of sensuality without exaggeration.

What time was it? Still three-twenty? Three-twenty? Why hadn't she set it up for three-thirty? What stupidity! Ângelo Marcos had gone to Salvador the previous afternoon and wouldn't be back for at least two more days. Bebel had finally managed to arrange another short stay on the island and was providing total cover in her usual competent manner. Everything was fine—so why that ridiculous idea of setting things up for four-thirty? Four-thirty, four-thirty, always that time; it's like a superstition. Or something from grandma's day: Screwing right after lunch causes congestion and the person either dies or ends up a cripple. Nonsense. Even more so because she hadn't had anything for lunch because it seemed as if her stomach had closed down, turned into a dried prune. Bebel had a martini first, and she decided to do the same. It went down so well that she quickly asked for another, and her eyes became moist and shining. But food, no way. She felt a tremendous lack of appetite as she picked at her plate with the end of the fork, across from Bebel, who was avidly eating rice with cowpeas in palm oil that Cornélio had made especially for her. Lord in heaven, what impatience! The hands of the clock weren't moving and Bebel was almost starting to become irritating with that *mmm-mmm*, closing her eyes and taking another helping. God, what a desire Ana Clara had to run away, flail her arms, do something, hit something!

"You don't know what you're missing," Bebel had said. "This rice is absolutely dazzling, a masterpiece."

"I know. But I can't put anything in my mouth or chew anything, much less swallow."

"Hey! Is all this a case of nerves? Calm down, girl, everything's going to be all right! Come have something; good food improves everything. And this dish is an aphrodisiac—everybody says so."

"It's not really nerves, it's a kind of impatience, anxiety, the feeling that the time will never pass. Why'd I tell him four-thirty?"

"Four-thirty is a perfectly decent hour. Three-thirty sort of seems like a student kind of thing, an adolescent amateur thing. Four-thirty, five is traditional, with the afternoon ending, a pleasant breeze, softer light—"

"I could've perfectly well said three-thirty, without the slightest problem."

"What a horrible thing. With all this hustle and bustle you'd think it was the first time you'd been together."

"It's like that, it's like that. I get so agitated— You're seeing it, I don't have to explain. I could've said three-thirty! So as a result it's not even one o'clock and I'm going to have to put up with the agony of waiting three and a half hours! I'm not cut out for doing nothing while I wait—know what I mean by nothing? I can't pay attention to anything; I just sink into anxiety."

"Aninha, have you stopped to think about this whole thing calmly? I mean, have you evaluated how it's evolving? Of all people I don't want to rattle your cage, but speaking as a friend and your collaborator in this whole affair, I think it's getting dangerous. The other day when I asked about it, you gave me some psychoanalytic b.s. without answering anything. But now I'm going to ask again and you're going to give me a direct answer, with no beating around the bush. Don't you think the guy's getting too serious? I've never seen you like this."

"Well, the sex—"

"That talk about sex doesn't cut it anymore. When it started, OK, but not any longer. Of course there's the sex thing, but there's a lot more to it than that. Sex by itself doesn't last like this, doesn't grow like this; there has to be something else."

"Well, of course I'm a little bit in love with him; without the spice of passion what's the point?"

"A little bit, my foot. You're in love. Admit it, woman, you're down for the count, drooling, on your hands and knees. Admit it!"

"No, it's not that bad. I like him and he turns me on and all that, but it's not like that, not that bad."

"Tell me something—what is passion? To reach a higher level than you're already at, you'd have to pump five bullets into Marquinhos and run off to Casablanca with João. What more does it take to characterize your condition? You're totally turned upside down, completely out of your mind, and you look like somebody on the verge of a breakdown. If that's not unbridled passion, then I don't know what passion is. And what about your conversation? Listen to yourself—it's nothing but João; he's all you talk about! Fine, but you have to see things clearly. I sincerely think you're trying to avoid facing the problem, but it's best to face it before some real nasty complication pops up."

"You really think so, Bebel? And I'm that obvious about it, you think?"

"Yes, yes. At least to me you are."

"You know he and I practically don't talk when we're together? We grab each other and practically don't speak. I've never told him I was in love with him, and he hasn't told me; we've never talked about it. Interesting, isn't it? Never, we haven't even exchanged a 'darling.' That's why I don't think it's passion, it's a kind of exaggerated sex thing, and—"

"You haven't said it because you don't want to admit it to yourself, of course. But now it's more like sweeping dirt under the rug than anything else. It doesn't do any good. Admit you're in love and take precautions. That's what worries me, you completely going ga-ga, letting yourself be swept along by events this way, and suddenly something happening to harm you, maybe permanently. You've got to open your eyes, open your eyes. Have you thought what could happen if you get into a situation where you can't handle things with Marquinhos?"

"That's true. You're right. It's getting to be a little like that. There are days when I can't even stand to look at him. And what about when he comes to me with that sugary air of his that he's affected since his illness? I even made up an attack of fever blisters to avoid kissing or anything to do with the mouth. I can't even think of putting my mouth there on him. It's so disgusting it kills me. I close my eyes and think of João, but it doesn't do any good; it's disgusting. The other day I almost spoke João's name. I got out the *J* but caught myself in time."

"That's awful! Rule number one, my dear, is never say anyone's name in bed. Any form of address except the name. After a certain stage in life, confusion is inevitable. But it goes to show you I'm right; you need to get oriented or whatever, and evaluate everything carefully."

Yes, it's true, Bebel was absolutely right. But she had replied that she'd think about the matter some other time; at that very moment she couldn't, she couldn't! And, as soon as Bebel finished lunch and said, with a semiobscene laugh, that from then on she would be in the small room off the veranda until it was time to come down and escort João Pedroso upstairs, she dashed to her room. She could take a long, quiet bath, even a bubble bath, but she could barely keep still under the shower. That was it: Wash her hair, of course, wash her hair with several hundred shampoos and a couple of hundred creme rinses, massage the roots, the full treatment. Then the dryer, to kill some time.

No, that doesn't take much time, and even before four o'clock she had washed out the small stain and pressed the dress with the travel iron, but not put it on. Naked and lightly fragrant, she caressed herself with her eyes closed and experienced the same excitation she had felt before, a deep fluttering rising from her groin and the inside of her clenched thighs, a burning that warmed her entire face, her breathing almost a gasp. Pushing aside the dress she had placed on the bed, she lay with her legs open and began to masturbate with both hands, one grasping her pubis and the other thrusting her index and middle fingers in short, quick movements. Turning her head from one side to the other faster and faster, moaning loudly and opening her mouth as if the muscles of her face had frozen in that position, she came once, then a second and a third time, finally rolling on the bed with a guttural sob until ending on her side, knees doubled up and hands still clutched between her thighs.

But she didn't relax, and she was still in practically the same condition, though dressed and made-up, when she opened the door for João Pedroso and forced herself to receive him standing still, with just a smile, until he, as soon as he closed the door, walked toward her with an erection that could be seen clearly through his pants and kissed and embraced her, drawing her to him by the buttocks with both hands. How was it possible that they got along so well from the start and better and better as time went on? She always thought about that, when she remembered the kisses like those they now exchanged, his mustache with the secret scent that revealed itself only at moments like this, his lips that she licked and sucked as if she depended on them for life. She rubbed against him, and he, crouching slightly, raised her skirt and did indeed show the expression that she expected when he saw before him the shiny and curly hairs of her pubis. Breathing rapidly, his eyes bulging slightly, his mouth opened in a gesture of inimitable desire. Caressing and pressing her buttocks, he gave her a long kiss between the thighs as she opened her legs and grasped his head. But he withdrew to look at her, holding her skirt as if raising the tent of a small circus.

"I don't know what to look at, I don't know what to look at!" he said in an altered voice, turning her around several times and then embracing her by the legs so powerfully that they fell onto the sofa in the suite's anteroom, he with his arms extended to avoid falling completely, she in a half-sitting position, her skirt around her hips. As he undid his belt, she decided to open his fly and impatiently began sucking him as soon as he undressed. She wanted to swallow him whole. She didn't know whether to suck him or stick her face into his balls, to sniff him and kiss his groin, whether she wanted him to come at once in her mouth so she could drink of him all she could—until he lifted her dress over her head and, in a way that also drove her wild, placed her prone, positioned a pillow at her back, mounted her smoothly at the thorax, and after a time lightly touching her breasts, thrust himself into her mouth and began to move back and forth as she moaned, clutching his thighs. He remained in that position for some time, and then, coming out of her with a small noise caused by her lips and tongue, ran his mouth down her stomach and began to suck her, while she moaned and ran her fingers through his hair.

"Put it in me, put it in, I can't take any more!" she screamed, raising him by his arms and pointedly looking at him erect and almost pulsating, the large head shining, a lance, a tree trunk, among pubic hair with an unforgettable aroma. Always a sublime moment, an indescribable instant, the time of penetration, a heaving jolt, an inexpressible thrust, and she with her legs wrapped around him, starting to come, to come repeatedly, until, as was their custom and their preference for the first time he came, he lifted her thighs and pushed himself into her until she could feel his balls and then, moaning, almost sobbing, he gave a few deep lunges and came to rest inside her. She could feel him throbbing and wetting her inside.

"My love, my love!" she said, holding him as tightly as she could and maintaining the embrace for a long time while she thought of how it was true that she really loved him, how the words had such deep meaning. And he, caressing her hair and speaking as if in a monologue, said it was difficult for him to believe it but he wanted to believe, because he loved her too and loved her in every way, not only because he enjoyed her and her company, but also because he desired her more and more and remembered everything they did together, remembered in a dazzling way how she raised her pretty little ass when he wanted to fuck her from behind, remembered biting her neck and afterward, when he entered her, entered her as deeply as he could, remembered seeing her so gracefully turn her face back toward him so he could kiss her mouth, remembered in a glorious way how he'd come in her mouth the first time, with her moaning and panting as if she wanted to take all his prick into her mouth, remembered everything, everything, everything, in every tiny detail. And for the first time, naked and embracing, they discussed everything that they had come to think they would never discuss, and he experienced truly exquisite happiness.

A great screw that black girl, better every time. A complete screw in every imaginable hole. What an ass! Really a beauty, and a piece of cake; from now on he was going to screw her always. What an ass! He'd forgotten how good the natives are in bed. The young black wench is a real live wire and knows everything, is game for anything, even a bit of slapping around, which always adds a little extra to the screwing and which he can't do at home because Ana Clara never let him. You don't go down on a black woman like that, but she's not interested in reciprocity; she gives head. With her it's mouth, ass, everything—it's wonderful. Period. All there was to it was to do like the other times: Get everything straightened out on the island, wait for her in Salvador, take her to the motel, and give her a little present afterward. A piece of cake. And she has a sister who's even more luscious than she is. He'd stick it to her too; there's nothing that a bit of do re mi won't take care of, especially in their situation and with their mother's interest. This stay on the island is working out better than expected.

Ângelo Marcos felt almost happy, drumming his fingers on the table in the restaurant and thinking of his performance that afternoon. A real hard-on. That little black gal is murder, but he had a lot of energy. Three times. Three. At his age that's nothing to sneeze at. Three. And it got hard enough the second time to ram it up the whore's ass, that sensational ass. People were right, giving up smoking makes you harder. Yeah, three times is quite a feat. Of course he was coming off a long dry spell, but even so it's impressive. Makes you feel like talking about it, but the guys think it's bullshit, especially the ones who can barely get it up and are lucky to knock some off once a week.

A week. It was that "a week" business that started the fight—and he creased his forehead at the memory. He'd been noticing something different about Ana Clara for some time now, including in bed. When she went to bed with him, that is, because she always seemed to have some excuse, from the traditional headache—something she'd never had, as she herself was fond of announcing—to extra-long menstruations, which she'd also never had. Nothing concrete, nothing he could put his finger on, but it was evident that something was wrong. At first he thought she knew about one of his escapades, but later he saw it couldn't be that, since there was no way for her to find out anything. And when he did manage to get her in bed, she wasn't the same woman; she seemed like a piece of meat, lying there inert and lifeless. Fever blisters, vaginitis, back pains, all sorts of things. He'd tried to be understanding, until the day, after he'd remarked, with a good-humored look on his face, that a husband had a right to his wife at least three times a week, and she had answered in that crude manner, so crude that she was sorry immediately, asked his forgiveness, said it was a joke, an unfortunate joke. But the harm had already been done. "Three times a year is too often for me," she'd said, and he got so irritated that he came close to hitting her. But he calmed down and that night tried having a conciliatory talk with her, which he planned to conclude with a little screwing. She, however, didn't even hear what he had to say, because she went to sleep, or pretended she went to sleep, and amid elbowing and small shoves, turned away from him, refusing to be awakened.

And it did no good to insist to the point of exasperation that she tell him what the problem was. No problem, she said, you're inventing things. But how could there be no problem if she was completely different? She knew she was different, why didn't she admit it and say right away what was wrong? She could be frank, bare her heart, it might be something he was unaware of and could correct. Nothing. And after a time she would make up some excuse and leave his presence. Nerve-racking. And from nerve-racking the atmosphere progressed to unbearable when, looking in her drawers for a hat she had borrowed, he came across two thick notebooks filled with her handwriting.

"What the hell is this?" he shouted as soon as he saw her, incredulous and so indignant that he couldn't remain seated, after spending a large part of the morning reading and rereading the notebooks until she returned from the beach.

"Those notebooks are mine. Where did you find them?"

"I know they're yours, I know they're yours! I—"

"Give me my notebooks. You have no right to snoop in my things. Give me my notebooks!"

"No! And I have every right to snoop; this isn't snooping, it's finding out about my wife's life. I have every right!"

"You don't have any right. Give me my notebooks, Ângelo Marcos. I'm serious."

"I know! I know you're serious! Listen to this gem, this exquisite gem: 'Perhaps, from the standpoint of the married woman who wants to run around outside the home but also wants to preserve the marriage, several lovers simultaneously is better than just one. It is possible that monopoly is harmful to marriage, besides which changing men—'"

"Give me those notebooks. You have no right to do this!"

"Stop saying I have no right to do it! I'm the one who knows about my rights. I have every right to demand clarification. My wife has taken to writing pornography—isn't that just great! Author of dirty books, isn't *that* just great! And on what experience is the lady basing herself? What's her research? Because, judging from this, her knowledge of whoring appears to be excellent."

"Give me the notebooks! Give me the notebooks! I never went snooping in anything of yours!"

"Because I don't have anything to snoop in. My life is completely open; I have no secrets. Much less this degenerate trash that I never imagined that a woman like you—"

"Give me those notebooks! Give me those notebooks!"

Yes, the notebooks did end up pretty shredded in the physical struggle for possession of them. And she even had the impudence to refer to one Suzana Friedman, Fondman, Foster, something like that, as if she were two people. This Suzana was the author, not she. She would have to be schizophrenic for that to wash. Still, that's not beyond the realm of possibility. She might be going off the deep end; she has a crazy aunt who spends her time in and out of the sanitarium, and they say her grandfather died a raving maniac. But how to convince her to get an examination? Well, the thing to do now is watch her behavior, because if it's insanity it'll show some very ugly signs. Maybe Bebel can help. No, no, that's no good. Well, we can see about that later. This was all he needed, to be married to a woman who's come unglued. Very strange pastime, that business of making up another personality, as she herself said, and writing that kind of stuff. But it might not be all that serious, might even be a perversion of hers that he'd never detected. If she weren't in Itaparica, which she no longer wanted to leave even for short trips, he might suspect something, but on the island there was no danger. Not only were there no men, but watchful eyes were around twenty-four hours a day. Yeah, the only thing was to await developments.

But the atmosphere became absolutely intolerable, among other reasons because, following the incident with the notebooks, she refused to speak to him and answered only when she could not avoid it, and then only in monosyllables. So intolerable that he decided to spend an indefinite period of time in Salvador. The black girl's mother, through whom the contact had been made, was a cleaning lady at City Hall; he could phone her at any time and the bed question was settled. He might stay a week or two. Maybe that way she'd take notice; maybe she'd suspect he was having an affair. Jealousy and suspicion are fine weapons when properly used. Yeah, an overly secure woman is bad news; there has to be a certain amount of insecurity so she won't be in the driver's seat or get a big head.

He looked around, pleased at not seeing anyone he knew, no one who might want to join him at his table or invite him to theirs. Waiting in a restaurant, without smoking or drinking, is a pain, a thought that had never occurred to him. "Between nine and nine-thirty," Nando had said. It was nine-twenty now, so he wasn't late. But he still could have arrived by now; a good conversation would at least help get these problems off his mind. Actually the dinner was more for business than friendship, because Nando was bringing that New York banker who handled his dollar-based investments. When he'd told Nando he was getting eight percent a year from his Nassau account, he was almost laughed at. "You're nuts," Nando said. "The way the American economy is going, soon that won't even keep up with inflation. You're nuts." Then, when the gringo showed up on one of his usual trips, Nando decided to act as go-between for the contact. And finally here they were, passing by the bar and coming toward him.

"Been here long?"

"No, maybe fifteen minutes."

"Let me introduce you. This is Abe Kaplan. Abe, this is the famous

Dr. Ângelo Marcos that I've been telling you so much about. Abe is married to a Brazilian, and he speaks Portuguese better than we do, so you don't have to use your English."

The American was nice, despite the habit of sticking his finger between his collar and his neck every thirty seconds. He loved Brazil, especially Bahia. Every year he took to the streets with a local Carnival group, from Friday to Sunday. He came especially from New York for it, accompanied by his wife Hannah, who was born here, in the Nazaré district.

"I'm aware of the problems, but it's still a great country, with many great qualities. And this city—" he said, making a fist and punching the air, "this city," he repeated, gesturing with his head, "is simply magical. I always tell Hannah that I have something of the Bahian in me. I really do."

Nando asked what they wanted to drink. Ângelo Marcos said he couldn't drink and Nando suggested at least a tiny bit of beer, what the hell, he was cured, he didn't feel anything the matter, a little beer couldn't hurt. Ângelo Marcos agreed; they ordered a small amount of beer, the American asked for gin in a glass rinsed with a dry martini, and Nando ordered whiskey on the rocks. After a short silence, Nando asked how things were going on the island. Fine, everything was fine on the island, nothing ever changes on the island. More silence, and after a slow sip from his gin, the American spoke. He knew about Ângelo Marcos's problem. Nando was right; it was a ridiculous return, practically something from the sixties. The panorama had changed greatly in the past few years. Ângelo Marcos asked if he worked with New York banks and he said he did. New York, Miami, San Francisco, Los Angeles, Zurich, Frankfurt, Luxembourg, Liechtenstein, Panama City, the Cayman Islands, the Channel Islands—how do you say "the Channel Islands" in Portuguese?—and so forth, because the range of services required by the complexity of the financial, economic, taxation, real estate, and even political structures demanded a network of varied and versatile activity. Ângelo Marcos couldn't imagine the complexity of certain operations. For example, in Ângelo Marcos's own case, he was sure that not only banking operations were involved. Many other options should be considered that depended on a very large number of factors and circumstances; the thing would have to be analyzed. Did Ângelo Marcos already have a firm in a convenient city, such as Panama, or just bank accounts in dollars? Just bank accounts? Then he was losing money and was having trouble moving money abroad. All this had to be handled through careful planning, which involved minimal risk. He would suggest, therefore, that they set up a meeting in his office in Salvador, just the two of them, for a preliminary study of the possibilities. His office, in the Commerce building, with a secretary and everything, was in permanent operation, even with him absent most of the time. And it was the best place for this kind of conversation, with absolute security. He knew it wasn't common, but every now and then someone had problems with the police and Internal Revenue because of deals like these, and it wasn't advisable to take risks, especially in the case of a public figure like Ângelo Marcos, who couldn't be exposed to scandal. They shouldn't talk about it here, where even the napkins had ears; throughout the world, conversations in restaurants are one of the most dangerous means of disclosure.

He found this last observation quite amusing and laughed, rapping the table lightly, and took another drink of gin. If Ângelo Marcos agreed, they could set a meeting for Thursday, two days from now; how was four o'clock? Perfect, perfect, he exclaimed when Ângelo Marcos agreed, and took from the inside pocket of his coat a gilt-edged appointment book in which he made a quick notation. Done. Now they could go on to more enjoyable matters, although of great importance, such as food, drink, women, and music.

And even if they had wanted to go on talking about business, they'd have had to change the subject anyway, for a laugh familiar to Nando and Ângelo Marcos was heard from the side of the bar hidden behind a column and, taking a few dance steps alongside the counter, appeared Tavinho, who immediately saw their table and concluded his dance with a flourish.

"Scoundrels! You didn't even call me! Blackguards! Good-for-nothings! Forming a cabal while I cultivate my solitude!"

He extended his arm, put it around a woman in a tight red-and-gold dress who was just behind him, and brought her to the table.

"*Con ustedes, Soledad, mi amante argentina!*" he stated, exhibiting the young woman.

No, of course she wasn't his Argentine lover, she was a Brazilian lover, he explained loudly after they had both sat down, and the woman shook her head and smiled in semi-embarrassment. Kathya, he said, K-A-T-H-Y-A—cute, isn't she? Ah, how nice to run into you all, it'd been a horrible week, a catastrophic weekend and now everything had taken a turn for the better, first with the settling of a pile of problems, then with Kathya coming on the scene, and, to cap the climax, running into his friends.

"Kathya," he said, pointing with the palm of his hand upward, "this is Dr. Fernando Caldas de Andrade Magalhães, a rich millionaire. And this is Dr. Ângelo Marcos Barreto, a just as rich millionaire."

"And this is my new American friend Abe Kaplan," Nando said, "a rich millionaire, ha-ha."

"Don't say that. I haven't made my first billion yet."

"But make it you shall, make it you shall. In the company of those two there you'll learn everything there is to know. The only reason they don't have a billion dollars is because there isn't a billion dollars in Bahia; this is a shithole. You know I've come up with the title of a samba for rich Bahians? The title is 'Peeling the Brie and Guzzling Cheap Chablis'—that is, coarseness with poverty. This is a shithole. But in America there's billions to burn, so learn from these two and you'll get there."

"That's where you're mistaken, Tavinho. We're going to learn from him. He's a financial consultant, one of the directors of Lewis & Strauss, and he knows everything about the long green."

"A financial consultant? I'm in the midst of wild beasts!"

"You could be one of Abe's clients too, Tavinho. No, seriously, because Abe is a whiz at this stuff. You could take advantage of the opportunity of him being here to make an appointment with him. I think it's worthwhile."

"If I had any dough. You know very well that the dough belongs to the old man, and the old man doesn't consult anybody. I don't even think he lets himself know how much money he has and what he does with it. No, unfortunately the only kind of adviser I need is an adviser to the lovelorn. I've been in a mess, my friend. I mean, now, with Kathya, I'm better—isn't she cute?—but I've been in a real mess. Your friend, Nandinho, that woman friend of yours, never again. I won't even get close. I prefer the company of a hydrophobic river otter."

"What friend? Ana Camila?"

"You mean Ana Camel. Ana Dromedary. Yeah, and on top of that, I was the one who moved out. There's nothing there that belongs to her except her crap and that collection of drawings that startled me every time I woke up to take a piss, when I ran into the ones she hung on the bedroom walls."

"Another separation?"

"No, this is the last one; you can take that to the bank."

"What number is this one?"

"This was number six. But there's not going to be a seventh. It doesn't work anymore. There's no way. In fact, she's already getting it on with another guy. I'm sure of it. When a marriage falls apart in bed, it falls apart in everything. That's the truth."

"That's true. I was married to somebody else, before Hannah, and it was the same thing. There's a Tennessee Williams character, I don't recall in which play, who bangs his fist on the bed and says 'When a marriage goes on the rocks, the rocks are here.' A great truth, a great truth."

"Yeah, for two months I'd been noticing how she was different, all standoffish, arrogant, full of excuses not to get close to me. Not to mention the days she'd wake up in destroyer mode and act in ways that would be considered offensive in a corral full of donkeys. It was obvious. I have some experience; I must have been cuckolded about eight times in my career, so I understand this business. When a woman takes to doing that, it's because she's putting out for some other guy. It never fails. She even claimed to have a fever blister so she wouldn't have to kiss me the last time I tried to grab her. I just don't want the bitch living there; that's taking it too far. Isn't that right? Not that. I've given her a deadline to move out."

"She said she had a fever blister, did she?"

"Judging by what she had to say, there must've been an epidemic of herpes simplex, which, come to think of it, in dealing with a cow is no surprise. 'I'm covered with blisters, Tavinho, ouch, oh, ouch, ouch, please!' You had to be there. And if it wasn't that, it was the old trick of migraine with nausea. She never had a migraine in her life. But that's the way it goes. How do they put it? I'm getting my life back together with Kathya—cute little thing—I'm a free and happy man and I love the apartment-hotel. Enough of that. This old habit of getting together to talk about women is real tacky. You may not believe it, but I'm going to have something to eat. What are you eating? Abe, would you like 'hearts and minds'?"

"What?"

"It's a dish Garcez, a friend of ours, invented. It's chicken hearts with beef brains. What do you think? OK, I'm going to have a sliced flank steak. Miguel, don't look at me like that again. It's not enough that you're the worst waiter in all of Salvador, you also have that expression on your face."

"It's because I know you're not going to eat the steak and then you'll blame the chef. Why don't you have some nice fish? You always like the fish."

"Is there anything harder to take than a waiter who knows what's best for us? You're a real S.O.B., you are. Very well, Miguel, what's the fish?"

"Grouper."

"Shark. All right, you con man, bring on the shark. Kathya will have *carpaccio*. Isn't it *carpaccio*, love? Let me do the ordering. Nando,

I'm paying for this shit, I've decided. I feel like celebrating. What'll our friend from the North have?"

"Flank steak seems like a good idea. Flank steak and a baked potato."

"Flank steak and a baked potato for *Mister* Kaplan, Miguel. Nando, I know—watercress salad, ribs, rice with parsley, and creamed spinach, which this time he'll say is shitty. Right? Right. And what about Dr. Ângelo Marcos? Dr. Ângelo Marcos! What happened, Marquinhos—did the price of cacao go down?"

"Huh? No, nothing. I was distracted, thinking. The beer didn't sit too well with me. Miguel, bring me a tonic water with a twist of lime and some ice. I don't think I'm going to eat; I have a touch of nausea."

He didn't, but he really wasn't hungry anymore, and he spent the rest of the dinner feigning interest in the conversation and laughing at what Tavinho said, though he wasn't paying attention. Using the excuse of nausea to leave before the dessert the American ordered, he went home. When he arrived, he couldn't immediately leave the car because one of the dogs had escaped to the garage and stood in front of it, growling. He had to blow the horn several times before a security guard came to the garage and led the dog away. Highly irritated, he said he was going to kill the animal, but his mind soon returned to where it had been earlier, and he went to bed but slept badly.

Black Rat bought it by being struck by a striped mullet, not from a bomb like his uncle. Mullet, as everyone knows, even if pretty dazed from a dynamite explosion, and especially if they're on the large side, should still be brought up with great care. Don't grab them from the front, because they'll slip through your hands and can hit a person in the pit of the stomach hard enough to kill. As in fact one killed Black Rat, who didn't heed the advice of the older men and, in his greed for fish, faced a thirteen-pound striped mullet that shot out like a cannonball and he fell stiff into the water and didn't come out again except for his wake. His uncle, on the other hand, actually did die from a bomb, blown to bits. In the company of his friend Ebinoel, who was lucky because the canoe was large and he was in the stern, while the other man set off blasts in front from the bow. It was a two-fish shot, because they would first knock out a school of saurel and then watch for the common jack that came to feed on the saurel scattered along the rocky bottom. Then the jack appeared sooner than they expected, he got flustered, didn't pay attention to the fuse, bit the cap distractedly, and the bomb blew up against his chest. Ebinoel was dazed, and to this day is half deaf and complains about a buzzing in the ears, but he suffered no serious effects, gathered as many pieces of his comrade as he could, and took them to his family in a sack. That was in 1956.

"Here on the island, people die from everything. None of that there talk 'bout certain kinds of deaths not happenin' here," said Crazy Jewfish, who since five o'clock had been doing research on the dead connected to the Market and the causes of their deaths. "You can't name no disease, includin' the most modern ones, that somebody around here ain't died of. Even some diseases that ain't really diseases kill people 'round here, like Blind Rooster, who had a pimple on his nose that turned into cancer and ate his face out and he died stinkin' and with his face all eat up. That from a pimple. Filu died from dropsy, Nandá from a hemorrhage, Ugly Roque from diabetes, Lazarão from typhus, Mosquete from TB, Fingernails from Chagas's disease, and Zoinho they say from AIDS. Even AIDS has shown up here, and Zoinho didn't betray his body, just the opposite. Everything is here. And now Quatinga's oldest grandson died of a cerebal tumor."

"Cerebral tumor."

"Of the brain. A tumor smack in the middle of his brain that they couldn't take out. He stayed in the hospital I don't know how long and died without ever knowin' nothing, in a comba."

"In a coma."

"Passed away. Quatinga said his case was rare. They even paid his hospital costs, the burial, and the tomb, so as they could keep his brain to study. Quatinga said it was some kind of earthworm in the brain, that's what the doctor said, 'ceptin' he, Quatinga, don't much believe it 'cause nobody ever heard of a' earthworm in a person's brain."

"Yes, but the doctor was right. It's not an earthworm, but it is a kind of worm. I heard about that case; I just didn't know it was Quatinga's grandson."

Lúcio Nemésio had made the right prognosis, of course. The boy was truly doomed. João Pedroso hit the counter lightly without saying anything else. It was clear that he wasn't to blame for what happened to the boy and therefore had no reason to feel guilty. But he didn't feel good; the news had been more unpleasant for him than it would normally have been.

In fact, everything was becoming unpleasant. He didn't want to leave Ana Clara's side, especially since that splendid afternoon when they talked so much and knew for certain they were in love. He was jealous, he was anxious, he was angry at Ângelo Marcos, although he never let it show, not even to her. And he was afraid of losing her, no matter what the circumstances, even if—as he sometimes fantasized hesitantly and nervously—they started living together. Especially if they started living together, even. Because he wasn't who she thought he was; he was in no way who she thought he was. He felt his ears burning when he recalled how she had praised him and when she'd said she admired him. Admired what? She didn't know who he was, she didn't know. He was nothing, and when she found out she would surely stop loving him.

Yes, everything was unpleasant. He remembered the last time he'd gone to sleep saying he would start a new life. For the nth time, like some people trying to quit smoking. He hadn't changed at all, except for his and Ana Clara's situation. The relationship itself had changed for the better, but everything else, for that very reason, had gotten worse.

"Has Quatinga gone out today?" he asked suddenly, without knowing why.

"Yes, but he should be back soon. He laid down a deep net yesterday and went to look for it over ten hours ago. He ought to be back soon."

He went to the ramp, looked in the direction of the spot marking the net, and saw Quatinga's raft appear in the distance. He waited impatiently, pacing from side to side on the pier until, fifteen minutes later, the boatman moored beside the ramp.

"Quatinga!" he shouted, even before they finished fastening the anchor. "I want to talk to you."

"I didn't bring anything today. Just a half dozen brim the crabs chewed up, that's it. I just stopped by to leave a couple for my mother, but I'm putting the boat away behind the fountain and I'll mend the net there later."

"But first I want to talk to you. Can't you come ashore for a minute? I'll buy you a beer."

"I don't want to get wet, João. Can't it be at noon or in the afternoon?"

"Two beers! And you're wearing trunks underneath. It's no big deal to strip to your trunks and come ashore. It's shallow there, all you'll get wet is your fanny. I have something to talk to you about that's of great interest to me."

Quatinga removed his pants and shirt, slipped off the side of the raft and waded to the ramp. What kind of mad rush was this, some problem?

"It's just this, Quatinga: Have you or anyone in your family consulted Bará da Misericórdia in the last few years?"

"Why do you want to know? Are you doing an investigation for Father Monteirinho? My youngest daughter is getting married, and I don't want any complications with the priest. He doesn't allow anybody to consult Bará."

"I'm no informer, Quatinga. The priest has nothing to do with this. The information is because of the death of your grandson."

"What's my grandson's death got to do with Bará? When he got sick they took him straight to the hospital. He wasn't treated by Bará. Might've been better if he was, 'cause I know from reliable sources he's cured lots of people. I don't believe that business about worms in the brain either."

"Has anyone in your family been treated by Bará?"

"Hey, man, go easy with that business. You're not going to tell Father Monteirinho, are you?"

"Of course not, I already told you I won't. It's just that I think I have a hunch about how your grandson got that disease."

"It won't do any good now; he's dead."

"But if my hunch is right, it may be that other people can avoid getting the same disease. So tell me, has anyone in your family consulted Bará?"

"My wife. My wife had a pain no doctor could find a cure for. So she went to Bará and he cured her in a week, with just tea and prayer."

"She stayed there a week?"

"Eight days. When she came back she was fine."

"And her health is good?"

"Strong as a mule, thank God. A mule for work. Doesn't even catch colds."

"But was she the only one in your family who consulted Bará? The boy who died was never with Bará?"

"Well, he must've been, 'cause he went with his grandmother to keep her company, 'cause when the pain'd hit her she couldn't stand to move around and needed somebody to help her."

"He was there the entire eight days?"

"Yes. He came back with her."

"Did he like dogs?"

"Never noticed. We don't have dogs at home. I can't stand dogs, think they're filthy, lousy animals who sniff and lick assholes and then come lick people."

"Exactly, exactly. You don't realize you've hit the nail on the head."

"I can't stand dogs, can't stand 'em."

"But you don't know about the boy."

"Well, every kid likes dogs. I don't know if he ran around with dogs in the street. We raised him pretty free—he didn't even go to school."

"When your wife was treated by Bará, did they kill a sheep?"

"A sheep?"

"They told me he usually has a sheep sacrificed."

"I don't know anything about that sheep business. She didn't say anything about a sheep, just about the tea and the prayers."

"Did Bará have a dog at the time? Can you say whether he had dogs and sheep there, at that time?"

"Beyond me. I was never there myself."

João Pedroso called Inocêncio from the storeroom, left money for three beers for Quatinga, went by the fish market and told Boa Morte and Nascimento he was leaving, and caught the bus for Amoreiras. He knew where several of the Little Hands lived, all in Amoreiras, and he also knew that most of them did nothing, except play dominoes, drink rum, and fish now and then. Some of them at least must be in the main square.

Two of them were in the square, talking about the lottery in a group under an oiti tree. João Pedroso greeted those he knew, put his hand on Little Hand 3's shoulder and asked to speak to him in private. They went to a bench on the other side of the square and João Pedroso asked about Bará's dogs. Yes, he'd always had dogs; he liked dogs a lot. But not sheep, and in fact he didn't always have sheep killed, just the opposite. The sheep were brought from right around there.

"And, the night before the sacrifice, do the sheep stay on his land?"

"Depends. Sometimes they stay there two or three days. Sometimes not."

"And what do they do with the dead sheep?"

"The heart is burned. The meat goes to the people, whoever's around."

"And the innards?"

"Well, sometimes one person or another wants them for a delicacy, but usually the people keep the meat and give the innards and belly to the dogs."

"Do they cook the innards before giving them to the dogs?"

"Man, since when does a dog care about anything being cooked, much less a mutt? It's raw—they eat everything raw, and they don't leave a thing."

"And when the sheep are waiting to be slaughtered, are they kept in the same place as the dogs?"

"Yes. Everything's in one place, except the dogs run loose and the sheep are tied on a long cord so they can graze."

"Do the dogs run over the grass they're grazing on?"

"Sure. The dogs are all over the place. You ever see a dog sit still?"

On the bus heading home, João Pedroso stuck his head slightly out the window, breathed deeply, and smiled. Suddenly, the echinococcosis mystery was practically solved. He would go to Lúcio Nemésio and tell him the news, and he would also go to Monteirinho. After all, if it could be proved that Bará's dogs were infected and were a menace to public health it would strike a blow against him, perhaps a definitive one. Monteirinho could take it to the mayor, or even to Ângelo Marcos, who was no longer minister of health but enjoyed great prestige. It was only necessary to be certain; maybe he should talk to Bará himself. Of course, talk to Bará, ask him about the sheep and the dogs, see things for himself before saying anything to Lúcio Nemésio.

What the devil had happened to him? He'd never found himself with such initiative and disposition like this; he seemed another person. Had he really done all that, this very morning? Yes, he had. Ever since Father Monteirinho had spoken to him of the dogs and sheep, he'd felt there might be some clue there but had done nothing, as always, not even reported his suspicion to the priest, in fear that he might want him to do something. Strange, strange. And what relief he felt, what a huge weight he had taken off his shoulders! No, not relief—almost an intense euphoria. Yes, a euphoria, a sense of lightness, confidence, and freedom. He hadn't realized before how much his way of acting, or rather of not acting, bothered him. Nor had he realized how easy it was to act; it was as easy as could be, it wasn't at all difficult. He took another deep breath, smiled again. Was everything really different or was it merely a momentary sensation? He couldn't deny that he had acted; it was a concrete thing. But had he changed? He had no idea, but he felt a certainty, a certainty he had never before experienced, that he would seek out Bará and carry this investigation forward. Now that he thought of it, why not take the step right now? He rose, spoke to the driver, and got out at the side of the highway. He was still close to Amoreiras and could walk back and ask one of the Little Hands to take him to Bará at the first opportunity, immediately if possible.

Walking back with a rapidity he knew was unnecessary but which he could not restrain, he arrived again at the square in Amoreiras, where he found Little Hand 3 in the same spot.

"Why all the rush, Mr. João? You lose something? You're almost red."

"No, it's nothing important. I just remembered to ask you for something. Can you take me to Bará?"

"The saint? You want to talk to him?"

"Of course I want to, Little Hand; otherwise I wouldn't ask you to take me there."

"For a consultation? Are you going to consult with him?"

"No, what foolishness. I don't want any kind of consultation. I have a matter to discuss with him."

"Is it the same matter he wanted to talk about with the priest and before that wanted to talk about with you?"

"No. More or less. Yes, yes, tell him that's what it is. Can it be today?"

"Not today. I have to talk to him first, so he can set up a time. There's lots of people living there, a regular pilgrimage."

"And when can you talk to him—today?"

"It's all that urgent?"

"Yes, it's very urgent."

"Then later today I'll go there and see if I can talk to him. Sometimes you can't talk to him direct, but if I say it's a message from you, maybe—"

"Say it, say it's a message from me, that I urgently need to talk to him. But don't jerk me around, Little Hand, go there as soon as you can. Don't worry, I'll give you something after you talk to him."

He banged on the roof supports of the bus stop, almost tapping his feet with excitement. He felt like going back to Little Hand 3 to reinforce his request, even started to do so, but he decided that was overdoing it and didn't go. Everything was underway, nothing hasty, no need to rush things too much. He cracked his knuckles, went to the corner to see if the bus was visible at the other end of the street, and decided to wait near the square, where he stood looking at the sea and thinking many thoughts about Ana Clara.

7

Despite everything, happiness. Yes, it was nothing else, though a happiness that, as always, could not be complete. But just Ângelo Marcos's extended absence cleared the air considerably. So good, so wonderful, so great! Her first thought upon awakening, almost an automatic, sudden dread, was of how to face the long, terribly painful hours in his company, and then immediately afterward, like a dawn suddenly lighting the night, came the memory that he wasn't there, he was away, far away, and he wouldn't arrive today, nor tomorrow, nor the day after. What a sense of relief! It was enough to make everything seem beautiful and stimulating, and Ana Clara sprang up, so happy that she crossed the bedroom swaying and singing.

Passion, passion, passion—passion so copious that new tastes burgeon from fruits, the air stings your nostrils, your step becomes light, song lyrics turn philosophical, crossing your legs generates unbearable heat, and every feeling is enhanced. Such confusion! That matter of Cacilda and the opossum, for example, which got to be ridiculous. Of course it was ridiculous; an opossum is an opossum, nobody can take an opossum, it's out of the question. And chicken is chicken, people eat chicken, that's what chicken is for. Cacilda was a tailless, scrawny little chicken, very nice, who had showed up still not fully grown. No one knew where she came from, and she had taken up residence outside the kitchen. When, after a month—by which time she was everyone's pet and esteemed by one and all—her owner came looking for her, Ana Clara refused to return her and paid three times what the woman asked.

Therefore, no one could think of anything but capital punishment for the opossum. But there was no need to go overboard like that; you'd think the world was coming to an end because of Cacilda's death. It was a day like those she was going through now, when she had awakened with an unbelievable appetite and gone to the kitchen thinking about breakfasts straight out of Hollywood, with everything mixed together in a colorful mélange, large glasses of orange juice, scrambled eggs with ham, whopping pieces of toast, jellies, cheeses, French bread and patés, everything, everything, everything—when she ran into Cornélio at the door to the pantry, drying his tears on his shirtsleeve. She found the scene amusing and felt like asking if he wasn't afraid he'd ruin his makeup, but he, after a sob, looked at her with bulging eyes and seemed on the verge of fainting.

"Cacilda!" he exclaimed, covering his face with his hands. "The opossum killed Cacilda, Dona Ana Clara!"

It was true. Beside the small enclosure where they kept the propane tanks and where she liked to spend the night lay her cadaver, a shapeless mass of feathers and blood. Poor Cacilda, of course, but Ana Clara reacted as if she had lost a relative, and she refused to eat anything. She went around almost the entire morning whimpering and with her chin trembling, and she flew into a fury against the opossum. When Edsonil said he'd seen the animal and that it was in the habit of appearing at night, walking along the top of the wall, she hardly recognized her own voice, shrill and nervous, demanding, in that case, that he set up an ambush and kill the opossum, kill that horrible murderer, even if was the last thing he did in his life.

A little after nine o'clock, she was upstairs and heard shouts from the rear patio. From the window she saw Edsonil with a club in his hand bringing the opossum to bay. He was seconded by Cornélio who did nothing but emit small screams and act as if he would flee at any moment. Ana Clara ran downstairs, where from behind Edsonil, she saw the animal. It looked like a horrid and disgusting large rat, baring its teeth and hissing against the wall.

"Kill it, kill it!" she screamed, and Edsonil clubbed the animal several times until it stopped writhing and lay curled on the ground, blood flowing from its half-open mouth.

"I'm going to take it home," Edsonil said. "My mother eats opossum."

"Your mother eats that disgusting animal?" Ana Clara said, drawing a little closer, and then she saw something moving in the opossum's belly. "There are things moving in its belly. How horrible!"

"They're its litter," Edsonil said. "It's a female and its belly was full of babies. They'll go in the stew too."

"But they're alive!"

"Yep, but they're going to die. They're going to die in any case, since they nurse there inside her belly."

"No, don't take her now. Let me leave, let me leave!"

Great. First, a veritable lying-in-state because of a simple flea-bitten chicken. Second, feeling like the queen of the heavies, the cruelest of the cruel, the greatest of all sinners against nature, washing her hands like a sleepwalker, unable to forget the sight of the opossum lying there with its belly squirming with tiny animals. Horrible, horrible.

Just confused feelings, that's what, totally blown out of proportion, all of it seemingly filtered through the violence of that passion, all of it magnified by her. Even Suzanna Fleischman had become hyperbolic, downright poisonous, after the incident of the notebooks. *Lie down with dogs, get up with fleas*, she had written with rancor, in a bad humor beyond belief, with not a conciliatory word to be found. Pages that made no sense, dealing with Ângelo Marcos's censorial fury. "With Only Scotch Tape, It's Impossible to Defend Outraged Dignity" was the title of the piece, written with a thick German pen in black ink and large, awkward letters that at times gouged the paper. And she had actually tried to fix with Scotch tape the crumpled, lacerated mass into which Ângelo Marcos had transformed most of the sheets in the two captured notebooks. First she ironed the crinkled pieces. The result was not good but even so, she got the adhesive tape and, on a table, attempted to join the fragments of each sheet. Useless; she'd never manage to put together that mutilated jigsaw puzzle of hundreds of pieces—and that was when she went into a fit of rage, stamped her feet, hit the back of an armchair repeatedly with both fists, and threw the remains of the notebooks onto the floor, to stomp them. "Son of a bitch, son of a bitch, son of a bitch" began the first, second, and third versions of the piece attacking Ângelo Marcos.

She threw all these out, but continued to the end of the fourth, which began in what she considered a moderate tone. Instead of "son of a bitch" three times, it read: "The son of a bitch, who in my opinion, I don't know why (perhaps because every man who gets off on hitting a woman in bed is a faggot—cf. this point later in greater depth), is a closet faggot, despite his ridiculous sexual escapades, thinks he can do more than he can." And, with irony and anger she proceeded with a kind of case study, using no names, only "he," "she," and "the other man." It was well-known what he was: a thieving, corrupt, cowardly, tightfisted, swaggering, closet fag; a lying, vain, tiresome, hypocritical, ignorant, repulsive con man, et cetera, et cetera, et cetera. She was an unknown quantity, given that she herself didn't know. But what seemed to emerge was that she was a weak-willed idiot; she was delineating the image of a perfect idiot who didn't know what to do with her life and tolerated the indignities he inflicted on her, including the supreme indignity: opening her legs for him. If he wanted her to get on hands and knees, she would, in order not to argue. She already had, she already had, on several occasions, and even after loving deeply for the first time, loving another man, would she still get on hands and knees, out of selfishness and cowardice? Of course idiocy and cowardice could be redeemed through an act of courage. And the act of courage is to tell that son of a bitch to go to hell, walk right up to him and tell him everything, with emphasis on his status as cuckold, say everything she thinks of him, tell him to stick his money up his ass and start a new life. And it didn't even take that much courage, because she'd have a companion in her new life, wouldn't she?

Ana Clara didn't want to think about that, and she closed the notebook in order not to reread the passages that most disturbed her. What about João? How would João react to it? She opened the notebook again and Suzanna Fleischman continued implacably. The existence of the other man merely made things easier, perhaps quite a bit, but determined nothing. Getting rid of the son of a bitch was an act of self-respect and decency; it was impossible not to see this with total clarity, unless, of course, she had neither decency nor self-respect. In other words, no character. The same as him. The same. The other man had nothing to do with the basic decision. Yes, he may have been the fuse, and he could come to be the support. If he went along with her separation, as he should, so much the better. If not, it was because he wasn't worth it, another loser in a trio of losers. It's not with Scotch tape that you defend integrity and the freedom of being what you want to be—it's through toughness, concluded Suzanna Fleischman dramatically. Every woman has the husband she deserves, and complaining without doing anything is shamelessness, and the woman who constantly complains about her husband has no shame.

"I completely disagree with Suzanna," Bebel had said, much to Ana Clara's surprise. "I think it's too precipitous; she's just piqued because Ângelo Marcos destroyed her notebooks. Do you recall the days of rationality? Well then, a little bit of rationality never hurt anyone, even though I know you've been as irrational as a water buffalo lately. All this started with your eyes wide open, with no commitments, a joyful thing, although—and I've already told you so—I saw you heading for this. OK, so you got bitten by the love bug; it even has a certain charm to it. Fine, but to me, doing what she suggests here is more than just irrational, it's insane. It's true that the business with the notebooks was a crappy thing to do. But to go from there to insulting him and throwing up to him that he's a cuckold, or whatever—all that's only going to hurt you. You'll come out looking like a prostitute and may even stop a bullet, all for a stupid and irrational moment of pleasure. And let's face it, you're not used to working, you don't know how to do practically anything and you'd be making a drastic change in your standard of living. You don't know how important that can be; I've seen a lot of people go down the tubes that way. And that's even if João doesn't catch a bullet too and goes for the deal, which you don't know for sure, because he suddenly might not agree to marriage, which wouldn't be surprising, considering he's been single all this time. And, if he does go along, you're going to spend your whole life here on the island, in this stagnation, without leaving it, without traveling, without any help. You'll forgive me, but Suzanna is sort of in the we'll-live-on-love mode, which has never worked out."

"It's not like that. João isn't poor."

"Compared with Marquinhos he is. More than poor, indigent. You can't imagine the difference, so stop being stupid. It's quite different being the wife of an important rich man and the wife of a fishmonger on the island, however well-connected that fishmonger is and however much his wife loves him. For God's sake, why can't you go on having João as a lover? Has he mentioned living with you?"

"No, we've never talked about the subject."

"So? Another sign he's not on the same wavelength."

"That, I don't know, but the question we're discussing here is important, the question of dignity. I really don't want to go to bed with Ângelo Marcos anymore."

"That will pass; it's just a phase, believe me. And while the phase lasts you can find a way around it. Ask Marquinhos for time, tell him you're going through a phase of mystic exploration, make up something or other. There has to be a way, Aninha. What you can't do is this act of madness. Or, at least think about it a little more. A lot more, in fact."

Yes, she would think, she would think one of these days, and she would finally have to face the problem. But she didn't want to think now; she preferred to remain in this half-crazy, ecstatic state, as if time had stopped, as if there would be no future. And she also wanted to enjoy the very welcome absence of Ângelo Marcos and the very easygoing companionship of João without pondering frightening future possibilities. Could it be that everything really was a phase, could it be that it would all pass and she would return to the same life with Ângelo Marcos?

No, no. Passion, passion, passion so overwhelming that, after her rage had subsided, she began writing lyrical divagations and even two poems. How is it possible never to feel, she wrote,

that your body on mine is all
and that inside me you are all and I am all
and that your kiss for me is all
and that all is something only if it is with you
and all begins when you penetrate me
and begins again when you rinse me?

"Rinse me" is no good, Ana Clara thought; it sounds like something out of a recipe. *After rinsing the chicken giblets well in salted water, leave them soaking in a marinate of fresh*—OK, so the poem may not be all that great, but everything seems like poetry and anything brings smiles and tears to the eyes.

yes, to the eyes the smallest thing brings tears
and anything brings laughter to the soul,
the world is nothing but the reflection
of all that I imagine in your face.

My, my, what a deliciously pompous thing. I'm turning into a regular decasyllabic lady Shakespeare. A fifth-rate lady Shakespeare, but still a lady Shakespeare. She had started reading poetry, something she had seldom done in the past. Just the other day, instead of going to the beach she had picked up one of those books in bible paper that Ângelo Marcos used for decoration and begun reading it without stopping, until almost two in the afternoon, from time to time letting out a small sob of emotion. When would he be back? She didn't know because she didn't want to know; he had already telephoned. He was rather cold, but she had pretended not to notice. He said nothing about his return and she didn't ask, as if afraid he might say "tomorrow." But the next time she *would* ask; she had no desire to be surprised by a sudden arrival. And she would treat him very well on the telephone, to avoid an argument, as she had been doing since the day he called from Salvador to say he wouldn't be back so soon, because he needed to make a business trip to São Paulo and take the opportunity for a checkup. She was so happy that she even falsely asked him not to take too long and said she regretted that he wouldn't have time to stop by the island before going to São Paulo. Yes, she'd send Edsonil with everything he'd requested; she'd like to be in Salvador, to help him with packing.

Monster, she thought, twirling a lock of hair between her fingers. Yes, monster, because she clearly remembered imagining, the day he left, that it wouldn't be a bad thing if the plane crashed, and all that kept her from fervently desiring it was concern for the other passengers. "But, I could very well be a rich widow," she said aloud, and went downstairs to the living room feeling like sliding down the handrail.

Normally, around six in the evening João Pedroso took his second bath of the day, put on bermudas, picked up a book, and headed to the Largo da Quitanda, to read and drink until about seven or eight. But that day he didn't want to drink anything, because, after a few days' wait, during which he had often cursed Little Hand 3, he was finally going to meet Bará da Misericórdia. Nine o'clock, Little Hand had said, promising to meet him at the square shortly before, to take him to Bará. João couldn't risk drinking too much and forgetting or not noticing important details. Therefore he wouldn't go to the square, in order not to expose himself to temptation, among other reasons because, as soon as he saw him, Luiz the Waiter, without asking, always placed a double shot of whiskey on the rocks before him. And then another, and another, and another, until, feeling drunk though still with reasonable self-control, João would return home or, quite infrequently, chat with Lúcio Nemésio.

But he had difficulty not going. Not because of the drink, which he now did not seem to need as much, but because he was impatient at that long, solitary wait. Previously, without a doubt, it wouldn't have bothered him as much, because he had become accustomed to solitude and, when he felt like talking and had no one to talk to, simply talked to himself. After he stopped his long, almost daily conversations with Monteirinho, he became accustomed to staying by himself at home. But not now. Now, despite his original reluctance to admit it, he considered himself shortchanged. Shortchanged, he thought angrily. Of course he wasn't married to Ana Clara, and in the last few days Ângelo Marcos's absence had greatly facilitated their meeting and they even came to speak of seeing each other openly, clinging to each other in the darkness of the Fortress Garden and strolling along the Boulevard holding hands. But more and more João felt it wasn't enough to be with her for only a few hours. It wasn't enough, especially after they began talking so much in bed. Just in bed isn't good enough—and in his irritation he kicked the leg of the desk.

He had a wife, after all. A strange thing, feeling married to Ana Clara, though forced to be with her like this. He felt married, attuned, confident, in need of her. He had never imagined it could happen to him, but it had. And for that very reason he considered himself shortchanged. Funny how they always called the husband the cuckold and the lover the cuckolder. In many cases that might be the truth, but in theirs it wasn't; he was the cuckold. He was the one who had to share the woman he loved with a man she didn't love but who demanded that she satisfy conjugal duties. He noticed how he was thinking in euphemistic terms, as if he refused to face the reality head on. Conjugal duties, my foot; it was bed, screwing, intimacy, everything. There were moments when he thought of asking her if she still did it with Ângelo Marcos and how that could be. But of course he wouldn't; that would be nothing but a coarse exercise in sadomasochism. How could they bear it, go on living the way they did, how could he bear the jealousy, the disrespect, and the anger that more and more assailed him? And what about the need he felt for her? Right now, he would like to be talking with her, chatting about the upcoming adventure, perhaps even going to Bará's in her company if she wanted to.

"Shit!" he exclaimed, standing up to get the book he had been trying to read, but he felt he wouldn't be able to stand intricate scientific writing and picked up a magazine. He sat down again, leafed through the magazine, was unable to pay attention to anything, and rose again to pace back and forth through the large old house. And he ended up walking mechanically in the direction of the Largo da Quitanda. It was still too early for Little Hand 3 to be there, but there would always be someone to make small talk with and forget the things that annoyed him.

Would he really forget, if only for a few moments? He didn't think so as he slowly descended the street, a tightness in his chest and full of uncertainty. Even if he had the courage to broach the subject with her—as he thought he would, sooner or later—wouldn't she think it foolish pretentiousness, a wacky idea? He stopped, head lowered, interlaced his fingers and cracked his knuckles. Anguish, genuine anguish—and he began walking again, as slowly as before, crushed by the certainty that he would be unable to refrain from speaking of the matter and by the near certainty of her refusal.

There were few people in the square, only a small group chatting on the benches under the chestnut tree and a couple sitting at one of the tables in the bar. Tamanca, Zé Nunes, the scribe, the owner of the pharmacy, and two fishermen. Topics: fish, the moon, the tide, the wind, dominoes. This last one was the worst of all, because he had never had the patience to play dominoes and understood nothing about the game. He approached the group; it was indeed dominoes, with Tamanca describing in minute detail the unfolding of a game in which, in partnership with João Grande, he had defeated Nicolau Cocota and Crazy Bertinho. A quadrille! A lighthouse set! A spinner! A skunk! João Pedroso tried to get interested but he didn't understand a thing and sat down facing the sun, which was beginning to set.

As the sky darkened, the subject turned from dominoes to soccer, which João understood to some extent. Nevertheless, he got up, looking at his watch, and decided he'd have something to drink after all. It was past seven. Little Hand would be arriving soon, so there wasn't time for him to get drunk. And in fact, when Little Hand did arrive, a little more than an hour later, João wasn't drunk; he was even feeling better than he had before, as if something promised him that everything would work out, beginning with the investigation at Bará's and ending with his exclusive winning of Ana Clara. And he would have made the entire trip to Bará's almost in a state of euphoria, despite the mud soaking into his shoes, had it not been that a feeling suddenly came to him similar to the times he'd seen the lizard with two tails. It wasn't as strong and as frightening, but in any case the trees and bushes seemed to begin vibrating malignantly, and the night became darker and menacing.

"Where are we?" he said, stopping with his hand on his forehead.

"A little further and we're there. In a little bit we'll be at the foot of the hill, and then all's we got to do is climb."

"Yes, but what is this place?"

"People call it Jackfruit Hollow. You feel anything?"

"Yes. No. It's not that I actually feel anything, but this place strikes me as odd, as if there were something there in the woods."

"Holy Mother, all you can do is cross yourself. This place is haunted. I don't like to come through here at night. When I came with Father Monteirinho, the whole time an owl was omenizing, and to this day I don't know what it was omenizing. I told the father I don't believe in those things, but I do. You want to go back? Later I can tell the saint that you couldn't come—some other time. If you want to, we can go back; it makes no difference to me."

"No, no. None of that," João Pedroso said, deciding that the sensation was imaginary, although from that moment on he tried not to look to the sides as they walked. Soon they climbed the hill and arrived at the jackfruit tree, beneath which Bará was waiting for them, illuminated by a string of lights and with a pair of dogs at his side.

"It is truly an immense pleasure, professor," he said, smiling and extending his hand to João Pedroso. "I feared that, owing to the recent meteorological inclemency that has rendered the road exceedingly inundated, you might desist from the visit, a visit that greatly honors me. Allow me to introduce myself. Sebastião Boanerges da Conceição, at your service. But it does not distress me to be called by the sobriquet of Bará, for over the years I have become habituated to such."

Everything was as Monteirinho had described it—the man, the house, the surroundings. And also his way of speaking; it was impossible not to be impressed by that abnormal fluency, especially when one took into account his complicated syntax and pedantic loquacity, which emerged in a sharp, somewhat effeminate voice. They sat in the living room. Bará apologized for the condition of the furniture, and Little Hand 3, upon a discreet look from him, got up and went outside, saying he was going to have some coffee.

"I have long been eager to have the good fortune to meet you," Bará said. "I lamented it greatly when, initially, you did not accept my invitation, which I extended, believe me, for motives that I judge to be in the interests of humanity. I am familiar with your intellectual reputation, professor, which is concealed behind a pallium of praiseworthy humility but which I know to be eminently deserved because of your knowledge of biological science."

"You're mistaken. My knowledge is quite superficial. I gave up science a long time ago."

"Very well, I accept your most modest assessment, but in any case your knowledge is immeasurably superior to mine. The problem that confronts me—"

"I know. Father Monteirinho told me."

"I fear that, in this case, the report has not been favorable to me. His Reverence viewed everything I said with vexed skepticism."

"I'm going to have to disappoint you, but I'm obligated to tell you that I entirely agree with the priest. Your story is too fantastic to be accepted without proof."

"Yes, I understand, but nonetheless, what I told him is absolutely veracious. Did he speak to you of the creatures, professor?"

"Yes, he did. He also mentioned a mysterious gypsy woman and other things equally hard to believe."

"Yes, but the gypsy, if she really is a gypsy, represents nothing more than an accessory, in the case in question."

"And you also doubt she's a gypsy?"

"I neither doubt nor abstain from doubting. What I insist upon is that it is not necessary to believe anything, shall we say, supernatural, for lack of a better word—it is not necessary to believe in anything from out of this world in order to accept the story. He spoke to you, therefore, about the creatures. What is your opinion?"

"None. I can't go around conjecturing about something I never saw and about whose existence I have strong doubts. Do you have some additional element besides what you told the priest? Some proof?"

"No, lamentably not. I have sought information by every means at my disposal, but the results have been fruitless. After the first contact that I had with the creatures and their mothers, every attempt to learn of their whereabouts met with failure. But I have reason to believe they are still on the island, or in its immediate vicinity. It would be very difficult for the women to move about in the company of the creatures without drawing attention. Furthermore, they are extremely poor and simple people, as could be easily apprehended from their appearance, behavior, and speech."

"All right, Mr. Bará, I don't want to call you a liar, but how can I have an opinion on something I never saw?"

"Perhaps if I reproduced the description that I gave to his Reverence, if I—"

"It wouldn't do any good, Mr. Bará; we'd still be in the same place. I can even accept that you've seen these creatures, but until you produce concrete evidence or, rather, until you can show me those creatures, I can't say anything."

"But you must think something can be done; otherwise you would not have come here."

"Well, I'm going to disappoint you again. What brings me here isn't that matter."

"No? But Florisvaldo, the friend who accompanied you here, gave me the clear impression that it was exactly that. He does not know precisely what the subject is, but he told me that the priest had surely spoken with you and that you had found the matter worthy of further inquiry."

"Wrong, Mr. Bará. I came here for another reason. I came to ask you some questions about certain practices, common at your worship site."

"I prefer that this humble property be referred to simply as my home, for it is nothing more. I am not a priest of any religion whatsoever, though I recognize that some judge me to be such. But that is not my fault; never have I arrogated such status to myself."

"Excuse me. I did not intend to offend you; I thought I was using the correct expression. But, as I started to say, I'm here to investigate the rise of a very rare disease among us and I have some clues that lead me to believe that the disease has something to do with your practices."

"I cannot believe that, professor. Even those habits of hygiene that our people do not observe, I have attempted to inculcate to them. If you wish to verify this, you will see that we make use of running water and adequate sanitary facilities, as well as insisting on generalized order and cleanliness."

"It's not a matter of that; it's something more complex. How many dogs do you have around here?"

"Countless; I would have to make an effort to list them all, among other reasons because I take in so-called mongrels that now and again come here in search of food and shelter. But I should tell you that, on the occasion of vaccination campaigns, I see to the inoculation of each of them."

"That's not it, Mr. Bará. Please wait a minute and I'll explain what we're talking about. You also sacrifice sheep, isn't that right?"

"I personally, no, but some of the people who come here do so. According to them—and I have no reason to doubt them, although I cannot prove it—under instructions transmitted by me."

"Ah, you transmit those instructions while you're in a trance?"

"If you wish to use that term. The fact is that, consciously, I never recall that or other instructions imputed to me."

"Well, it doesn't matter anyway. The fact is that the sheep are sacrificed, as you have just admitted. Are these sacrifices frequent?"

"No, they are occasional. Perhaps eight or ten a year."

"And, according to what I'm told, the meat is distributed among various people. Are the innards given to the dogs?"

"Yes, frequently—"

"Mr. Bará, I think that both your dogs and your sheep—"

"I do not raise sheep; they are obtained from people who have flocks nearby, a handful of people. Because sheep are not very common here, sometimes they are brought from the outside, from Nazaré das Farinhas, for example."

"But most of them are from right here."

"Yes. Some people in the environs keep two or three sheep, for slaughter."

"It's like this, Mr. Bará: Sheep can be intermediate hosts for a worm whose adult form lives in the intestines of dogs. When the dog defecates, there are eggs from that worm in the feces. If someone accidentally ingests something contaminated with the eggs, he is also infected by the worm. A true cycle is established with the sheep. They eat grass contaminated with the eggs, become intermediate hosts, their intestines are eaten by dogs, who become intermediate hosts, defecate, the sheep eat, and so forth. But man can enter the process as well. This is because he may not only unwittingly eat something contaminated but may also pet a dog that has licked itself and then eat something without washing his hands and thus ingest eggs. This is very serious because those eggs go on to form cysts in the person's system, cysts that can settle in any organ of the body, such as the liver and lungs. And the problem is that there have already been several cases of it here, including one that caused death, although it's not a common disease among us, for one thing because we have very few sheep. And I'm inclined to believe that your dogs are contaminated and are causing the outbreak of these cases. The boy who died with a cyst in his brain spent a few days here, in the company of his grandmother."

"Yes, I remember a lady who spent, I believe, a week here, in the company of her grandson."

"Exactly."

"And the child passed away? But, that is terrible, profoundly to be lamented."

"Yes, it is. I only wanted to make sure of everything and report to you that an investigation will be made. It's a question of public health."

"But, I have no objection, if we are dealing with the welfare of the people. I am merely concerned with the fate of my dogs. If the result is positive, will they have to be sacrificed?"

"I don't know, Mr. Bará. I don't understand such things. I don't know about the effective means of combating the worm; I'm neither a parasitologist nor an epidemiologist, nor anything like it. I just received some information and decided to investigate. Now I'm going to hand the matter over to the proper authorities. But it's obvious there'll be certain consequences for you, I don't know what kind, perhaps a prohibition of continuing your activities; I don't really know. As I already told you, I don't understand the subject. My part ends here."

"It is not without its element of irony that the origin of the greater part of the sheep that you believe brought the sickness was precisely the hospital."

"The hospital? Does the hospital raise sheep?"

"Not at present, I believe. But in the beginning, after the construction of some new wings, there was a small flock that they later donated to the people in the vicinity. Some raised the ovines for a time, while others ate them."

"That *is* curious. And where might the hospital's sheep have come from?"

"I am completely at a loss."

"Curious, very curious. Well, Mr. Bará, I appreciate your generosity in receiving me and am sorry my visit hasn't been exactly a pleasant one."

"Do not worry, professor. You are carrying out a civic duty. Believe me that I harbor not the slightest resentment. What must be, must be."

"That's true. Well . . ."

It was already rather dark when they descended the hill. Little Hand 3 observed with pleasure that the owl hadn't hooted on either leg of the journey, but João Pedroso didn't answer because throughout nearly the entire route he again sensed that malevolent presence.

"But Augusta Street is always crowded, and the video store is just two blocks from here, open day and night," Nando said. "If we're talking about danger, we could be robbed right here in the hotel. It wouldn't be the first time it happened. You turn into a real hillbilly when you get to Rio or São Paulo; you'd think you'd never traveled in your life."

"It's pointless. I don't rent a car or go on foot, only by taxi. Especially since Tavinho got mugged, because now I'm basing myself on statistics. He and I were the last ones in our circle who hadn't been mugged. Now I'm the last. I mean, one of these days they'll get me; it's inevitable. But just because it's inevitable doesn't mean I'm going to put myself at risk. No, not at all. Trust me and call that escort service; we'll pay the girls, have dinner with them right here, bring them up to the room and screw. It's very simple; there's no reason at all to go out."

They had met at Nando's office a few days earlier, specifically to make arrangements for the trip to São Paulo, when Tavinho called and asked if he could stop by—he had to talk, had to be with friends. A horrifying story, he said when he arrived, pale, trembling, and with a bandage on his forehead. Around ten in the evening, as he was getting ready to leave, one cheek already shaved and the other still unshaved, there was a knock on the door and he thought it was Kathya, whom the people at the reception desk knew and who came up without being announced on the intercom, so he didn't look through the peephole and opened the door. He found himself looking down the barrel of a .38 in the hand of an enormous guy, followed by a large black man with a short rifle. He didn't say anything, but he took a blow to the forehead with the side of the revolver, and the two entered and asked where the money was. What money, he answered, I don't have any money, and the guy smacked him in the forehead again, sufficient to drench him in blood and require four stitches later. They pushed him onto the bed, where they tied him up, then proceeded to turn the apartment upside down. They took the credit cards, the checkbooks, the chain, the gold Rolex, the pocket Audemars Piguet, the television set, two ten-gram envelopes, the clothes in the armoire, they took every goddamn thing. They stayed in the building till 2:00 A.M.; they cleaned out everything, screwed several women—including Kathya, who had the bad luck to arrive fifteen minutes after they'd taken over the reception desk, cut the phone lines, and locked the building's staff in the storeroom; she was gang banged by two of them, right in the reception area. They beat up several people, ate and shit in the restaurant, and carted away what they ripped off in three large station wagons. The police said there were eleven of them, all with large-caliber revolvers and heavy artillery; one even had a grenade. As soon as the old man kicks off, Tavinho had said, I'm selling everything that's coming to me and leaving this shithole. I'm going to go live in Alaska. Anything beats this crap here. Maybe only rural Haiti and Lower Gabon are a bit worse.

"Look, I'm not going, and nobody can make me. Phone the girls. Ask if they have two real young ones for me, a blond and a brunette, who also go down on each other. I'm in the mood for an orgy."

"Not me. I was never into that orgy stuff. All I want is one."

"Ah, you don't know what you're missing. There's nothing lovelier than two pretty women going down on each other in front of you."

"I've seen it. It doesn't show me anything. I'm past that phase. But there's no accounting for taste. I'll ask for your two, don't worry. I've used this service before; it's the best in São Paulo and accepts all major credit cards, so we can spend as much as we like. The phone number's in my appointment book."

"Aren't you afraid Bebel will get her hands on that book?"

"Only if I were stupid enough to put down the name of the escort service. Isn't the name Top Escort Service? Well, here's the name of my good friend in São Paulo, Tadeu Orico Prado—T.O.P., get it? Leave it to me; I'll talk to Tadeu and set up our evening."

He picked up the phone and arranged everything. Perfect, three girls, all knockout university students, would be there in about an hour, entirely in line with specifications, and the men would wait for them in the Golden Grill, the hotel's main restaurant. And, while Nando went to bathe and get ready, Ângelo Marcos put his feet on the bed, locked his fingers behind his neck, and thought how this São Paulo trip was turning out better than expected, even in relation to Ana Clara—which, as a matter of fact, he had foreseen. The strategy worked more quickly than he'd hoped, from the first day. When he phoned her, advising that he was going to São Paulo and wouldn't even stop by the island first, he sensed that she immediately softened her behavior and treated him with an amiability, even a fondness, that she hadn't shown for a long time. The only thing she didn't do was to ask him not to leave. She was startled, of course, by her husband suddenly not being under her thumb like this. And she must have been even more startled later because, after arriving in São Paulo, he let two days go by without any word, only phoning on the third day and even then very quickly and in a tone that, if not cold, was also not affectionate. She was as sweet as could be at the other end of the line, a real 180-degree change, a change that became more accentuated in the days that followed, to the point that they were now practically as they had been in good times, at least on the telephone.

That's it, all right; you can't give a woman too much slack. This talk about equality, feminism, et cetera and so forth is disproved by the facts. A woman only likes a macho; it's a biological given and you can't escape it. She can be as independent as she wants, as open-minded as she wants, as modern as she wants, but if the man falls into that stupidity of treating her as an equal, he's asking for it. There are dozens of examples to demonstrate that it's undeniable. After the illness, he had begun paying too much attention to her, made things too easy for her, and you saw what that led to. In a way it was even a good thing that she'd written the notebooks because, if he hadn't found those writings, it might have been too late by the time he tried to get things back on track. Those notebooks were the clearest sign that she was losing interest in him and, if it weren't for the isolation of the island, might have started some kind of affair. Women don't have a very sound head; they're instinctive creatures functioning much more on a hormonal and animal basis than one of intellect. There are no exceptions, and anybody who thinks otherwise is in for a surprise. If the guy doesn't skillfully manipulate that irrational characteristic of their behavior, they become insecure and light out to fulfill their instinctive necessities in any way possible. A woman is female, as old Palmeiras used to say back at the university. Never forget that, he would say, in those memorable bull sessions in the cafeteria: A woman is female. First a female, second a female, third a female, then a person. And, as he liked to repeat, there is no such thing as a serious woman in the classical sense, only women who haven't been handed the right line.

Luckily, on the island there were no lines and no men giving lines. Who could fill those requirements? Some of the doctors at the hospital? Never. Besides their rarely coming to town, she thinks they're all insignificant pains in the ass. Who else? João Pedroso? Never. Not only because of her—she was always a snob and would rather die than put out for a fishmonger—but also him—a friend and a decent, respectful guy, shy and maybe a latent fag, past forty; he's never been married, and doesn't run around with women. End of list. Besides which, on the island everything is known and everything is gossiped about, as she herself constantly complains. Where would she meet her lover—on the street? In a car? Only if it were in her own house, but she'd never have the courage to do that, if only because of the servants.

No, it was stupid. Forget that stuff about a lover; that problem's been overcome. Stupid, stupid. Really and truly overcome, so much that, contrary to his initial intention, he would take her a gift. In the afternoon he'd gone to the superchic jewelry store in the lobby of the hotel and, without blinking, spent an incalculable fortune for a necklace, bracelet, and earring set, aquamarine in white gold, which she preferred to the yellow. Besides being a fantastic gift to which no woman could be indifferent, it was also an excellent investment, a lifelong patrimony, because naturally he wouldn't let her keep it if there were a separation or some serious problem.

And speaking of investment, that constituted another positive aspect of the trip. After long conversations and analyses with the American, who was really a shark when it came to finance and accounting, the advantage of liquidating most of his holdings in the São Paulo stock market, as well as his bearer bonds, in order to invest in dollars outside the country, was clear. Among other reasons, because to trust this shitty economy, which one of these days would fall to pieces along with everything else, is crazy, and if a guy doesn't look out he'll be heading the same way as the country, that is, down the drain. And since all, every last one, of his blocks of stock were up, the dumping was a total success. Nando, in a joking tone that nevertheless betrayed a dash of envy, even cursed such luck, which he never had. In reality it wouldn't have been necessary to go to São Paulo to close the deal, but it had been worthwhile, not only to give Ana Clara a jolt, but also because for some reason it was more stimulating, more invigorating and satisfying, to make money firsthand in São Paulo than in Bahia. Economically and financially, Bahia is a downer. Making money in São Paulo is like a Bahian soccer team doing well against teams from the South; it's a kind of consecration. Come down to their home turf and cart away their green. And furthermore, São Paulo, unlike what Paulistas themselves keep saying, is a fantastic city, a city where everything works, nobody is an incompetent idiot like practically everybody in Bahia, you eat well, you fuck well, you can find anything. In addition, there was the checkup. A real checkup can only be done in São Paulo, everybody knows that. Compared to the hospitals and medical centers here, the ones in Bahia are medieval infirmaries. And everything had gone marvelously, following a battery of impressive examinations. A surprising recovery, excellent overall condition for his age, minimal recommendations that were much milder than those for most of his friends: moderate habits, no smoking, a bit of exercise, low cholesterol food, and a few other trifles.

Ângelo Marcos sprang up, suddenly invaded by a wave of euphoric energy that made him feel like shouting. Yes, he was a happy man, a fully accomplished man, with everything that he sought within his grasp. He strutted to the bathroom, where Nando, with the door open, was retouching his hairdo and putting a fragrant gel on his face.

"Fine, man, you're beautiful, a veritable matinee idol, so let's go. And why're you so concerned with your appearance when the main attraction tonight is going to have everybody naked?"

"The girls aren't here yet. No need to rush."

"We can talk in the restaurant bar. It beats being cooped up here."

"Marquinhos, I was thinking. Aren't you afraid of AIDS? Here in São Paulo, you know, AIDS is nothing to laugh at."

"C'mon, man, this AIDS thing is badly misrepresented. There's a lot of hypocrisy among doctors because of pressure from faggots. In my day faggots disguised themselves; they were ashamed of being fags. Not now; now they have organizations, hold demonstrations, want rights and who knows what all. The doctors, so they won't be pestered and criticized by them, keep on compromising and talking in ambiguities. But in reality everybody knows that the only way to get AIDS is to take it up the ass or suck cock. Speaking as a doctor, let me tell you what the first signs of AIDS are: a weight on your back and heavy breathing on the back of your neck. Get it? How can healthy vaginal tissue transmit anything? It's made to stretch. It's true that I haven't opened a goddamn medical book in years, but I'm certain that repeated injuries are needed, multiple exposures, bodies weakened by drugs or orgies, and so on. And it's been proven that a lot of sperm in the rectal mucous membrane finally depresses immunological response. That is, you not only have to take it in the ass, you have to take it in the ass a lot. None of that AIDS crap. There's no AIDS around; you can dip your wick with no sweat."

"But it's always a worry. I read in a magazine that in Africa, for instance, a lot of heterosexuals get it."

"That's a lie. I mean, partially a lie. I'd like to know what statistic you can rely on in Africa, where most of the blacks shit in the jungle and don't even know what glass and paper are. And blacks really go for ass-fucking, everybody knows that. Not to mention their conditions of hygiene, with everybody having chancres on their cocks and pussies, syphilis, leprosy, elephantiasis, a shitpot of things. So infection is inevitable. It's not that bad, my dear Dr. Fernando, so don't be ridiculous. Let's apply the coup de grace to this downer of a conversation: If you haven't taken it up the ass, you have no need to fear AIDS. Have you ever taken it up the ass?"

"Not me."

"Neither have I. Therefore, to the wars!"

An extraordinary night. Real beauties these São Paulo whores, truly refined girls with excellent conversation. In Bahia they would be ladies. You could take them anywhere because they don't behave badly, just the opposite. They were exactly what the men had ordered, the blond and brunette for Ângelo Marcos and another brunette for Nando, with the most spectacular ass of the three, which left Ângelo Marcos a bit envious. He decided to get her name and call her next time. They spent some time in the hotel bar but finally decided to go out. Gabi, Ângelo Marcos's brunette, of Italian descent, mentioned Italian food, which aroused everyone's appetite. They went in two taxis, Ângelo Marcos seated in the back of his between the two girls. What breasts the blond had, a pair of veritable sculptures with a downy fuzz between them that drove him wild. He couldn't resist; he put his arm around her and stuck his hand down her blouse. On his left, the other woman moved and, noticing her skirt was halfway up her thighs, he caressed her knee and ran his hand upward, as she deliciously opened her legs. He even thought about calling off the dinner but decided that was gauche and contented himself with an ever more frenetic frottage until they arrived at the restaurant, a place worthy of any European metropolis, with a decor of the highest caliber. They almost didn't get in, because they didn't have reservations, but Nando, with the greatest class and utmost discretion, slapped a fifty-dollar bill in the maître d's hand and a corner table appeared instantly, exactly what they wanted.

A wild evening! Naked with the two women in his room at the hotel, Ângelo Marcos dived into bed between them, and one began to rub herself against his behind, while the other sucked him. What a sensation! And when they went down on each other? And him having them get on their hands and knees side by side and then sticking it to first one then the other in rotation? He came in both of them and could still get it up to continue the fun and games all night, though he didn't come again. He liked it so much that when they left, after daybreak, he couldn't immediately fall asleep. He lay in bed on his back, thinking about what an elegant night of pleasure he'd had, from the meal to the women—it's such things that make for total fulfillment of the refined, polished man.

Waiting until eleven o'clock, when Father Monteirinho would be through with his morning tasks at the church and working in the parish house, João Pedroso suddenly decided to open the center drawer of his desk and take out an album, not a photo album but an album of letters written in a small hand, almost printed, all of them addressed to him. They were his father's letters, the written supplement to what he had said when João lived in his house, which never ceased to assail him wherever he went and made him feel he was in a permanent hell of recrimination and guilt. There was the letter about the law school admissions test, which João had refused to take, an act the old man considered one of cowardice and betrayal. The letter about a real man's character. The letter about failure. The one containing João's biography, beginning with a childhood in which weakness of will and inertia were already evident. The one from his desolate old age. The one about permanent disappointment. And dozens of others, each remembered with its own special grief.

João closed the album but kept it in his hands. Why had he saved those letters so carefully? Why, despite the fact that it was painful for him and that he did so amid quivers and nervous interruptions, did he reread them? He didn't know why. But now he knew something else; he knew he didn't want to read them again, ever. He had come to see them, at last, as simple resentful insults, envious and unhealthy, coming from a man who, in spite of being his father, had never liked him, a man who, while thinking himself superior, was in reality petty, autocratic, frustrated, and repressed. In one way or another, João had always known that, but he had grown so accustomed to seeing things happen as his father had predicted that he had never questioned it. He remembered the day of his death. João had felt nothing. He refused to see the deceased, hid from most of the visitors, and went to the funeral solely because as an only son there was no way he could not go. He had often asked himself if he was not totally insensitive—as his father had in fact accused him several times—because of his indifference to the death of someone who, after all, had sired and raised him. And he had spent his entire life tortured by the Fourth Commandment. No. In the first place, he had never dishonored his father in any sense, always leading an upright if inactive life. Nor had he dishonored his mother, though secretly stifling great anger at her for never having opposed his father's acts of violence and injustice and never having defended her son against absurd accusations. In the second place, seeing the truth was not to dishonor. If a guy is the son of a confirmed thief and recognizes that his father is a thief, he isn't dishonoring his father. And in the third and last place, enough!

He looked at the album without opening it. "I'll never open this piece of shit again," he said aloud, clutching and almost crumpling the letters. But as he was about to replace the album in the drawer he stayed his arm in midmotion. No, why keep the thing? What kind of morbid masochism is this? What was so important in those pedantic and lying documents that should have been buried with him? Of course, João thought: Burn them. He got up, imagining how he would burn the album and leave only trampled ashes. He decided he would build a small bonfire in the backyard. Some twigs, some dead leaves, kerosene or alcohol on top, and fire. He found a small bottle of kerosene in the cabinet under the sink and marched out to the yard with the sober air of someone taking part in an important ceremony. He selected a spot in the middle of the grass, threw the album onto it and was about to open the bottle of kerosene, but suddenly he felt this was too much solemnity for getting rid of an unimportant collection of nonsense, picked up the album, went back to the house and, upon arriving at the kitchen door, removed the garbage can lid and dropped it in.

It was almost eleven, and, hands in his pockets and in a very good mood, he set out for the parish house. Everything was changing. Even the estrangement between him and Monteirinho, it now seemed to him, though he recognized he could see no concrete reason for it, was something that had been surmounted. Yes, he would get back his friend and the fellowship; he didn't know how, but he was sure of it. He briefly rehearsed what he would say to him. Perhaps a certain suspense, a certain playful dramatics. And he was still imagining how he would begin, when he arrived at the gate of the parish house.

"With your permission, Chico," he said to Chico Frade, Monteirinho's sacristan and secretary, who was on the vestibule chatting with two old women. "I think Father Monteirinho is expecting me. I sent a message."

Indeed he was, he could go right in, he belonged there. The priest was burrowed in the main sitting room upstairs, doing the orphanage accounts. João Pedroso found the door ajar, knocked lightly twice, and the priest raised his eyes from a confused mass of ruled paper.

"Why don't you get a calculator?" João Pedroso said, entering and stopping before the priest's desk. "You're going to go crazy with all those accounts you're always doing."

"I can't get the hang of machines. And I'm good at multiplication tables and arithmetic; I always was. But, what a surprise! How are you? From the moment I received your message I've been dying of curiosity. And I had a hunch: It has something to do with Bará, doesn't it? Have you found out anything?"

"I have, yes indeed."

"Sit down and tell me about it. Have you learned anything about the supposed creatures?"

"The creatures? No, not about the creatures. I was there and he gave me the same pitch he gave you—that he saw the creatures, all that, but without a bit of proof. I also think it's bunk."

"But did you unmask some fraud on his part?"

"No, I didn't unmask a fraud of any kind."

"Then, what is it? Stop being so mysterious!"

"I'm not being mysterious at all. You're the one who keeps peppering me with questions and not letting me talk."

"You're right, you're right. Go ahead."

"You're going to be so happy with the news that you might well offer me a drink. It's already past eleven, my time for drinking a little something before lunch. And today I'm having lunch with Lúcio Nemésio at the hospital, and at the hospital they don't serve alcoholic beverages. A horrible thing, but I'm only going because the subject interests Lúcio Nemésio too, and I think he's going to help you. So, do I get that drink or not?"

"Besides being mysterious, you're committing blackmail. You know very well I have no whiskey here in the office."

"But downstairs you do; that I know. Want me to go get it?"

Monteirinho sighed, went to the head of the stairs, called Chico Frade and asked him to bring the whiskey bottle, ice, and a glass. João Pedroso, despite the priest's impatience, only began to speak after taking the first swallow. But he was less indirect than he'd planned to be and quickly summarized the story of the echinococcosis and the visit to Bará. He was almost certain that the focus of the disease had to do with Bará's activities and that his dogs were hosts of the worm and were contaminating people, maybe even him. That of course meant that Public Health could act against the sorcerer and perhaps also meant he'd be forced to suspend his practices or face removal from where he was. He was going to talk to Lúcio Nemésio, who in all certainty would take measures. And, if suspicions were confirmed, Lúcio Nemésio, and probably Ângelo Marcos as well, could head the steps to be taken against the sorcerer. What did he think of that?

"You're right," the priest said. "A most lovely piece of news. Most lovely. The hand of Providence is helping the Church. When are you going to resume the investigation?"

"I'm not going to resume the investigation; I'm not equipped to do so. It requires specialized knowledge, specialized techniques and methodologies. I'm going to speak with Lúcio Nemésio. The hospital is state-run, so he can send people there to Bará's worship site to examine the dogs and do whatever has to be done, including closing down the site, whatever. There must be lots of things within their power. I don't understand in the least the laws governing the subject, but I'm sure something can be done."

When he left, he stopped in front of an oiti tree in the Largo da Quitanda because he couldn't restrain the impulse to admire the great tree, solid as a stone tower and at the same time alive and vibrant, inhabited by dozens of birds and millions of other beings and swaying its tiny leaves against the bluest of skies. He would have stayed there longer if not for a rustling that he noticed in the groin of the tree and the sudden appearance of the head of a large lizard among the leaves and twigs accumulated there. Did it have two tails, like that other one? Was it him again? He went up to the trunk of the oiti and walked around it, hoping to catch a rear view of the lizard, but the animal disappeared into the upper branches with such velocity that he couldn't see it. Could it be him? Why did he think there was just one, rather than several? Why didn't he simply forget about it? Why did it always bring him that feeling, practically forgotten but now reinvigorated, that something was terribly wrong and that a tangible evil throbbed in the things around him? He rubbed his head, squeezed his neck, and left almost in a run for the bus stop.

As soon as he got off the bus, he found Lúcio Nemésio standing at the main gate to the hospital, inspecting the construction of a septic tank and complaining that he even had to know about septic tanks, because if he didn't keep an eye on them everything would turn out wrong, and you don't mess around with a hospital septic tank. He gave a few more orders but didn't take long. The tank was almost ready; they could stop by his office, talk in peace, and then go up to the cafeteria. They hadn't seen each other for some time; one would think they were living in a large city. He had a pile of work at the hospital, which besides everything else is a veritable Sisyphean torture, because the majority of the patients that leave cured come down with exactly the same disease again; it's a bit frustrating. But, say, what's this? What makes the human oyster, João Pedroso, leave his lodgings to honor him with a visit to the hospital?

"I think I've discovered the key to the echinococcosis mystery," João Pedroso said after they were seated in his office.

"You've what? Did you hear that the boy, the one I spoke to you about, died?"

"Yes, I heard. He's the grandson of Quatinga, a fisherman friend of mine."

"Poor kid. There was nothing we could do for him. But you've solved the mystery? Do tell! I'm going to award you the Hospital Merit Medal, which doesn't exist but which I hereby create. How did it come about?"

"Well, I'm not totally certain, but I think I've found the answer. You've heard of Bará, the one that people call a saint, Bará da Misericórdia?"

"Yes, yes."

"He makes sacrifices of sheep. In those sacrifices they burn the sheep's heart, but the meat is distributed for eating, including the intestines. And the intestines are often fed raw to the dogs. He has lots of dogs at his worship site. Quatinga's grandson once spent a week at the site along with his grandmother. I started putting two and two together. . . . I'd be willing to bet that if they do a study of the people with echinococcosis who came here, all of them had contact with Bará. With his dogs, I mean."

"Fantastic! A beautiful working hypothesis. I'll send a social worker to verify it. It won't be difficult; there are very few cases. A beautiful hypothesis, and good news you bring me. If it's a localized, circumscribed focus like that, it'll be easy to eliminate. I'm not familiar with the methodology of such work, but I can get a sanitation expert from the Ministry, or a special team."

"The only thing that doesn't fit was what you told me about the sheep. You remember, you said you didn't know of any Rio Grande sheep around here. Isn't the disease common in the South, in Argentina, Uruguay, et cetera? In fact, there's one curious datum: Bará told me the hospital gave away some sheep. But evidently you didn't know anything about it. It must be a lie on his part, but why would he make up such a story?"

"Well, it might have been three or four years ago, when I was in the United States for more than six months. The lab people raise some animals there, and so do the gringos, but I never heard of a single sheep. But I'm going to look into it; it's not without its interesting aspects. If I can get this damned intercom to work, I'll talk to Dona Salete right now, so she can see to it—Dona Salete, I'd like a favor from you. Please verify whether, during the time I was away in the United States, there were any sheep here."

"I don't have to verify it, Dr. Nemésio. I know about the sheep. They came with Dr. Grimes, but later it seems he decided he didn't need them anymore and gave them to the families of patients at the hospital. I know because he asked me to choose the families and make the donations. There were fifteen or twenty rams and ewes."

"Thank you very much, Dona Salete. Dr. Grimes, eh? Of course, of course! The complete solution, my dear Dr. João Pedroso: Dr. Grimes's sheep were from Rio Grande. They had to be, because earlier Dr. Grimes, who came here in my absence, was working in Argentina."

"But why the devil did he bring the sheep? Was he developing some project involving sheep?"

"English eccentricity, weirdness; he's sort of off the wall. He was probably using the sheep for serological reactions and became attached to them; the English are like that."

"But if he was attached to them, why did he give them all away, especially if he knew most of them would be eaten?"

"I don't know. Maybe he was shocked at the poverty and hunger of people around here and decided that they needed the sheep more than he did. I don't know; you'd have to ask him."

"Why don't you ask?"

"I can't. He's in Germany and won't be back till next year."

"Yes, that business with the sheep is strange. My curiosity's aroused. What did you say this Dr. Grimes does?"

"Huh? Oh, he's a microbiologist. He does some kind of research with the other gringos. I don't follow it."

"And he worked with sheep, eh? Interesting."

"You'll forgive me, but I don't find it so interesting. Sheep may not be the most frequently used animal in medical research, but they are used. He may have inoculated the beasts with bacteria of some kind and wanted to see the results. How should I know?"

"Yes. Right. Of course."

But Lúcio Nemésio did not appear very calm, after the revelation. He changed the subject, turning to the contacts he would make to get a special team from the Health Ministry, from which he went on to discourse at great length on the stupidity of the bureaucracy. At lunch, which was rushed because the doctor had a lot to do in the afternoon and didn't stop looking at his watch, João, who was finding him odd, spoke of the creatures seen by Bará, and he almost choked, though he quickly regained his composure.

"What happened?" João asked.

"I never mend my ways and I never learn to chew correctly. I think I choked on a piece of chicken cartilage."

"I had the impression that you were startled when I mentioned the creatures."

"Startled? Why would I be startled by that crazy tale? No, it went down the wrong pipe, you can be sure of that."

Lúcio Nemésio didn't ask any questions about the creatures, spent the rest of the lunch in virtual silence, and said good-bye to João Pedroso even before the after-lunch coffee, thanking him for his cooperation and apologizing for the rush. Pensive, João Pedroso took the elevator down, and he remained pensive throughout the bus trip home. And he was still intrigued and distracted when, on getting off at the last stop, he almost tripped over two pug puppies being led by Rosário, Nemésio's wife.

"Sorry, Dona Rosário. I nearly stepped on your puppies."

"Not mine, Lúcio's."

"I didn't know he liked dogs."

"He doesn't like them all that much. They were given to him, but actually I'm the one who takes care of them. I think they're quite cute. Don't you?"

"Yes, I do. Funny, I never see them when I go to visit Lúcio."

"They weren't here; they were at my daughter's house. That's why you never saw them."

"What are their names? Do they respond when you call?"

"Yes, they do. This one here is Watson and the other one is Crick."

"What?"

"Watson and Crick. Lúcio's idea. I thought it was great. They're English and they really do look like a Watson and Crick."

"Watson and Crick . . . Funny . . ."

"Yes, I think so too."

"But not for the same reason. It's just that— Well, it's not important."

"Their walk is getting behind schedule. I have to be on my way. Good day to you, João. A pleasure to see you. Let's go, boys."

João stood under the shelter and leaned against a post. Of course it could all be coincidental, just an impression, but if he was intrigued before, now he was more so. Why the devil had Lúcio Nemésio given the dogs those names? Why Watson and Crick?

8

She was astonished. Flabbergasted. Stupefied, not understanding anything. She never expected a reaction like that, never. She hadn't planned to talk with him so soon after his return from São Paulo, but the situation became untenable on the very first day. She had always been very regular and had counted on getting her period on the day he returned, God's blessing. But her period didn't come, and there was no way to pretend, because sometimes he took Modess in stride and he'd catch on to the deception. As indication of how far these things can go: She even thought of putting in a tampon and wearing a sanitary napkin stained with ketchup—really! Actually, the only reason she didn't do so was because there was no ketchup in the house, and that was the truth. Her repugnance had become absolutely insurmountable.

She had made a serious effort to keep things under control for a time, but she hadn't correctly calculated her tolerance, which basically depended on the help of her period in much greater measure than she had foreseen. What a sacrifice that ardent kiss when he arrived was—fortunately, it was a weekend and Bebel and Nando came with him and good manners dictated that they not stand there sucking each other in front of the others, as she herself said, with all possible delicateness. And to make things worse, fierce opposition from Bebel.

"Don't give me that 'it's disgusting' stuff. Stop acting like a lunatic!" she had screamed, extremely irritated. "Stop acting like a prima donna. You've flipped out completely, and I do mean completely! Aninha, are you sure you're not sick? Have you had a fever, or maybe hallucinations?"

"There's no way, Bebel, no way! You can't imagine the torture. What am I going to do tonight? Just thinking about it makes my skin crawl."

"Tie one on. Do anything, but what you can't do is go on with what you're thinking. It's the most off-the-wall act of insanity of your entire life! Throw away a comfortable marriage, with money and status, to soon be sorting shrimp in the Market for your husband's customers? Where's your head, woman? Where'd you ever see such a thing?"

"I think you're exaggerating everything. Even if life here is a bit monotonous, I've gotten used to it. Salvador isn't far, and João isn't so poor."

"Yes, but that brings up another aspect. Have you talked to João?"

"No, not yet. But—"

"You haven't talked to him yet? My God in heaven, it's worse than I thought. It's stark raving madness, the kind for asylums, Thorazine, and shock treatments. Aninha, for God's sake, can't you see you're acting like a total maniac and trying to destroy your life? How can you do something like this without talking to the other party? And if he bails out, what then?"

"I don't think he's going to bail out; I think he's going to go along."

"You think, you think, you think. You have to be sure! Or rather, you don't have to be sure of anything, what you have to do is forget this world-class stupidity! So you think he'll go along, do you? How wonderful: You *think*."

"But, even if I didn't, I'd separate from Marquinhos anyway. It's not just because of João that I want a separation; it's for myself. I can't take any more."

"Aninha, do something for yourself. This will pass; it's just a phase. Everybody goes through it once or twice in their lives; it's normal. What you can't do is lose your sense of judgment like this. Take some time; go on a trip together. Travel is excellent for these things. Do something to save yourself, girl!"

"I already thought about taking some time, but it's hard, Bebel! You can't imagine how hard it is."

"All right, I believe you. But it's not impossible."

"Look, if I'm suffering like this because of tonight, just think what I'll go through during that time."

"I told you, tonight you tie one on, close your eyes, and face it. A woman doesn't have to get anything up to screw; it may be vulgar, but fortunately it's the truth. Tying one on'll make everything easier, and then maybe things won't go so badly; maybe tomorrow'll be another day. Am I right or am I right? You even have a pretext for a binge—his arrival, getting back together, that stuff. Did he already give you the gift?"

"What gift?"

"He's going to give you a gift. He's going to give you a gift; there's going to be touchy-feely. Remember, you *are* married to him. You let him court you, you went out with him, danced with him, did everything with him, so he can't be a monster. Go on, give yourself a chance and stop being so finicky."

So she did everything she could not to be finicky, and she did tie one on. Not a big one, but enough to make the wings of her nose go numb. She ran her thumb and index finger along her nose and couldn't feel it. It wasn't difficult; she had champagne, supposedly opened to celebrate Ângelo Marcos's return, lots of champagne, with strong encouragement from Bebel, who got a bit smashed herself, raised her skirt a few times, and said half a dozen dumb things that led Nando to say good night and go to sleep early, followed quickly by her.

And then came the terrifying part. First, kisses and more kisses in the bedroom, squeezes, and all the rest. She decided she would moan—not moans of pleasure, moans of actual suffering. And she moaned and moaned, while he massaged her bottom like a baker kneading dough and sucked her breasts, panting, until she discovered that her moans were giving him pleasure, after which she was unable to emit a single sound. Horrible to tell, yes, they went to bed. First he pulled down her panties, gasping even more loudly than before. And then he grabbed her by the hips and sank his face between her thighs, doing a thing with his tongue that she had never liked and that did nothing except cause an uncomfortable tickle but now irritated her so much that, even while preferring to be as far away as possible, she pulled his head toward her, partly to rid herself of that ridiculous itching, partly in the hope that he would suffocate. But he didn't suffocate, and he nosed about her in such an unbearable manner that she was forced to interrupt it and—the mother of all shamelessness—scream *my looove, my looove* in a voice caught in her throat, the code to indicate she had come, which she had used in the time when they got along. But she rued having done so, because, his cock dripping that repugnant fluid that had always made her close her eyes before taking it into her mouth, he lay prone, pulled her head down and rubbed his glans against her lips, then stuck it into her mouth and left it there like someone who wanted to come that way. No, no! He couldn't come like that. Barely holding back her uncontrollable nausea, she pushed him away, opened her legs, and had him penetrate her, while she kept her eyes tightly closed, clutching his back, wishing he would die, and waited, her face averted, until he finished, which he did with his habitual grunt and the almost rough push backwards with which he customarily withdrew immediately afterward, rolling on his side to lie panting, belly up, until, God willing, he fell asleep.

God was willing, thank God, and she got up, not making a sound, and, gripping with the tips of her fingers the sheet onto which had dripped what he had spurted into her, she used the same sheet to clean the inside of her thighs, then threw it into the dirty clothes hamper and went to take a long and meticulous shower before returning to the bed, to sleep as far as possible from him, with her back turned. She awoke, much earlier than she expected, with an awful taste in her mouth and decided to get out of bed and occupy herself to the fullest extent possible; luckily, Bebel was there to help. After all, holding on was her idea, so she had to help. And since she couldn't see João, she had to rely on Bebel. What a horrible situation!

The gift just made everything worse. How could she keep the gift? She was getting ready to go shopping and spend the entire morning at the supermarket and the vegetable vendors' when he, also getting up somewhat earlier than usual, appeared still in his pajamas and handed her a package, much heavier than its size would suggest. A little souvenir from São Paulo, he said, affecting a modest laugh. She was disconcerted, and for a second felt like saying she didn't want it. But she managed to say "Oh!" and opened the package. Three elegant cases. Inside, earrings, a necklace, and a bracelet, all in horrible taste, scandalous aquamarines in white gold done by jewelers with Parkinson's disease and surrounded by annoying circles of small diamonds. "White gold," he said, "the kind you like."

That was when she broke into tears and—what a terrible thing—he thought it was from emotion about the gift, but of course it wasn't; it was tears of anger and frustration, anger and frustration even greater because she couldn't reject the hug he gave her and was obliged to cry with her head on his shoulder. Fortunately, he hadn't brushed his teeth yet and had the decency to spare her his morning dragon breath, not attempting to kiss her on the mouth. She didn't remember how she thanked him for the lovely jewels, still sobbing. He finally left to do his ablutions and she put on dark glasses and a scarf on her head, got into the station wagon, and drove off with the tires squealing. On the way she had another crying attack, so strong that she stopped at the side of the road and dissolved into tears, her head leaning against the wheel. Shit, shit, shit! Why couldn't things be simple? Why do you have to do, not what you want, but what other people want? It wasn't Bebel's life, it was hers, hers! She had the impulse to turn the car around and go back and settle the matter once and for all, to return the jewels and say why she couldn't keep them. She wouldn't mention João, mainly because she didn't have the right to without consulting him, but she would say she wanted a separation, period. She pulled back onto the highway and got as far as putting the car into reverse, but changed her mind. No, not all worked up and looking like she'd been crying. It should be a cold thing, among other reasons because he might have a violent reaction, and probably would. She needed to be calm and in control of herself.

She spent the morning at the supermarket, filling several carts with an indecent quantity of purchases, including gifts for the servants and the servants' children, an orgy. But the morning wasn't over yet, and she decided she'd first have a leisurely lunch in the restaurant next door and then, one by one, go through the stalls of fruits, greens, and pottery lined up in front of her. She managed to make it to noon, the time she had for some reason decided upon. Was she calm now? Yes. Before pulling away, she lowered the small mirror behind the sun visor and checked her appearance. Everything OK; her eyes were no longer red, everything back to normal. Fine, but maybe she should rehearse a little. Marquinhos, I have a very serious matter to discuss with you. Yes, that was the best formula; no need to come up with some better introduction, no sense trying to improve on the traditional. I have a very serious matter to discuss with you. Sit down. I've been giving it a lot of thought and have come to a conclusion: I want a separation. Would it be all right like that? Maybe not. It was pretty sudden; he might get startled and have a very violent reaction.

And she was right. He began by turning pale and having a crying fit, his hand on his head and his eyes fixed on her. I can't believe it, I can't believe it. Why, why? He began to open the door as if to leave, changed his mind, closed the door, came back and stood before her. Why, why?

She tried to be gentle. At first she avoided saying she no longer loved him and used a half-existential, half-psychoanalytical approach, saying that she wanted to study, go back to the university, make some sense out of a hitherto empty existence, blah-blah-blah, et cetera, et cetera. But he appeared to find these arguments unacceptable, or else didn't hear them, because he kept on reciting the same "why, why?"

"Well, there's no love anymore," she finally said. "That's it: There's no love anymore, neither on my part nor yours. Admit it."

"What do you mean, no more love? How can you say that after the night we had together?"

"I'm saying it because it's true."

"But that's not possible. Are these some of Bebel's crazy ideas? Was it Bebel who put this in your head? I'll get that bitch! She'll see what I'll do to her for meddling in other people's marriages, that—"

"Stop it, Marquinhos. Bebel is against it."

"She's against it? Ah, so Bebel already knows about it. The matter was fully discussed, and the cuckold, the cuckold here!—the great cuckold!—the cuckold is, like always, the last to know. Oh, oh, oh! It hurts! It really hurts! It hurts! Who is the guy? Aninha, for God's sake, I have a right to know. I'm not going to do anything to him, I promise, but I have to know!"

"I want a separation in any case, Marquinhos. With a man or without one."

"But there's another guy. Of course there's another guy. You have to tell me who he is!"

"I'm telling you, the reason is that there's no love left."

In fact, it was that. Technically it wasn't a lie. But neither was it the whole truth, the real truth, and she had to ward off an endless assault, amid tears, sighs, panting groans, and tragic expressions. I beg you, I beg you, a supplication I offer down on my knees! What about his exemplary behavior on the São Paulo trip, because of his respect and love for her? He could easily have fooled around—he *should* have fooled around—but no. The sucker, sap, clown, the good little boy, the screw-at-home, the stupid impassioned husband hadn't done anything. He'd been like a monk, caring for the health and patrimony of his family. More tears and ohs and ahs and dramatic expressions, which for her was a full dress rehearsal for purgatory. A lovely moment, he comes traipsing downstairs with the jewels that she'd said she couldn't accept and, with one of the ugliest expressions so far, implored her to accept them, to give him another chance; after all, how could she throw away like this, so unceremoniously, without a second thought, years and years of living together and of love? Another chance, another chance; love hasn't died, we'll travel, take a trip to Europe, two months, three months, we'll see Paris again! And more weeping and grimaces and pleases—awful, awful. There was even an appeal to Christian charity.

But she remained firm. Firm even in the face of disapproval from Bebel, who, when she heard the news, was almost beside herself and fought, actually fought with her. Distressing, but true. Her presence wasn't going to be of any help at all, so it was a good thing she left with Nando as a sign of protest, or something of the sort. Later things would be set straight, because, after a repetitious and unbearable siege, Ana Clara ended up agreeing to give Ângelo Marcos the time he'd been asking for in whimpers. But with certain conditions, all of which he eagerly agreed to, including the one that gave her veto power over sexual relations as long as she felt as she did. Some time, thirty days, more than enough time. She even regretted having accepted such a long period of time, but it was too late to suggest a different one. Not only would it be disagreeable, but she also didn't want him to start up again with his lamentations and wailing entreaties. She never thought it would come to this, but live and learn. Astonished. Flabbergasted. Stupefied. Aninha, my love, do you know I decided to cook for you today? Give me strength.

Even more strength, because he wouldn't leave her side, nor did there seem any chance he'd go to Salvador any time soon. He was totally dedicated to Operation Reconquest, so unctuous he was a veritable tube of foul-smelling Vaseline, impossible to tolerate for more than five minutes at a time, tops. No, she had to do something to talk with João; she couldn't wait for some stroke of luck or remain in this situation the whole blessed time she was granting Ângelo Marcos. Of course—the most obvious things are the most difficult to see. Obvious, obvious. Why couldn't she just go naturally to the fish market, where her presence would be considered normal, and personally give João a message? Sure, it's silly to become all thumbs; things are really so simple if you want them to be. She goes there, hands over the note, and that's that. But what will the note say? Nothing about the affair; that's not something you put in a note, or a letter, or even a book. The note will merely contain a message of love and set up a meeting. A meeting where? At his house, by golly, why not?

This time João Pedroso didn't need any of the Little Hands to take him to Bará. He knew the road now, and the invitation this time was explicit: Bará had proof of the existence of the creatures and was willing to show it privately to João Pedroso. He was also afraid and requested earnestly that absolute secrecy be maintained about everything. The facts had changed greatly, and he was truly afraid. Remembering the part of the note where he had spoken of that fear, João Pedroso regretted not having called one of the Little Hands to accompany him. He was actually frightened by the dark and deserted road, illuminated only by his small flashlight. And the truth was that he preferred having company. He'd never been through there by himself, and he felt nervous and apprehensive for no visible reason. And he was also in a bad humor, spoiling for a fight, without patience for anything, irritated by everything. Now that Ângelo Marcos had returned from his trip and seemed inclined to never again leave the island, he couldn't see Ana Clara anymore. He had spent several nights sleeping badly, trying to come up with a plan to be with her, at least to talk to her alone, but didn't hit upon anything. He could not, nor did he want to, talk with her in front of her husband. It was more and more an intolerable situation, all that pretending, that unreal conversation, that embarrassment behind every word or gesture. In fact, he couldn't stand being with Ângelo Marcos under any circumstances; he had to make an effort not to turn his back and leave without a word. He had the impulse to tell him everything immediately and settle things once and for all. He had the feeling he would do something crazy. When, with an affability that made João Pedroso feel like hitting him, Ângelo Marcos invited him to another fishing party on his boat, he made up a lie in order not to go. He didn't want to go. He was jealous, he was angry, he couldn't tolerate this situation.

He doubted once again that he'd have the courage to tell Ana Clara he was thinking about their living together, married or not, but together, just the two of them. He was still afraid of her answer. And, despite not depending directly on the fish market, with what he had inherited from his family, he didn't have a millionth of Ângelo Marcos's money—and how could a woman used to that type of life come down so abruptly in standard of living? It's useless to say it doesn't matter, because it does; lack of money changes people. Could she have money of her own, independently of Ângelo Marcos? If she did, it would make things easier. She could provide for herself many of the things to which she was accustomed. But she might very well not have, and under the circumstances everyone would think he didn't want to give her anything. How could he not want to? It would be hell. In other words, on top of the separation, she was threatened with being penniless. In exchange for what? In exchange for this, here? All right, but he couldn't refrain from telling her, he couldn't. He'd have to find a way.

Distracted, he didn't realize he had come to Bará's hill and he stopped only after he had already gone past it. He looked at his watch—nine o'clock; he was on time. He turned around, climbed, passed the jackfruit tree, and found Bará at the door, leaning on his cane and looking very serious. He went to him, and Bará, without saying anything, bowed slightly, indicated the door with his extended hand, and stood aside.

"A very good evening, Dr. João Pedroso," he said after they were seated. "I am exceedingly grateful for your coming. This time, I think that the situation has become extremely aggravated and I judge that the case demands a strategy of secrecy. The men from the hospital were here."

"Yes, the echinococcosis case. I imagined as much; I was the one who passed the information along to them. I'm very sorry, Mr. Bará, but it's necessary to investigate the disease here, and if the results are positive, there's no way you can escape the consequences. And, honestly, even if I could do something to avoid it, I wouldn't. But is that why you called me here? I have your note in my pocket. The note says—"

"I remember perfectly the content of the missive, Dr. João Pedroso.

It was not to free myself from the sanitation authorities that I invited you; resort to such recourse is not my wont. The reason for my invitation is that found in the note, as you will see. I referred to the men from the hospital perhaps inadvertently, outside the logical order with which I intended to conduct my exposition to you. Perhaps it is because I find myself prey to intense nervousness, based on my belief that something portentously evil is happening. And part of that nervousness, perchance the greatest part, surely the greatest part, owes to the visit of those men from the hospital. Not because of the illness, as I already told you. They did in fact take some dogs for laboratory examination, but they seemed less, far less interested in the dogs than in a certain piece of information. When you were with the authorities, did you speak of the creatures?"

"No, no, I didn't. There was no need."

"Very curious, then. In that case, could the priest have said anything?"

"Wait a minute. On second thought, I did say something. Of course I did, but I mentioned it casually, not as an accusation, because you already know my position on those creatures. But now that you tell me this— Interesting. Did they ask about the creatures?"

"They asked repeatedly. And, although lying disturbs me and I have an absolute aversion to it, in this case I lied to them. I denied the creatures' existence, denied everything, and pretended not to understand."

"I don't get it. Why did you lie? Weren't you quite interested that the story about the creatures be investigated?"

"I was and I am. But I did not trust them. I distrusted their looks, their manner and gestures, their acts, their words. They seemed to me like pursuers, they acted as if they wished to capture the creatures, about whose existence they seemed to have no doubt—even without my showing them the proof, naturally, that I now have at my disposal. As I had already observed that the creatures' mothers behaved as if they were being pursued, I added, as they say, two and two and concluded that by lying I would be protecting those wretched women and their children. Believe me, Dr. João Pedroso, the men from the hospital, the ones who asked about the creatures, were sinister pursuers; I am absolutely convinced. That must be why, just now, I spoke of them beforehand."

"And the proof? Where's the proof?"

"You will have it soon. First, let me explain that I understand nothing of the art and techniques of photography. I had a simple camera purchased, equivalent to what in olden times was called a box camera but with the advantage that its simplicity was appropriate to my ignorance and its price to my exiguous means. I was always certain that I would see the creatures again, and I decided to carry the camera with me when I had notice of them. And I did. And I saw them again. And I photographed them. It was already getting dark and their mothers, especially one of them, tried to assail me because of the camera. I had great difficulty in fleeing, but fortunately I was mounted."

"Later you can tell the details, but now show me the photos. Now I'm really interested."

Bará rose, went down the corridor, and returned holding a yellow envelope. Really, he should emphasize that the photographs were not very good. He had managed to take four, and two of them were little more than badly focused blurs. But the other two, especially one of them, were much clearer. By Dr. João Pedroso's leave, he would like to present the photos one by one, from the worst to the best.

The first and second were indeed little more than blurs. On the left of the first could be seen what appeared to be the wall of a house of bamboo, and, on the right side, half crouching, a form that could be a person but could also be an animal or even an object. The second was almost the same as the first, with the difference that the form was more toward the center of the frame and seemed to have raised its head at the moment the shutter went off, though its features weren't visible, with the exception of the open mouth in which appeared crooked and very large teeth. The third one startled João Pedroso, who took it under a light. The torso, half in profile, of a very strange boy appeared quite visibly, though poorly lighted. A very flat nose, almost imperceptible, quite accentuated inferior prognathism, strange shapes.

"What enormous ears! And what's that on its face—hair?"

"Yes, hair. This one is hairier, the others much less so. I never had time to observe carefully, but I believe there are many differences between them; they are similar but visibly different. And here is the fourth photo."

João Pedroso shuddered and almost dropped the photo. Very well focused, though partially obscured by what was apparently the arm of a black woman, was a frontal view of a face that caught him unawares, a face unlike any he had seen before, an expression that gave him gooseflesh. What was different about that face? Yes, it was a human face, but not a human face. It was frightened, its eyes bulging, the skin wrinkled above the lower lip, the hairs on the cheeks standing on end, its strange teeth exposed, gigantic fanlike ears, and a very wide nose. Could it be a sorcerer's trick, some young boy in disguise? But it did not appear to be; it appeared terrifyingly real. It couldn't be a monkey, for no monkey would have that skin in the places where there was no hair. It also couldn't be a monkey, because there was no monkey with that face. And there was no boy with that face; there couldn't be.

"Where— Where, my God in heaven— What a strange thing, his look, what a strange thing . . . Where did you take these photos?"

"In Matange. They were hiding in the thickest woods there in Matange, in a place that one can reach only by foot or on the back of a beast of burden, and even then with extreme difficulty."

"And was it the gypsy who took you?"

"No, it was not. And that is another aggravating factor of the case. Several people know of their existence. The one who saw them in Matange was an armadillo hunter, who informed me and, although I asked him to keep it secret, told me that he had spoken to other people before me. It was he who took me there. I have done everything possible to prevent any publicity on the subject, but I am extremely skeptical of achieving success."

"Have you been back since then?"

"Yes. They are no longer there. Nothing is there except the skeleton of their hiding place. I fear for those wretched women. I am sure that, sooner or later, the men from the hospital will find them and then I do not know what they will do, but I anticipate nothing good."

"But, do you think the hospital has knowledge of the creatures?"

"I think more than that. Perhaps you consider me given to flights of fancy, but I am imbued with the conviction that it is something that originated there, something that they created there that escaped. You are under no obligation to take this into account, of course, but that is also the gypsy woman's conviction. She may not really be a gypsy, but she said something truly interesting. She said she hates those men because they are the same type of people who tried to exterminate the gypsies. Is that not interesting? *I* thought so."

"I'm becoming confused from all this, really confused. I can't believe it. Do you know anything else about them?"

"No, nothing, only what I saw and what I presume. But I am absolutely certain of what I saw and of what I presume. Do you understand now why I consider this of interest to all of humanity, as I told the priest?"

"Yes, of course, but—I can't believe it. This . . ."

And he went on stammering for a time, the photos in his hands, until he decided to ask to borrow them. He needed to talk with the priest, listen to his opinion. He wanted to think it over, see what could be done to clear up the mystery. Bará agreed, merely reiterating his appeal for secrecy, to which João Pedroso acquiesced, leaving without knowing what to think.

Back at home, he picked up the photos and spent a long time examining them under a strong light. He used a magnifying glass, but the film's grain was large, and the increase in size didn't help. It didn't look like a trick, but then he knew nothing about trick photography. On the other hand, Bará sounded sincere and genuinely apprehensive. What a crazy story! And the hospital—could there be something to Bará's suspicions? He really didn't know what to think.

"I don't know, I really don't know what to think," he told Father

Monteirinho for the third time, after knocking at his door shortly before daybreak to tell him about events and show him the photos.

"If you don't know, just imagine me," the priest said, after taking another look at one of the photos and turning it face down. "This photo, this one here, is in fact disturbing; I don't like to look at it. My God, can it be? I'm like you; I don't know what to think. I alternate between thinking it's all a crude hoax and something truly grave. And, if the hospital is really involved, does Lúcio Nemésio know about it?"

"That's the problem. It strikes me as impossible for Lúcio Nemésio to be involved in creating monsters. But the fact is that he's the only one I told. And he didn't pay much attention; he even seemed not to have heard properly what I'd said, preoccupied with a choking incident at the time."

"He could have faked not paying attention."

"True, true. In reality, even the choking may have been the consequence of his surprise at the information. If the creatures really disappeared from the hospital, they must have gone looking for them and then given up, believing they were far away. And now that they've found out they're still on the island . . . Can it be? My God, can it be? I can't believe it; there has to be some explanation for all this. Sure; even if I don't know why, it might still be a trick on Bará's part."

"That's true. That charlatan is probably capable of anything."

"You know, this time, he seemed sincere to me? And his fear also seemed sincere. And the truth is, I must admit, now that I think about the matter, there are certain things about Lúcio Nemésio that are at the very least curious and even intriguing. I know he's a brilliant doctor and a great surgeon, but I always thought he knew more biology, embryology, genetics, those things, than is common among doctors; at times he speaks with the assurance and knowledge of a specialist. I always thought it was a kind of hobby, but now I don't know; we have to be suspicious. And you know what those two dogs of his are called, the ones I saw the other day with Dona Rosário? Watson and Crick. I know you don't know what that means, so I'll explain. Watson and Crick are the names of two researchers who discovered the helicoidal structure of DNA, the double helix. In fact, it's customary to give the names of one of them to each of the helices. Why would it enter his head to name the two puppies precisely Watson and Crick? Why would exactly those two names be on his mind? It's circumstantial but, in light of what we know now . . . "

"And there's that talk about the sheep being from the hospital, as you told me."

"That's right. I noticed something different about him when he told me about this Dr. Grimes, the man with the sheep. Maybe he was lying, or not telling the complete truth. And, to bring sheep from such distance, from another country, just for serological reactions? I don't understand such things, but it seems excessive."

"Yes, there are some odd things, there really are. But as you said, it's all circumstantial. It may all be some perfectly explainable piece of foolishness. Can't they be mutant monkeys that they used in labs for experiments, like guinea pigs?"

"Know what I'm going to do? I'm going to ask him. That's what I'll do; I'll ask him."

"Do you think he'll tell you?"

"If there's nothing more to it, as I hope there isn't, he'll tell me. He already knows the stories of the creatures in any case, so I won't be breaking my promise of secrecy to Bará. Yes, that's it; I'm going to talk with him."

João Pedroso phoned the hospital shortly after eight and didn't succeed in talking to Lúcio Nemésio. Dona Salete explained that he had gone to Rio to participate in a conference and take care of a number of tasks; he would be back in a few days. Would he like to leave a message? No, no message, but he'd like to use the opportunity to confirm a piece of information: What was Dr. Grimes's specialty again, the man with the sheep? Embryology? But Dr. Lúcio Nemésio had said he was a microbiologist.

"Well, I thought he was an embryologist, but if Dr. Lúcio said he was a microbiologist, he must be right. Dr. Lúcio is always right," Dona

Salete said, and João Pedroso said good-bye and hung up, his hand remaining suspended over the telephone for a long time.

"No kidding," João Pedroso said after explaining to Ana Clara why his bed was so large. "I swear this bed really belonged to my great-uncle, on my mother's side, who used to sleep with two women—two sisters, in fact. So he had a special bed made, which I found falling apart on his ranch and had restored for myself. Uncle Dodô, a great man, he left two grieving widows."

"How incredible, for that time! Uncle Dodô must have been a wild man. But even so, it's too much; it's a football field."

"If you want, we can move to an old bed I have there inside. If you're into a sound track of creaking springs there's nothing like it."

"Bedsprings! I haven't heard about bedsprings in years! One of these days we'll try the bedsprings; I want to. But today let's stay in Uncle Dodô's. I love getting close to the edge and rolling on top of you, *ro-o-o-lling*! My love! My sweet love, my obsession, my macho, my man, my love! Oh, the passion!"

So easy! To be sure, they had set up complicated security schemes, extremely detailed plans, synchronized watches, all those great things from spy films. Thrilling. At exactly such and such a time I go through the front door and open the back door and leave it open, then you come out of the alley when no one is around, and then you carefully . . . Yes, but there wasn't really the need for any of it; everything had been quite easy. First the note that she handed him, with all naturalness, at the Market, after taking much longer than necessary to choose and buy a grouper from him. She was, so to speak, a bit naughty. She even squeezed his rear twice when, under the pretext of looking for a shark in one of the freezers, she slipped away with him down one of the Market's passageways. And when he bent over to look at the fish, she found a way to lean against him. He turned crimson and she felt like kissing him, but did not, as conditions of course didn't permit it. She watched as Boa Morte cleaned the fish and only then, after rattling on for a time, got the money and the note and handed both to João. She had to wink a couple of times, because he wanted to give her the fish as a gift, but he finally perceived that frenetic blinking and took the money and the note. The note read:

> *My dearly beloved,*
>
> *I am dying of loneliness, I think of nothing else, I'm dying of loneliness, I'm dying of loneliness, I'm dying of loneliness, I'm dying of loneliness, I'm dying of loneliness and passion. I want you only for me, at every hour, all the time, I think of only that, I'm dying of love, I'm dying of loneliness, I'm dying of passion, I'm dying of the desire to embrace you. I ADORE YOU! ADORE, ADORE, ADORE, ADORE! I CAN'T BEAR LIVING WITHOUT YOU!*
>
> *I'm not going to wait for things to happen so I can see you and have you, I'm not going to remain in this anguish and anxiety seeing each moment of life, when I could be with you, pass never to return. No, life is short and we've already lost a lot of time, all that time when we didn't yet know each other. We're going to meet. I have a diabolical plan (I'm good at diabolical plans, watch out for me—my man has to toe the line). I'll call you this afternoon, at three o'clock sharp, so we can make plans. But I'm a step ahead of you. If you asked that classical question, "Your place or mine?" my answer would be "Your place, darling." Kisses, kisses, kisses, everything, all of me, everything, everything, everything!*
>
> *Your wife,*
> *A.C.*

He had a stupid look on his face when he saw the white piece of paper folded among the bills and was about to return it, but she winked again and whispered "It's for you." She asked Boa Morte to carry the fish to the car, said "Ciao, João" in a way that she knew aroused him and left, swaying her hips only the tiniest bit.

The phone call couldn't be from the house, naturally, especially now that Ângelo Marcos, thinking she didn't notice, had gone into an obsessive crisis of watching her and was suspicious of everything, with seemingly innocent little questions followed by pacifying gestures with which he pretended to be asking from mere curiosity. At times like that, Bebel's logistical support was sorely missed. But soon the support would no longer be needed, because, whether Ângelo Marcos was ready or not, the separation would be absolutely final; there was no longer any turning back. Was Bebel going to break off with her? What a stupid idea! Well, one problem at a time. First the phone call. She managed to get away by herself and went unabashedly to the Grande Hotel in dark glasses and a hat with her hair tucked underneath, asked to use the telephone, and despite a light-skinned mulatto at the desk not taking his eyes off her, talked for a long time with João. Actually, not all that long, but enough to exchange sighs and brief declarations of love, and, most important, set up the first rendezvous at his house. A degree of sangfroid was necessary to wait for the time Ângelo Marcos took the nap to which he had fortunately become addicted, although, to do him justice, he was very punctual, starting to snore at precisely two-thirty. And that was it; everything else meshed quickly, as easy as could be, no problem.

"Don't you think things are a lot simpler than they seem?" she said, shoving one of her legs under João's. "This is the third time we've gotten together here without the slightest problem. And soon the complications will be over for good, because his time limit has to run out, even if it seems to last an eternity."

"You're right, we complicate things. First, the separation, which judging by appearances isn't going to be all that big a deal. Neither is our living together here; just the opposite. I'm even going to have the house straightened up to receive you, a few small repairs, new paint, cleaning, things like that. I can't forget how I thought that almost impossible, how I tortured myself, wanting to talk to you about it and afraid of your answer."

"You're really silly, aren't you? In that note I gave you at the Market I made all that clear. Remember how I signed it? 'Your wife.' And I called you 'my man,' don't you remember? I even thought I was being forward, before talking with you."

"Yes, but at the time I thought it was just a manner of speaking. Now I see it wasn't. These are things you only see afterwards."

"In any case it doesn't matter, because everything's going to proceed without problems. I even have the impression that he's beginning to resign himself. It's been several days since he's bugged me with that whining for me not to leave."

But it wasn't quite like that, for, a little more than half an hour later, when she was back home and sitting on the large upstairs veranda and scribbling some Suzanna Fleischman notes, he burst in from the inner room, livid, holding an envelope and a sheet of paper.

"Liar! Liar! A man kills over things like this, you know that? He kills!"

"What is it? I don't understand anything."

"Kills, you hear? Kills!"

He strode toward her with the hand holding the envelope raised as if to strike her. He halted midway, still pale and his lips so white that they could hardly be distinguished from the rest of his face, and started to hand her the paper.

"No!" he screamed. "No, ah no. I'm not going to give you this to read. The way you've shown yourself to be a perfect tramp, liar, and wretch, you might get rid of it. You're a liar, a liar! I'm not giving this to you; it's proof, concrete evidence, and I'm keeping it. Liar, liar, of all things. I'm speechless. I don't know what to say. A man kills over things like this, did you know that? Kills!"

"Ângelo Marcos, will you please stop insulting me and tell me what you're talking about. In the first place, I won't allow you to say those things to me; there's no longer anything between us that gives you that right, and even if there were, I don't like being insulted. Show some respect."

"I'm your husband!"

"That's what you say, but I don't consider myself your wife anymore and you know that very well."

"In any case, it doesn't matter whether you consider yourself my wife or not for me to call you a liar, because that's what you are. Lying, betraying, deceiving, disloyal, hypocritical. I, I, I—I can't find the words to say what I want to, God in heaven. What you did, I never imagined such a thing could happen to me. Great God in heaven, I must be having a nightmare. When you denied it, I believed your denial, I believed because I thought you still retained a shred of decency. And now, now— A man kills over something like this, you know that? Kills!"

"Would you please explain what's going on. I don't understand a thing. What's that in your hand—a letter?"

"Listen, just listen. How wonderful, how beautiful. See how you've managed to discredit me. 'Dear friend Dr. Ângelo Marcos Barreto: These lines are from a friend and admirer who deeply regrets the delicate situation in which you find yourself, being stabbed in the back. If you ask your wife about her whereabouts last Thursday you will get an unpleasant surprise. Ask her in whose house she spent the afternoon and who with, and—'"

"I don't believe it! An anonymous letter? Is that an anonymous letter? That's all we needed, an anonymous letter! Let me see that."

"Absolutely not! It's not leaving my hand!"

"And you believe in anonymous letters?"

"Just because it's anonymous doesn't mean it's not true. Where did you go on Thursday and where were you today? Because, when I woke up, you still hadn't gotten back."

"None of your business. I'm not a prisoner. I go where I want, and I don't have to answer to you."

"If you have nothing to hide, there's no reason not to tell me. You're going to tell me, you're going to tell me; I'm not going to be made a mockery of like this, the whole town laughing and calling me a cuckold behind my back. You're going to tell me; even if I have to beat it out of you, you're going to tell me!"

"Don't raise your hand to me! If you hit me you'll be sorry!"

"You're the one who'll be sorry unless you tell me! You're the one who'll be sorry!"

Yes, on second thought, maybe this was the best time to tell him. Not because of his yelling and the look on his face that indicated he was on the verge of attacking her with blows and kicks, but because this was as good a time as any. The moment had come to put a definitive end to this ridiculous and exhausting business. Why not? And maybe it was a chance to hasten the end of the waiting period, which didn't make the least bit of sense. Despite all the confusion and the threat of violence she was surprisingly calm, perhaps even triumphantly calm. What could happen to her? She looked him straight in the eye, took a deep breath, and asked him in a deliberate voice to control himself, sit down, and listen. She hadn't lied when she'd said she didn't want a separation because of another man. She wanted a separation in any case, as there were no longer even the slightest conditions, on her part, for them to live together. But, yes, there was a man. She hadn't said anything in order not to offend his self-esteem, not that there was any reason for his self-esteem to be offended, because she explicitly and manifestly no longer considered herself his wife, even before the day she first spoke to him about a separation. But, since he insisted, there *was* a man.

He almost leapt up, walked half aimlessly and staggering about the veranda, came back to a spot beside the sofa where he had been sitting and collapsed onto it, his legs sagging and hiding his face in his hands.

"Oh! Oh! Oh!" he exclaimed after a time, uncovering his face and looking at her with moist eyes. "It hurts, it hurts, it hurts, you can't imagine how it hurts. Oh, oh, oh, my God, how can you do this to me? How long has this been going on?"

"More or less since the day I discovered I didn't want to continue being married to you."

"Do you understand the seriousness of this? Do you know what you did and are doing? Oh, oh, oh!"

He got up again, paced the length of the veranda several times, smacking his hands into his palms, cracking his knuckles and clutching the sides of his head, and finally halting in front of her.

"Who is he?" he asked, taking the letter from the pocket where he had put it. "Who is he?"

"I'm not going to say now. Later I will, but I have to talk with him first. The matter affects him too, and without his knowing about it I'm not going to say."

"Oh yes you are! You are! You're going to tell me right now. I have a right to know! You have to tell me!"

"You don't have a right to know. If I tell you, as I've promised, it's because I want to."

"Ana Clara, good God above, suddenly a guy discovers he's lived I don't know how many years with a stranger. I don't know you anymore; maybe I never did, my God!"

"I think I agree with you on that point. We never really knew each other."

"But why don't you want to tell me? You think I'm going to do something to him?"

"I don't know, but that's not the reason. It's because I don't think it's right to tell now. I already said I'll tell you only after talking with him, and that's what I'm going to do."

"I don't believe this is happening, I don't believe it! I hear it and I don't believe it. Suddenly the world is crumbling, suddenly everything seems like a hallucination. Oh, oh, oh, oh, oh!"

"Ângelo Marcos, calm down. You're making an unnecessary tragedy out of this. You already knew I wanted a separation. You knew I don't love you anymore. And you don't love me; admit it. It's all wounded ego, but there's no reason for it. I'm not insulting you, I didn't do anything to humiliate you, and I never tried to diminish you. Not at all."

"You never did anything? You can look me in the eye and say you never did anything?"

"No, I didn't. It would be worse if I hadn't come to you to talk to you honestly and laid the cards on the table. I understand you're upset, but the whole thing can be seen calmly and rationally. It's something we can face in a civilized way, like adults."

"That kind of talk is very nice for other people, but it won't work with me. How can I stay calm, how can I stay calm?"

"Maybe, if you agree to waive the remainder of the time you asked for and I move out, things might get better for you."

"Never! Either you tell me this very minute who the guy is or there won't be any separation! No separation, you hear me—you're going to stay right here, you're not going anywhere!"

"Stop talking as if you were my owner. There's nothing you can do to prevent the separation. In fact, considering your machismo, it's even better for you that I leave at once. Let's cool down and discuss this like civilized people. Separation is inevitable, so why keep putting it off?"

"No, no, I'm not giving up any part of the waiting period. I'm not letting go of it, and I hope you have the decency to honor your promise."

But his tone had changed, as if suddenly he really had decided to remain calm. She felt encouraged to continue her arguments, but he claimed he needed to breathe and think a little, and, taking his leave in a surprisingly courteous manner, he left the veranda, saying they would talk later. He went to his office, locked the door, and sat at the desk, staring straight ahead. Yes, it was natural that he would be upset after that blow, but now that the initial impact was over, there was no reason to act like an emotional idiot. A man like him, with vast life experience and superior intelligence, couldn't lose the battle to an airhead whose sole cleverness was only what she derived from her gall. He remembered a chapter from an American book about personal decision-making processes, which he had read not so long ago. Of course, of course—he'd carefully and methodically analyze every resource at his disposal in order to confront the crisis and orient events according to his will and interests. Of course, of course.

Less than half an hour later, he was already preparing in his head what he would say to Ana Clara, which naturally would have no relation whatsoever to what he'd really decided to do. No losing his cool. He would stop accusing her and merely assume the pained and shaken attitude that the situation called for. He wouldn't continue to insist on knowing the name of the other man, but neither would he waive the waiting period, which was indispensable to the success of the plan—which, incidentally, couldn't be simpler. Another trip to São Paulo, this time much quicker than the last, to look for the best private detective specializing in these matters; there should be several very good ones there. He wanted nothing to do with Bahian detectives, who in addition to their presumable incompetence of a high order, would further expose him to the risk of the thing being spread about. Salvador is still basically a small town, and loves to gossip. Yes, São Paulo, São Paulo, hurray for São Paulo. This way, without any fuss, he would in a very short time have the name of the sonofabitch, along with proof of adultery that could later be used in a trial, if it should come to that. Perfect. And afterwards . . . Yes, what he would do afterwards was already decided too, but he didn't want to go over that in his head now. One step at a time was the way to proceed. Ana Clara didn't know who she was dealing with, he thought, standing up with a small smile of contentment and returning to the veranda.

"I've thought it over and I've calmed down," he said, with a hangdog air and his voice somewhat weak. "You're right. There's no reason for making a scene; it was just the initial impact. After all, it was a very powerful blow. And still is, in fact. But you're right. I'm going to leave you for a few days, go to Salvador and maybe to São Paulo. It seems like a way of recycling myself a bit. Maybe—who knows?—you'll even miss me a little, because, because—because I still haven't given up on winning you back. Something has to happen to prevent your leaving me. You're wrong about just one thing: I never stopped loving you. I never have, and I never will. I'm a wounded man who asks for nothing more than the right to battle on a while longer for what is his. Even if you told me the other man's name, I wouldn't do anything to him. I would just try to find something in my favor, as I am trying. But you can keep your secret. I understand. I understand."

He spoke a little longer, gave her a light kiss on the forehead, said he was going for a walk through the Fortress Garden, and left. She remained seated, the sheaf of notes in her hand and her brow furrowed. Very odd, that turnabout, very odd indeed. It was even possible that it was sincere, but she couldn't let down her guard. Suddenly, thanks to some unknown busybody, everything that had been so simple had become complicated again. With him gone there was nothing to hinder her meeting João, but there was the busybody. What if, in the next anonymous letter the busybody named João? Now for sure she'd never tell Ângelo Marcos his name; that gentleness of his could be a trick so he could commit an act of violence as soon as he had the information. No, no. A delicate situation. Think, think. And think fast, because even if his time period were greater, things were about to become untenable, because for several days she had known with certainty that she was expecting João's child, a child that, as all the couple's friends would know, could not be Ângelo Marcos's, who had had a vasectomy many years ago.

Despite being in something of a rush, João Pedroso stopped at the edge of the ramp at the Largo da Quitanda to admire the colors of every hue that the sun in the ten o'clock sky was creating, both on the water filled with canoes and rafts and on the trees, houses, and people bustling about. It was a Sunday with every characteristic of Sunday, a festive air, smells and tastes felt, anticipated, and remembered, a cow lying beneath the chestnut tree placidly chewing its cud. He approached it, caressed its brow, and stood there at length watching it circumspectly await the wads of food that periodically rose in its throat, and rippled the brilliant, silky leather of its neck. "Cow," he said, imitating the way a cowhand would speak, "*Ê-boi*!" And it seemed to understand, raising its head for an instant and staring at him with those large eyes and heavy lashes. "*Ê-boi,*" he repeated, feeling a tenderness toward the enormous animal, who had also shown up in the square to take part in Sunday. He spent a long time contemplating the cow, until a din in the distance made him turn his eyes to the canal, where the water was breaking into dozens of metallic reflections caused by a blanket of frantic mullets jumping and almost flying before a ravenous common jack, of which could be seen from time to time only its rapidly moving yellow tail. At the edge of the pier a group of boys yelled and applauded as the pursuit of the mullet continued out to sea until it disappeared among the poles and buoys in the distance. João Pedroso thought he would like to be a painter. He would like to let time go by and just stand there, transferring visions and deliriums to canvas. And he stood there for a few minutes without moving, executing an enormous painting in his head.

But he remembered that he'd set the meeting for ten o'clock and he was already late. "See you later, cow," he said between his teeth, then headed down the Largo, turning the corner toward Lúcio Nemésio's house. He patted his shirt pocket, felt Bará's photos and started to take them out to look at them again but stopped, almost as if he lacked the courage. Yes, he would have to see them again shortly, but now it seemed as if to look at them would ruin the day; it wouldn't help. He recalled that he'd thought about asking Monteirinho to go to Nemésio with him but had decided against it. In the presence of the priest, to whom the doctor wasn't close, he perhaps wouldn't get the answers he sought. But would there actually be any answers? Why didn't he give the whole thing up? Why not just live his life, now on the verge of such a radical change? Why did he want to investigate that crazy story? He didn't really know. Maybe he didn't really have the will to know, merely the desire.

"Sorry I'm late," he said when he entered the office of Lúcio Nemésio, who was sitting at a desk, slowly turning a large globe of the earth lighted from inside, and who rose when he arrived. "I made friends with a cow and spent a bit of time talking with it."

"You made friends with a cow?"

"Yes. On my way through the Largo da Quitanda I saw a cow lying down, chewing its cud. So I stood there enjoying the cud-chewing and I think I underwent a minor philosophical crisis in its presence."

"Interesting. I'm rather philosophical today myself. Except that my company wasn't a cow; it was that globe. Do you find the earth pretty?"

"Yes, yes, I do. Not only in those photographs taken from space but right here on the surface as well. Of course we make a great effort to spoil everything, but it's a nice little planet, very tidy and very orderly."

"That's because you don't live in the Arctic Circle. I expected that would be your opinion; it's more or less the universal consensus. But a being whose organic structure wasn't based on carbon compounds and water and who had a metabolism completely different from ours would consider this to be hell itself. For that matter, since you certainly believe in hell, you can very well imagine hell as an atmosphere of methane and lakes of sulfuric acid, or some such thing. That beauty you allude to exists because it is in the things that, in one form or another, meet our needs. Have you read Spinoza?"

"No."

"I was reading him, some time ago. He wastes his breath on those propositions involving God, from absolutely gratuitous premises, even if his God is less unbelievable than yours. It's not a person, and it doesn't butt into our lives. In fact I don't really understand why he even needs God to develop his reasoning; it's a generalized habit among those types. Even when you practically don't believe in God you have to resort to him as a conceptual category. I've had it with that. But, as to beauty, I think he hits the nail on the head. Of course—beauty isn't in the nature of objects but in our own subjectivity. I was thinking about that as I spun the globe. I don't find anything tidy; I think it could be vastly improved, especially ourselves. Take nationality. I look at those colored stains that define states and nations and I'm convinced it's total stupidity. Patriotism, languages more beautiful than others, people prettier than others, whatever. The only relevant differences are the intellectual and technological stage; the rest is complete foolishness. I myself don't divide anyone into Brazilians and non-Brazilians; I divide, for example, into feebleminded and non-feebleminded, scoundrels and nonscoundrels, the competent and the incompetent, and so on."

Yes, but he didn't want to go on in a monologue; some other day they would discuss the topic. What was the great subject of the conversation? He'd become curious. Some new discovery about echinococcosis? He had already sent some people from the hospital to Bará's worship site; the work was underway, and they'd soon have the first results.

João Pedroso had some difficulty in beginning, as if he harbored a certain fear about what he might learn. He remained silent for a few moments, looking at Lúcio Nemésio's attentive and almost jovial face. Should he show the photos right away? No, perhaps the best idea was to use them as the final weapon if Lúcio Nemésio denied the hospital's interest in the creatures or claimed to have no knowledge of the matter. And he began by speaking of Bará's initial invitation, the visit by the priest, and his own visit. He was on the alert for any change in the other man's physiognomy, but Lúcio Nemésio merely removed his reading glasses, which previously had been perched on the end of his nose, and leaned back, his hands crossed over his stomach, without interrupting João Pedroso a single time.

"Well," he concluded, "that's it. I thought it would be of interest to you. I thought it would—no, I'm sure of it. But I'm also sure there's a perfectly reasonable explanation for everything. I must be seeing things."

"Are you certain that these creatures were actually seen?" Lúcio Nemésio asked, with the same impassive expression. "Here on the island?"

"More or less. If these photographs that I brought with me aren't a trick, I'm forced to admit that I've seen them."

For the first time, Lúcio Nemésio appeared disturbed, because he abruptly lurched backward as if he had suffered a small shock, and reached out his hand to take the photos more quickly than he would have otherwise. He put on his glasses and spent a great deal of time examining each one, biting his lower lip.

"Who took these photos?"

"Bará himself. I borrowed them and am showing them to you in confidence, because he asked me to keep it secret."

"Interesting, interesting. Where did he take the photos?"

"Matange, in the middle of the woods. But when he went back, the creatures and their mothers weren't there anymore."

Lúcio Nemésio rose, went to the window, placed his hands on the sill and stood there a long time looking at the sea, which unveiled itself beyond the crowns of the tamarind trees at the edge of the docks. At one point he appeared about to turn, but he resumed his previous position and continued without saying anything. João Pedroso became nervous, thought about asking him something, but preferred to wait, fiddling with the photos that had been left on the desk. Despite all the Sunday movement down below, there was a great silence there where they stood, broken only by the almost inaudible drone of a strange machine beside the desk, which João Pedroso was not familiar with and had only now noticed. The sun, behind Lúcio Nemésio's head, made his rather disheveled white hair look like a kind of luminous halo. Finally, he left the window and sat down again, but this time with his torso erect and his hands gripping the edge of the desk, like an orator preparing to make a formal statement.

"No, João, you're not seeing things," he said, in a voice lower than before, and João Pedroso felt something like a palpitation. "I was thinking over there about how I would answer you. I confess that it occurred to me to claim complete ignorance of the matter, but then I decided against it, for three reasons. First, trying to make up a false version would not only be too laborious, but also you would probably not be convinced. Second, I have confidence in your scientific spirit and admiration for your learning, although I'm constantly surprised at your religious convictions, as you know. Third, and in one way most important, there's something that may shock you, but I'm being completely frank with you: What I'm going to tell you is absolutely confidential and therefore I'm telling you only because I know it will go no further, independently of your will, at least in a form that might affect the project that I'm about to describe to you. If you ask me why I'm sure of that, I'll tell you only that I'm sure, or I wouldn't tell you anything. I merely hope that I never have to prove that certainty to you. I'm not sure about your reaction, but if it's negative, I should emphasize that it won't do any good in any case. I shall under no circumstances permit this project to be harmed. But before getting on to the principal matter, I have a preliminary question: Now that you have perceived the importance of the thing, do you really want to know what's going on?"

João Pedroso, his heart racing, did not answer at once. He had suddenly become frightened and even felt the urge to flee. Despite having the photos in front of him, he refused to look at them again. Lúcio Nemésio stopped talking and merely looked at him fixedly, until, his throat tight, he stammered "Yes, yes."

"I lied to you when I said Dr. Grimes is a microbiologist," Lúcio Nemésio said. "In reality he's an embryologist and is part of a team carrying out a project of the greatest complexity, one that involves specialists of various types. After you asked me about him, I informed myself about the sheep. He was doing experiments with sheep embryos at the blastocyst stage. It's a genetic transfer technique in which cells are injected into the blastocyst and, so to speak, colonize the embryo. But that only produces transgenics of the mosaic type, which doesn't interest us because in the mosaics—"

"You mean the work is with genetic engineering?"

"Yes, though the existence of those creatures, as you naturally must have already gathered, is not the fruit of genetic engineering. Those beings are created through certain, shall we say, relatively simple techniques of fertilization and embryological manipulation that basically require only patience. But we're studying their genome, not only here but in other centers, since a project like this is too complex for us to carry out by ourselves, of course. Our part, in relation to the production of hybrids, for the time being is done. They're no longer here, with the exception of those three, who will soon be found and sent to the same place as the others. Which reminds me, by the way, that nothing would be found to directly link them to the hospital, in case it were submitted to inspection—something I would scarcely allow, as a matter of principle. We have their genetic material stockpiled, naturally, but it can only be identified by the team responsible and no one else. And we continue our work, to which unfortunately you are opposed because of sheer obscurantism and—forgive my saying it—superstition. You'd be surprised at some of our victories, in coordination with other centers. For example, in the production of transgenic animals we apply techniques that the gringos call 'differential interference microscopy'; we don't use centrifuges anymore. In a certain manner, these techniques are at the heart of a survival rate of transgenic ova superior—greatly superior—to those obtained by other researchers. Generally, in large mammals, where the cytoplasm in the ova gets in the way of manipulation, the rate is around one percent. But here we're already close to five percent and rising. The creatures, as you call them, are hybrids, not actually transgenic animals, although our intention is to produce some of these animals from their genetic material. At the same time, they're a project parallel to the genetic projects and also a convergent project. This work, obviously, involving from one hundred thousand to two hundred thousand genes, is not a simple thing, but in the future, the prediction is that we won't use conventional fertilization processes for their production but, yes, direct genetic manipulation, though I must admit that's still pretty far off. I know you're aware of this, but you don't know about the progress we've made. The most unexpected transgenic animals can already be produced, even between species biologically quite diverse—man with lizard, for example."

"Man with what? Did you say lizard?"

"Yes, I said lizard, just as it could be a parrot. It was just an example."

"And has anybody been doing experiments with lizards here?"

"Not that I know of. Unless it was some nut testing a hypothesis on his own time. But not that I know of. Why?"

"Nothing. But I want to hear more of this story. Lúcio, I'm absolutely dumbstruck. I can't believe all this. And you—"

"Believe it, because it's true. There are similar experiments in other centers, some of which work in coordination with us. Our center was chosen to carry out this type of work because it offers very good conditions. In spite of the immense backwardness and poverty of the region, there's a large city nearby, capable of handling a great many things. And here we have at our disposal women whose uteruses we can use for the fixation of the egg. As you can imagine, it's rather difficult to convince a woman to gestate and give birth to a, shall we say, aberrant baby. The choice was limited to monkeys, of course, female chimpanzees. That, however, handicaps important aspects of the research, because, raised by a monkey, the creature's development is sure to be different from what it would be if it were raised by a natural human mother. And there are the processes of socialization, learning, et cetera, that can only be studied correctly in such conditions. We chose black women. Not from any prejudice on our part but because, in a way, of the overall prejudice. We chose black women because white society thinks blacks are like monkeys. That can prevent certain practical problems. We also gave preference to black women who were genetically alopecic, except for the hair on their heads and a bit on the pubis. By doing so, I think we managed to minimize a bit the problem of the creature's fur, which is surprisingly accentuated. We applied a battery of ovulatory hormones to the women, frequently obtaining three or four ovules per ovulation and that way we achieved better indices of success in the insemination."

"But the women, the women! Used as guinea pigs, forced to lend their bodies to those experiments! How can anyone do such a thing?"

"Guinea pigs, yes, but you know very well that use of human guinea pigs is quite common in many cases; I see no problem in it. For one thing, it's not like you said. They weren't forced; all of them agreed fully with the terms of the project."

"I don't believe that, of course. If it were so, three of them wouldn't have run away."

"It was all a misunderstanding. One of the women, who led the others, is a little unbalanced and was undergoing treatment. But I'm sure they'll be easily persuaded to return. With us they're in a situation that affords them many advantages, of all kinds. They're treated quite well, in every sense."

"Great God in heaven, I can't believe it! Lúcio, don't you see the monstrosity of all this? My God, Lúcio, it's not true. You're joking with me!"

But, attaching no importance to João Pedroso's bulging eyes and paleness, he said it was not a joke. And he continued to talk, as if he took pleasure in giving that exposition in the most minute and objective manner possible, in a tone utterly devoid of emotion. It wasn't a question of some Brave New World type of project. The intention, at least for now, wasn't the production of large numbers of the creatures, among other reasons because of the objections they would have to confront from reactionary forces, i.e., most of society. It was a question of creating a limited number of them, a number already attained, for a series of studies. The hypothetical utility was great, from setting up organ banks to testing of medicines and vaccines. In addition to, of course, more sophisticated steps still impossible but perfectly within the realm of conjecture, such as the use of neuronic structures instead of certain chips, in electronic circuits, with vast implications for processing capacity and the development of artificial intelligence.

No, no, of course they weren't people; they were animals, children of monkeys. And, as animals, anything could be done to them. João Pedroso himself, who loved animals, nevertheless told of eating even cats. And he would eat the cow with which he had made friends. And he would collaborate professionally, if such were the case, in developing breeds better suited for slaughter. Also, he thought nothing about chickens on poultry farms having their beaks clipped and being raised in tiny cubicles like veritable machines transforming vegetable protein into animal protein, which was in fact what they were, all hypocrisy aside—a hypocrisy reflected even in the euphemisms used to devour the flesh of cadavers. Even killing an animal is nobly designated as "slaughter" and not "killing." Slaughtered chickens, not dead chickens. Cattle on the hoof, not living cattle, before being killed, and so forth.

The soul again? What is the soul? In any case, being an animal and not a man, the creature, according to those who believe in the soul, has no soul. And even taking into account the argument of God and evolution, there is nothing in the project, technically, that contradicts either God or evolution. God created the world and with it, evolution. Fine. Man is the fruit of that evolution and therefore whatever is fruit of him is also, indirectly, the fruit of evolution. A logically unanswerable argument, whatever João Pedroso might say. The creatures were the fruit of evolution the same as modern varieties of corn, cattle, et cetera. And if God creates everything in this world, the creatures also came from him, like mules and other hybrids. And, one way or another, it was a program that would benefit an incalculable number of people, so superstitious objections couldn't be allowed to get in the way. Man is only one part in a thousand of a biomass of two thousand billion tons, but he should develop the capacity of total control over that biomass, using it for his total and exclusive benefit.

"We still have to find out if people want that benefit," João Pedroso said, now feeling a mixture of fear and anger and asking himself whether Lúcio Nemésio wasn't mad, raving mad. "People should be consulted. People don't consider themselves merely particles of one part in a thousand of the earth's biomass."

"But that's what they are. And that business about consulting them is superstitious claptrap. No one should be consulted; no one understands enough about the subject to guide these decisions. There's nothing more ridiculous than the so-called ignorant masses having an opinion on something they don't understand and superseding the opinion of those who do understand. It's the same as that leveling and demagogic chicanery that lets students and semi-illiterate employees elect university presidents, department heads, and professors. Democracy is a farce, and you know that very well. What does an elected president understand about the matters he decides upon—nuclear physics, electric power, transportation, agriculture, public finance, et cetera, et cetera, et cetera? Nothing, of course. The ones who decide are the appointed advisers, the specialists. And that's how it should be; the ones to decide are those who understand. This democracy stuff is really just superstition, an obsolete fetish, just like nationalism, the fatherland concept and such."

"Lúcio, I'll tell you what I think. What I think is that you're mad, completely mad. And you were wrong when you said I wouldn't pass anything on. It's my duty to pass everything on, to do all I can to impede this monstrosity, and I'm going to."

"I'm not the least bit crazy. You're the one who's crazy, prisoner of a bunch of ridiculous notions devoid of rationality," Lúcio Nemésio said, picking up the photos as if shuffling a deck of cards and, with a casual gesture, throwing them into the machine beside the desk.

"What's that you did with the photos?"

"This machine is American. It's very useful when you're involved in a project like mine. It's called a paper shredder. When you put paper in, it reduces it to very thin strips. The paper turns to shavings, more or less. That's what I've just done to your photos, which should be sufficient to show I wasn't joking when I told you I wouldn't permit anything to harm the project."

"You can't do that!"

"I just did."

"The photos don't belong to you! This is an unspeakable act of violence!"

"Perhaps, but it's as I told you. I'm very sorry you've made the decision that you've made, which is a disappointment to me, although to a certain extent I expected it."

"Lúcio, you can be sure that I'm going to fight against this, you'll see!"

"It won't do any good; it's a waste of time. Or maybe more than that."

"Are you threatening me?"

"Not I. You're the one who's threatening me, by threatening my project."

"I'm going to fight, I'm going to fight!"

"Do whatever you like. As I've already said, I would much prefer that it not happen. You wanted to know about things, and I told you the truth. But that's no reason, I repeat, for me to permit the project to be harmed."

"You're crazy, Lúcio, crazy, completely crazy."

João Pedroso left without saying good-bye, almost in a run. Lúcio Nemésio got up, walked after him to the door, stopped trying to keep up with him, and went back to his desk. He turned off the paper shredder, examined the unrecognizable remains of the photos, sat for a long time in thought, his hand on his chin, then picked up the phone.

"Dona Salete? Forgive my bothering you on your day off, but an emergency has arisen. Call the entire staff of both annexes. I want to hold a quick meeting. I'm going to the Hospital right now. Find the secretary of health in Salvador; I want to talk to him. I'm going to need a team of sanitation control workers this very day. And call the shock people from our own team also; they'll go with the control workers. And also get hold of the judge; I need a court order to take certain steps at a *candomblé* site where there's a focus of a very serious disease. We have to eliminate it."

He gave further instructions, hung up the telephone, put on a jacket with leather patches on the elbows, went downstairs, got in his car and drove to the hospital. If this was how João Pedroso wanted it, this was how it would be.

9

Yes, the story had been printed. To be sure, in a newspaper with a limited circulation and it was very different from what they wanted, but at least it was something. Father Monteirinho took the paper from João Pedroso's hands again and read the headline: "Creation of Genetic Monsters Denounced on the Island." Two photos with captions, one of Bará—"Healer says the proof has disappeared"—and another of João Pedroso—"Biologist affirms his certainty of the existence of the monsters." The text, which both read several times with anger and displeasure, was far from convincing. Despite the caption under his photo, João Pedroso was mentioned as "a fish vendor, although claiming to be a graduate biologist." And all the information, which he had passed along in as much detail and with as much clarity as he could, was garbled, beginning with the headline, an incomprehensible and contradictory series of howlers. And there was just one reference to the hospital: "At that nosocomial facility a receptionist informed us that the administration became aware of the fact only through the reporter and that the story was so absurd as not to merit comment."

"I'm beginning to think it would've been better not to have the coverage," João Pedroso said. "I think this hurts rather than helps us."

But what else could they have done? Immediately after his conversation with Lúcio Nemésio, João Pedroso had burst breathlessly into the parish house, in such a state that Monteirinho put down the silverware on the plate from which he was having lunch and asked if he was having a heart attack.

"Maybe I am, maybe I am. But finish your lunch and I'll tell you. Go on, finish your lunch, finish it, go on!"

"Sit down. I'll order a plate for you."

"No, no, I don't want anything. I can't even think about food."

"But, what happened? You're completely beside yourself, with your eyes bulging, your hair every which way. Were you in a fight with someone?"

"No, no. No, Monteirinho, it's nothing like that. Finish your lunch. Go ahead, finish it!"

"I'm done. How can I eat lunch with you standing there looking as if you'd seen a couple of hundred apparitions? Dona Marta, please, you may clear the table. Let's get out of here, João. Let's go to the library and talk."

"I didn't mean to interrupt your lunch. Forgive me."

"It's all right. No matter, I don't like roast beef all that much in any case, and a little fasting now and then is good for you."

In the library, with trembling hands João Pedroso lit a cigarette, took two deep drags, and told of his conversation with Lúcio Nemésio.

"I can't believe it," the priest said. "I can't. It's too monstrous to be true."

"But it is true, it is! He told me all that, insisting it wasn't a joke."

"But don't you think he'd be running too big a risk in telling you those things? After all, he can't guarantee you won't go spreading it around."

"No, he says he's running no risk at all. I don't know, he seems like he's crazy, like he took pleasure in telling me all that, as if it were a question of professional pride. And he repeated several times that he was absolutely sure I couldn't do anything."

"What about the photos?"

"Oh, I forgot to tell you that. You can't imagine what happened. I committed the enormous stupidity of showing him the photos. And then, at the end of the conversation, he very casually took the photos from the top of the desk and threw all three of them into a machine he has to destroy papers and documents."

"He what? My God!"

"Just what you heard. The photos were reduced to tiny shreds."

"But there are negatives, aren't there? Bará must have the negatives."

"That's right! Yes, Bará! Wait, could it be that Lúcio Nemésio plans to take some action against Bará? Of course he does. If he was capable of destroying the photos in that cynical manner, of course he's going to do something, of course he is!"

"Yes, everything indicates as much. Among other reasons, because he has the excuse of that disease whose focus you say is at the worship site."

"That's true. I have to go there right now. Lend me your jeep. I'll go by jeep as far as I can and then run to the site."

"I can't. The jeep is in the repair shop with a broken radiator. Pepeu said it'd be ready tomorrow."

"No, it has to be ready today. I have to talk with Bará now; it's the only chance to do something to expose this business."

"But today's Sunday. Pepeu must be around somewhere, drinking rum after fishing."

"Yeah, but he's going to have to work something out. I'm on my way; I can't afford to lose any time."

He emptied his glass and headed down Direita Street almost in a sprint. Pepeu usually drank rum in one of the bars in the Largo da Quitanda and must surely be there. But he wasn't. He was at a *feijoada* lunch at Honorino's house. On the hill, near Raul Grande's place. And where was Raul Grande's place? More or less near the church. João Pedroso offered a boy money to take him there, climbed the hill so quickly that he almost couldn't speak when he arrived at the top and finally located Honorino's house. No, he didn't want to have a drink, some other time. He just urgently needed to talk to Pepeu; where was he? He'd gone for beer and wouldn't be long. João Pedroso, responding with only gestures and an embarrassed smile to what they told him, waited at the window for what seemed an eternity, until, some ten minutes later, Pepeu, staggering a bit, appeared at the corner carrying a sack filled with bottles.

"Pepeu! I have to talk to you! It's urgent!"

He began talking while he was still in the street. Pepeu seemed to have trouble understanding him. He'd had a few, it was Sunday, what could be all that urgent? It wouldn't do any good to mess around with the radiator in the priest's jeep, which incidentally also had problems with its starter motor. The radiator wasn't any good; it had more holes than a sieve and needed to be replaced. Pepeu was going to buy one Monday in Salvador. But João Pedroso insisted; there had to be a way, even if it meant adapting the radiator of one of the junk cars that he knew were kept at the garage for just that purpose, so their parts could be used for repairs.

"It'll be one godawful sloppy job," Pepeu said. "I can't guarantee a thing."

"It's all right. You don't have to guarantee it; I'll take responsibility."

"Can't we have lunch first? The *feijoada*'s about ready, and it's Honorino's birthday. He's my buddy and might take offense."

"No. Don't worry about him being offended. I'll talk to him."

Honorino was indeed not offended, but he'd had a few himself and insisted on explaining, amid remembrances of his youth, that he wasn't a man who took offense at nothing, because when he did take offense, watch out. Things got rough, and he didn't run from anything. When he got offended—his wife could testify to that, right, Vicentina?—he could take on three or four men, as he'd done before, more than once. Now, he'd be offended, speaking as a friend, if João Pedroso didn't have at least a sip of rum before leaving—none of that factory-bottled booze, but pure rum, the best Santo Amaro, made at the still of a buddy of his, great stuff. João Pedroso, feeling like screaming in exasperation, raised the glass, touched it to Honorino's, took a swallow and, after again shaking hands and exchanging embraces, managed to leave with Pepeu.

At the entrance to the garage, another contretemps: Pepeu had forgotten the key to the gate back at Honorino's, in his knapsack. There was a duplicate, but it was inside, which is the same as there not being one. They could send a boy to pick up the knapsack; it wouldn't take long, and he'd be back in fifteen minutes. Meanwhile they would go on enjoying Sunday by having a nice beer across the street. No, no, none of that. Then they'd have to climb over the wall. But how could they, a smooth wall of that height? A ladder; somebody could lend them a ladder.

They found a ladder after João Pedroso made a frenetic door-to-door search along the street and, finally, Pepeu climbed the wall, spent a considerable time inside looking for the duplicate key, and opened the gate. The priest's radiator was in sad shape, no good for anything. Well, now to see what could be found, and after Pepeu spent what seemed like hours sifting through a pile of parts, scrap, and junk, he found what he was looking for.

"Will it take long?"

"A while. It's gonna be real jury-rigged. I don't know if this hose will fit. Think I'll have to make a cut here at the intake and see if I can put on a clamp."

Once the radiator was installed—with Pepeu saying the whole time that it wasn't going to work and that the water would boil—the motor wouldn't catch. João Pedroso went back to the street to recruit people to push the jeep, and after some four tries and several noisy shudders, it started. Despite appearing to cough frequently, it ran reasonably well and João Pedroso was feeling better, when, still a long way from the turnoff to Misericórdia, in the middle of the deserted highway, he heard a high pitched sound and steam began to pour from the sides of the hood and the jeep came to a halt in a kind of collapse.

There was nothing that could be done except to walk along the highway where the heat from the asphalt raised visible waves of warm air. João Pedroso pushed the jeep to the side of the road, did what he could to close the half-ruined windows, and, without looking back, took off at a quick pace for Misericórdia. After arriving at the turnoff he would still have the entire long road to the hillock where Bará lived. Was there time? There must be, there must. After all, it was Sunday for Lúcio Nemésio too. He couldn't possibly be that fast.

But he was. At the foot of the hill, in the middle of a small cluster of people, were two station wagons and two police cars. Around them were soldiers and some men dressed in white. A police lieutenant, who seemed to be in charge, his arms crossed and with an air of impatience, was listening to what an agitated man, who kept repeating "It's not possible, it's not possible," was telling him.

"Not only is it possible, it's already done," the lieutenant said. "This is a menace to public health and a center of faith healing, an illegal practice of medicine. It is closed down and will continue to be off limits. We have orders from the Sanitation Control, from Public Health, and from a judge."

"But it's not possible. It's not possible!"

"Either you withdraw or I'll be forced to have you arrested. You can't interfere in a police matter."

A soldier who was behind the lieutenant stepped in front of him and nudged the man with the end of his billy club—"Move along, move along, there's nothing else for anybody to do here." João Pedroso approached the lieutenant, said "Good afternoon, lieutenant," and asked what was going on. Nothing was going on, they'd just gotten orders to support a Public Health operation to interdict the place. Only the resident, his family, and his employees could remain, and then under watch, so that the entering of persons seeking the healer could be prevented. There was a focus of an extremely serious disease there that had already caused the death of several people. João Pedroso asked if he couldn't go up to speak to the healer and the lieutenant said no, no one could go up.

"But I was the one who discovered the focus of the disease. I'm collaborating on this case."

"Got any documentation on you?"

"No, but you can check with Dr. Lúcio Nemésio, at the hospital. I need to go up to verify a few things. It's urgent. If I don't go up now, we're going to lose several important leads."

The lieutenant hesitated, looking at João Pedroso as if making an assessment. There were radios in the vehicles, but they couldn't be used to communicate with the hospital administration. Couldn't he come back later, after the confusion had died down? In a little while the people around there would calm down and disperse; it wouldn't be long. But João insisted, and the lieutenant, taking off his kepi and drying out the sweatband with a dirty handkerchief, finally made a conciliatory motion. "Go ahead; go on. But don't take long."

Bará was in the living room, sunk in an armchair. When he saw João, he gave signs of rising, but merely straightened slightly and remained seated. He apologized; that blessed withered leg, besides not being good for anything, ached from time to time. João Pedroso should make himself at home—despite the danger of contamination from the tenebrous disease that had been found there. He apologized again, this time for having spoken in an ironic tone to one who did not deserve it, but he was embittered, very embittered. Not so much for the fact that he was going to be prosecuted for illegal practice of medicine, nor for their having interdicted that which they called a worship site, not even because of the certainty he would be forced to leave there and go to another place. In a way, it made no difference; he could live anywhere, and it wasn't the first time it had happened. And if they arrested him, he had the strong hope that they would let him take books to his cell, so he would not experience a great difference between there inside and here outside. But he lamented, greatly lamented that now they could not raise a finger in relation to the problem of the creatures. The house had been rifled and the photo negatives had disappeared. Good thing the prints were in João Pedroso's possession, because if he had kept them they would have been apprehended too—and João, feeling like weeping and flooded with shame, collapsed onto the sofa.

Now, looking at the newspaper for the thousandth time, in Monteirinho's company, he recalled how he really had ended up almost sobbing after telling Bará what had happened during his visit to Lúcio Nemésio, a visit which he regretted because of its consequences for Bará but which had at least yielded confirmation of his suspicions. Yes, everything was terrible, far more terrible than he had imagined. But they weren't lost; they were going to fight—at least he was going to fight, for he felt responsible for it all, and would have fought even if he didn't. Lúcio Nemésio would of course begin a wide search throughout the island to find the creatures and their mothers. But he too would begin a search; he knew the island quite well, he would get hold of a car, a horse, a mule, whatever was necessary. And he would find witnesses, like those people Bará believed had at least heard of the creatures. Even without more concrete proof he could get the matter investigated and affect public opinion. He had no experience in that, but he was going to fight, with the priest's help, with the support of Bará's followers, with every weapon he could find. And as for Bará himself, there must be some legal step that could be taken, an injunction, habeas corpus, some such thing. João Pedroso was determined to carry it forward.

"Yes," Father Monteirinho said, "You're succeeding in helping Bará, but we're getting nowhere with the problem of the creatures, which is the main thing. Even the witnesses we found for the reporter only made things worse, as you see in that story—one of them saying they were animals with the face of a sloth, others saying they had scales on their backs, a veritable festival of imagination. I even think that some of them are deliberately lying, just to get into the newspapers."

"Don't mention newspapers to me. I never thought it would be so difficult to get something in the papers. They all promised to send reporters here, but that rag there is the only one that followed through. Could the hand of Lúcio Nemésio be behind it?"

"It's quite possible; he knows everyone. Oh! The phone, the phone! Is it possible no one's inside to answer the phone? Excuse me; the phone has that irritating quality: When it rings, it interrupts anything. It would even interrupt the Sermon on the Mount."

"It's all right. I'll go get today's papers, which should be out by now. Go answer your phone; I'm going down to the newsstand."

Still inside the newsstand, he opened the first section of all the newspapers, scanned each page, and initially found nothing concerning the case. Keep calm, you've got to keep calm; keep calm and you'll find something. It's not possible that nothing was printed. He placed the papers on the counter and decided to examine them slowly. Of course; here was a note, in a column on the second page. "Dangerous Healer. Healers and sorcerers have much more power than is believed. Not magic powers, which are for the naive and ignorant. But concrete powers, such as the case of one Bará da Misericórdia, who is now the object—or creator—of sensationalist claims about supposed monsters that are being created at the Freyre da Costa Regional Hospital on the island. What has happened is that the sorcerer hopes through this trick to resist the action taken by Public Health, which accuses him not only of the illegal practice of medicine but, perhaps more serious still, also of disseminating through his rituals a new disease, till now unknown in the area, that has attacked several victims, some fatally. The frightening thing about all this is, as suggested above, the power exercised by this sorcerer, who even has the support of the local priest, Father Olavo Bento Monteiro, who confirms his allegations about the monsters."

Sons of bitches. Another short piece here, the sons of bitches. "Irreverence. Irreverence in our people is not limited to residents of Rio de Janeiro, it's everywhere. Right now, on the island, the fishmonger and alleged biologist João Pedroso, who gave an absurd interview about the existence of monkey children on the island, is being called João the Monkey and Cheetah's Husband around the island." The sons of bitches! And it was a lie; no one was calling him by any kind of nickname. Sons of bitches. And more articles, both short and longer; now he'd come across a lot of them. An interview with Lúcio Nemésio. Faith healing, echinococcosis, superstition, involvement of the well-meaning with an excess of faith. "The hospital does carry out research, yes—research of a high order and of vital interest to society, nothing as patently absurd as the development of exotic beings. This a figment of the imagination of a, shall we say, creative charlatan. And we didn't seize any photographs; ours aren't photographic laboratories. All the material seized—including five dogs, a sheep, and other objects without value—was catalogued and can be seen by anyone." The son of a bitch. More short items, more items all of the same type. The sons of bitches, the sons of bitches.

"A son of a bitch, that Lúcio Nemésio," he said when he finally got to the priest's house, after walking slowly around the newsstand, stopping from time to time with his eyes on the papers. "Excuse me for using dirty words with a priest, but son of a bitch is the only name for it, the only possible expression. What's wrong? Why that look? Have you seen the papers too?"

"No, I haven't seen the newspapers. And I don't think I want to; what just happened is bad enough."

"What just happened?"

"That phone call. That phone call from the assistant bishop of the Archdiocese. He gave me a horrible dressing down for being involved with faith healers and sorcerers. I tried to explain, but he only redoubled the dressing down. And he ordered me to go there to speak with him, surely to call me on the carpet personally, or worse."

João Pedroso threw the newspapers onto the seat of a chair. Now this. He looked at the priest with sympathy, started to say something but didn't know what to say. He placed his hand on his shoulder, then walked about the living room for a short time, and finally said he was going out to think and would be back later. He picked up the newspapers, gathered them into a crumpled mass, and left without a word. On the street, after standing motionless for a long time, not knowing where to go, he decided he would go home and call Ana Clara. Ângelo Marcos could return at any moment, and he needed to see her, very much needed to see her, whoever might be suspicious of the phone call—in any case, sooner or later their situation was going to define itself once and for all.

* * *

The detective had insisted on obtaining more proof before making his report, but he had already indicated that he knew who Ana Clara's lover was, and Ângelo Marcos forced him to spit it out at once, by giving him an under-the-table bonus that made his eyes bug out. And as soon as he began to talk, Ângelo Marcos thought he was literally going to faint and even clutched the armrest of a chair. Impossible! Absurd, it was impossible! But it wasn't, and there were the photos, as clear as could be, taken with an excellent telephoto lens, near close-ups of Ana Clara going shamelessly into João Pedroso's house and, before clearing the threshold, bending over and leaving it patently obvious that she was kissing the person who'd opened the door—João Pedroso, naturally, despite the detective coming out with some line from an American-style movie, you couldn't be sure and all that stuff, until Ângelo Marcos said that was all the certainty he needed and dispensed with his services.

But what gall that shameless little whore had! And that bastard João, with that shit-eating face and that faggy shyness of his and, to top it off, now a total laughingstock because of some monkey children he says exist and everybody knows are something he and a discredited faith healer made up. A cheap souse, a shitty fishmonger, walking scum, a failure in the profession he claims to have a degree in, but— But, but as Granny Dalvinha used to say, the only reason a woman doesn't go to bed with a toad is because she can't tell the male from the female. If she could, there'd even be women for toads. João Pedroso? Of all people, João Pedroso? He couldn't conceive of any greater discrediting. No, no. Killing him was the only way.

Killing him *was* the only way, of course. Not a figure of speech—actually killing, liquidating. He'd never had any doubt about it, from the time he'd learned the truth: a definitive vanishing. Not her. He'd think about her later; it still depended on a lot of things. But that son of a bitch would find no forgiveness. A professional job, perfectly clean. He already had a plan: Kill him and throw him in the ocean, weighted down so the corpse would never be found. Complete disappearance;

no dumping the body somewhere for Ana Clara to suspect him and cause problems. Nothing like that. Totally disappeared, vanished from the face of the earth, vaporized. It'd be nice to cremate the son of a bitch and throw the ashes in the toilet, but unfortunately that wasn't possible. Filling the bastard with lead and throwing him into the sea was really the best solution.

He already had the executor of the plan in mind; he hadn't even needed to think about it. He also insisted, for sentimental reasons, so to speak, on participating, but in a supporting role. In the leading role would be Boaventura, of course. The telephone number of his plantation had long been on a slip of paper that he kept in his wallet. He would call immediately, as soon as he had an opportunity. It couldn't be from the house; he didn't want that unusual phone call to show up in his bill. It would have to be from a public phone, and late at night, not only to be sure he would find Boaventura at home, but also so there would be no one about, thinking it strange that he'd be using a pay phone with so many telephones at his disposal. Yeah, it wasn't going to be a problem; it's paranoia to think anyone would be intrigued by his using a public phone. What foolishness, it could be a call to his own house, some kind of emergency. Yes, he'd call from a pay phone, collect; he was sure Boaventura would accept the call at once. A simple message: I need you, bring the most modern and sophisticated equipment, get a room at the Grande Hotel and come for a friendly stay—a plantation owner in Goiás and a colleague in the Rural Democratic Union, nothing suspicious in that. And after the job, Boaventura could spend a few days on the island, so there wouldn't be any simultaneity between his departure and the dispatching of João.

Live and learn. João Pedroso! Putting horns on him, sticking it to his wife, her underneath him with her legs open, maybe even taking it in the ass. Yeah, that happens; there are women who won't let their husband come in their mouths but let their lover, who don't give their ass to their husband and give it to their lover. It had happened to him, more than once. She certainly must tell João the same thing that Conceição, for example, had told him so many times: I've never done this with my husband; I only do it with you— That sort of thing. Humiliating, there couldn't be anything more humiliating; you need a lot of self-control not to blow up, a whole lot of self-control. Yeah, that's right. And that business would have gone on indefinitely if he hadn't hired the detective and sent him ahead, because it's possible that with him on the island they wouldn't have had the gall to meet in such a cynical fashion. But the detective came, disguised as a photographer for a tourist agency, and he already knew everything about her, knew where the house was, what the cars were like, already had her photo, everything, everything. He didn't waste any time, and he quickly discovered the sordid truth. That son of a bitch screwing her without a care in the world, and the clown here paying for everything and even suffering because of her. But she's going to take such a beating that she'll learn once and for all. And in the best-case scenario she'll live forever with the certainty that he had something to do with João's disappearance, without being able to prove a thing. She'll go crazy.

To think that, though he was now calm and under control, he'd almost ruined everything that morning when the maid, who was working in the living room while he read the newspapers, handed him the phone and said it was Mr. João Pedroso. He couldn't control himself and jumped, which startled the maid and caused her to ask, her hand over the speaker, if she should say he wasn't in.

"No, no! I'm in! I'm in!" he said, after taking the phone out of her hand and also covering it. "I'm in! Now, if you don't mind."

He waited for the maid to close the door, and he perceived how nervous he had become, his heart racing and a very cold sweat wetting his forehead and neck. What was it? Was he afraid of the son of a bitch? Was he going to talk to him stuttering, all tongue-tied? It wasn't possible, not that too! And he even swallowed saliva and took a deep breath, willing to have it out with the bastard, tell him he wasn't a fool and threaten him viva voce. He uncovered the phone, opened his mouth, but checked himself in time. No, he'd really be a fool if he did that;

then revenge would be impossible and events would take a completely different direction. No, no, nothing hasty; self-control, self-control—although at the beginning of the phone call his voice sounded rather strained.

"Hello, João, how's it going? We haven't talked for a long time; we have to get together. Anything new? Lots of fish around?"

"No, nothing new. I mean, I needed to talk to you, today if possible."

"You—You need to talk to me? Has—Has something happened?"

"Well, you must have already heard about it. At least Ana Clara must have told you."

"Ana Clara? Is it about Ana Clara? No, she didn't tell me anything, she didn't say anything at all."

"But you must have heard talk about it, even being away. There was a lot in the newspapers about the matter."

"Oh, you mean—Ah, yes, good. Right. Yes, you mean that business about the monkey children? You're mixed up in that, aren't you? But, man, are you taking that stuff seriously? To me it's a joke. Have you yourself seen these monkey men?"

"No, I haven't seen any monkey man. Personally, I haven't seen one, and I never said I did."

"I got the impression from what I read in one of the papers that you said you had."

"Yes, a lot of nonsense came out in the papers. I'm sorry I ever went to the newspapers. I think it was hasty on my part and only made things worse. But look, Ângelo Marcos, I'm certain those creatures exist, and I even have hopes of finding them, because as I see it, they're still out there. I needed to talk to you about this. The matter is serious, and I'll explain it to you personally."

"Talking to me isn't a problem, João, you know that. I feel like an old friend of yours. But honesty compels me to tell you that this story, however much I like and respect you, is kind of hard to swallow. I can't believe—"

"At least let me explain. Believe me, it wasn't easy for me to ask you to take an interest in the matter, but it's because of the graveness of the fact, not for myself. If it were for me I wouldn't bother you, but it's of public interest, of vital public interest, and after all you're a public man who has dedicated his whole life to public service."

"All right, João, let's have a talk; it doesn't cost anything. Want to come by here tonight, around eight-thirty or nine?"

"OK, if it has to be at night, fine."

"It's because I have a lot of things to do today, and at this very moment I was heading out the door. You almost didn't catch me in. A few hours won't make any difference, will it?"

Before the phone call he wasn't on his way out at all, but now that the bastard, with that gall of his, had had the nerve to ask for his support, he thought he could do him even more harm—how, he didn't know—and help discredit him before his death. Maybe that was a good idea, because then many would speculate that his disappearance had been a flight; everybody knows running away is in his temperament. Yes, yes, maybe even Ana Clara would think that and then feel abandoned and betrayed—excellent, excellent. Do anything for that son of a bitch? Never, but what gall, what hypocrisy!

He looked up the number of Lúcio Nemésio's office at the hospital and spoke with Dona Salete. Lúcio Nemésio was in a meeting now in another wing of the hospital—was it anything urgent? If it were urgent, maybe she could do something. No, it wasn't urgent, but could Lúcio Nemésio perhaps see him later this afternoon at any time? Dona Salete said she was sure he could, because his calendar wasn't very crowded in the afternoon, after the cancellation of two other meetings. But in any case she would call back shortly to confirm.

She telephoned half an hour later and confirmed. Was five o'clock all right? It was perfect, and now, at a bit past three, he was preparing to amuse himself until time to leave for the hospital by doing something he had abruptly put aside some time ago. Killing sparrows. He'd had an idea he couldn't resist, despite finding it a trifle imprudent. His mouth watering like the other times, he picked up the rifle and went down to the patio. The birds shouldn't be skittish; they'd probably already forgotten the rifle. He loaded the clip, cocked the rifle, and went to the area by the garbage cans, around which several of them were pecking. He chose one of the largest ones and fired. At first he was disappointed, for the sparrow sprang up, fell to the ground, and quickly took flight in the same direction as the others. But it didn't make it over the wall and fell in a corner of the patio. A beauty of a shot, although the bird, as he confirmed while preparing the coup de grace, wasn't dead yet. He thought about crushing it with his foot but felt disgusted and gave it two shots in the head. He got a dustpan from beside the cans, took a plastic bag from his pocket and threw the sparrow's corpse inside.

After many other attempts, he had wounded two more, one in the wing and the other in the back. He had difficulty picking them up from the ground because they ran, thrashed about, and pecked furiously. But he succeeded in pushing them into the bag, without bothering to finish them off. Since he was going to store them in the freezer in the basement, they would die anyway, turn into Popsicles, so it wasn't necessary to keep firing at point-blank range, which always made him fear a ricochet. And that was that; three was enough, a fine harvest. He looked at the time: past four-thirty. Soon he'd leave for the hospital. But he had time to go calmly to the freezer, down there where no one ever went, to close the bag with the sparrows, and put it in, leaning against one of the sides. The birds squirmed in the sack and he thought it would be interesting if the freezer had a glass window so he could witness the freezing. Well, it was time to leave anyway, and he went to get the car from the garage. As he passed through the small room adjoining the living room, he met Ana Clara, who had just finished locking something in the dresser drawer. Must be those Suzanna Frischmann notebooks; she spends all her time ensconced in corners writing. That is, when she isn't fucking João Pedroso, of course. The face of a saint, innocent, an angel. She smiled at him—the cynical, amoral, insensitive cynic. He smiled back at her.

"Know something?" he said as casually as he could. "João Pedroso is coming over tonight."

"João Pedroso? You called him?"

"No, he called me, this morning. I forgot to tell you earlier."

"And what does he want?"

"I don't quite know. It appears he wants my support for that craziness about the monkey men that he dreamed up. As far as I'm concerned, he's nuts, out of his mind. For that matter, I never thought he was all there."

"I'm not sure those creatures don't exist. João is a very competent guy."

"What's this, Ana Clara? You too? João is just a shit-ass fish vendor like any other, with a thin veneer of what he says he learned at the university, but he might well have learned it from almanacs; what he has is almanac culture."

"You didn't used to think that way."

"Yes, but with familiarity I caught on. He's a piece of shit, an alcoholic failure."

"I disagree. That's your opinion. But anyway, you shouldn't talk like that. After all, he's your friend."

"But I'm not saying it in public. I'm saying it in my own house, to my wife. Can't I even make a frank comment in the intimacy of my home?"

"You're right, Ângelo Marcos, fine. If you don't mind, I have some things to take care of."

"I'm going out."

"I noticed. You have the car keys in your hand. Dinner's at eight."

The cynical, shameless little whore. She has the guts to say that son of a bitch, who in league with her knifes him in the back with the greatest audacity, is his friend? And she even comes to his defense! Unbelievable. How far is she capable of going, to what amoral, unscrupulous abyss? But, when he mentioned João Pedroso, it was evident that she got a bit rattled. Just for a second, but she did get rattled. The dirty little whore. And she didn't even want to know where he was going, more or less dressed up and at this hour of the afternoon, the time for clandestine rendezvous. She didn't even want to know. Total indifference, disdain. All right, all right, we'll see who laughs last.

He got into the car, irritated, and pulled out with an abrupt reverse without looking to the sides. Once on the road, however, he calmed down and began driving at a little above twenty-five miles per hour, looking at the landscape and humming. He couldn't say he was happy, but he was at least content with himself, acting in a cool and objective manner, as the situation demanded. No, he wasn't unhappy, he was the master of events, absolutely in control. As he blew the horn for the parking gate at the hospital to open, he waited, smiling, and greeted the attendant affably.

At the very outset of the conversation with Lúcio Nemésio, who was incidentally in a very good mood and extraordinarily friendly, he had difficulty in approaching the subject. He didn't know how to bring it up without running the risk of arousing irritation. But Lúcio Nemésio himself finally was first to speak of the creatures. As Ângelo Marcos expected, he denied everything. But he denied it in such a way that his face seemed to indicate the opposite of his words, as if he were amusing himself with it all. Ângelo Marcos was suspicious and said that if there were even a small bit of truth in it, he was in favor and found it a fascinating experiment. Lúcio Nemésio could have confidence in him.

"I know," Lúcio Nemésio said. "It's not a question of confidence or lack of confidence. The truth is that we have none of those monkey children here."

"But João Pedroso is absolutely convinced they exist. Just today he called me and is going to come by the house, undoubtedly to ask for my support. That's why I came to talk to you. If I can be of help in anything, I'm at your disposal. Naturally I'm not going to side with him."

"João Pedroso is a good man, but he's a superstitious religious type, which allowed him to be taken in by the tricks of a sensationalist healer. And even if you wanted to, you couldn't support him, because there's nothing to support."

"But, as I've already said, I'd never do that. I would never harm the progress of science. Just the opposite—I think João Pedroso and the healer ought to be discredited for good; what they're doing is unacceptable. What do you think I should do?"

"Nothing. You don't have to do anything. They're already discredited. No one believes them, and they'll never succeed in proving any of their allegations."

"Hasn't this hurt the hospital, hurt some project?"

"It hasn't hurt anything. Everything is completely normal."

"Anyway, I wanted to convey to you my willingness to help you in any way possible. Where I am concerned, this hospital will always have a defender. I'm proud of it too."

"Thank you very much, Ângelo Marcos, I know that. Thank you very much."

He remained a while longer, chatting awkwardly and without finding a way of mentioning the creatures again, until he saw the old man was about to excuse himself and ask him to leave. Ângelo Marcos made his good-byes effusively and headed back as slowly as he had come, driving with one hand on the wheel and the other on his chin. Of course the old man knew a lot more he didn't want to talk about. That way of speaking, almost ironic, almost ridiculing, and those excessively detailed and technical explanations to explain why they couldn't be producing hybrids and working with genetics at the hospital. And those foreign foundations don't do anything without an ulterior motive. Both of them have ties to large chemical and pharmaceutical industries; it's obvious there is great commercial interest in the work being done in the hospital's labs. Now that he thought about it, he would be doing them a favor to get rid of João Pedroso. He ought to be rewarded for it; that was the only fair thing to do. He was more and more certain that Lúcio Nemésio had hidden something from him, and when he stopped in the garage he felt envious of him. There was something fishy there, no doubt of it.

He went into the house, straight to the basement, opened the freezer, picked up the bag of sparrows, and shook it. Three ice cubes inside, everything OK. Dinner would be ready at eight, as Ana Clara had said, with that shit-eating air she had affected when she spoke to him. There was time, therefore, to go upstairs, smoke a joint, and relax. And then have dinner, forcing Ana Clara to talk and offer opinions while they awaited João Pedroso's visit, which he was beginning to think would be interesting and even useful; it took care of a small problem for him.

João Pedroso looked at his watch for the third time. Only five minutes had gone by since the second time; it still wasn't even seven-thirty. Ana Clara was against the visit and had even gotten rather excited and raised her voice, as she had never done before. What an idea, especially now that Ângelo Marcos's waiting period was nearing its end. What an awkward situation! Awkward in every sense. For example, she couldn't say she was happy about João begging favors from Ângelo Marcos. It was very unseemly, almost humiliating.

"In the first place, I'm not going to beg," João had said. "I'm going to lay out the problem to him, which isn't a problem of mine but a problem for everybody, for humanity itself."

"All right, you've already said that. But I'm sure it won't do any good to talk to him; he's not going to be moved. You're only going to subject yourself to embarrassment. And me too, of course. What an awful situation! Not before, but ever since we agreed to live together, I've been ill at ease. It's going to be very unpleasant. Later he's going to throw it all up to me; it'll be hell."

"Yes, but it's necessary. I don't know anyone. I have no prestige—just the opposite. I'm even kind of discredited because of that stuff in the newspapers. So I need his help. The people need his help and anyone else he can enlist."

"You say it's not your problem, but you act as if it were. Since you got involved in this business you're completely different—nervous, restless, almost aggressive—"

"I'm being aggressive, am I? Sorry, I hadn't noticed."

"It doesn't matter. I understand. But I think you could stay calmer and even begin to prepare yourself for the possibility—to me, the most likely one—that you won't be able to do anything. It's not what I want, of course, but you should be prepared for it. Lúcio Nemésio is powerful and influential, and the priest may be transferred from here because of this story. Your situation isn't good; it's more or less hopeless, isn't it?"

"Maybe, but I would consider it a terrible defeat. I could never accept losing out in this. The defeat would destroy me."

"I think you're exaggerating, João. It can't be like that. You have to be realistic and see things as they are and not how you want them to be."

"That's easy to say. If you had seen those photos and heard Lúcio Nemésio's sinister conversation, your skin would still be creeping from fear. Do you have any idea, any idea at all, of what this means?"

He remembered how he had spoken then, for over an hour, excited and almost feverish, and how she had been right about his emotional state. Yes, he was being aggressive, and there were moments when she irritated him and he was more or less gruff. Interesting, she had never irritated him before, even when she came out with that playful teasing of which she was perhaps a little too fond. Now, however, he thought she didn't comprehend the gravity of what he was saying and making known, and even found her somewhat indifferent, insensitive to the calamity. But they said good-bye with copious hugs and kisses, and the visit was confirmed despite her insistence that it was a terrible idea.

Seven-thirty, at last. Yes, but there was still at least an hour ahead of him. Was he nervous? He certainly was. He could pull out, couldn't he? Ana Clara was probably right: The conversation would end up accomplishing nothing. Maybe it was perfectly idiotic, as the other initiatives had been, beginning with the newspapers. What did Monteirinho think about it? No, he wouldn't ask the poor priest anything; he couldn't get him further involved in this. He was up to his neck in problems with the Archdiocese and fearful of being transferred to one of those parishes where the only way to get there is on muleback or by helicopter.

He placed his hand on the telephone. It was easy; all he had to do was call Ângelo Marcos and cancel the visit, thank him for his attention and maintain the distance that decency required. He picked up the phone but immediately replaced it on the hook. No, giving up was just one more withdrawal. He'd promised himself he would try every recourse, however remote the chances of its working; he wasn't going to withdraw once again. But he was nervous, very nervous, and decided the best thing to do was spend the remaining time walking aimlessly or reading something in the square.

He knew he shouldn't drink, but, what the devil, he needed a couple of drinks to calm down; after all, he couldn't arrive at Ângelo Marcos's house all shitting in his pants and hesitant. He signaled Luiz the Waiter, ordered a whiskey with lots of ice but changed his mind as soon as he spoke and—why not, since he was going to have another anyway?—said he wanted his usual double. And less than fifteen minutes later he had ordered the second, followed by the third around eight-ten, and one for the road, drunk hurriedly, at eight-twenty.

Yes, alcohol does have a calming effect. From the time he finished the second glass, he'd felt his nervousness diminishing. But was he all right? He wasn't, as he confirmed when he rose from the table and took some time to gain his balance. Not really drunk, certainly, but quite a bit drunker than he'd foreseen. A little high. Shit! He breathed deeply several times, rubbed his temples, and bit his lower lip forcefully. Shit! Well, he was starting to get better now. The dizziness had been mostly from changing position; he'd been sitting a long time and had gotten up suddenly. He straightened his shirt, hitched up his pants, tossed the magazine he had been reading into the wastebasket, and, thinking how ridiculous it was to drink not to get nervous, then get nervous precisely because he'd been drinking, he began walking toward the home of Ângelo Marcos.

. . . Who, incidentally, was feeling very good, truly very good, stretched out on a chaise longue on the upstairs veranda and smoking a Jamaican cigar, while Ana Clara pretended to calmly watch a film on the TV projection screen. Excellent tobacco, a cigar and a half. For the price it ought to be wrapped in gold, but it's worth it; everything that's good is worth it. He raised his upper body a bit to look at the street below. Wasn't it time for that son of a bitch to show up? Yes, it was; there he was, approaching from along the tamarind trees and, judging by his walk, half in the bag. He must have gotten nervous and hung one on for Dutch courage like a good son of a bitch. Well, let's go down and receive the illustrious personage.

Up close, João Pedroso seemed less drunk than from a distance, but he was visibly high. And flustered, awkward, full of sickly grins. Ana Clara came down, giving João a peck on the cheek, the cheap, cynical whore. His blood boiled, but cool it; they're not going to get the best of this. Yes, wouldn't the distinguished guest like another drink? Since he's already started to tie one on, he could very well finish it; there was no shortage of booze, and much better than what he was used to pouring down his throat, real whiskey and not Brazilian rotgut and Old Stroessner. He didn't say this, of course, but he thought it as he offered João whiskey. Strangely, he refused, but Ângelo Marcos acted as if he hadn't heard and went to the bar, where he poured an enormous amount of scotch over three ice cubes, then brought the glass and stuck it in his hand.

"Twenty years old," he said with an exaggerated smile. "Not too shabby. You're going to like it. I won't join you because I can't. Ana Clara, would you like anything, sweetheart?"

"Thank you. Will you make me a martini?"

"Of course, dear. Semidry, isn't it?"

Little kisses for Ana Clara, hugs, a husband's affection. The son of a bitch would just have to put up with it; this wasn't his territory. If she told him she didn't do it with her husband anymore, now he'd be in doubt. More caresses, a few looks, and some pats. And the little whore couldn't do a thing either—this really was enjoyable, as he had anticipated. He returned with the martini—another little kiss and a rubbing of her arm, close to the breast. Could they talk there in the living room, or did João want a secret session behind closed doors, Top Secret type? What gall those two had, what a couple of sons of bitches, now so uncomfortable—beautiful!

Well, since João was taking so long to speak, preferring to sit there with a stupid look on his face, having one drink after the other, he would broach the subject himself. He knew what the subject was, of course; João had told him on the phone. He was going to be frank, just as he had been on the telephone. He didn't really believe the story; João was laboring under a misconception. And they shouldn't think he was saying this without foundation, purely from preconceived notions. Just this afternoon he had taken the care to seek out Lúcio Nemésio at the hospital and he had convincingly denied everything. Not only denied it but offered evidence, though the burden of proof was not on him.

"You mean, if you want to, you can make an inspection of the hospital, go completely through it?"

"I didn't go as far as asking in those terms, João, but I believe so."

"Then will you make that inspection? We can't miss this opportunity. Will you?"

"João, again I'm going to be frank. It's tough to be frank sometimes, but I'm going to be. It's my makeup; I can't be any other way. I like you very much, but I'm also friends, very close friends, with Lúcio Nemésio, for whom I have the greatest respect and consideration. I can't put that friendship in jeopardy by doubting his word and trying to find out if he's lying. I know he isn't lying, and he has the right to expect that of me. I know he isn't lying."

He didn't know any such thing, of course, and he had problems in avoiding showing excessive interest in certain details when João, pretty drunk and his tongue suddenly loose, made a kind of apocalyptic and pathetic speech in which he told of his conversation with Lúcio Nemésio, spoke of the fugitive mothers and their monstrous children, and of the indescribable violence committed against the poor in the region. Suddenly, Ângelo Marcos was absolutely certain that Lúcio Nemésio had lied to him and had told João the truth.

"João, forgive me, please forgive me, but I can't believe it."

"But João is right about one thing, Marquinhos. You could make that visit. I think that, as a visit, there'd be no problem. A visit doesn't offend anyone, and Lúcio Nemésio might even like it, if he really has nothing to hide."

"No, Aninha. Forgive me, but it's out of the question, absolutely out of the question."

Wonderful details, "Marquinhos" here, "Aninha" there, right in front of the son of a bitch, who was plainly nervous as hell. Drunker and drunker, he could no longer offer counterarguments and just sat there looking stupid like some kind of nitwit. And she must be perceiving the piece of shit she preferred to her husband. A tremendous pleasure in denying, elegantly, eloquently, and nicely, what he was asking. Such a visit was impossible. It seemed he had set aside the night for making excuses for his frankness, but he must do so once again. And frankly, his position didn't allow him to expose himself to the same ridicule—again, pardon the frankness, a thousand pardons—as João. And they should consider that João didn't have a public image to maintain, as did he. Imagine the disaster it would be, a disaster of irrecoverable consequences. If there were proof, fine. But, under the circumstances . . .

It was obvious that João was telling the truth. Lúcio Nemésio had some kind of fantastic scheme, that was it—vaccines, organ banks, enzymes, hormones, proteins of every type, an unimaginable infinity of applications, a gold mine. There had to be a way for him to get in on it. He began almost to daydream, imagining what that way might be, a trifle irritated because João, speaking in a grotesquely emotional tone, wouldn't let him think. He needed to find a way to ask questions without giving himself away. He needed information, not that bleeding-heart twaddle about man as a moral being and about the existence of a soul in such creatures and about mothers threatened with kidnap and private imprisonment by the hospital—as if it weren't a good deal for a poverty-stricken black woman like that to have the best to eat, to sleep in a bed with a mattress and be treated like a person instead of wandering around the woods without even the money to buy the seasoning for the third-rate fish stew that she spent the entire day mired in the swamp to catch. Give me a goddamn break. And what the hell was this? Now he was crying? He was asking to be forgiven because he was crying, in gushes and grimaces? Horrible! Crying, just look. What is this, man, there's no reason to cry. The world's not coming to an end. Those creatures don't exist; you yourself say you never laid eyes on them. What foolishness. Have another, go on, it'll calm you down.

Crying. Crying like a lamb, in front of Ana Clara. A lovely sight for her, that bastard with the look of a faggot, crying with that face of his like some saintly reformed whore. Crying and so drunk he couldn't stay on his feet when, after regaining his control a bit, but with his chin still trembling, he decided to leave. There it was, one more useful thing that had come from this excellent visit: the pretext to go out and take care of a couple of matters. He would play the magnanimous role and leave with João Pedroso to help him in case he fell. Despite the short distance, he would take him to the car; he insisted. Looking at the other man with what now seemed to be very close to rage, João Pedroso refused. But he was too drunk to resist Ângelo Marcos, who held him by the elbow, took him to the car parked in the yard, installed him in the passenger's seat, and asked Ana Clara to get the keys. In the meantime, he went quickly down to the basement, retrieved the frozen sparrows, went back up to the patio, and threw the bag into the back seat before Ana Clara returned.

"I'll be right back, sweetheart," he said, kissing her on the cheek because she turned her mouth away.

"So long, Ana Clara. I'm sorry," João said, his words emerging thickly.

"It's all right, João."

Shameless little whore. This time she'd screwed up; they'd both screwed up. A classic confrontation between a superior man and trash, right under her nose. And how about her audacity at sitting beside him, eh? Really, great cynicism. And this son of a bitch, if he weren't so drunk, would end up wanting to resort to physical aggression. In the moment just before he left, he had a mean look, as if he'd like to punch somebody. That's all we need; first you screw another man's wife and then you beat him up. Yeah, it was bound to happen, sooner or later; one more reason to get rid of him.

"Are you going in here or through the side gate?" he asked when they arrived at João's house, but João was asleep and Ângelo Marcos had to shake him to wake him up.

"What is it?"

"We've arrived. Isn't this your house?"

"Huh? Yeah, yes, of course it is. Yes, of course. Thank you very much. Good night."

Ângelo Marcos remained at the wheel throughout the very lengthy time that João Pedroso, stumbling, took to go around the car, make his way to the door, manage to open it, and practically fall inside. João also took such a long time to close the door that Ângelo Marcos, in his impatience, actually thought about going to help him; he didn't want to be away too long and arouse Ana Clara's suspicions. But the door finally shut with a bang and a light went on inside, a sign that the rummy had at least succeeded in dragging himself down the corridor. Trying not to make any noise, Ângelo Marcos got out of the car, picked up the bag of sparrows, tore open the upper part, and dumped its contents on the doorstep. In the morning they would be thawed, and he wanted João to come across them when he left his house. He greatly wanted him to see those three dead sparrows there and think about them. He didn't only want him to die, he wanted him, one way or another, to be afraid of dying, to feel anguish and be terrified before dying. It mattered little if he connected the sparrows to the story about the killer—in fact, that was precisely the desired effect. He couldn't prove anything anyway; they were merely dead sparrows like dozens of others that showed up on the sidewalks, equally dead, after a rainstorm, for example.

Back in the car, Ângelo Marcos drove toward Campo Formoso and parked. It was totally deserted and the pay phone stood like a beneficent obelisk. He took the telephone number from his wallet and dialed collect. Boaventura was at home and accepted the call at once, said he would come immediately, everything was understood. Fine, fine. Now to return home calmly, listen to a little music, and talk with Ana Clara about what a damned fool João is.

"I think I'm on the same path," Father Monteirinho answered when João Pedroso, upon returning the key to his jeep, told him he wasn't distinguishing the real from the imaginary and that, at times, he thought he'd died and was in hell. "This whole story is causing me one grief after another. Dom Túlio almost threatened me with excommunication, and I had to listen to it all in silence, of course. What was I going to say? It must be a nightmare, mustn't it? I've had nightmares so real that when I woke up it took a long time to convince myself that I wasn't really in that nightmarish situation. And what's worse, I'm almost certain I'm going to be transferred, in a matter of days. I even know who the priest is they're thinking about bringing in my place. I've met him."

"Monteirinho, this makes me even more bananas. I never should have involved you in this. All I do is screw up."

Yes, all he did *was* screw up, time after time—like getting plastered the night of the talk with Ângelo Marcos and conducting himself in that depressing fashion. He had crashed in the room next to the living room, which he never used, because he couldn't take another step. And he'd awakened around five-thirty, at first not remembering what had happened the night before. But, after killing an infernal thirst with almost an entire bottle of cold water, he gradually remembered and felt indescribable shame, the desire to disappear, the desire to be nowhere. How could he have done it?

But he had done it, and there was no way to run away from himself. What must Ana Clara be thinking? What a question—of course she must be ashamed and disappointed, very disappointed. Perhaps disappointed beyond recovery. No, it wasn't like that; it was a serious slip-up but it wasn't the end of the world. The worst thing was that he couldn't come up with a way to be with her, even if only to talk, now that Ângelo Marcos seemed inclined to never leave the island again. And, when he did meet her, what would he say to her?

He went into the bathroom, passed by the mirror in the built-in cabinet, and stopped to look at himself. Bags under his eyes, a grayish beard, a defeated and unhappy look. What shit. He stood there for a long time, looking at himself as if he were another person, some strange guy on the other side. Right, a stranger, a dejected and unfamiliar nincompoop. It had seemed he would spend the entire morning there, motionless before the mirror, when an irrepressible wave of nausea made him vomit, straight into the basin, a greenish, fetid slime. He finished vomiting, sweating heavily and his eyes watering, cleaned the basin, and went into the shower, where he shaved by touch in order to not have to look at himself in the mirror again.

He thought about eating something but decided he couldn't tolerate anything in his stomach, except coffee, which he drank punctuated by grimaces. Well, he wasn't going to sit around all day rehashing what had happened. In the end, Ana Clara would understand—a moment of weakness, that type of thing. But the problem of the creatures—that would continue to torment him, and the only way to confront the torment was to keep on trying to do something. He'd had no success at all with Ângelo Marcos, but he could look for other people. He could find the creatures before the men from the hospital. And then, with a start, he remembered he had set up a talk that morning with Bará, who despite having won a preliminary hearing had decided to move away for good, perhaps to Cachoeira or Nazaré das Farinhas. João saw the hour; he still had lots of time. Of course, before leaving, Bará wanted to see him; perhaps he might have some new idea.

What could explain those three dead sparrows he found on his doorstep when he went out later to return the jeep borrowed from the priest and to meet Bará? Two and a half sparrows, rather, because one of them had been gnawed by some animal or other and all that was left was the head and legs. Strange place for sparrows to come to die, especially three at once. It wasn't voodoo rites; no one does that with sparrows. But just sparrows, nothing else? He kicked the cadavers to the curb. Lots of puddles in the streets; it must have rained heavily during the morning hours and he hadn't heard it because he was soused. Sure, it had rained heavily, something frightened them out of the oiti tree, and the wind and rain blew them here. But three at once? Well, it wasn't impossible, and he was getting ready to leave when an almost forgotten memory leapt into his head and he turned pale. Good God, could it be? No, no, it couldn't; it was too crazy. But the story of the sparrows told by Ângelo Marcos wouldn't leave his head, the story of the killer who started out by killing sparrows. But how could that type of threat occur to Ângelo Marcos if he considered himself his friend and he knew nothing about the affair with Ana Clara? Or did he? No, no, he couldn't know; they had been exceedingly discreet. Or had they? Betrayal from Bebel, now that she was so estranged from Ana Clara? And why, if he planned to kill him, would Ângelo Marcos give himself away beforehand? Yes, of course, the sparrows proved nothing; it wasn't even possible to say if it was Ângelo Marcos who put them there. Or was he only trying to frighten him? Or was it just a prank, perhaps even a prank done by some other person, a young boy's mischief? Of course, it was all paranoid foolishness, nothing to do with Ângelo Marcos, kids' doings or something from the rain. And, anyway, where would Ângelo Marcos get sparrows and find a way to put them on his doorstep? Yeah, nonsense. But João Pedroso drove the entire route to the vicinity of Bará's house with a furrowed brow, feeling agonized and unable to think about what they would discuss at the meeting.

A meeting that proved to be more discouraging and melancholy than he had anticipated, because Bará assured him that the hospital had captured the fugitives some days earlier, though he himself had learned of it only a few hours ago. João Pedroso refused to believe it at first, but Bará insisted there was no room for doubt. He was absolutely sure of it; the station wagons from the hospital had been seen everywhere at the periphery of the woods, since the day they invaded his house. Two days later, the movement ceased, naturally because they had attained their objective; otherwise they wouldn't have given up so easily. The two of them could forget about finding the creatures, for he had the intuitive certainty that there were no more of them even in the custody of the hospital. He felt that Lúcio Nemésio had spoken with such frankness to João for several reasons—vanity, arrogance, showing off, or even insanity—but one reason was that which the doctor had insinuated: The creatures were there only temporarily. By now they must have been transported to another of their organization's centers. Perhaps the three mothers had fled because they knew of the transfer and didn't want to go, as other creatures and their mothers must have gone. No, they would never get near those creatures.

João Pedroso persisted a bit in his doubt, but he soon concluded that Bará was right, as he had been other times. True, they wouldn't have given up the search so early; they won every time, they were formidable, and they had surely captured the fugitives. He sighed, got up, lit a cigarette, and uttered a curse. Yes, it seemed there wasn't any way out, and Bará was the living image of the whole situation. He pointed to some pieces of furniture in a pile, next to crates with wrapped objects, and asked if the move was underway. In a sad tone, Bará said yes, he would leave for Cachoeira the next day. João wanted to make some comment, but nothing occurred to him and he allowed himself to be caught up in the almost funereal air of the setting. Until Bará, excusing himself, said he needed to work on the preparation for the move and must therefore say good-bye. He shook João's hand and thanked him for the help he had given and the confidence he had lately showed in him. João embraced him at length, said nothing, and left. He didn't feel well; he didn't feel well at all.

"And you don't see certain interesting aspects in all this?" Father Monteirinho asked, after João returned the keys to the jeep, sat down, and told him of his visit to Bará.

"Interesting aspects? If you call one licking after another an 'interesting aspect,' I guess so."

"No, that's not what I'm referring to. It's just that I was never able to swallow that talk about the gypsy woman, this business of Bará, all those things. It's true, the existence of the creatures is another problem. But remember that the only evidence of their existence, the only concrete evidence, was those photos, which Bará may very well have faked. And now he says that the creatures were taken away. Couldn't that be because he knows there never were any such creatures and that, if by chance they forced a complete inspection of the hospital, they wouldn't find anything?"

"What about my conversation with Lúcio Nemésio?"

"Couldn't it be he was playing some kind of joke on you? Knowing there were no creatures and that therefore he was risking nothing, he might have decided to tell you that story, a kind of horror story."

"Monteirinho, you surprise me. What about the immediate invasion of Bará's house, and on a Sunday at that—was that a joke? And the disappearance of the negatives? And the campaign of ridicule in the newspapers? And the conversation itself, the conversation! I know it wasn't a lie; I was there and saw it in his eyes! And how is it that a man with a background in general surgery, however good that background, can be so familiar with such matters, the familiarity of one who has frequent contact with them? I know that what he told me is the truth. I know it!"

"All that's very relative, João. For example, Bará may have destroyed the negatives himself so a possible examination wouldn't show them to be fakes."

"Monteirinho, I'm really finding you strange, very strange. I'm telling you in all seriousness: I'm going to dedicate my life to unraveling this business, my life!"

"That's where I think you should act more realistically. You're taking too much to heart something about which, when all is said and done, there are doubts. Maybe you should stop hitting your head against the wall and resign yourself to the fact that you're never going to know—"

"You too? You too? Not you, you can't!"

"What do mean, you too? Who else told you that?"

"It's irrelevant; forget it. The truly interesting thing is that you used to be so horrified by the photos of the creatures and by what Lúcio Nemésio is doing, and now you act as if everything were natural, as if there weren't anything horrible at all."

"That's not fair. You know it's not that. It's because I really do have doubts; there are moments when everything really seems to be something made up by the sorcerer, as I always suspected."

"Monteirinho, in reality what you're saying is that Divine Providence, wishing to intervene in the problem of the creatures, wouldn't act through a person like Bará. Do you know that's real arrogance?"

"I don't see any arrogance at all. I don't see why I should place any faith in a common charlatan."

"Bará is no common charlatan; he's an interesting guy."

"That's right: an interesting charlatan, but a charlatan nonetheless. I still have doubts about him."

"And doubts about me?"

"It's not a matter of doubting you."

"Of course it is."

"It's not! It's only because you're so obsessed, you act so hastily, you don't see things calmly, and don't analyze all the possibilities."

"And how do you expect me to act calmly when I'm sure of what I'm talking about? How can you want me to sit here with my arms folded? Especially a guy like me, who never did anything in his life? You remember my sin, don't you? Of course you do. You don't want to let me redeem my sin, Monteirinho. That's what you want, just think!"

Yes, that's what he wants, João thought angrily, after an argument that became more and more severe, until he decided to leave, saying good-bye curtly and slamming the door. Almost noon, the sun hot, the air still and a mortal solitude in which everyone in the street looked like figures from another dimension that he wouldn't be able to touch and who didn't see him. He sat at his usual table, in the Largo da Quitanda, and Luiz the Waiter asked if he wanted to send for the newspapers. He didn't; all he wanted was to drink. A surreal situation; he felt himself outside the world. Maybe Monteirinho's question was justified: Was all this actually happening? Where was he really? What was really happening? What did "really" mean?

He'd thought of drinking quickly to become intoxicated, but he changed his mind when the glass arrived. For a long time he did not raise it to his lips, twirling it between both hands. The sparrows. He'd like to have someone's opinion about the sparrows. But he couldn't talk with Monteirinho because he didn't want to embarrass him, since the matter involved Ana Clara. And he couldn't talk to Ana Clara because it wasn't possible to be with her. Damn, that situation has to be resolved, and then there's the business of the deadline and all the rest. Well, maybe she'd come up with something; she was always more ingenious than he. Confusion, confusion. He picked up the glass, took a sip, and as he raised his eyes toward the sea before him, he noticed that a heat front was forming, strange for that season and that time of day. Nothing moved, not a wave, not a fish, not a boat, not the static mist that hid the other side of the bay and softened the outlines of the buoys along the ramp. Although he had to squint and his eyes hurt a little, he looked at the shining steel ball that the sun formed on the water, as if it were God's eye fixed upon him. He turned his head, looked about; it was a heat front just like the one when the boys had brought him the lizard with two tails. Yes, now he was certain that the other two-tailed lizard, the one at the elementary school, really was laughing; of course it was laughing. Maybe not actually at him, but he surely was part of a general laughter, a kind of laughter of nature. He couldn't explain it, not even to himself, but he was certain: It was a lizard that smiled.

The only difference between the two heat fronts was that this one didn't bring with it that odd fear he'd felt previously. Now he wasn't afraid, and even felt a kind of peace, incomprehensible for someone with his problems. But he did feel that peace, and again he tried to look into the sun's reflection, which he did not succeed in doing, because Father Monteirinho appeared before him.

"I was looking for you," he said. "I want to apologize. I know how much this means to you. Forgive me for certain things I said."

"I was also thinking about looking for you, to apologize. Forgive me. Especially because I feel responsible for this mess you're in. Forgive me too. Sit down. Want something to drink?"

"A soft drink."

"A *guaraná*. You know, Monteirinho, I was thinking of something that seems kind of stupid, but isn't. I was thinking that this business of us believing man is God's favorite child is monumental insolence. In essence, we're not favorite children at all, we're what we make of ourselves, whatever we make of ourselves. I don't know if you understand me. Either we bring ourselves close to God, or we confront not His hatred, because He has no hatred, but His indifference. And I believe He is more and more indifferent, not because of Him, but because of us. Believe me, Monteirinho, the lizard will smile. Man is by definition a moral being, and when he ceases to be a moral being, he can only claim to be a child of God *latu sensu*, like any animal or plant, but not *strictu sensu*. The image, but not the likeness. And the image is the least important thing, because God is all the images. Believe me, man, He's indifferent; it's *our* problem. Besides that, He is nontemporal, so for Him all time is the present; time is our problem also. I understood all that now. I understood quite well looking at this heat front, looking at the sun reflected on the water and remembering certain things. Time is our problem too, as well as what we do with ourselves and with what's around us—which is the same thing. Time is merely the translation of our effort to integrate ourselves with Him, or in other words, with nontemporality. The soul is mortal, my dear Monteirinho. You die, it's gone. The only one who doesn't die is the one who goes to

Glory. And the Church can't do a thing; the Church is outside of people! It has to be inside!"

"How much have you had to drink?"

"Not even half a glass. It's nothing like that, Olavo Bento. I'm lucid; I've never been more lucid in my life. But it's a lucidity that pains me. I feel like some kind of prophet, like one of those heavy hitters from the Old Testament. Verily I say unto you, He is indifferent. We've made all this shit we see around us, and by making ourselves this shit we've alienated ourselves from Him; it's elementary reasoning. It's not He who is alienated, but us. And the lizard will smile, believe me."

"I don't understand. What lizard?"

"Nothing, nothing, my dear Reverend, nothing at all. Remember, my dear Reverend, even if the creatures never existed here, somewhere they exist and will exist, along with many other things of the same kind. No one will be able to prevent it. Do you agree?"

"I may agree, but I have faith that humanity—"

"If you agree, go pray! The lizard will smile! Now that I know that God is indifferent, I'm no longer afraid!"

And he continued to talk, paying no heed to the astonishment of the priest, who, concerned, left only after João decided to go home and have lunch.

10

He had told Monteirinho he was going to disappear, but he wasn't. He wasn't about to disappear; suddenly everything had changed. For several days after his binge, with no word from Ana Clara and feeling increasingly frustrated at the disappearance of the creatures, João Pedroso remained in morose despair and, unlike what he would have done in other circumstances, did not even pray. He was ashamed of God. Even Ana Clara's phone call didn't lift his spirits at first, for he was afraid she was calling to say she no longer loved him. He assumed a defensive attitude, which must have sounded strange to her, full of evasions and pauses, speaking of defeat and frustration. Now he was concerned about having acted that way, especially because the call had been hurried and nervous, since she was speaking from her house, taking advantage of a providential absence of Ângelo Marcos's. Yes, but it didn't constitute a major problem, and he would be very different when he met her. And that would be sooner than he'd expected, in fact, though under rather mysterious circumstances. In the call she had said in two days, that would be tomorrow, Ângelo Marcos was going out on the boat, in the company of a friend, a plantation owner, who was spending a few days on the island. They wanted to take a cruise and use the opportunity to transport to Salvador some antiques that the friend had been buying and crating—lots of old knickknacks from trunks to sewing machines and irons—and which he now wanted to ship to his city. So tomorrow they would meet. That was what João Pedroso thought until he found the note on his door. A bit mysterious also, only a typed strip of paper saying "Midnight, at Areia do Sete, at the mastodon." Had Ângelo Marcos moved his trip ahead to this evening? And why at Areia do Sete? Perhaps because of the romantic tradition; people always met there for romance. Mischievousness on her part. Of course, totally deserted, especially at this time of year, with the summer houses empty. Sure, it could be that Ângelo Marcos had decided to leave in the evening and she, worried or anxious because of his manner on the phone, perhaps couldn't bear waiting till the following day. It could also be that she suddenly suspected that this hasty trip was a ruse. Well, in any case she must have her reasons; he would be there.

Everything changed, yes; everything was cleared up after the phone call and the note. Ângelo Marcos's time period was almost over and the sense of desperation had evaporated. Not the obsession; the obsession continued. He was going to fight against it, do what he could. Now, for some reason, he was confident. He had thought it over and seen that the struggle wasn't against a specific target, like Lúcio Nemésio's projects. It was against all projects of that type or that spirit. Therefore, in his book he probably wouldn't even mention Lúcio Nemésio or the hospital. Yes, his book. He was going to write a book, and he had already laid out a plan of bibliographic research and begun to note down a few themes and ideas, disordered for the time being. Political and economic power over the evolution of species, especially the human. If man controls evolution, it will be dictated by those who hold power. Does power know what's best for the species, or merely what's best for its own short-term interest? The sociology of genetics. The ethics of genetics. Dictatorships programming official genetic standards. Now that the child can be specified, here are the government's specifications. Unlawful to have a child who doesn't meet the specifications, unpatriotic. Predetermination of sex: Cultures where, because of dowries or some other reason, it's bad business to have a daughter, and only males will be produced; opposite cultures will only produce females. Overpopulation of one or the other, thirty men per woman (and an entire economy built on the fact, with most women millionaires); the government intervenes:

Henceforth it is forbidden to have a male child, females only. Predetermination of abilities. The government plan establishes quotas, based on statistical projections, to adequately meet future labor needs. In free-market economies, parents will study these projections and invest in the production of children with more lucrative abilities. Various ways to use all this to finish the job of crippling the Third World. Monopoly-controlled pools of superior genes, like today's poultry farm chickens. Support for dictatorships that manipulate the genetic profile of the population according to the ruling interest. Supplying gametes for their barbarous ends. Patents for substances and procedures aimed at eliminating defects of genetic origin. Whoever wants to be sure his child won't inherit any defects can pay the fee. Rich countries with perfect generations and us teeming with every type of genetically-related health problem and buying medicine and contraptions from them to treat ourselves.

All he had to do was sit down and write the notes and he wouldn't stop scribbling, one idea following on the other's heels. But he couldn't get too enthusiastic; he had to give the book a sober tone that would avoid any similarity to pseudoscientific literature of the sensationalist type. He looked at the volumes lined up in his bookcase. Did he still know how to work with them? Yes, he did, and he had to get hold of several others; he had to have a bibliography that was at least reasonably up to date. Old Madeira's imported books shop must still exist, perhaps in the hands of his sons. Right, go to Salvador, take a look at old Madeira's catalogs, order the books, subscribe to some magazines. He rubbed his hands and smiled. Things were calm now, none of that hysterical reaction to the existence of the creatures, which had only served to wear him down. No, a book, a solid work, the beginning of a movement that would surely attract followers. A book that he would in any case publish, even at his own expense.

When he left, shortly before midnight, he was happy. He buttoned his jacket against the cold wind, and, eagerly looking forward to embracing and kissing Ana Clara for the first time in so many days, he took the Boulevard to walk to Areia do Sete. As he had foreseen, there was no one in the street, nothing, not a dog, not a cat, only the clicking sounds of the animals of the lowland in their grottoes. A few fireflies among the branches of the tamarind trees, the wind increasingly colder. He turned the corner at the pier, and went along it to Areia do Sete. With difficulty, because it was very dark, he made out the mastodon, the name she gave the large diesel station wagon that she liked to drive from time to time. He quickened his step, trying unsuccessfully to spot her inside the vehicle. When he was two steps from the car, he stopped, suddenly remembering the dead sparrows. Why hadn't he thought of that? Why had he acted so unwisely? But then, João Pedroso, you do nothing right, nothing at all! As sure as anything, it wasn't Ana Clara, it was Ângelo Marcos, in the station wagon. He hadn't taken the threat seriously, and now what would happen? Hesitating between turning back and verifying whether his suspicion was correct, he finally stepped a bit closer. He thought of calling her, but if it were not she, that would give her away.

"Ângelo Marcos?"

"No," a hoarse voice said from inside the car, and two .45 caliber bullets, shot from a pistol with a silencer, ripped through João Pedroso's heart. He died instantly and fell to the sidewalk beside the station wagon, from which a man emerged, picked him up and, with little difficulty, deposited him into a large plastic-lined crate in the back of the wagon among several others of the same type. He put padlocks on the three staples, cleaned up the bloodstains with a rag that he then threw into the sea, got back into the car and headed for the Grande Hotel, where he drove into the lot, parked, locked the car, and went up to his room.

At home, seated in his office with the TV on, Ângelo Marcos looked at the clock. Obviously everything had worked out; Boaventura was a consummate professional. Sensational, that idea about the antiques, which he'd had as soon as he found out the details of the job. As for that aspect of it, the plan left nothing to worry about. Taken aboard the launch, the crate containing João Pedroso's body—and, thinking about it, Ângelo Marcos shuddered and felt his mouth watering, as had happened when he killed sparrows—would be thrown into a deep part of the bay with lead weights so it would sink and never be found. By now, if everything had gone as planned, João Pedroso should already be in the back of the station wagon lent to Boaventura, properly packed away and awaiting shipment at 7:00 A.M. Excited, Ângelo Marcos felt like getting up and walking around the room, but he had to keep calm, because Ana Clara was still awake, writing in the small room, and mustn't suspect anything. Had she telephoned him? Certainly, of course she had; she wasn't going to miss a rare chance like that, which he himself had created by making up a story about a friend who might have arrived in his sailboat and dropped anchor at the new bridge. So he went out and stayed away from the house for a time. Or had she suspected something about that trip, coming out of nowhere and entirely contrary to what she expected of him? No, it really wasn't all that much out of nowhere, he had explained: He owed that friend favors; he couldn't deny him anything. It was an annoyance, but he really couldn't say no to him. Had she bought it? There was always room for doubt. Just as there was, incidentally, in several other aspects of the plan, because they depended on luck to a much greater extent than they liked, but there wasn't time; he couldn't wait for her to go live with João Pedroso, as with total certainty they must have already agreed to do. The thing was to act right away, take some risks. No, no, everything would work out—everything *was* working out.

Well, no point in staying here agonizing in front of the TV, where some cretin with the face of an asthmatic prophet was babbling a chain of stupidities about the environment, to which he paid no attention but which still annoyed him. He needed to go to sleep; he had to get up early the next morning. Boaventura would be down there with the station wagon and the antiques at 7:00 A.M. He had to get to the Market early to buy bait, because if some boat came by as they stopped to dump the body, they would pretend they were fishing until it left. It was off-season, midweek, probably there wouldn't be any boats, but better safe than sorry. And just the two of them would go, of course; the crew was on the other side, presumably setting out for the return trip. Yes, get some sleep, despite thinking he was going to have difficulty in dropping off. He got up, turned out the ceiling light, leaving a lamp on, passed by the half-open door of the small room, stopped and said good night to Ana Clara, without entering. She answered "Good night," and he went to the bedroom where he had been sleeping alone since the height of the crisis.

He thought about taking a sleeping pill, but he was afraid he wouldn't wake up at the appointed time, even with an alarm clock, as had happened more than once. He should have spoken with Cornélio or someone else to call him shortly after six, but he hadn't. Too bad. He had some trouble with the buttons of the digital alarm clock but managed to set it for six-fifteen. At seven he would be ready, down below. He lay about in his undershorts, turned on at low volume the FM radio with built-in speakers in the headboard, turned out the light, and went to bed. Odd, the same song that was playing on the radio at the hotel when he'd met Boaventura the last time was playing in his room. The same song—and he felt an erection swell the fly of his shorts.

Since Boaventura's arrival there had been nothing physical between them, just the occasional emergence of a certain climate quickly dispelled by averted eyes, changes of subject or trips to the balcony. But, that day, Boaventura had arrived earlier than scheduled, and when Ângelo Marcos called the room, he said he still had to shower, but why didn't he come up? He went up, and Boaventura opened the door wearing bermudas and no shirt. He'd take a quick shower; Ângelo Marcos should make himself comfortable. They were showing some excellent programs about animals on the TV. But Ângelo Marcos said he found such programs boring, asked permission, and turned off the TV, turned on the radio, and sat down in the armchair at the bathroom door, which Boaventura did not shut. Not only did he not shut it, he left it open enough so that, from the chair, he could be seen in the shower. What similarity to that other hotel, that other time! The air was charged with sex, with uncontrolled desire! And Ângelo Marcos, after squirming in the chair and gripping its arms, got up, already unbuttoning his shirt, stripped, and went to join the other man in the shower. They embraced, kissed, and rubbed soap on each other, delaying tenderly between the legs and behind. Then they dried each other quickly and, still a little wet and tousled, fell onto the bed and rolled about, intertwined. Adroitly, Ângelo Marcos, after they had given each other pleasure for several minutes, avoided letting Boaventura penetrate him, because now he was afraid, and, in a state of excitement that made him tremble, he lowered his mouth to the other man's crotch and sucked voluptuously, kissing his groin from time to time and resting his face in it. Boaventura, kneeling in the bed, began making back-and-forth movements, and then Ângelo Marcos took him in his mouth as far as he could, waiting, his prostate burning with desire and mad with pleasure, for him to come—which happened immediately afterward, in thick gushes of sperm into his throat that he swallowed almost thirstily, while Boaventura, gripping his head forcefully, moaned and collapsed to one side.

He hadn't needed anything else for him to come as well, and now he remembered, feeling the same desire, though less intense, as when, moaning more loudly each time, Boaventura had suddenly halted his thrusts and simply grasped his head, penetrating his mouth as far as he could—a clear sign he was going to come—the burning increased and a spasm contracted his pubis, and while the other ejaculated in him, he ejaculated onto the carpet on which he was kneeling. What a moment of ecstasy—although, immediately afterward, a certain awkwardness came over them. But only afterward, not before; before it was that uncontrollable lust, like this which assailed him now, with the music exacerbating the memory. And he sucked the fingers of his left hand to remember Boaventura, and masturbated until he came on the edge of the sheet, immediately rolling onto his back and falling asleep shortly afterward.

He slept much better than he expected, and when the alarm buzzed, he was already half dozing, half awake. He rose in a good mood, with an enthusiasm that reminded him of his childhood, when he would get up knowing he had a new toy or a special day ahead of him. A special day. And when he left the bedroom, shaved, showered, and dressed to go out, he even hummed as he went down for breakfast. He was very hungry and decided to make a radical break from his diet. Two fried eggs, that's it. Two fried eggs, the yolks not too hard, three fried sausages, lots of bread and butter. He ate everything, drank three cups of coffee with biscuits and jelly, and even thought of smoking a cigarette. No, not a cigarette. This feeling of well-being was enough, from having eaten what he really wanted for the first time in so long.

He left the house at precisely the moment the station wagon driven by Boaventura was entering the courtyard. He felt an instant of anxiety, but Boaventura, even before he stopped, smiled and gave him the thumbs-up sign. Everything under control; they could leave immediately. And they needed to, for the tide was going to turn into a huge ebb tide soon, and if they got any further behind, they might not be able to bring the boat up alongside the dock at the Market, and that would be a problem. Edsonil and two of his brothers, called the day before, must already be waiting for them at the ramp to load the crates. After leaving a message for Ana Clara, who was still sleeping, Ângelo Marcos went inside, picked up a few accoutrements, sat down beside Boaventura, and they pulled away.

No problem. They found bait when they arrived; the black men were at their places, and it was simple to arrange a pirogue for Ângelo Marcos to go to the boat and maneuver it back to the dock. The blacks had little difficulty with the crates, despite some of them, like the one with João Pedroso—Ângelo Marcos knew which one it was and almost smiled when it was lowered onto the boat—being rather heavy. Once the boat was loaded and the blacks had released the lines, Boaventura leapt for the passageway as Ângelo Marcos maneuvered spectacularly around the large buoy and set out for Salvador, in the mouth of the outgoing waters, with the tide.

But they didn't follow a direct route, because they needed to first arrive at the spot where they could unload the coffin, which Boaventura was now piercing in several places with a brace and bit. At two points he drilled holes in a circle and managed to make openings approximately six inches in diameter, explaining that all the holes were so the crate would fill with water, and the two larger ones were for fish and crabs to get in and finish the job. He quickly ran lines through some of the small holes and tied several lead weights on them, at the sides of the crate.

"Done," he said, looking with satisfaction at the result. "Ready for shipment. All that's left is to push it over the side."

"Push it right there. It's pretty deep here."

They didn't even have to come to a full stop. Ângelo Marcos put the boat in slow ahead, turned on the autopilot, looked around, saw nothing but the outlines of the bay and the island coast, and went down to help Boaventura throw the crate, now quite heavy because of the lead, into the sea. They spread a canvas over the side of the boat in order not to scratch it, and with some difficulty hoisted the crate, which immediately tumbled into the water and sank with a rapidity that was somewhat disappointing. A certain sense of anticlimax—was that it, everything over with in this insipid manner? Yes, that was it, everything over with; it was almost no fun. Ângelo Marcos looked at Boaventura and gripped his hand. He went back to the wheel and accelerated again, looking back, in an effort that he knew to be futile, to mark the spot where he had left that son of a bitch's corpse.

At eleven the truck from the transport company had already come to the Yacht Club to pick up Boaventura's antiques, and Ângelo Marcos decided to phone Ana Clara. He said nothing to give away the pleasure the call gave him, a pleasure he had anticipated and which he now enjoyed with greater intensity than he had foreseen. He spoke in a cordial and unconcerned voice. He just wanted to let her know that his friend and he were going to stay and have lunch in the city with some other friends and wouldn't be back until late afternoon. Was everything all right? Yes, yes, it was, but he felt from her tone that it wasn't. And he was right, because, nervous and irritated, she couldn't understand why João Pedroso didn't answer his phone, and she was inclined to go to his house, whatever it led to.

* * *

Ana Clara stopped in the middle of the conversation she was having with Cornélio about dinner and almost began to cry. No, not to cry—to bellow, to bellow like a cow, to scream like a woman possessed, throwing herself against the wall, pulling her hair, tearing her flesh, rolling on the floor, and gnawing the table legs. What was she doing there, what kind of absurdity was this? What an insane farce, what horror! What was going on? What did all this mean? Did anything make sense? Her chin quivered and her eyes swam, but she bit her tongue and got herself under control. Yes, Cornélio, but it wasn't a Lion's Club party, so no stroganoff, for God's sake! And none of those thick fillets surrounded by peas, heart of palm, and asparagus that pass for food at politicians' banquets. No, something decent. That large snook from the freezer, baked whole. And a large steak made with fillet, several omelets. Rice, manioc garnish, cassava purée, cowpea salad, a few more cheery things, and voilà, a proper dinner. Ambrosia, compote of cashew fruit, guava paste with cheese and those smelly little cheeses that should be taken from the fridge half an hour early so they can become even smellier.

It was good that Cornélio neither whined nor argued; if he had, she really would have screamed. Life seemed to hang by a thread these days, something was always on the verge of disintegrating, and this dinner was the last straw. A going-away party for that plantation owner friend of Ângelo Marcos's, an oleaginous and slippery type with a smile like a crocodile. And Lúcio Nemésio and Rosário as well. Good lord! And her totally lost, not knowing what to think, or what to do, or where to go, or whom to talk to—pregnant, alone, desperate, full of hate, frustration, and suspicion. What madness; no one said anything, no one said a thing, João gone, wiped from the face of the earth, and no one did anything. Could he really have run away, gone mad? Where could he be? His fishermen went to the police, Boa Morte had told her. An agent searched João's house without finding a lead but was willing to call the Bureau of Security and ask them to take an interest, although it was a case with which he was already more than familiar. It happens every day: A guy goes out to buy cigarettes and nobody ever lays eyes on him again. You get cases like that every day. The thing to do was contact his relatives, if he had any, and wait; there was nothing to be done.

Nothing to be done, nothing to be done! What do you mean, nothing to be done? It wasn't possible for the world to have crumbled so abruptly, precisely now that everything seemed to be heading for the best conceivable outcome. Despair, despair, total disorientation, absolute confusion—wouldn't it be better to die? The time period completed, with her still there in that indescribable situation, even forced to listen to Ângelo Marcos's sarcasm. God in heaven, there had be to be something within her reach, there had to be some kind of solution for her life. Despite their estrangement, she had attempted to talk to Bebel, but as always happens when you need someone, she was in Europe. Despair, despair, despair inside, outside, on all sides.

By now she had abandoned most of her precautions and no longer thought of the possibility of Ângelo Marcos surprising her on the several occasions when she went by João's house and even when she posted herself in front of it like a statue for hours at a time. She had also sought out the priest. The priest seemed not to like her, but to hell with him, she needed to talk with someone about the mystery. But he too knew nothing, and apparently he agreed with the police detective, believing that João had gone into crisis over the story of the monkey children and had decided to disappear; he had been talking about it lately—and she recalled, with unbearable anguish, that he had said something like that in their last phone call. But he couldn't, he couldn't disappear. Could it be possible that he was that different from what she thought? Could he be just what he appeared when he'd abased himself by getting plastered in Ângelo Marcos's presence? Good God, good God, what to do, what to think?

But she had to stay calm, had to control herself, had to make a cold assessment. The only way out of this was to consider all aspects of the situation objectively and then take action. To think, using Suzanna

Fleischman's method, the "worst-case scenario" method. Think of absolutely the worst thing that can happen and then you see that you can survive; in the end everything works out. Yes, the first step to gaining psychological peace is think of the worst that can happen. It isn't easy; it takes imagination, logical reasoning, and intuition. And she would stay calm; she had to stay calm. She couldn't sink deeper and deeper into that impotent hopelessness.

But how could she stay calm during that horrible dinner in which all of them seemed odious and suspect to her? She did her best to pay attention to the conversation and be nice, but every so often their faces seemed to separate from their bodies and float in the air like pathetic balloons. She didn't want to pretend she wasn't feeling well in order to leave; she wanted to be well mannered, but at each moment the impulse became stronger to flee and never see any of them again, never again. Instead of that supposed flight, João might have been assassinated by one of them. Maybe Ângelo Marcos, with that repellent expression of happiness and making his habitual unfunny funny remarks, had received another anonymous letter, this time mentioning João by name. And what about Lúcio Nemésio? If that story about the hospital was true, wouldn't he be capable of having João eliminated? No, of course not; it was all crazy, delirium. But, in any case, she was having difficulty, ever more difficulty, in remaining in their company.

"This snook reminds me of one I caught near the mouth of the Paraguaçu," Ângelo Marcos told Lúcio Nemésio. "A real beauty. I caught three that day, one of them a little bigger than this one. A lot bigger, actually, a fifteen- or seventeen-pounder. You don't fish, do you, professor?"

"No. For me, fish is a foodstuff you buy at the fish market."

"Too bad; otherwise we could go fishing together on the boat. Although my best fishing buddy, who knows everything there is to know about the waters around here, seems to have decided to disappear. You heard about it, didn't you? João Pedroso vanished without a trace."

"Yes, I heard. It didn't really surprise me, because João Pedroso was always rather disturbed, rather odd, and lately he was worse, even a bit mythomaniacal. Even though he made up that whole story, I bear him no grudge. I still like him and I'm worried, because I feel he may have gone mad once and for all."

"So do I. Nobody vanishes like that, without a word, only crazy people. And there's also the drinking problem; he drinks like a fish. Just the other day, here at the house, he got so soused that I had to drive him home."

"Have the police discovered anything? Stupid question. Of course not, because they don't pay any attention to people who disappear, unless it's a kidnapping or murder. And I absolutely refuse to believe João was kidnapped or murdered. I can't imagine who'd do such a thing. Our own João Pedroso . . . What is it, dear? What's wrong, Dona Ana, are you feeling ill? Why so pale?"

"Migraine," Ana Clara said, her voice faltering and her head spinning. She rose quickly, stammered an apology, and ran to her room, where she locked herself in, fell onto the bed, and began to cry. A few minutes later she got up, dizzy and still crying, rummaged through a drawer and removed two small medicine bottles—a tranquilizer and some sleeping pills. But before she could decide which to take, she remembered her pregnancy. She couldn't use those medicines; they were undoubtedly the type that harmed the fetus. Yes, the child in her belly, now a child without a father. Could it be possible? Was that really it? She was fantasizing so much about that child, never desired before and now so wanted. She had been sure it would be a boy and he'd learn to fish with his father. She imagined herself teaching him things. What despair, what horrible anguish—and she fell onto the bed again to sob.

And it was still in bed, although no longer lying on her stomach, but staring at the ceiling with a fixed gaze and an empty expression, that Ângelo Marcos found her after knocking on the door several times without an answer. He came into the room; she appeared not to have noticed his presence, even when he went up to the bed, leaned over, and asked if the migraine was any better. She didn't say anything, and he repeated the question a few times, with the same result. Then she sat up in bed with an abrupt movement, stared at him in rage, and said she didn't want to talk to him about anything. She told him to leave, to get out and never look for her again.

"Go away, go away, go away!" she screamed, standing up and shaking her fists. "Go away!"

"Calm down, Ana Clara. I just came to see how you're getting along. Before they left, everybody was worried about you, as I am. That's the only reason I came. No offense intended."

"Yes, there is! Yes, there is! Everything about you is offensive! Go away! Go away, please! Leave me alone!"

"All right, but I see no reason for you to be in such a condition."

"What do you know about my condition? What do you know about my condition? You have nothing to do with my condition, you know that? Nothing!"

"I don't understand the reason, but I understand enough to see that it's a quasi-hysterical condition. Hysteria pure and simple, in fact."

"No, not a hysterical condition! I'm going to tell you what my condition is. My condition is expectant—isn't that the way they put it? That's right, an expectant condition, did you hear that?"

"I don't understand."

"You never understand anything I tell you. Expectant condition, expectant condition, a condition of pregnancy. Now do you understand? I'm pregnant! Pregnant! I'm going to have a child. You understand now? I'm preg-nant!"

"You're what?"

"For the love of God, Ângelo Marcos, go away. Please, leave me alone. Go away. I don't want to look at you."

"Oh no. Now you're going to explain all this in detail. You said you're pregnant?"

"Isn't that what you heard?"

It was, of course, but he still insisted on confirming it several times, each time making ever more dramatic gestures and sudden pauses in his pacing back and forth. This was incredible. So she was pregnant by the man who was her lover. Her lack of good sense, her irresponsibility, and lack of character had come to that point? And she still thought he had no right to know who that man was? Who was he?

She answered, and he had the same reaction as when he learned of her pregnancy. João Pedroso, João Pedroso? Absolutely unbelievable! João Pedroso? That bastard, that scum, simulating friendship, winning his confidence, only to later stab him in the back! And he'd even been hypocritical enough, when already his wife's lover, to come and ask for support and favors. A greater act of vileness was impossible! No, it could only be a tasteless joke; this wasn't happening! And just look at what a humiliating and degrading situation she had descended to, by her own hand. After impregnating her, the wretch had refused to take responsibility and had run away. Run away as he had run away all his life, in order not to have to face reality—the coward, the scum, the bastard! She must be feeling very good, pregnant by him and unable to harbor the slightest hope of ever seeing him again because he had run away—you patsy, you fool, you cheap whore, you idiot! The child, naturally, would never be born. When was she getting the abortion?

"Abortion? You must be crazy. I'm not getting an abortion, I'm going to have my child."

"No, you're the one who's crazy. Of course you're going to get an abortion. You can't have that child."

"And why can't I? Obviously I can. I make my own decisions, and I've decided I'm going to have my child."

"Oh no, oh no you're not! You most certainly are not! You know perfectly well that I had a vasectomy, and my friends know it too. I'm not going to lose face like that!"

"One thing has nothing to do with the other. The child isn't yours anyway, and I never had any intention of telling anyone it's yours. There's no loss of face involved; it happens every day. A married woman falls in love with another man, leaves her husband, and has a child with that other man."

"But you didn't leave me! You got pregnant by another man in the confines of your marriage!"

"I didn't leave because you wouldn't let me. But I'm leaving."

"You're leaving—how? How, since that bastard disappeared, abandoned you, with his mess in your belly?"

"That's my problem, and besides that, this disappearance is temporary. He must be away taking care of some urgent matter. I'm certain he's coming back."

"Well, I'm just as certain he's not coming back. A coward like that, a weakling, a man without moral fiber, a drunk—like hell he's coming back. Don't hold your breath. He's off boozing in Rondônia or some such place, until he knocks up the next damned fool woman and moves on to Bolivia."

"I've already said that's my problem. You have nothing to do with it."

"With the child, I do! The child affects me, affects my honor, my reputation, my dignity! You're not going to have that child!"

"That's enough! Go away! Leave me alone! Enough! Get out of my sight! You irritate me, and I have nothing to say to you. Get out!"

"You're not going to have that child, you brazen whore, you bitch, you common whore. You're not going to discredit me, you two-bit whore, you're not going to discredit me!"

"Ângelo Marcos, don't you dare raise your hand to me. Don't be stupid enough to strike me!"

"Whore! Shameless whore!"

He launched himself toward her with his right hand, palm outward, in the air, but she grabbed him by the wrists, kicked him in the shin, and after a moment's hesitation during which he rubbed the spot of the blow, she snatched the keys from the dresser top and ran out. He ran after her but was unable to overtake her and merely witnessed, from a few yards away, the instant her shoe caught on one of the steps of the stairs and she tumbled to the first floor, where, after attempting weakly to move her torso, she remained lying in a twisted position.

The hospital, of course. She deserved that fall, deserved even more, but he didn't want to be accused of negligence. He called Cornélio to help carry her to a car—to save time, the same one whose keys she had grabbed before running out. He felt her pulse; not as weak as he had imagined. Well, in any case he wouldn't know what to do to help her, and he might even do something to make it worse. On the other hand, couldn't moving her aggravate any trauma? He stood up, thinking of phoning the hospital and asking for an ambulance, when she changed positions with a groan and tried to sit up, not succeeding until he helped her.

"Better not to move much. Where does it hurt?"

"My foot. My foot, my head, and my stomach."

"Do you think you can make it to the car with help, or do you want me to call an ambulance?"

"I don't know. I don't know. I'm dizzy. Oh!"

"I think it's best to call the ambulance. Treatment here starts en route. When I tell them who I am, they'll be here in five minutes."

In nine, actually. And Ângelo Marcos got in the car to follow them, arriving just after they had taken Ana Clara inside. At the admissions desk, great courtesy—she seemed all right, she was quite lucid and looked good, for one who'd suffered an accident. Wouldn't he like to watch the examinations? No, he wouldn't. He got very nervous when something happened to a member of the family; he preferred to remain downstairs, in the waiting room.

He didn't leave the hospital until much later, after he had walked miles around the waiting room and the garden and had leafed through every magazine he'd found. Despite the wait, he didn't leave unhappy—just the opposite; he left very happy. She had fractured a small bone in her ankle, a trifling fracture that was now in a cast. She'd taken a blow to the head, but it was nothing more than a lump and a slight dizziness; it hadn't been a real concussion. She was in there, sedated, among other reasons because the doctor said she had become very nervous and agitated as soon as she learned she'd lost the child. She kept repeating that she was an opossum, the doctor said; did Ângelo Marcos know what that meant? No, he didn't know, and though he didn't tell the doctor, he had no desire to know. But there was no way to refuse to take a look at her, which wasn't very difficult, because she was sleeping, though her face was strangely contracted. He stayed beside her for a short time, said good-bye to the doctor, and returned home, thinking how good it was that the thing he had wished for so much, while in the waiting room, had come to pass. Now he was free of that worrisome problem of the pregnancy. God is great.

"Bonkers," Tavinho said. "Not bonkers where they strap you down and pump a gallon of tranquilizer into your veins, but still bonkers, completely bonkers."

"It's not that bad," Bebel said. "At first, yes, she did seem a lot worse. When I got back from Europe, I thought she was going to die—pale, kind of emaciated, with that cast on her foot and the crutch, refusing to talk, refusing to eat, a real mean depression, to the point that I thought about going to stay with her for a time, from fear she'd commit suicide. But not now; now she's fine. She's got some pretty weird habits, but you could say they're just eccentricities. No, she's not bonkers, not at all."

"Then I don't know what you mean by bonkers. Don't you remember that day at her house when I said something about us going fishing on the island? I was talking to her and it looked like she wasn't listening. I repeated: 'What say, Ana Clara, why don't we go on another fishing trip on the island?' Not a word out of her. It was like I was completely invisible and inaudible. That bugged me, so I nudged her arm: 'Hey, Ana Clara, don't you hear me? Hey, Ana Clara, what do you say to another fishing trip, on the island?' You heard it, you and Nando. You both heard what she answered. She had almost a look of rage on her face and she said: 'I can't stand the island and I hate boats.' "

"Yeah, I know. I knew it already; she'd told me that before."

"And it didn't shock you? How can that be? She used to love the island."

"Beats me. Maybe because of the accident. I don't know, people change. And she just suddenly changed."

"Come off it, Bebel. Later I mentioned that friend of yours, that guy who showed us the fishing places—what's his name?"

"João Pedroso."

"Right. I mentioned him and she got up, straightened her hair, and said: 'I don't remember any of that. You have a very fertile imagination, Tavinho.' And she walked away."

"Yes, I know. Very strange, but it's not enough to prove she's crazy. Maybe she wants to forget something; such things happen. Besides which, she hit her head, in the accident."

"Just a very minor blow; Marquinhos told me. And he also told me she's bonkers, and that the doctor prescribed a real cocktail of pills for her."

"Well, the fact is that she's still my friend, and an excellent friend at that. I enjoy her company immensely and I don't see anything crazy about her."

"Fine, fine. Let's not fight over it. C'mere and give me a kiss, c'mere. Sexy! You know, every day I think you're sexier. I never get tired of screwing you. It's better now than when we were married, isn't it? How come we took so long to start getting together?"

"Because you were snorting all the time and the least you'd have done was tell Nando at the first opportunity."

"But you yourself always said you told Nando everything."

"Not in your case. In your case I made an exception. I don't think it'd go over well with him. It's better to leave things the way they are, in secret. Don't even think, not for a minute, not for a fraction of a second, of saying anything to Nando."

"Of course, of course, love. I not only promised, I've given up snorting too. There's no danger."

"Sometimes I wonder about your reform. I—"

"Hey, forget it. No need to wonder about anything. I'm a serious man. C'mere, c'mere. Let me feel that ass, that fantastic ass! Oh, you sexy woman!"

There was no avoiding one last lay for the road, which incidentally was great. Tavinho was showing real talent in bed—who'd have thought it? But the result was that she was late leaving his apartment. She needed to write down a few things to do the next day, she needed to make calls to a lot of people and it was already past five, and there wouldn't be time for everything. The following day wouldn't necessarily be too late, but time was getting short and the party had to be absolutely impeccable, without the slightest flaw. It called for her exclusive dedication and, therefore, no extracurricular distractions—that is, no Tavinho until after the party. Everything was going well, and so forth and so on, but not only mustn't the organizing of the party be hampered; the truth was that she was seeing Tavinho too often. Three times last week, a major overindulgence. Eventually Nando was going to get suspicious, and that mustn't happen. No, no one could know of the affair, except possibly Ana Clara.

Or could she? What if she suddenly went off her head for good? For now, Tavinho was wrong; she was under control, practically normal. Make that entirely normal, except maybe to someone who knew her intimately before. She hadn't fallen back into a depression, like in those first days. No, not the first days—the first two or three months. Thinking back, it seemed she'd never recover. Really sad. At that time she hadn't yet become amnesiac—if she really did have amnesia, this odd amnesia that seemed a bit too specific. Back then, when she felt like talking to Bebel, she related everything that now she no longer remembers. She told all about the pregnancy and the miscarriage and how, for a few days, she had terrible nightmares in which she was an opossum that they'd once clubbed to death and that was carrying its immature offspring in its pouch. And then she'd cry, sometimes for days on end, as she also cried when she spoke of João Pedroso, about whom she alternated, as if reciting a litany, between saying that she forgave him and didn't forgive him, forgave and didn't forgive, forgave and didn't forgive. As for Marquinhos, she did not speak his name, calling him merely "he," and she would lock herself in when he was at home. But she explained that she hadn't changed her mind about leaving him, she just lacked the energy to do so—and then she would cry again and call herself a despicable person, a worm, an insect that didn't deserve to live. It was at that time that Bebel decided to spend a few days in her company, afraid she might kill herself. But when she arrived at her house to discuss the matter, she got an enormous surprise, because, wearing denim overalls, with garden shears in her hand and a mason's trowel stuck in her rear pocket, pieces of leaves clinging to her sweating face and her hair piled on top of her head, she received her with a smile from ear to ear, hugging her without touching her with her hands, which were dirty with soil.

"Suzanna Fleischman!" she exclaimed, bubbling. "I've been writing since six in the morning, and I decided to give my head a rest and do a little gardening."

"How marvelous. I can't believe it. You look so well! I don't believe it, for someone who three days ago— But how wonderful, Aninha, you're like another person. It's a miracle."

"I'm not *like* another person; I *am* another person. I'm not Ana Clara, I'm Suzanna Fleischman. You know me."

"Yes, I know. But you're also Ana Clara."

"No. I'm exclusively Suzanna Fleischman. Ana Clara is someone else."

"Yes, but—"

It took some time for Bebel to realize that she was serious and that she no longer thought of herself as Ana Clara, only as Suzanna Fleischman. Naturally she knew—as she confided with a sly expression—that the others thought she was Ana Clara. So she pretended, just for convenience, that she was Ana Clara. It was all a trick, a way for Suzanna not to be pestered. For example, of course Suzanna didn't get along with Ângelo Marcos—she had total contempt for him—but in front of the others she spoke with him, and no one suspected anything.

"And what about the separation? Are you going ahead with the separation?"

"What separation? The only one who can separate from him is Ana Clara. I don't have anything to do with him; I was never married to him. He supports me. I have no material cares. It's as if he were my patron. And in fact it's very little for him to do to expiate all the bad things he did, does, and will do, that absolute scoundrel. I even maintain he's queer—always did think so—and doesn't have the courage to face reality."

"And do you think Ana Clara will get a separation?"

"Oh, I don't know. I'm coming to the conclusion that Ana Clara is a weakling, a wimpy little princess without a brain in her head. Separate, my foot. She's hopeless. She deserves that fragrant lowlife—stinking lowlife, I mean."

"Good thing, because João Pedroso has disappeared and, independent of my being against it, for her to face the separation all alone would have been very difficult."

"What João Pedroso? I don't understand what you're talking about."

"Anin—Suzanna—Suzanna, are you serious? You don't know anything about João Pedroso?"

"You can call me Aninha, everybody does, and I'm used to it. Now, as for that João, of course I don't know anything about him. I have the vague impression that I've heard of him, but I've forgotten and have no desire to remember. It's hard work, and I need to occupy my mind with other things. I've lots of projects, really all kinds of projects; you have to see them. I'm truly inspired. Let's go to my office. I decided to put together a real office, a writer's office, and I'm going to learn to type so I can write directly on the machine. Let's go to my office so I can show you some things. Everything's just beginning, even a soap opera I'm writing. A soap!"

On the desk, among a profusion of pads, pens of every kind, staplers, punches, paperweights and dozens of small office items, was a stiff-cover notebook with a white label glued to the front, which read "The

Adventures of Amanda Cienfuegos, or Badness Rewarded: A work moral and educational, containing lessons on Love, Money, and Happiness without Work." This Amanda Cienfuegos was a fantastic woman, extremely pretty, sexy as could be, out for what she could get, and vulgar. She became a millionaire by screwing and putting horns on everybody and then marrying the king and putting horns on him too. Told like that, it might seem not to have anything of interest, but she could guarantee it would be excellent. But that wasn't the main project; the main project was to rewrite Machiavelli. Yes indeed, rewrite Machiavelli! She'd heard of *The Prince*. So she decided, without knowing exactly how or why, to nose around in those virgin collections of the son of a bitch, and at once she came across *The Prince*. A tiny little book, she read it all in a couple of hours—wonderful. At first she'd thought merely of parodying it by writing a book with the title *Theory and Practice of the Shrewd Woman*. No, not that. So she crossed out that woman-and-power stuff and decided to confront rewriting the beast. *The Princess—Machiavelli for Women*. How was that for a title? She thought it excellent. She wouldn't start in order but with the parts she considered most interesting, like the one about obtaining principalities through double-dealing. Fantastic, fantastic—tremendous ideas. When it was ready, Bebel would be the first to see it. And publication was guaranteed; the louse would pay for it, of course. It was his obligation. Pick one of those publishing houses in Rio or São Paulo, the prestigious ones, give the guys some dough, and publish the book. No publication party; she'd already decided how her literary career would go. She'd be the mysterious type; no one would know the identity of Suzanna Fleischman, only those who already knew—Bebel and the bastard. No photographs, no interviews, total mystery. Oh, so much to do, so exciting! After gardening she was going to eat something—her stomach was hollow from hunger, hunger for turnovers, hunger for a sandwich, hunger for a chicken croquette, everything that was crap—and then hit the notebooks again; Amanda was on her way to getting ready for the first dirty trick of a very long series.

Even after she became accustomed, it sometimes took Bebel a

while to know if she was talking to Ana Clara or to Suzanna, because when she called her Ana, she still responded, even if at the moment she was Suzanna, with her trick of pretending she was Ana, although there was also their clothes and the way they got ready, always a bit different. Suzanna had pulled Ana Clara out of her depression once and for all, because when Suzanna suddenly disappeared and Ana Clara returned, she was quite different. Talkative, a spendthrift, brash, somewhat frivolous, funny, smiling, and festive, although with many new odd things about her, like refusing to hear of the island or the boat, getting nauseated if she saw or smelled fresh fish, and, like Suzanna, claiming to have absolutely no recollection of João Pedroso. Well, you find it strange at first, but you get used to it. The alternation between Ana Clara and Suzanna ended up making little difference. Just the opposite: It made their friendship more fun and gave it more variety. In some way, the two continued to be the same person, friendly, pleasant, a confidante, certainly a lot better than in the days when she had decided to commit that folly of going to live with a fish vendor and was even talking and thinking like him.

Everything's changed for the better, Bebel thought when, shortly after five, she parked the car in the garage and dashed to Nando's office, which he was using as the center for the party preparations. Lists and more lists, millions of lists, an infernal state of confusion. Anxiety to start the work at once; there were times when she had the impression that she'd never manage to get everything done. She went to the bedroom, put on some light clothes, and returned almost at a run. She picked up the first list, made a show of irritation as if about to throw it in the wastebasket, and changed her mind in mid-gesture. Ângelo Marcos's list of guests. A few acceptable people, but many of low extraction. Why had she had the unfortunate idea of asking him for a list? Well, he was enjoying great prestige and might even be a candidate for governor, a kind of compromise choice in the dogfight that the internal dispute in the party was turning into.

Ângelo Marcos had in fact entered one of the best phases of his life, even where Ana Clara was concerned. Surprisingly, he had learned to live with her on her terms and was getting along quite well. Well, maybe not so surprisingly, because everyone knew about his relationship with Mônica Leitão Sobral, who by now was practically a kept woman. So, as Ana Clara didn't mind and Suzanna Fleischman occupied herself with her crazy writings, things were very convenient for him. And he might actually be a candidate, maybe even get elected. Yeah, Bebel thought, let's send His Excellency's invitations. The political types would segregate themselves naturally and she would create two basic settings, which would facilitate the division at the party. On one side, the squares. On the other, the real party. Everything had to go right; she was staking everything on this party—Nando's fortieth birthday. Everything had to be truly perfect.

And everything did in fact turn out almost perfect. The house seemed like an illuminated palace in the middle of the garden and lawn, the pool was out of a fairy tale, there was an orchestra on the large veranda, a discotheque sound system downstairs, she and Ana Clara looking very beautiful and very turned on, there was an impeccable division between the with-it crowd and the squares, the nearby bathrooms were filled with people snorting, and the tables over there were occupied by the stiffs; everything was truly above criticism. The only problem occurred around three in the morning, when a group of armed men tried to cross the security area separating the garden from the outside wall and carry out a robbery. But the dogs and the guards did their job, as well as the alarms that Nando installed, and even the police arrived without delay, engaging in a gun battle with the robbers, killing two, wounding three, and dispersing the rest. Nando did not refuse interviews to the newspapers the following day. Just the opposite: He insisted, because he thought that by letting it be known how well protected his house was, it would discourage future robberies. And he took advantage of the opportunity to denounce the lack of security in Brazilian cities and demonstrate his support for instituting the death penalty as the only means of containing the wave of violence. In the society pages, the spotlight was on Bebel Magalhães. At the moment when shots were popping outside, the orchestra stopped and a certain panic began taking hold, she said she suddenly remembered the sinking of the *Titanic*, when the musicians continued playing as the ship went down, and grabbed the maestro by the sleeve and ordered the music to resume as if nothing were happening. She was greatly applauded for her courage and sangfroid.

At afternoon's end, after hovering in spirals over the crests of the low waves along the old bridge, a majestic and deliberate waterfowl dived suddenly, drawing in its large wings, and became an arrow that plunged and emerged some distance ahead, a fish glistening in its beak. Father Monteirinho, standing beside the dock to admire the bird, smiled and sighed. He needed the walk and the fresh air, needed it much more than he had been aware of before. How different was the parish he now occupied, in the backlands some 350 miles from here, another world. The sea magnified the horizon; it was freedom, the sensation that there will always be the other side, always a way out. He sighed again, and resumed the walk he had begun as soon as he'd arrived in the small city he hadn't seen for months. The old walk from the time he had lived here, a time that now seemed so long ago, the old routine. Which, by the way, might end today at the Largo da Quitanda, a few dozen yards from where he was. Yes, why not? He would finish at the square, choose a table facing the sunset, order a beer—no, not a beer, a whiskey, in honor of old times—and cultivate the bittersweet melancholy that was sure to come to him, amid nostalgic memories and old feelings.

It was still Luiz the Waiter. Of course it was; why should it be anyone else? But in fact everything appeared so remote to him that he was surprised to see the same things, as if so much time had passed that everything had to be different. But it wasn't. There was no difference at all. With the square almost deserted, he sat in exactly the place he had expected to find unoccupied, ordered a whiskey with a little water and ice, and fixed his eyes on the horizon before him, where the sun was a red semicircle among frayed clouds. The whiskey arrived. Night was falling rapidly; only a few streetlights on the square came on, and Monteirinho became enveloped in a soft penumbra, experiencing in reality the melancholy he had anticipated.

Beginning to sip the second whiskey and promising himself he wouldn't have a third, although he wanted to, he thought how, if not for Luiz the Waiter occasionally passing by and two voices talking from a spot he couldn't pinpoint, it was possible to think he was all alone in the world, immobile in time, detached from everything, close to God. A new moon, the sky dark; he changed position slightly in the chair to see the stars more comfortably and became irritated when his eyes were dazzled by the headlights of a car that pulled up on the other side and were pointing toward his table. He protected his eyes with his hand, but the light still bothered him, and the car's occupant appeared neither to wish to get out, nor to turn off the lights. He was thinking about complaining, when the lights were finally turned off and a corpulent form emerged from the car, headed to a nearby table, sat down, and was transformed into a black silhouette contrasting with the whitewashed trunk of the oiti tree behind it.

Monteirinho was again looking at the sky when he sensed that the man was staring at him. He was wearing a hat, which accentuated the darkness surrounding his face, but it was impossible not to realize the direction of his persistent gaze. Who was the guy, and what did he mean by that unpleasant look? Yes, more and more unpleasant, causing him to squirm in his chair and want to get up and go somewhere else. How silly; he couldn't even be sure the man actually had his eyes glued on him. It might be just an impression. No, it wasn't. But it was also only the look of a stranger; there was no reason to have taken it as hostile. But he had. If not hostile, at least not friendly. Perhaps not even that, but certainly unpleasant. Yes, unpleasant. And not only the look, but also its owner, even though he couldn't see his features. Maybe he could move to another table behind the chestnut tree, where that look couldn't reach him, but before he could decide, he was startled, for the stranger rose and came toward him with rapid steps.

"Good evening," he said, and Monteirinho was startled to see who it was. "You're Father Monteirinho, aren't you? We were never introduced, but naturally I know you rather well by name. And by sight."

"I know you too, by name and by sight. You're Dr. Lúcio Nemésio, director of the hospital, aren't you? When you arrived, I didn't recognize you, maybe the hat—"

"Yes, well, it's me. Pleased to meet you. Do you mind if I sit down in your company for a bit?"

Yes, he did mind. The other man was speaking in a friendly manner and there was no call for mistreating him, but because of the memory of the story about the creatures and the possibility that they actually existed, his presence upset Monteirinho. Not to mention the awkwardness because, after all, they had traded accusations publicly, even if the main fight had been with João Pedroso. But he answered that of course he didn't mind, and Lúcio Nemésio returned briefly to his table, got his glass, and sat down across from Monteirinho. He hadn't seen the priest in a long time—had he been traveling or some such thing?

"No. Transferred. I'm in another diocese, in Santa Maria da Vitória."

"Santa Maria da Vitória? Pretty far, eh?"

"That's true. Very far."

"And you're going around the island, out of nostalgia."

"No, it's not that, actually. I miss it, but that's not why I came. I came to pick up some things of mine that I left here temporarily until I could get settled in Santa Maria da Vitória. I've taken care of everything and I go back tomorrow."

"You must be finding it strange that I came over to speak with you. After that problem of João Pedroso's accusations, which you supported, you might think there's some animosity on my part. There is none, I can assure you. It was a mistake, which I perfectly understand."

"I saw the photos."

"What photos?"

"The ones you destroyed."

"The photos meant nothing. They were crude forgeries."

"But you destroyed them."

"Because I didn't want to be bothered anymore having to give interviews to stupid reporters, just to clear up a fraud of which you were the victims."

"That's not quite what João Pedroso told me."

"You know our João is a troubled man. Even so, I like him and harbor no grudge against him either, because of that episode. On the contrary: I'm worried about him. That's why I came to you. I thought that, as his friend, you might have some news of him. Do you know where he is?"

"I haven't the slightest idea. Sometimes I even think he may have been killed."

"Killed? Who could want to kill him? Who would benefit from his death?"

"I don't know. It's all speculation, things that pass through my head, and it's irresponsible to speak them aloud."

"That hypothesis never occurred to me. I think he's alive and I'd like to know where."

"Dr. Nemésio, what I'm about to say to you is not intended to be the least bit aggressive, let me make that clear. It's not my intention to offend you or accuse you, but I cannot refrain from asking you this question. The truth is that if you and João were initially friends, you later broke off under unpleasant circumstances in which you spoke badly of him and he of you. Which leads one to believe that your curiosity as to his whereabouts is based less on friendship, as you say, than on self-interest. This is the question: Deep down, aren't you concerned about finding him in order to learn what he's doing to expose the existence of the creatures?"

"Forgive me, Father, I also don't wish to offend you, but that's nonsense. For one thing, even if you don't believe in my sincerity, the objective truth is that nothing João Pedroso does can impede the march of events. A process is underway, an inexorable and irreversible process.

The many João Pedrosos who will doubtless appear can at most slightly affect one aspect or another."

"I confess that, at a certain moment, I had doubts about what João told me. I even had a falling out with him as a result of it, but now you seem to be admitting everything he said. The way you're talking—"

"I'm not admitting anything; I'm speaking of the course of scientific evolution. What João Pedroso and you denounced as monstrous and unthinkable not only is neither, it's also inevitable. That type of project and others, related to it, are already being conducted in various centers."

"Are you saying that such a monkey man exists?"

"Yes, it does. Or if it doesn't already exist, it should and will exist."

"And you truly don't consider it a monstrosity, an aberration?"

"Absolutely not. It's just a new animal, one that opens immense perspectives of progress in several fields of knowledge, both basic and applied. Man needed that animal, and when he had the ability, created it, that's all. We're still a long way from being able to build such an animal genetically, so hybridization was the recourse adopted. In the future, that animal can be perfected through strictly genetic means, at the molecular level itself."

"Can that animal also be used as a guinea pig?"

"Naturally, just like any other animal."

"But wouldn't it have the right to refuse to be a guinea pig?"

"How so? An animal has no rights; that's the crazy notion of some ignorant ecologist. If animals had rights, a wildcat would have the right to eat you, as would a cow, if it were a carnivore. But it's you who have the right to eat a cow, not vice versa."

"And what about the right not to suffer? Don't they have the right not to suffer?"

"No. Man, who among other things is the only animal capable of the concept of suffering, is the one who, perhaps, has the right not to witness what he judges, with or without foundation, to be the suffering of an animal. Animals have no rights whatsoever; only people have rights.

Besides that, in normal laboratory conditions, that suffering thing is very relative; efforts are made to avoid it, because it's stressful and stress introduces physiological reactions often undesirable for the maintenance of experimental conditions."

"Dr. Nemésio, as João told me, you don't believe in God, which creates a gulf between us, but there must be some humanist content in your background; it's not possible for there not to be. Don't you find it terrible for a hybrid of human being and animal to be created and, on top of that, to call that hybrid 'just a new animal'?"

"No, because as you yourself said, I don't believe in God; in other words, I don't believe we're the fruit of the divine breath. To me, we're animals, rather primitive but intelligent and dominant and with possibilities for progress. My humanism is because I'm a man, of course. If the dominant species were the gorilla and I were a gorilla, I would be a gorillist. Man is only a temporary species on a temporary planet in a temporary universe, and the least he can do for himself is utilize his intelligence to maintain his power over nature as long as possible. The rest is wishful thinking or superstition, or both. Society, starting now, is beginning to control its elements rationally and is going to be able to free itself from various problems previously beyond its control. I think we're going to achieve an extremely high degree of control—not in the near future, of course, but sooner or later we will."

"I see in that hybrid and in other things of the kind a rejection by man of his semblance to God. I see power, so often corrupt, as it is in Brazil, perpetrating ever greater monstrosities and perpetuating itself in a vile manner."

"As for the semblance to God, I think you and I depart from irreconcilable premises. But in any case I have difficulty understanding how one can conceive an absolute being with a beard, mustache, and hair in his nose."

"You know that's not what I'm referring to. I'm referring to consciousness, which is our semblance to the Creator. You materialists have never succeeding in explaining consciousness."

"Nor have you. You merely transferred the problem."

"I don't wish to discuss questions of faith with you; to me that's not important, nor is it for you. But look at the moral problem it entails, the political problem. Political power shaping humanity and nature."

"That's inevitable. Whoever's here is here; whoever isn't won't get here. Power today has at its disposal such instruments that it has definitively implanted itself. It's never really going to change hands, and the tendency is for this to become more pronounced. That's good. It means greater possibilities of rational control. There will be no revolution nor any radical alteration in the power structure, not among nations, not among social classes. In that sense, it's the end of history. I always say that democracy is a superstitious myth, along with equality and other clichés. It's a long time since democracy has been practiced anywhere, except microscopically, and we have to turn that situation to our favor—that is, by perfecting mankind in every way possible."

"To me, that means extinguishing mankind as we know it. To me, it is man becoming the enemy of man, allowing the adversary he carries within himself to triumph by making him turn against himself. It's as if it were the work of Satan."

"Yes, Satan, ha, ha! Satan means 'enemy,' doesn't it? In that case, I would be Satan, or at least a satan, as I believe there's some controversy in the Church itself about whether there is one or several satans. That's funny, excuse me for laughing, very funny indeed—Satan. Well, look, I accept your inference and I think it technically correct. I *am* an enemy of God, although I consider him a fictitious enemy. All of you arranged for me that fictitious enemy that I have to fight. It's a type of radical humanism, actual rebellion. Enough of this business of kneeling down to an invisible, unprovable, and absurd spirit, in grotesque practices and rituals. Enough of handing everything over to the hands of God; we have to grasp things with our own hands, even deciding when we want to die instead of giving in to a masochistic and agonizing wait from which not even theists escape, for despite their immortality they too are afraid to die. There is no God, and if there is one, it's necessary to take away his power. He's been incompetent; for an omnipotent being his performance has been very unsatisfactory. And so, given the preceding, you are right: I am in fact Satan. You're right; it's more than logical."

He laughed again, a guffaw that shook the whole of his massive body and left Monteirinho feeling that he really was dealing with the voice of Darkness and of the Enemy. As the laughter gradually subsided, Monteirinho drank in a few swallows all that remained of his forgotten whiskey and was afraid he would begin speaking again, was afraid of the darkness, almost went into a panic. He rose, trying to look at Lúcio Nemésio's face as little as possible, said good-bye with a word and a gesture, and left hurriedly, hearing him still replying to the good-bye and saying that he understood perfectly the reverend's withdrawal; it wasn't good for a priest to be in the company of Satan.

Vade retro, thought Monteirinho, back in the bedroom at the parish house where he was staying. He said the same words again, feeling both afraid and ridiculous. No, why ridiculous? All of this really *was* terrible, and more terrible still for happening in that irresistible form, as Lúcio Nemésio had said so convincingly. João Pedroso had tried to resist and had been eliminated. Yes, had been eliminated; now he was sure of it, though he couldn't prove it, though he could never say anything to anyone. He was certain, absolutely certain that João had been killed through Ângelo Marcos's doing when he discovered he was being betrayed. He didn't know how, but he had been. And thus that agent of Evil carried out his mission, removed an obstacle. Everything fit; Evil had enjoyed a great victory. He would dedicate his life, João had said, he would dedicate his life to the struggle against it. But he had only lost his life, martyred anonymously.

Could the complete victory of Evil be possible? The evil that comes from within man; evil is what comes from man, not what enters into him, as in the Gospel. Pride, total hubris, absolute freedom, absolute sin. Was God really indifferent? Why was all this happening? No, God wasn't indifferent, but man is just one of His creatures and, if they turn against themselves, it is not beholden upon Him to do anything; there are many other of His creatures in the universe who do not turn away from Him like this, and everything on the face of the earth can change, under His eternal eyes. Monteirinho kneeled and prayed fervently and at length for humanity, until he fell asleep and had a dream in intense colors from which he awoke trembling and sweating, in which God spoke to him as He spoke to Job and asked him hath the rain a father and who was the father of the rain and where was he when He laid the foundations of the earth.

It was rainy at daybreak, but as he finished breakfast, said good-bye, and left, carrying his small valise, the sun appeared and took command of the entire sky, which became extraordinarily blue. Above the roof of the nuns' house was a late full moon, very white and almost brilliant, the smooth sea reflected the color of the sky, the marine birds roosted on posts and pilings, in the distance were the delicate deltas of the sails of the fishing boats that skimmed solemnly over the clear water—and Monteirinho, who had awakened to sadness, felt even sadder. He had to leave, and leave even more perplexed and discouraged, to live like one merely surrendering to his fate. He came to the end of the line, found no bus, and waited under the shelter. Everything was immobile, four or five people were scattered along the benches in the park, dogs slept in corners, and an acacia in full yellow bloom stood at the end of the street. About three yards from him, a rustling in one of the flower beds broke the silence and he went to see what it was. It was a large greenish, iridescent lizard, which stuck its head out from a clump of daisies and looked at him, repeatedly exhibiting and retracting its tongue. João Pedroso's lizard, the lizard that smiled, the lizard that would smile even more? It wasn't possible for a lizard to smile, but the truth is that, after drawing a little closer, Monteirinho felt there really was something like a smile enveloping the animal, and that it wasn't smiling at him but was mocking him. He recalled the fear that had assailed João Pedroso, and slowly that same fear, a fear similar to that which Lúcio Nemésio had engendered in him, attacked him too. Could it be the two-tailed lizard, the one João Pedroso had seen? Could there be such a coincidence—and if there could, what did it mean? He noticed that behind the lizard the clump of flowers was lower, and he considered going around it to see whether it really did have two tails. But he desisted after the first step. It was the same lizard, surely it was, but he lacked the courage to prove that certainty to himself—and meanwhile the animal in some way smiled, yes, smiled. And frightened him immensely, but despite his wishes, and however distressed and besieged and fearful he felt, he was unable to take his eyes off it, and it was with great relief that he boarded the bus that had just stopped to meet its timetable, and sat down in a spot from which it was impossible to see it, although he knew that never could he truly escape it.

João Ubaldo Ribeiro was born in 1941 on the island of Itaparica in the state of Bahia, Brazil. He received an LL.B. from the School of Law of the Federal University of Bahia and a master's degree in public administration from UCLA and has worked as a journalist and a teacher. He is the author of several novels, including *Sergeant Getúlio* and *An Invincible Memory*, both of which he translated into English. He now lives in Rio de Janeiro.